F. Max Müller

Rig-Veda-sanhita

Vol. I.: The Sacred Hymns of the Brahmans

F. Max Müller

Rig-Veda-sanhita
Vol. I.: The Sacred Hymns of the Brahmans

ISBN/EAN: 9783744778732

Printed in Europe, USA, Canada, Australia, Japan

Cover: Foto ©Andreas Hilbeck / pixelio.de

More available books at **www.hansebooks.com**

RIG-VEDA-SANHITA.

THE SACRED HYMNS OF THE BRAHMANS

TRANSLATED AND EXPLAINED

BY

F. MAX MÜLLER, M.A., LL.D.

FELLOW OF ALL SOULS COLLEGE;
PROFESSOR OF COMPARATIVE PHILOLOGY AT OXFORD;
FOREIGN MEMBER OF THE INSTITUTE OF FRANCE, ETC., ETC.

VOL. I.

HYMNS TO THE MARUTS OR THE STORM-GODS.

LONDON:

TRÜBNER AND CO., 60, PATERNOSTER ROW.

1869.

To the Memory

OF

COLEBROOKE, ROSEN, BURNOUF,

THE THREE FOUNDERS

OF VEDIC SCHOLARSHIP IN EUROPE.

PREFACE.

WHEN some twenty years ago I decided on undertaking the first edition of the two texts and the commentary of the Rig-veda, I little expected that it would fall to my lot to publish also what may, without presumption, be called the first translation of the ancient sacred hymns of the Brahmans. Such is the charm of deciphering step by step the dark and helpless utterances of the early poets of India, and discovering from time to time behind words that for years seemed unintelligible, the simple though strange expressions of primitive thought and primitive faith, that it required no small amount of self-denial to decide in favour of devoting a life to the publishing of the materials rather than to the drawing of the results which those materials supply to the student of ancient language and ancient religion. Even five and twenty years ago, and without waiting for the publication of Sâyana's commentary, much might have been achieved in the interpretation of the hymns of the Rig-veda. With the MSS. then

accessible in the principal libraries of Europe, a
tolerably correct text of the Sanhitâ might have
been published, and these ancient relics of a primitive
religion might have been at least partially deciphered
and translated in the same way in which ancient
inscriptions are deciphered and translated, viz. by
a careful collection of all grammatical forms, and
by a complete intercomparison of all passages in
which the same words and the same phrases occur.
When I resolved to devote my leisure to a critical
edition of the text and commentary of the Rig-
veda rather than to an independent study of that
text, it was chiefly from a conviction that the
traditional interpretation of the Rig-veda, as em-
bodied in the commentary of Sâyana and other
works of a similar character, could not be neglected
with impunity, and that sooner or later a complete
edition of these works would be recognized as a
necessity. It was better therefore to begin with the
beginning, though it seemed hard sometimes to spend
forty years in the wilderness instead of rushing
straight into the promised land.

It is well known to those who have followed
my literary publications that I never entertained
any exaggerated opinion as to the value of the
traditional interpretation of the Veda, handed down
in the theological schools of India, and preserved
to us in the great commentary of Sâyana. More
than twenty years ago, when it required more
courage to speak out than now, I expressed my

opinion on that subject in no ambiguous language,
and was blamed for it by some of those who now
speak of Sâyana as a mere drag in the progress
of Vedic scholarship. A drag, however, is sometimes more conducive to the safe advancement of
learning than a whip; and those who recollect the
history of Vedic scholarship during the last five
and twenty years, know best that, with all its
faults and weaknesses, Sâyana's commentary was a
sine quâ non for a scholarlike study of the Rig-
veda. I do not wonder that others who have more
recently entered on that study are inclined to speak
disparagingly of the scholastic interpretations of
Sâyana. They hardly know how much we all owe
to his guidance in effecting our first entrance into
this fortress of Vedic language and Vedic religion,
and how much even they, without being aware of
it, are indebted to that Indian Eustathius. I do
not withdraw an opinion which I expressed many
years ago, and for which I was much blamed at
the time, that Sâyana in many cases teaches us
how the Veda ought not to be, rather than how it
ought to be understood. But for all that, who
does not know how much assistance may be derived
from a first translation, even though it is imperfect,
nay, how often the very mistakes of our predecessors help us in finding the right track? If we
can now walk without Sâyana, we ought to bear
in mind that five and twenty years ago we could
not have made even our first steps, we could never,

at least, have gained a firm footing, without his leading strings. If therefore we can now see further than he could, let us not forget that we are standing on his shoulders.

I do not regret in the least the time which I have devoted to the somewhat tedious work of editing the commentary of Sâya*n*a, and editing it according to the strictest rules of critical scholarship. The Veda, I feel convinced, will occupy scholars for centuries to come, and will take and maintain for ever its position as the most ancient of books in the library of mankind. Such a book, and the commentary of such a book, should be edited once for all; and unless some unexpected discovery is made of more ancient MSS., I do not anticipate that any future Bekker or Dindorf will find much to glean for a new edition of Sâya*n*a, or that the text, as restored by me from a collation of the best MSS. accessible in Europe, will ever be materially shaken*. It has taken

---

* Since the publication of the first volume of the Rig-veda, many new MSS. have come before me, partly copied for me, partly lent to me for a time by scholars in India, but every one of them belonged clearly to one of the three families which I have described in my introduction to the first volume of the Rig-veda. In the beginning of the first Ash*t*aka, and occasionally at the beginning of other Ash*t*akas, likewise in the commentary on hymns which were studied by native scholars with particular interest, various readings occur in some MSS., which seem at first to betoken an independent source, but which are in reality mere marginal notes, due to more or less learned students of

a long time, I know; but those who find fault
with me for the delay, should remember that few
scholars, if any, have worked for others more than
I have done in copying and editing Sanskrit texts,

---

these MSS. Thus after verse 3 of the introduction one MS.
reads : sa prâha nripatim râgan, sâyanâryo mamânugah, sarvam
vetty esha vedânâm vyâkhyâtritvena yugyatâm. The same MS.,
after verse 4, adds : ityukto mâdhavâryena virabukkamahîpatih,
anvasât sâyanâkâryam vedârthasya prakâsane.

I had for a time some hope that MSS. written in Grantha
or other South-Indian alphabets might have preserved an independent text of Sâyana, but from some specimens of a
Grantha MS. collated for me by Mr. Eggeling, I do not think
that even this hope is meant to be realised. The MS. in
question contains a few independent various readings, such as
are found in all MSS., and owe their origin clearly to the
jottings of individual students. When at the end of verse 6,
I found the independent reading, vyutpannas tâvatâ sarvâ riko
vyâkhyâtum arhati, I expected that other various readings of
the same character might follow. But after a few additions
in the beginning, and those clearly taken from other parts of
Sâyana's commentary, nothing of real importance could be
gleaned from that MS. I may mention as more important
specimens of marginal notes that, before the first punah kidrisam,
on page 44, line 24, this MS. reads : athavâ yagñasya devam
iti sambandhah, yagñasya prakâsakam ityarthah, purohitam iti
prithagviseshanam. And again, page 44, line 26, before punah
kidrisam, this MS. adds : athavâ ritvigam ritvigvid (vad) yagña-
nirvâhakam hotâram devânâm âhvâtâram ; tathâ ratnadhâtamam.
In the same line, after ratnânâm, we read ramaniyadhanânâm vâ,
taken from page 46, line 2. Various readings like these, however,
occur on the first sheets only, soon after the MS. follows the usual
and recognized text. For the later Ashtakas, where all the MSS.
are very deficient, and where an independent authority would be
of real use, no Grantha MS. has as yet been discovered.

and that after all one cannot give up the whole of one's life to the collation of Oriental MSS. and the correction of proof-sheets. The two concluding volumes have long been ready for Press, and as soon as I can find leisure, they too shall be printed and published.

In now venturing to publish the first volume of my translation of the Rig-veda, I am fully aware that the fate which awaits it will be very different from that of my edition of the text and commentary. It is a mere contribution towards a better understanding of the Vedic hymns, and though I hope it may give in the main a right rendering of the sense of the Vedic poets, I feel convinced that on many points my translation is liable to correction, and will sooner or later be replaced by a more satisfactory one. It is difficult to explain to those who have not themselves worked at the Veda, how it is that, though we may understand almost every word, yet we find it so difficult to lay hold of a whole chain of connected thought, and to discover expressions that will not throw a wrong shade on the original features of the ancient words of the Veda. We have, on the one hand, to avoid giving to our translations too modern a character, or paraphrasing instead of translating; while, on the other, we cannot retain expressions which, if literally rendered in English or any modern tongue, would have an air of quaintness or absurdity totally foreign to the intention of the ancient poets. There are, as all Vedic scholars know, whole verses which, as yet, yield no sense whatever. There are words the meaning of which we can only guess. Here, no doubt, a continued study will remove some of our difficulties, and many a passage that is now dark, will receive light hereafter from a happy combination. Much has already been achieved by the efforts of European scholars, but much more remains to be done; and our only chance of seeing any rapid progress made lies, I believe, in communicating freely what every one has found out by himself, and not minding if others point out to us that we have overlooked the very passage that would at once have solved our difficulties, that our conjectures were unnecessary, and our emendations wrong. True and honest scholars whose conscience tells them that they have done their best, and who care for the subject on which they are engaged more than for the praise of benevolent or the blame of malignant critics, ought not to take any notice of merely frivolous censure. There are mistakes, no doubt, of which we ought to be ashamed, and for which the only *amende honorable* we can make is to openly confess and retract them. But there are others, particularly in a subject like Vedic interpretation, which we should forgive, as we wish to be forgiven. This can be done without lowering the standard of true scholarship or vitiating the healthy tone of scientific morality. Kindness and gentleness are not

incompatible with earnestness,—far from it!—and
where these elements are wanting, not only is
the joy embittered which is the inherent reward
of all *bonâ fide* work, but selfishness, malignity,
aye, even untruthfulness, gain the upper hand, and
the healthy growth of science is stunted. While
in my translation of the Veda and in the remarks
that I have to make in the course of my commentary, I shall frequently differ from other scholars,
I hope I shall never say an unkind word of men
who have done their best, and who have done
what they have done in a truly scholarlike, that
is, in a humble spirit. It would be unpleasant,
even were it possible within the limits assigned, to
criticise every opinion that has been put forward
on the meaning of certain words or on the construction of certain verses of the Veda. I prefer,
as much as possible, to vindicate my own translation, instead of examining the translations of other
scholars, whether Indian or European. Sâyana's
translation, as rendered into English by Professor
Wilson, is before the world. Let those who take
an interest in these matters compare it with the
translation here proposed. In order to give readers
who do not possess that translation, an opportunity
of comparing it with my own, I have for a few
hymns printed that as well as the translations of
Langlois and Benfey on the same page with my
own. Everybody will thus be enabled to judge
of the peculiar character of each of these transla-

tions. That of Sâyana represents the tradition of
India; that of Langlois is the ingenious, but
thoroughly uncritical, guess-work of a man of taste;
that of Benfey is the rendering of a scholar, who
has carefully worked out the history of some
words, but who assigns to other words either the
traditional meaning recorded by Sâyana, or a conjectural meaning which, however, would not always
stand the test of an intercomparison of all passages
in which these words occur. I may say, in general,
that Sâyana's translation was of great use to me
in the beginning, though it seldom afforded help
for the really difficult passages. Langlois' translation has hardly ever yielded real assistance, while
I sincerely regret that Benfey's rendering does not
extend beyond the first Mandala.

It may sound self-contradictory, if, after confessing
the help which I derived from these translations,
I venture to call my own the first translation of
the Rig-veda. The word translation, however, has
many meanings. I mean by translation, not a mere
rendering of the hymns of the Rig-veda into
English, French, or German, but a full account of
the reasons which justify the translator in assigning such a power to such a word, and such a
meaning to such a sentence. I mean by translation
a real deciphering, a work like that which Burnouf
performed in his first attempts at a translation
of the Avesta,—a *traduction raisonnée*, if such an
expression may be used. Without such a process,

without a running commentary, a mere translation of the ancient hymns of the Brahmans will never lead to any solid results. Even if the translator has discovered the right meaning of a word or of a whole sentence, his mere translation does not help us much, unless he shows us the process by which he has arrived at it, unless he places before us the *pièces justificatives* of his final judgment. The Veda teems with words that require a justification; not so much the words which occur but once or twice, though many of these are difficult enough, but rather the common words and particles, which occur again and again, which we understand to a certain point, and can render in a vague way, but which must be defined before they can be translated, and before they can convey to us any real and tangible meaning. It was out of the question in a translation of this character to attempt either an imitation of the original rhythm or metre, or to introduce the totally foreign element of rhyming. Such translations may follow by and by: at present a metrical translation would only be an excuse for an inaccurate translation.

While engaged in collecting the evidence on which the meaning of every word and every sentence must be founded, I have derived the most important assistance from the Sanskrit Dictionary of Professors Boehtlingk and Roth, which has been in course of publication during the last sixteen years. The Vedic portion of that Dictionary may,

I believe, be taken as the almost exclusive work of Professor Roth, and as such, for the sake of brevity, I shall treat it in my notes. It would be ungrateful were I not to acknowledge most fully the real benefit which this publication has conferred on every student of Sanskrit, and my only regret is that its publication has not proceeded more rapidly, so that even now years will elapse before we can hope to see it finished. But my sincere admiration for the work performed by the compilers of that Dictionary does not prevent me from differing, in many cases, from the explanations of Vedic words given by Professor Roth. If I do not always criticise Professor Roth's explanations when I differ from him, the reason is obvious. A dictionary without a full translation of each passage, or without a justification of the meanings assigned to each word, is only a preliminary step to a translation. It represents a first classification of the meanings of the same word in different passages, but it gives us no means of judging how, according to the opinion of the compiler, the meaning of each single word should be made to fit the general sense of a whole sentence. I do not say this in disparagement, for, in a dictionary, it can hardly be otherwise; I only refer to it in order to explain the difficulty I felt whenever I differed from Professor Roth, and was yet unable to tell how the meaning assigned by him to certain words would be justified by the author of the Dictionary himself. On this ground

I have throughout preferred to explain every step by which I arrived at my own renderings, rather than to write a running criticism of Professor Roth's Dictionary. My obligations to him I like to express thus once for all, by stating that whenever I found that I agreed with him, I felt greatly assured as to the soundness of my own rendering, while whenever I differed from him, I never did so without careful consideration.

The works, however, which I have hitherto mentioned, though the most important, are by no means the only ones that have been of use to me in preparing my translation of the Rig-veda. The numerous articles on certain hymns, verses, or single words occurring in the Rig-veda, published by Vedic scholars in Europe and India during the last thirty years, were read by me at the time of their publication, and have helped me to overcome difficulties, the very existence of which is now forgotten. If I go back still further, I feel that in grappling with the first and the greatest of difficulties in the study of the Veda, I and many others are more deeply indebted than it is possible to say, to one whose early loss has been one of the greatest misfortunes to Sanskrit scholarship. It was in Burnouf's lectures that we first learnt what the Veda was, and how it should form the foundation of all our studies. Not only did he most liberally communicate to his pupils his valuable MSS., and teach us how to use these tools, but the results of his own

experience were freely placed at our service, we were
warned against researches which he knew to be
useless, we were encouraged in undertakings which
he knew to be full of promise. His minute analysis of long passages of Sâyana, his independent
interpretations of the text of the hymns, his comparisons between the words and grammatical forms,
the thoughts and legends of the Veda and Avesta,
his brilliant divination checked by an inexorable
sense of truth, and his dry logical method enlivened
by sallies of humour and sparks of imaginative
genius, though not easily forgotten and always
remembered with gratitude, are now beyond the
reach of praise or blame. Were I to criticise what
he or other scholars have said and written many
years ago, they might justly complain of such
criticism. It is no longer necessary to prove that
Nâbhânedishtha cannot mean 'new relatives,' or that
there never was a race of Etendhras, or that the
angels of the Bible are in no way connected with
the Aṅgiras of the Vedic hymns ; and it would,
on the other hand, be a mere waste of time, were
I to attempt to find out who first discovered that
in the Veda *deva* does not always mean *divine*,
but sometimes means *brilliant*. In fact, it could
not be done. In a new subject like that of the
interpretation of the Veda, there are certain things
which everybody discovers who has eyes to see.
Their discovery requires so little research that it
seems almost an insult to say that they were dis-

covered by this or that scholar. Take, for instance,
the peculiar pronunciation of certain words, rendered
necessary by the requirements of Vedic metres. I
believe that my learned friend Professor Kuhn was
one of the first to call general attention to the fact
that semivowels must frequently be changed into
their corresponding vowels, and that long vowels
must sometimes be pronounced as two syllables. It
is clear, however, from Rosen's notes to the first
Ash*t*aka (i. 1, 8), that he, too, was perfectly aware
of this fact, and that he recognized the prevalence
of this rule, not only with regard to semivowels
(see his note to Rv. i. 2, 9) and long vowels which
are the result of Sandhi, but likewise with regard
to others that occur in the body of a word. 'Ani-
madverte,' he writes, 'tres syllabas postremas vocis
adhvarâ*n*âm dipodiæ iambicæ munus sustinentes,
penultima syllaba præter iambi prioris arsin, thesin
quoque sequentis pedis ferente. Satis frequentia
sunt, in hac præsertim dipodiæ iambicæ sede,
exempla syllabæ natura longæ in tres moras pro-
ductæ. De qua re nihil quidem memoratum
invenio apud Pingalam aliosque qui de arte
metrica scripserunt : sed numeros ita, ut modo
dictum est, computandos esse, taciti agnoscere
videntur, quum versus una syllaba mancus non
eos offendat.'

Now this is exactly the case. The ancient grammarians, as we shall see, teach distinctly that where
two vowels have coalesced into one according to

the rules of Sandhi, they may be pronounced as
two syllables; and though they do not teach the
same with regard to semivowels and long vowels
occurring in the body of the word, yet they tacitly
recognize that rule, by frequently taking its effects
for granted. Thus in Sûtra 950 of the Prâtisâkhya,
verse ix. 111, 1, is called an Atyashti, and the first
pâda is said to consist of twelve syllables. In order
to get this number, the author must have read,

ăyā̆ rŭ́k̆ā̆ hărĭnyā̆ pŭ̄nā̆naḥ.

Immediately after, verse iv. 1, 3, is called a Dhriti,
and the first pâda must again have twelve syllables.
Here therefore the author takes it for granted that
we should read,

săkhē̄ săkhā̆yăm ăbhy̆ ā̆ vāvṛ̆ītsvā̄ *.

No one, in fact, with any ear for rhythm, whether
Saunaka and Piṅgala, or Rosen and Kuhn, could
have helped observing these rules when reading the
Veda. But it is quite a different case when we
come to the question as to which words admit of
such protracted pronunciation, and which do not.
Here one scholar may differ from another according
to the view he takes of the character of Vedic

---

* See also Sûtra 937 seq. I cannot find any authority for the
statement of Professor Kuhn (Beiträge, vol. iii. p. 114) that according to the Rik-prâtisâkhya it is the *first* semivowel that must be
dissolved, unless he referred to the remarks of the commentator
to Sûtra 973.

metres, and here one has to take careful account
of the minute and ingenious observations contained
in numerous articles by Professors Kuhn, Bollensen,
Grassmann, and others. With regard to the interpretation of certain words and sentences, too, it may
happen that explanations which have taxed the
ingenuity of some scholars to the utmost, seem to
others so self-evident that they would hardly think
of quoting anybody's name in support of them, to
say nothing of the endless and useless work it would
entail, were we obliged always to find out who was
the first to propose this or that interpretation. It
is impossible here to lay down general rules :—each
scholar must be guided by his own sense of justice to
others and by self-respect. Let us take one instance.
From the first time that I read the fourth hymn
of the Rig-veda, I translated the fifth and sixth
verses :

utá bruvantu na*h* nídah níh anyátah kit árata,
    dádhánáh índre ít dúvah,
utá na*h* su-bhágán aríh voké̇yu*h* dasma krishtáyah,
    syáma ít índrasya sármani.

1. Whether our enemies say, 'Move away elsewhere, you who offer worship to Indra only,'—

2. Or whether, O mighty one, all people call us
blessed : may we always remain in the keeping of
Indra.

About the general sense of this passage I imagined
there could be no doubt, although one word in it,
viz. arí*h*, required an explanation. Yet the variety

of interpretations proposed by different scholars is extraordinary. First, if we look to Sâyana, he translates :

1. May our priests praise Indra! O enemies, go away from this place, and also from another place! Our priests (may praise Indra), they who are always performing worship for Indra.

2. O destroyer of enemies! may the enemy call us possessed of wealth ; how much more, friendly people! May we be in the happiness of Indra !

Professor Wilson did not follow Sâyana closely, but translated :

1. Let our ministers, earnestly performing his worship, exclaim : Depart, ye revilers, from hence and every other place (where he is adored).

2. Destroyer of foes, let our enemies say we are prosperous : let men (congratulate us). May we ever abide in the felicity (derived from the favour) of Indra.

Langlois translated :

1. Que (ces amis), en fêtant Indra, puissent dire : Vous, qui êtes nos adversaires, retirez-vous loin d'ici.

2. Que nos ennemis nous appellent des hommes fortunés, placés que nous sommes sous la protection d'Indra.

Stevenson translated :

1. Let all men again join in praising Indra. Avaunt ye profane scoffers, remove from hence, and from every other place, while we perform the rites of Indra.

2. O foe-destroyer, (through thy favour) even our enemies speak peaceably to us, the possessors of wealth ; what wonder then if other men do so. Let us ever enjoy the happiness which springs from Indra's blessing.

Professor Benfey translated :

1. And let the scoffers say, They are rejected by every one else, therefore they celebrate Indra alone.

2. And may the enemy and the country proclaim us as happy, O destroyer, if we are only in Indra's keeping.

Professor Roth, s. v. anyátah, took this word rightly in the sense of 'to a different place,' and must therefore have taken that sentence 'move away elsewhere' in the same sense in which I take it. Later, however, s. v. ar, he corrected himself, and proposed to translate the same words by 'you neglect something else.'

Professor Bollensen (Orient und Occident, vol. ii. p. 462), adopting to a certain extent the second rendering of Professor Roth in preference to that of Professor Benfey, endeavoured to show that the 'something else which is neglected,' is not something indefinite, but the worship of all the other gods, except Indra.

It might, no doubt, be said that every one of these translations contains something that is right, though mixed up with a great deal that is wrong ; but to attempt for every verse of the Veda to quote and to criticise every previous translation, would be an invidious and useless task. In the case just quoted, it might seem right to state that Professor Bollensen was the first to see that ari*h* should be joined with k*r*ish*t*áya*h*, and that he therefore proposed to alter it to ari*h*, as a nom. plur. But on referring to Rosen, I find that, to a certain extent, he had anticipated Professor Bollensen's remark, for though, in his cautious way, he abstained from altering the text, yet he remarked : Possitne ari*h* pluralis esse, contracta terminatione, pro araya*h* ?

After these preliminary remarks I have to say a few words on the general plan of my translation.

I do not attempt as yet a translation of the whole of the Rig-veda, and I therefore considered myself at liberty to group the hymns according to the deities to which they are addressed. By this process, I believe, a great advantage is gained. We see at one glance all that has been said of a certain god, and we gain a more complete insight into his nature and character. Something of the same kind had been attempted by the original collectors of the ten books, for it can hardly be by accident that each of them begins with hymns addressed to Agni, and that these are followed by hymns addressed to Indra. The only exception to this rule is the eighth Ma*nd*ala, for the ninth being devoted to one deity, to Soma, can hardly be accounted an exception. But if we take the Rig-veda as a whole, we find hymns, addressed to the

same deities, not only scattered about in different
books, but not even grouped together when they
occur in one and the same book.   Here, as we
lose nothing by giving up the old arrangement,
we are surely at liberty, for our own purposes,
to put together such hymns as have a common
object, and to place before the reader as much
material as possible for an exhaustive study of each
individual deity.

I give for each hymn the Sanskrit original in
what is known as the Pada text, i. e. the text in
which all words (pada) stand by themselves, as
they do in Greek or Latin, without being joined
together according to the rules of Sandhi.   The
text in which the words are thus joined, as they
are in all other Sanskrit texts, is called the Sanhitâ
text.   Whether the Pada or the Sanhitâ text be
the more ancient, may seem difficult to settle.   As
far as I can judge, they seem to me, in their present form, the product of the same period of
Vedic scholarship.   The Prâtisâkhyas, it is true,
start from the Pada text, take it, as it were, for
granted, and devote their rules to the explanation of
those changes which that text undergoes in being
changed into the Sanhitâ text.   But, on the other
hand, the Pada text in some cases clearly presupposes the Sanhitâ text.   It leaves out passages
which are repeated more than once, while the
Sanhitâ text always repeats these passages; it
abstains from dividing the termination of the loca-

tive plural su, whenever in the Sanhitâ text, i. e.
according to the rules of Sandhi, it becomes shu ;
hence nadîshu, agishu, but ap-su ; and it gives
short vowels instead of the long ones of the Sanhitâ, even in cases where the long vowels are
justified by the rules of the Vedic language. It
is certain, in fact, that neither the Pada nor the
Sanhitâ text, as we now possess them, represent
the original text of the Veda. Both show clear
traces of scholastic influences. But if we try to
restore the original form of the Vedic hymns, we
shall certainly arrive at some kind of Pada text
rather than at a Sanhitâ text ; nay, even in their
present form, the original metre and rhythm of
the ancient hymns of the *R*ishis are far more
perceptible when the words are divided, than when
we join them together throughout according to the
rules of Sandhi. Lastly, for practical purposes,
the Pada text is far superior to the Sanhitâ text
in which the final and initial letters, that is, the
most important letters of words, are constantly
disguised, and liable therefore to different interpretations. Although in some passages we may
differ from the interpretation adopted by the
Pada text, and although certain Vedic words have,
no doubt, been wrongly analysed and divided by
*S*âkalya, yet such cases are comparatively few, and
where they occur, they are interesting as carrying
us back to the earliest attempts of Vedic scholarship. In the vast majority of cases the divided

text, with a few such rules as we have to observe
in reading Latin, nay, even in reading Pali verses,
brings us certainly much nearer to the original
utterance of the ancient *R*ishis than the amalga-
mated text.

The critical principles by which I have been
guided in editing for the first time the text of
the Rig-veda, require a few words of explanation,
as they have lately been challenged on grounds
which, I think, rest on a complete misapprehension
of my previous statements on this subject.

As far as we are able to judge at present, we
can hardly speak of various readings in the Vedic
hymns, in the usual sense of that word. Various
readings to be gathered from a collation of different MSS., now accessible to us, there are none.
After collating a considerable number of MSS., I
have succeeded, I believe, in fixing on three representative MSS., as described in the preface to the
first volume of my edition of the Rig-veda. Even
these MSS. are not free from blunders,—for what
MS. is?—but these blunders have no claim to the
title of various readings. They are *lapsus calami*,
and no more; and, what is important, they have not
become traditional*.

---

* Thus x. 101, 2, one of the Pada MSS. (P. 2) reads distinctly
ya*gñâm* prá kri*n*uta sakhâya*h*, but all the other MSS. have
nayata, and there can be little doubt that it was the frequent
repetition of the verb kri in this verse which led the writer
to substitute kri*n*uta for nayata. No other MS., as far as I

The text, as deduced from the best MSS. of the Sanhitâ text, can be controlled by four independent checks. The first is, of course, a collation of the best MSS. of the Sanhitâ text.

The second check to be applied to the Sanhitâ text is a comparison with the Pada text, of which, again, I possessed at least one excellent MS., and several more modern copies.

am aware, repeats this blunder. In ix. 86, 34, the writer of the same MS. puts ra*g*asi instead of dhâvasi, because his eye was caught by râ*g*â in the preceding line. x. 16, 5, the same MS. reads sám ga*kkh*asva instead of ga*kkh*atâm, which is supported by S. 1, S. 2, P. 1, while S. 3. has a peculiar and more important reading, ga*kkh*atât. x. 67, 6, the same MS. P. 2. has ví *k*akartha instead of ví *k*akarta.

A number of various readings which have been gleaned from Pandit Târânâtha's Tulâdânâdipaddhati (see Trübner's American and Oriental Literary Record, July 31, 1868) belong to the same class. They may be due either to the copyists of the MSS. which Pandit Târânâtha used while compiling his work, or they may by accident have crept into his own MS. Anyhow, not one of them is supported either by the best MSS. accessible in Europe, or by any passage in the Prâtisâkhya.

Rv. ix. 11, 2, read devayu   instead of devayu*h* †.

ix. 11, 4,	„	ar*k*ata	„	ar*k*ate †.
ix. 14, 2,	„	yadi sabandhava*h*	„	yaddîptabandhava*h* †.
ix. 16, 3,	„	anaptam	„	anuptam †.
ix. 17, 2,	„	suvânâsa	„	stuvânâsa †.
ix. 21, 2,	„	prav*ri*nvanto	„	prav*ri*nvato †.
ix. 48, 2,	„	sa*m*v*ri*kta	„	sa*m*yukta †.
ix. 49, 1,	„	no 'pâm	„	no yâm †.
ix. 54, 3,	„	sûrya*h*	„	sûryam †.
ix. 59, 3,	„	sîda ni	„	sîdati †.

† As printed by Pandit Târânâtha.

The third check was a comparison of this text with Sâyana's commentary, or rather with the text which is presupposed by that commentary. In the few cases where the Pada text seemed to differ from the Sanhitâ text, a note was added to that effect, in the various readings of my edition; and the same was done, at least in all important cases, where Sâyana clearly followed a text at variance with our own.

The fourth check was a comparison of any doubtful passage with the numerous passages quoted in the Prâtisâkhya.

These were the principles by which I was guided in the critical restoration of the text of the Rigveda, and I believe I may say that the text as printed by me is more correct than any MS. now accessible, more trustworthy than the text followed by Sâyana, and in all important points identically the same with that text which the authors of the Prâtisâkhya followed in their critical researches in the fifth or sixth century before our era. I believe that starting from that date our text of the Veda is better authenticated, and supported by a more perfect *apparatus criticus*, than the text of any Greek or Latin author, and I do not think that diplomatic criticism can ever go beyond what has been achieved in the constitution of the text of the Vedic hymns.

Far be it from me to say that the *editio princeps* of the text thus constituted was printed without mistakes. But most of these mistakes are mistakes

which no attentive reader could fail to detect. Cases
like ii. 35, 1, where *góģishat* instead of *góshishat*
was printed three times, so as to perplex even
Professor Roth, or ii. 12, 14, where *sasumânâm*
occurs three times instead of *sasamânâm*, are, I
believe, of rare occurrence. Nor do I think that,
unless some quite unexpected discoveries are made,
there ever will be a new critical edition, or, as
we call it in Germany, a new recension of the
hymns of the Rig-veda. If by collating new MSS.,
or by a careful study of the Prâtisâkhya, or by
conjectural emendations, a more correct text could
have been produced, we may be certain that a
critical scholar like Professor Aufrecht would have
given us such a text. But after carefully collating
several MSS. of Professor Wilson's collection, and
after enjoying the advantage of Professor Weber's
assistance in collating the MSS. of the Royal
Library at Berlin, and after a minute study of the
Prâtisâkhya, he frankly states that in the text of
the Rig-veda, transcribed in Roman letters, which he
printed at Berlin, he followed my edition, and that
he had to correct but a small number of misprints.
For the two Mandalas which I had not yet published, I lent him the very MSS. on which my
edition is founded; and there will be accordingly
but few passages in these two concluding Mandalas,
which I have still to publish, where the text will
materially differ from that of his Romanised transcript.

No one, I should think, who is at all acquainted with the rules of diplomatic criticism, would easily bring himself to touch a text resting on such authorities as the text of the Rig-veda. What would a Greek scholar give, if he could say of Homer that his text was in every word, in every syllable, in every vowel, in every accent, the same as the text used by Peisistratos in the sixth century B.C.! A text thus preserved in its integrity for so many centuries, must remain for ever the authoritative text of the Veda.

To remove, for instance, the hymns 49–59 in the eighth Man*d*ala ·from their proper place, or count them by themselves as Vâlakhilya * hymns, seems to me little short of a critical sacrilege. Why Sâya*n*a does not explain these hymns, I con-

---

* The earliest interpretation of the name Vâlakhilya is found i n the Taittirîya-âra*n*yaka i. 23. We are told that Pra*g*âpati created the world, and in the process of creation the following interlude occurs :

sa tapo 'tapyata. sa tapas taptvâ *s*ariram adhûnuta. tasya yan mâ*m*sam âsît tato 'ru*n*â*h* ketavo vâtarasanâ *r*ishaya udatish*th*an. ye nakhâ*h*, te vaikhânasâ*h*. ye bâlâ*h*, te bâlakhilyâ*h*.

He burned with emotion. Having burnt with emotion, he shook his body. From what was his flesh, the *R*ishis, called Aru*n*as, Ketus, and Vâtarasanas, sprang forth. His nails became the Vaikhânasas, his hairs the Bâlakhilyas.

The author of this allegory therefore took bâla or vâla in vâlakhilya, not in the sense of child, but identified it with bâla, hair.

The commentator remarks with regard to tapas : nâtra tapa upavâsâdirûpam, ki*m*tu srash*t*avya*m* vastu kîd*r*isam iti paryâlo*k*anarûpam.

fess I do not know*; but whatever the reason was, it was not because they did not exist at his time, or because he thought them spurious. They are regularly counted in Kâtyâyana's Sarvânukrama, though here the same accident has happened. One commentator, Sha*d*gurusishya, the one most commonly used, does not explain them; but another commentator, *G*agannâtha, does explain them, exactly as they occur in the Sarvânukrama, only leaving out hymn 58. That these hymns had something peculiar in the eyes of native scholars, is clear enough. They may for a time have formed a separate collection, they may have been considered of more modern origin. I shall go even further than those who remove these hymns from the place which they have occupied for more than two thousand years. I admit they disturb the regularity both of the Ma*n*d*ala and the Ash*t*aka divisions, and I have pointed out myself that they are not counted in the ancient Anukrama*n*îs ascribed to *S*aunaka; (History of Ancient Sanskrit Literature, p. 220.) But, on the other hand, verses taken from these hymns occur in all the other Vedas†; the hymns

---

* A similar omission was pointed out by Professor Roth. Verses 21–24 of the 53rd hymn of the third Ma*n*d*ala, which contain imprecations against Vasish*t*ha, are left out by the writer of a Pada MS., and by a copyist of Sâya*n*a's commentary, probably because they both belonged to the family of Vasish*t*ha. See my edition of the Rig-veda, vol. ii. p. lvi, Notes.

† This is a criterion of some importance, and it might have

themselves are never included in the collections of
Parisishtas or Khilas or apocryphal hymns, nor does
Kâtyâyana ever mention mere Khilas in his Sarvânukrama. Eight of them are mentioned in the Bri-
haddevatâ, without any allusion to their apocryphal
character :

Parâny ashtau tu sûktâny rishînâm tigmategasâm,
Aindrâny atra tu shadvimsah pragâtho bahudaivatah.
Rig antyâgner akety agnih sûryam antyapado gagau.
Praskanvas ka prishadhras ka prâdâd yad vastu
    kimkana
Bhûrîd iti tu sûktâbhyâm akhilam parikîrtitam.
Aindrâny ubhayam ity atra shal âgneyât parâni tu.

'The next eight hymns belong to Rishis of keen
intellect *; they are addressed to Indra, but the
26th Pragâtha (viii. 54, 3–4, which verses form the
26th couplet, if counting from viii. 49, 1) is addressed to many gods. The last verse (of these
eight hymns), viii. 56, 5, beginning with the words
akety agnih, is addressed to Agni, and the last

---

been mentioned, for instance, by Professor Bollensen in his interesting article on the Dvipadâ Virâg hymns ascribed to
Parâsara (i. 65–70) that not a single verse of them occurs in
any of the other Vedas.

* Lest Saunaka be suspected of having applied this epithet,
tigmategas, to the Vâlakhilyas in order to fill the verse (pâda-
pûranârtham), I may point out that the same epithet is applied
to the Vâlakhilyas in the Maitry-upanishad 2, 3. The nom. plur.
which occurs there is tigmategasâh, and the commentator remarks :
tigmategasas tivrategaso 'tyûrgitaprabhâvâh; tegasâ ityevamvidha
etakkhâkhâsanketapâthas khândasah sarvatra.

foot celebrates Sûrya. Whatsoever Praskanva and
Prishadhra gave (or, if we read prishadhrâya, whatever Praskanva gave to Prishadhra), all that is
celebrated in the two hymns beginning with bhûrit.
After the hymn addressed to Agni (viii. 60, 1), there
follow six hymns addressed to Indra, beginning with
ubhayam.'

But the most important point of all is this, that
these hymns, which exist both in the Pada and
Sanhitâ texts, are quoted by the Prâtisâkhya, not
only for general purposes, but for special passages
occurring in them, and nowhere else. Thus in
Sûtra 154, hetáyah is quoted as one of the few
words which does not require the elision of a following short a. In order to appreciate what is
implied by this special quotation, it is necessary
to have a clear insight into the mechanism of the
Prâtisâkhya. Its chief object is to bring under
general categories the changes which the separate
words of the Pada text undergo when joined together in the Ârshî Sanhitâ, and to do this with
the utmost brevity possible. Now the Sandhi rules,
as observed in the Sanhitâ of the Rig-veda, are by
no means so uniform and regular as they are in
later Sanskrit, and hence it is sometimes extremely
difficult to bring all the exceptional cases under
more or less general rules. In our passage the
author of the Prâtisâkhya endeavours to comprehend all the passages where an initial a in the
Veda is not elided after a final e or o. In ordinary

Sanskrit it would be always elided, in the Sanhitâ it is sometimes elided, and sometimes not. Thus the Prâtisâkhya begins in Sûtra 139 by stating that if the short a stands at the beginning of a pâda or foot, it is always elided. Why it should be always elided in the very place where the metre most strongly requires that it should be pronounced, does not concern the author of the Prâtisâkhya. He is a statistician, not a grammarian, and he therefore simply adds in Sûtra 153 the only three exceptional passages where the a, under these very circumstances, happens to be not elided. He then proceeds in Sûtra 139 to state that a is elided even in the middle of a pâda, provided it be light, followed by y or v, and these, y or v, again followed by a light vowel. Hence the Sanhitâ writes te 'vădan, so 'yăm, but not sikshanto 'vratam, for here the a of avratam is heavy; nor mitramaho 'vadyât, for here the a following the v is heavy.

Then follows again an extension of this rule, viz. in the case of words ending in âvo. After these, a short a, even if followed by other consonants besides y or v, may be elided, but the other conditions must be fulfilled, i. e. the short a must be light, and the vowel of the next syllable must again be light. Thus the Sanhitâ writes indeed gâvo 'bhïta*h*, but not gâvo 'gman, because here the a is heavy, being followed by two consonants.

After this, a more general rule, or, more correctly, a more comprehensive observation is made, viz. that under all circumstances initial a is elided, if the preceding word ends in aye, aya*h*, ave, or ava*h*. As might be expected, however, so large a class must have numerous exceptions, and these can only be collected by quoting every word ending in these syllables, or every passage in which the exceptions occur. Before these exceptions are enumerated, some other more or less general observations are made, providing for the elision of initial a. Initial a, according to Sûtra 142, is to be elided if the preceding word is va*h*, and if this va*h* is preceded by â, na, pra, kva, *k*itra*h*, savitâ, eva, or ka*h*. There is, of course, no intelligible reason why, if these words precede va*h*, the next a should be elided. It is a mere statement of facts, and, generally speaking, these statements are minutely accurate. There is probably no verse in the whole of the Rig-veda where an initial a after va*h* is elided, unless these very words precede, or unless some other observation has been made to provide for the elision of the a. For instance, in v. 25, 1, we find va*h* preceded by a*kkh*a, which is not among the words just mentioned, and here the Saṅhitâ does not elide the a of agnim, which follows after va*h*. After all these more or less general observations as to the elision of an initial a are thus exhausted, the author of the Prâtisâkhya descends into particulars, and gives lists, first, of words the initial a of which is always elided; secondly, of words which, if preceding, require under

all circumstances the elision of the initial a of the
next word, whatever may have been said to the contrary in the preceding Sûtras. Afterwards, he gives
a number of passages which defy all rules, and must
be given on their own merits, and as they stand
in the Sanhitâ. Lastly, follow special exceptions to
the more or less general rules given before. And
here, among these special exceptions, we see that
the author of the Prâtisâkhya finds it necessary to
quote a passage from a Vâlakhilya hymn in which
hetáyah occurs, i. e. a word ending in ayah, and
where, in defiance of Sûtra 149, which required the
elision of a following initial a under all circumstances (sarvathâ), the initial a of asya is not elided;
viii. 50, 2, Sanhitâ, satǎnîkâ hetáyo asya. It might
be objected that the Prâtisâkhya only quotes hetáyah
as an exceptional word, and does not refer directly
to the verse in the Vâlakhilya hymn. But for-
tunately hetáyah occurs but twice in the whole of
the Rig-veda; and in the other passage where it
occurs, i. 190, 4, neither the rule nor the exception
as to the elision of an initial a, could apply. The
author of the Prâtisâkhya therefore makes no distinction between the Vâlakhilya and any other hymns
of the Rig-veda, and he would have considered his
phonetic statistics equally at fault, if it had been
possible to quote one single passage from the hymns
viii. 49 to 59, as contravening his observations, as if
such passages had been alleged from the hymns of
Vasishtha or Visvâmitra.

It would lead me too far, were I to enter here into similar cases in support of the fact that the Prâtisâkhya makes no distinction between the Vâlakhilya and any other hymns of the Rig-veda-sanhitâ*. But I doubt whether the bearing of this fact has ever been fully realised. Here we see that the absence of the elision of a short a which follows after a word ending in aya*h*, was considered of sufficient importance to be recorded in a special rule, because in most cases the Sanhitâ elides an initial a, if preceded by a word ending in aya*h*. What does this prove? It proves, unless all our views on the chronology of Vedic literature are wrong, that in the fifth century B. C. at least, or previously rather to the time when the Prâtisâkhya was composed, both the Pada and the Sanhitâ texts were so firmly settled that it was impossible, for the sake of uniformity or regularity, to omit one single short a ; and it proves *à fortiori*, that the hymn in which that irregular short a occurs, formed at that time part of the Vedic canon. I confess I feel sometimes frightened by the stringency of this argument, and I should like to see a possibility by which we could explain the addition, not of the Vâlakhilya hymns only, but of other much more modern sounding hymns, at a later time than the period of the Prâtisâkhyas. But until that possi-

---

* The Prâtisâkhya takes into account both the *S*âkala and Bâshkala *s*âkhâs, as may be seen from Sûtra 1057.

bility is shown, we must abide by our own conclusions; and then I ask, who is the critic who
would dare to tamper with a canon of scripture of
which every iota was settled before the time of
Cyrus, and which we possess in exactly that form
in which it is described to us by the authors of
the Prâtisâkhyas? I say again, that I am not free
from misgivings on the subject, and my critical
conscience would be far better satisfied if we could
ascribe the Prâtisâkhya and all it presupposes to a
much later date. But until that is done, the fact
remains that the two divergent texts, the Pada
and Sanhitâ, which we now possess, existed, as we
now possess them, previous to the time of the
Prâtisâkhya: they have not diverged nor varied
since, and the vertex to which they point, starting
from the distance of the two texts as measured
by the Prâtisâkhya, carries us back far beyond the
time of Saunaka, if we wish to determine the date
of the first authorised collection of the hymns, both
in their Pada and in their Sanhitâ form.

Instances abound, if we compare the Pada and
Sanhitâ texts, where, if uniformity between the two
texts had been the object of the scholars of the
ancient Parishads, the lengthening or shortening of
a vowel would at once have removed the apparent
discordance between the two traditional texts. Nor
should it be supposed that such minute discord-
ances between the two, as the length or shortness
of a vowel, were always rendered necessary by the

requirements of the metre, and that for that reason
the ancient students or the later copyists of the
Veda abstained from altering the peculiar spelling
of words, which seemed required by the exigencies
of the metre in the Sanhitâ text, but not in the Pada
text. Though this may be true in some cases, it is
not so in all. There are short vowels in the Sanhitâ
where, according to grammar, we expect long vowels,
and where, according to metre, there was no necessity
for shortening them. Yet in these very places all the
MSS. of the Sanhitâ text give the irregular short,
and all the MSS. of the Pada text the regular long
vowel, and the authors of the Prâtisâkhyas bear
witness that the same minute difference existed at
their own time, nay, previous to their own time. In
vii. 60, 12, the Sanhitâ text gives:

iyám deva puróhitir yuvábhyâm yagñéshu mitrâ-
varunâv akâri.

This primacy, O (two) gods, was made for you
two, O Mitra and Varuna, at the sacrifices!

Here it is quite clear that deva is meant for a
dual, and ought to have been devâ or devau. The
metre does not require a short syllable, and yet
all the Sanhitâ MSS. read devă, and all the Pada
MSS. read devâ; and what is more important, the
authors of the Prâtisâkhya had to register this small
divergence of the two texts, which existed in their
time as it exists in our own *.

---

* See Prâtisâkhya, Sûtra 309 seq., where several more instances
of the same kind are given.

Nor let it be supposed, that the writers of our MSS. were so careful and so conscientious that they would, when copying MSS., regulate every consonant or vowel according to the rules of the Prâtisâkhya. This is by no means the case. The writers of Vedic MSS. are on the whole more accurate than the writers of other MSS., but their learning does not seem to extend to a knowledge of the minute rules of the Prâtisâkhya, and they will commit occasionally the very mistakes against which they are warned by the Prâtisâkhya. Thus the Prâtisâkhya (Sûtra 799) warns the students against a common mistake of changing vaiyasva into vayyasva, i. e. by changing ai to a, and doubling the semivowel y. But this very mistake occurs in S. 2, and another MS. gives vaiyyasva. See p. xlvii.

If these arguments are sound, if nothing can be said against the critical principles by which I have been guided in editing the text of the Rig-veda, if the fourfold check, described above, fulfils every requirement that could be made for restoring that text which was known to Sâyana, and which was known, probably 2000 years earlier, to the authors of the Prâtisâkhyas, what can be the motives, it may fairly be asked, of those who clamour for a new and more critical edition, and who imagine that the *editio princeps* of the Rig-veda will share the fate of most of the *editiones principes* of the Greek and Roman classics, and be supplanted by new editions founded on the collation of other MSS. ? No one could have rejoiced more sincerely than I did at the publication of the Romanised transliteration of the Rig-veda, carried out with so much patience and accuracy by Professor Aufrecht. It showed that there was a growing interest in this, the only true Veda; it showed that even those who could not read Sanskrit in the original Devanâgarî, wished to have access to the original text of these ancient hymns; it showed that the study of the Veda had a future before it like no other book of Sanskrit literature. My learned friend Professor Aufrecht has been most unfairly charged with having printed this Romanised text *me insciente vel invito*. My edition of the Rig-veda is *publici juris*, like any edition of Homer or Plato, and anybody might have reprinted it either in Roman or Devanâgarî letters. But far from keeping me in ignorance of his useful enterprise, Professor Aufrecht applied to me for the loan of the MSS. of the two Mandalas which I had not yet published, and I lent them to him most gladly because, by seeing them printed at once, I felt far less guilty in delaying the publication of the last volumes of my edition of the text and commentary. Nor could anything have been more honourable than the way in which Professor Aufrecht speaks of the true relation of his Romanised text to my edition. That there are misprints, and I, speaking for myself, ought to say mistakes also, in my edition of the Rig-veda, I

know but too well; and if Professor Aufrecht, after
carefully transcribing every word, could honestly say
that their number is small, I doubt whether other
scholars will be able to prove that their number
is large.   I believe I may with the same honesty
return Professor Aufrecht's compliment, and considering the great difficulty of avoiding misprints
in Romanised transcripts, I have always thought
and I have always said that his reprint of the
hymns of the Veda is remarkably correct and accurate. What, however, I must protest against, and
what, I feel sure, Professor Aufrecht himself would
equally protest against, is the supposition, and
more than supposition of certain scholars, that
wherever his Latin transcript varies from my own
Devanâgarî text, Professor Aufrecht is right, and
I am wrong, that his various readings rest on the
authority of new MSS., and constitute in fact a
new recension of the Vedic hymns. Against this
supposition I must protest most strongly, not for
my own sake, but for the sake of the old book,
and, still more, for the sake of the truth. No doubt
it is natural to suppose that where a later edition
differs from a former edition, it does so intentionally;
and I do not complain of those who, without being
able to have recourse to MSS. in order to test
the authority of various readings, concluded that
wherever the new text differed from the old, it was
because the old text was at fault. In order to satisfy
my own conscience on this point, I have collated a

number of passages where Professor Aufrecht's text differs from my own, and I feel satisfied that in the vast majority of cases, I am right and he is wrong, and that his variations do not rest on the authority of MSS. I must not shrink from the duty of making good this assertion, and I therefore proceed to an examination of such passages as have occurred to me on occasionally referring to his text, pointing out the readings both where he is right, and where he is wrong. The differences between the two texts may appear trifling, but I shall not avail myself of that plea. On the contrary, I quite agree with those scholars who hold that in truly critical scholarship there is nothing trifling. Besides, it is in the nature of the case that what may, by a stretch of the word, be called various readings in the Veda, must be confined to single letters or accents, and can but seldom extend to whole words, and never to whole sentences. I must therefore beg my readers to have patience while I endeavour to show that the text of the Rig-veda, as first published by me, though by no means faultless, was nevertheless not edited in so perfunctory a manner as some learned critics seem to suppose, and that it will not be easy to supplant it either by a collation of new MSS., such as are accessible at present, or by occasional references to the Prâtisâkhya.

I begin with some mistakes of my own, mistakes which I might have avoided, if I had always consulted the Prâtisâkhya, where single words or whole passages of the Veda are quoted. Some of these mistakes have been removed by Professor Aufrecht, others appear in his transcript as they appear in my own edition.

I need hardly point out passages where palpable misprints in my edition have been repeated in Professor Aufrecht's text. I mean by palpable misprints, cases where a glance at the Pada text or at the Sanhitâ text or a reference to Sâyana's commentary would show at once what was intended. Thus, for instance, in vi. 15, 3, vridhé, as I had printed in the Sanhitâ, was clearly a misprint for vridhó, as may be seen from the Pada, which gives vridháh, and from Sâyana. Here, though Professor Aufrecht repeats vridhé, I think it hardly necessary to show that the authority of the best MSS. (S. 2. alone contains a correction of vridhó to vridhé) is in favour of vridháh, whatever we may think of the relative value of these two readings. One must be careful, however, in a text like that of the Vedic hymns, where the presence or absence of a single letter or accent begins to become the object of the most learned and painstaking discussions, not to claim too large an indulgence for misprints. A misprint in the Sanhitâ, if repeated in the Pada, or if admitted even in the commentary of Sâyana, though it need not be put down to the editor's deplorable ignorance, becomes yet a serious matter, and I willingly take all the blame which is justly due for occasional accidents of this character. Such are, for instance, ii. 12, 14, sasa-mânâm instead of sasamânâm; i. 124, 4, sudhyúva*h*, in the Pada, instead of sundhyúva*h*; and the substitution in several places of a short u instead of a long û in such forms as sûsâvâma, when occurring in the Pada; cf. i. 166, 14; 167, 9.

It is clear from Sûtra 819 and 163, 5, that the two words ûti índra in iv. 29, 1, should not be joined together, but that in the Sanhitâ the hiatus should remain. Hence ûtíndra, as printed in my edition and repeated in Professor Aufrecht's, should be corrected, and the hiatus be preserved, as it is in the fourth verse of the same hymn, ûtí itthâ. MSS. S. 1, S. 3. are right; in S. 2. the words are joined.

It follows from Sûtra 799 that to double the y in vaiyasva is a mistake, but a mistake which had to be pointed out and guarded against as early as the time of the Prâtisâkhya. In viii. 26, 11, therefore, vaiyyasvásya, as printed in my edition and repeated in Professor Aufrecht's, should be changed to vaiyasvásya. MSS. S. 1, S. 3. are right, likewise P. 1, P. 2; but S. 2. has the double mistake vay-yasvásya, as described in the Prâtisâkhya; another MS. of Wilson's has vaiyy. The same applies to viii. 23, 24, and viii. 24, 23. P. 1. admits the mistaken spelling vayyasva.

Some corrections that ought to be made in the Padapâ*th*a only, as printed in my edition, are pointed out in a note to Sûtra 738 of the Prâtisâkhya. Thus, according to Sûtra 583, 6, *srûyắh* in the Pada text of ii. 10, 2, should be changed to *sruyắh*. MSS. P. 1, P. 2. have the short u.

In v. 7, 8, I had printed *sûkih* shma, leaving the a of shma short in accordance with the Prâtisâkhya, Sûtra 514, where a string of words is given before which sma must not be lengthened, and where under No. II. we find yásmai. Professor Aufrecht has altered this, and gives the â as long, which is wrong. The MSS. S. 1, S. 2, S. 3. have the short a.

Another word before which sma ought not to be lengthened is mắvate. Hence, according to Sûtra 514, 14, I ought not to have printed in vi. 65, 4, shmâ mắvate, but shma mắvate. Here Professor Aufrecht has retained the long â, which is wrong. MSS. S. 1, S. 2, S. 3. have the short a.

It follows from Sûtra 499 that in i. 138, 4, we should not lengthen the vowel of sú. Hence, instead of asyắ û shû *na* úpa sâtáye, as printed in my edition and repeated by Professor Aufrecht, we should read asyắ û shú *na* úpa sâtáye. S. 1, S. 2, S. 3. have short u.

In vii. 31, 4, I had by mistake printed viddhí instead of viddhî. The same reading is adopted by Professor Aufrecht (ii. p. 24), but the authority of the Prâtisâkhya, Sûtra 445, can hardly be overruled. S. 1, S. 2, S. 3. have viddhî.

While in cases like these, the Prâtisâkhya is an authority which, as far as I can judge, ought to overrule the authority of every MS., however ancient, we must in other cases depend either on the testimony of the best MSS. or be guided, in fixing on the right reading, by Sâyana and the rules of grammar. I shall therefore, in cases where I cannot consider Professor Aufrecht's readings as authoritative improvements, have to give my reasons why I adhere to the readings which I had originally adopted.

In v. 9, 4, I had printed by mistake purú yó instead of purû yó. I had, however, corrected this misprint in my edition of the Prâtisâkhya, 393, 532. Professor Aufrecht decides in favour of purú with a short u, but against the authority of the MSS., S. 1, S. 2, S. 3, which have purû.

It was certainly a great mistake of mine, though it may seem more excusable in a Romanised transcript, that I did not follow the writers of the best MSS. in their use of the Avagraha, or, I should rather say, of that sign which, as far as the Veda is concerned, is very wrongly designated by the name of Avagraha. Avagraha, according to the Prâtisâkhya, never occurs in the Sanhitâ text, but is the name given to that halt, stoppage, or pause which in the Pada text separates the component parts of compound words. That pause has the length of one short vowel, i. e. one mâtrâ. Of course, nothing is said by the Prâtisâkhya as to how the pause should be represented graphically, but it is several times alluded to as of importance in the recitation and accentuation of the Veda. What we have been in the habit of calling Avagraha is by the writers of certain MSS. of the Sanhitâ text used as the sign of the Vivritti or hiatus. This hiatus, however, is very different from the Avagraha, for while the Avagraha has the length of one mâtrâ, the Vivritti or hiatus has the length of $\frac{1}{4}$ mâtrâ, if the two vowels are short; of $\frac{1}{2}$ mâtrâ, if either vowel is long; of $\frac{3}{4}$ mâtrâ, if both vowels are long. Now I have several times called attention to the fact that though this hiatus is marked in certain MSS. by the sign s, I have in my edition omitted it, because I thought that the hiatus spoke for itself and did not require a sign to attract the attention of European readers; while, on the contrary, I have inserted that sign where MSS. hardly ever use it, viz. when a short initial a is elided after a final e or o; (see my re-marks on pp. 36, 39, of my edition of the Prâtisâkhya.) Although I thought, and still think, that this use of the sign s is more useful for practical purposes, yet I regret that, in this one particular, I should have deviated from the authority of the best MSS., and caused some misunderstandings on the part of those who have made use of my edition. If, for instance, I had placed the sign of the Vivritti, the s, in its proper place, or if, at least, I had not inserted it where, as we say, the initial a has been elided after e or o, Professor Bollensen would have seen at once that the authors of the Prâtisâkhyas fully agree with him in looking on this change, not as an elision, but as a contraction. If, as sometimes

happens, final o or e remain unchanged before initial short a, this is called the Pañkâla and Prâkya
padavṛitti (Sûtra 137). If, on the contrary, final o or
e become one (ekîbhavati) with the initial short a, this
is called the Abhinihita sandhi (Sûtra 138). While
the former, the hiatus of the Pañkâla and Eastern
schools, is marked by the writers of several MSS.
by the sign s, the Abhinihita sandhi, being a sandhi,
is not marked by any sign*.

i. 3, 12. rấgati (Aufr. p. 2) instead of râgati (M. M.
vol. i. p. 75) is wrong.

i. 7, 9. ya ékaḥ (Aufr. p. 5) should be yấ ékaḥ
(M. M. vol. i. p. 110), because the relative pronoun is
never without an accent. The relative particle yathâ
may be without an accent, if it stands at the end
of a pâda; and though there are exceptions to this
rule, yet in viii. 21, 5, where Professor Aufrecht gives
yấthâ, the MSS. are unanimous in favour of yathâ
(M. M. vol. iv. p. 480). See Phit-sûtra, ed. Kielhorn,
p. 54.

i. 10, 11. â tấ (Aufr. p. 7) should be ấ tấ (M. M.
vol. i. p. 139), because â is never without the
accent.

i. 10, 12. gúshtâḥ, which Professor Aufrecht specially
mentions as having no final Visarga in the Pada, has
the Visarga in all the MSS., (Aufr. p. 7, M. M. vol. i.
p. 140.)

---

* As to the system or want of system, according to which the
Abhinihita sandhi takes place in the Saṇhitâ, see p. xxxv seq.

i. 11, 4. kávir (Aufr. p. 7) should be kavír (M. M. vol. i. p. 143).

i. 22, 8. read rắdhâmsi.

i. 40, 1 and 6. There is no excuse for the accent either on tvémahe or on vókema, while sắkẫñ in i. 51, 11, ought to have the accent on the first syllable.

i. 49, 3. Rosen was right in not eliding the a in divó ántebhyaḥ. S. 1, S. 2, S. 3. preserve the initial a, nor does the Prâtisâkhya anywhere provide for its suppression.

i. 54, 8. kshátram (Aufr. p. 46) is a mere misprint for kshatrám.

i. 55, 7. vandanasrúd (Aufr. p. 47) instead of vandanasrud (M. M. vol. i. p. 514) is wrong.

i. 57, 2. samắsîta instead of samásita had been corrected in my reprint of the first Mandala, published at Leipzig. See Bollensen, Zeitschrift der D. M. G., vol. xxii. p. 626.

i. 61, 7. read víshṇuḥ; i. 64, 2. read súkayaḥ; i. 64, 5. read dhŭtayaḥ.

i. 61, 16. Rosen had rightly printed hâriyoganâ with a long â both in the Sanhitâ and Pada texts, and I ought not to have given the short a instead. All the MSS., S. 1, S. 2, S. 3, P. 1, and P. 2, give the long â. Professor Aufrecht gives the short a in the Pada, which is wrong.

i. 67, 2 (4). vidántim (M. M. vol. i. p. 594) is perfectly right, as far as the authority of the MSS. and of Sâyaṇa is concerned, and should not have been altered to vindántim (Aufr. p. 57).

i. 72, 2. read vatsâm ; i. 72, 6. read pasûñ ; i. 76, 3. read dhákshy ; i. 82, 1. read yadâ.

i. 83, 3. Rosen was right in giving ásam*y*atta*h*. I gave ásam*y*ata*h* on the authority of P. 1, but all the other MSS. have tt.

i. 84, 1. indra (Aufr. p. 68) cannot have the accent on the first syllable, because it does not stand at the beginning of a pâda (M. M. vol. i. p. 677). The same applies to índra, vi. 41, 4, (Aufr. p. 429) instead of indra (M. M. vol. iii. p. 734); to ágne, i. 140, 12, (Aufr. p. 130) instead of agne (M. M. vol. ii. p. 133). In iii. 36, 3, on the contrary, indra, being at the head of a pâda, ought to have the accent on the first syllable, índra (M. M. vol. ii. p. 855), not indra (Aufr. p. 249). The same mistake occurs again, iii. 36, 10, (Aufr. p. 250); iv. 32, 7, (Aufr. p. 305); iv. 32, 12, (Aufr. p. 305); viii. 3, 12, (Aufr. ii. p. 86). In v. 61, 1, nara*h* should have no accent; whereas in vii. 91, 3, it should have the accent on the first syllable. In viii. 8, 19, vipanyû should have no accent, and Professor Aufrecht gives it correctly in the notes, where he has likewise very properly removed the Avagraha which I had inserted.

i. 88, 1. read yâta (M. M. vol. i. p. 708), not yâtha (Aufr. p. 72).

i. 90, 1. read *rig*unîtî̇ ; i. 94, 11. read yavasâ̇do (M. M. vol. i. p. 766), not yayasâ̇do (Aufr. p. 80).

i. 118, 9. abhibhŭtim (Aufr. p. 105) instead of abhí̇bhûtim (M. M. vol. i. p. 957) cannot be right, considering that in all other passages abhí̇bhûti has the accent on the second syllable. S. 1, S. 2, S. 3. have the accent on the i.

i. 128, 4. ghritasrîr (Aufr. p. 117) instead of ghritasrîr (M. M. vol. ii. p. 52) is wrong.

i. 144, 2. read párîvritâ*h* (M. M. vol. ii. p. 155) instead of parîvritâ*h* (Aufr. p. 133).

i. 145, 5. Professor Aufrecht (p. 134) gives upamasyãm, both in the Sanhitâ and Pada texts, as having the accent on the last syllable. I had placed the accent on the penultimate, (Pada, upa-mâsyâm, vol. ii. p. 161,) and whatever may be the reading of other MSS., this is the only possible accentuation. S. 1, S. 2, S. 3. have the right accent.

i. 148, 4. pûrû*ni* (Aufr. p. 136) instead of purû*ni* (M. M. vol. ii. p. 170) does not rest, as far as I know, on the authority of any MSS. S. 1, S. 2, S. 3. have purû*ni*.

i. 151, 7. gak*kh*atho (Aufr. p. 137) should be gák*kh*atho (M. M. vol. ii. p. 181).

i. 161, 12. All the Pada MSS. read prá ábravît, separating the two words and accentuating each. Though the accent is irregular, yet, considering the peculiar construction of the verse, in which prá and pró are used as adverbs rather than as prepositions, I should not venture with Professor Aufrecht (p. 144) to write prá abravît.

i. 163, 11. dhrá*gi*man (Aufr. p. 147) instead of dhrá*gi*mân (M. M. vol. ii. p. 245) is wrong.

i. 163, 13. gamyâ (Aufr. p. 148) instead of gamyâ (M. M. vol. ii. p. 246) is wrong.

i. 164, 17. read páre*na* (M. M. vol. ii. p. 259) instead of paró*na* (Aufr. p. 149).

i. 164, 38. The first *k*ikyú*h* ought to have the accent, and has it in all the MSS., (Aufr. p. 151, M. M. vol. ii. p. 278.)

i. 165, 5. A mere change of accent may seem a small matter, yet it is frequently of the highest importance in the interpretation of the Veda. Thus in i. 165, 5, I had, in accordance with the MSS. S. 1, S. 2, S. 3, printed étân (vol. ii. p. 293) with the accent on the first syllable. Professor Aufrecht alters this into etăn (p. 153), which, no doubt, would be the right form, if it were intended for the accusative plural of the pronoun, but not if it is meant, as it is here, for the accusative plural of éta, the speckled deer of the Maruts.

i. 165, 15. yâsish*t*a (Aufr. p. 154) instead of yâsîsh*t*a (M. M. vol. ii. p. 298) is not supported by any MSS.

i. 169, 7, instead of patayánta (Aufr. p. 158), read patáyanta (M. M. vol. ii. p. 322).

i. 174, 7. kúyâvâ*k*am (Aufr. p. 162) should be kúya-vâ*k*am (M. M. vol. ii. p. 340).

i. 177, 1. yuktắ, which I had adopted from MS. S. 3 (prima manu), is not supported by other MSS., though P. 2. reads yuttkắ. Professor Aufrecht, who had retained yuktắ in the text, has afterwards corrected it to yuktvắ, and in this he was right. In i. 177, 2, gâhi for yâhi is wrong.

i. 188, 4. astrinan (Aufr. p. 171) instead of ast*r*i*n*an (M. M. vol. ii. p. 395) can only be a misprint.

ii. 29, 6. kártâd (Aufr. p. 203) instead of kartắd (M. M. vol. ii. p. 560) is wrong.

ii. 40, 4. *k*akra (Aufr. p. 214) instead of *k*akrá (M. M. vol. ii. p. 614) is wrong.

iii. 7, 7. gu*h* (Aufr. p. 226) instead of gú*h* (M. M. vol. ii. p. 666) is wrong ; likewise iii. 30, 10. gâ*h* (Aufr. p. 241) instead of gấ*h* (M. M. vol. ii. p. 792).

iii. 17, 1. i*g*yate (Aufr. p. 232) instead of a*g*yate (M. M. vol. ii. p. 722) is impossible.

iii. 47, 1. Professor Aufrecht (p. 256) puts the nominative índro instead of the vocative indra, which I had given (vol. ii. p. 902). I doubt whether any MSS. support that change (S. 1, S. 2, S. 3. have indra), but it is clear that Sâya*n*a takes indra as a vocative, and likewise the Nirukta.

iii. 50, 2. Professor Aufrecht (p. 258) gives asya, both in the Sanhitâ and Pada, without the accent on the last syllable. But all the MSS. that I know (S. 1, S. 2, S. 3, P. 1, P. 2), give it with the accent on the last syllable (M. M. vol. ii. p. 912), and this no doubt is right. The same mistake occurs again in iii. 51, 10, (Aufr. p. 259); iv. 5, 11, (Aufr. p. 281); iv. 36, 2, (Aufr. p. 309); v. 12, 3, (Aufr. p. 337); while in viii. 103, 9, (Aufr. ii. p. 195) the MSS. consistently give asya as unaccented, whereas Professor Aufrecht, in this very passage, places the accent on the last syllable. On the same page (p. 259) amandau, in the Pada, is a misprint for ámandau.

iii. 53, 18. asi (Aufr. p. 262) instead of ási (M. M. vol. ii. p. 934) is wrong, because hí requires that the accent should remain on ási. S. 1, S. 2, S. 3, P. 1, P. 2. have ási.

iv. 4, 7. svá ā́yushe (Aufr. p. 279) instead of svá ā́yushi (M. M. vol. iii. p. 37) is not supported by any good MSS., nor required by the sense of the passage. S. 1, S. 2, S. 3, P. 1, P. 2. have ā́yushi.

iv. 5, 7. árupitam, in the Pada, (Aufr. p. 280) instead of ắrupitam (M. M. vol. iii. p. 45) is right, as had been shown in the Prâtisâkhya, Sûtra 179, though by a misprint the long â of the Sanhitâ had been put in the place of the short a of the Pada.

iv. 5, 9. read gaúh (M. M. vol. iii. p. 46) instead of góh (Aufr. p. 281).

iv. 15, 2. yắti, with the accent on the first syllable, is supported by all MSS. against yâti (Aufr. p. 287). The same applies to yắti in iv. 29, 2, and to várante in iv. 31, 9.

iv. 18, 11. amî, without any accent (Aufr. p. 293), instead of amî (M. M. vol. iii. p. 105) is wrong, because amî is never unaccented.

iv. 21, 9. no, without an accent (Aufr. p. 296), instead of nó (M. M. vol. iii. p. 120) is wrong.

iv. 26, 3. átithigvam (Aufr. p. 300) instead of atithigvám (M. M. vol. iii. p. 140) and vi. 47, 22. átithigvasya (Aufr. p. 437) instead of atithigvásya (M. M. vol. iii. p. 776) are wrong, for atithigvá never occurs again except with the accent on the last syllable. The MSS. do not vary. Nor do they vary in the accentuation of kútsa: hence kutsám (Aufr. p. 300) should be kútsam (M. M. vol. iii. p. 139).

iv. 3ʔ, 6. Professor Aufrecht (p. 309) has altered the accent of ắvishu*h* into âvishú*h*, but the MSS. are unanimous in favour of ắvishu*h* (M. M. vol. iii. p. 181).

Again in iv. 41, 9, the MSS. support the accentuation of ágman (M. M. vol. iii. p. 200), while Professor Aufrecht (p. 313) has altered it to agman.

iv. 42, 9. ádâsat, being preceded by hí, ought to have the accent ; (Aufrecht, p. 314, has adâsat without the accent.) For the same reason, v. 29, 3, ávindat (M. M. vol. iii. p. 342) ought not to have been altered to avindat (Aufr. p. 344).

iv. 50, 4. vyóman is a misprint for vyòman.

v. 15, 5. Professor Aufrecht (p. 338) writes dîrghám instead of dógham (M. M. vol. iii. p. 314). This, no doubt, was done intentionally, and not by accident, as we see from the change of accent. But dógham, though it occurs but once, is supported in this place by all the best MSS., and has been accepted by Professor Roth in his Dictionary.

v. 34, 4. práyato (Aufr. p. 351) instead of práyatâ (M. M. vol. iii. p. 371) is wrong.

v. 42, 9. visármâ*n*am (Aufr. p. 358) instead of visar-mâ*n*am (M. M. vol. iii. p. 402) is wrong.

v. 44, 4. parva*n*ó (Aufr. p. 360) instead of pravo*n*ó (M. M. vol. iii. p. 415) is wrong.

v. 83, 4. vânti (Aufr. p. 389) instead of vắnti (M. M. vol. iii. p. 554) is supported by no MSS.

v. 85, 6. âsiñ*k*antî*h* (Aufr. p. 391) instead of âsiñ*k*ántî*h* (M. M. vol. iii. p. 560) is not supported

either by MSS. or by grammar, as siṅk belongs to
the Tud-class. On the same grounds ishǎyantaḥ,
vi. 16, 27 (M. M. vol. iii. p. 638), ought not to have
been changed to ishayántaḥ (Aufr. p. 408), nor vi. 24, 7,
avakarsáyanti (M. M. vol. iii. p. 687) into avakǎrsa-
yanti (Aufr. p. 418).

vi. 46, 10. read girvaṇas (M. M. vol. iii. p. 763)
instead of gírvaṇas (Aufr. p. 435).

vi. 60, 10. kriṇoti (Aufr. p. 450) instead of kriṇóti
(M. M. vol. iii. p. 839) is wrong.

vii. 40, 4. aryamǎ ǎpaḥ (Aufr. ii. p. 35), in the
Pada, instead of aryamǎ ápaḥ (M. M. vol. iv. p. 81)
is wrong.

vii. 51, 1. âdityânǎm (Aufr. ii. p. 40) instead of
âdityǎnâm (M. M. vol. iv. p. 103) is wrong.

vii. 64, 2. ilǎm (Aufr. ii. p. 50) instead of ílâm (M. M.
vol. iv. p. 146) is wrong. In the same verse gopâḥ in
the Pada should be changed in my edition to gopâ.

vii. 66, 5. yó (Aufr. ii. p. 51) instead of yé (M. M.
vol. iv. p. 151) is indeed supported by S. 3, but
evidently untenable on account of atipíprati.

vii. 72, 3. In abudhran Professor Aufrecht has
properly altered the wrong spelling abudhnan; and,
as far as the authority of the best MSS. is concerned
(S. 1, S. 2, S. 3), he is also right in putting a final ṅ,
although Professor Bollensen prefers the dental n;
(Zeitschrift der D. M. G., vol. xxii. p. 599.) The fact
is that Vedic MSS. use the Anusvâra dot for final
nasals before all class-letters, and leave it to us
to interpret that dot according to the letter which

follows. Before I felt quite certain on this point,
I have in several cases retained the dot, as given
by the MSS., instead of changing it, as I ought
to have done according to my system of writing
Devanâgarî, into the corresponding nasal, provided
it represents an original n. In i. 71, 1, S. 2, S. 3.
have the dot in *agushran*, but S. 1. has dental n. In
ix. 87, 5, as*r*igran has the dot ; i. e. S. 1. has the dot,
and n*kh*, dental n joined to *kh* ; S. 2. has n*kh* without
the dot before the n ; S. 3. has the dot, and then *kh*.
In iv. 24, 6, the spelling of the Sanhitâ ávivena*m* tám
would leave it doubtful whether we ought to read
ávivenan tám or ávivenam tám ; S. 1. and S. 3. read
ávivena*m* tám, but S. 2. has ávivenan tám ; P. 2. has
ávi-venan tám, and P. 1. had the same originally,
though a later hand changed it to ávi-vena*m* tá*m*.
In iv. 25, 3, on the contrary, S. 1. and S. 3. write
ávivena*m* ; S. 2. ávivenam ; P. 1. and P. 2. ávi-vena*m*.
What is intended is clear enough, viz. ávi-venan in
iv. 24, 6 ; ávi-venam in iv. 25, 3.

vii. 73, 1. a*s*vinâ (Aufr. ii. p. 56) instead of a*s*vínâ
(M. M. vol. iv. p. 176) is wrong. On the same page,
dhíshn*y*e, vii. 72, 3, should have the accent on the
first syllable.

vii. 77, 1. In this verse, which has been so often
discussed (see Kuhn, Beiträge, vol. iii. p. 472 ; Boehtlingk and Roth, Dictionary, vol. ii. p. 968 ; Bollensen,
Orient und Occident, vol. ii. p. 463), all the MSS.
which I know, read *k*aráyai, and not either *k*aráthai
nor *g*aráyai.

viii. 2, 29. kîrí*n*am (Aufr. ii. p. 84) instead of kârí*n*am
(M. M. vol. iv. p. 308) does not rest on the authority
of any MSS., nor is it supported by Sâya*n*a.

viii. 9, 9. Professor Aufrecht has altered the very
important form â*k*u*k*yuvîmâhi (M. M. vol. iv. p. 389)
to â*k*u*k*yavîmâhi (ii. p. 98). The question is whether
this was done intentionally and on the authority of
any MSS. My own MSS. support the form â*k*u*k*yuvîmâhi, and I see that Professor Roth accepts this
form.

viii. 32, 14. âyántâram (Aufr. ii. p. 129) instead of
âyantâram (M. M. vol. iv. p. 567) is wrong.

viii. 47, 15. dushvápnyam (Aufr. ii. p. 150) is not
so correct as du*h*shvápnyam (M. M. vol. iv. p. 660),
or, better, dushshvápnyam (Prâtisâkhya, Sûtras 255
and 364), though it is perfectly true that the MSS.
write dushvápnyam.

In the ninth and tenth Ma*n*dalas I have not to
defend myself, and I need not therefore give a
list of the passages where I think that Professor
Aufrecht's text is not supported by the best MSS.
My own edition of these Ma*n*dalas will soon be
published, and I need hardly say that where it differs from Professor Aufrecht's text, I am prepared to
show that I had the best authorities on my side.

Having said so much in vindication of the text
of the Rig-veda as published by me, and in defence
of my principles of criticism which seem to me so
self-evident as hardly to deserve the name of *cano-
nes critici*, I feel bound at the same time both to

acknowledge some inaccuracies that have occurred in the index at the end of each volume, and to defend some entries in that index which have been challenged without sufficient cause.

It has been supposed that in the index at the end of my fourth volume, the seventeenth verse of the 34th hymn in the seventh Ma*n*dala has been wrongly assigned to Ahi Budhnya, and that one half only of that verse should have been reserved for that deity. I do not deny that we should be justified in deriving that sense from the words of the Anukrama*n*ikâ, but I cannot admit that my own interpretation is untenable. As Sâya*n*a does not speak authoritatively on the subject, I followed the authority of Sha*d*gurusishya. This commentator of the Anukrama*n*ikâ says : atra *k*a abg*â*m ukthair ahim gr*i*nîsha ity ardhar*k*o 'bg*a*nâmno devasya stuti*h*; mâ no 'hir budhnya ity ardhar*k*o 'hirbudh-nyanâmno devasya*. Another commentator says : abg*â*m ukthair ardhar*k*o 'hi*h*; uttaro mâ no 'hir ity ahir budhnya*h*. From this we learn that both commentators looked upon the Dvipadâs as ardhar*k*as or half-verses, and ascribed the whole of verse 16 to Ahir abg*â*h, the whole of verse 17 to Ahir budhnya*h*. It will be seen from an accurate examination of Sâya*n*a's commentary on verse 17, that in the second interpretation of the second half of verse 17, he

---

labours to show that in this portion, too, Ahir budhnya*h* may be considered as the deity.

It is perfectly right to say that the words of the Anukrama*n*ikâ, ab*g*âm ahe*h*, signify that the verse beginning with ab*g*âm, belongs to Ahi. But there was no misprint in my index. It will be seen that Sha*d*guru*s*ishya goes even beyond me, and calls that deity simply Ab*g*a, leaving out Ahi altogether, as understood. I was anxious to show the distinction between Ab*g*â Ahi*h* and Ahir Budhnya*h*, as the deities of the two successive verses, and I did not expect that any reader could possibly misinterpret my entry.

With regard to hymns 91 and 92 of the seventh Ma*nd*ala, it is true, that in the index I did not mention that certain verses in which two deities are mentioned (91, 2; 4–7; 92, 2), must be considered as addressed not to Vâyu alone, but to Vâyu and Indra. It will be seen from Sâya*n*a's introduction to hymn 90, that he, too, wrongly limits the sentence of the Anukrama*n*ikâ, aindryas *k*a yâ dvivaduktâ*h*, to the fifth and following verses of hymn 90, and that he never alludes to this proviso again in his introductory remarks to hymns 91 and 92, though, of course, he explains the verses, in which a dual occurs, as addressed to two deities, viz. Indra and Vâyu. The same omission, whether intentional or unintentional, occurs in Sha*d*guru*s*ishya's commentary. The other commentary, however, assigns the verses of the three hymns rightly. The subject has evidently been one

that excited attention in very early days, for in the
Aitareya-brâhma*n*a, v. 20, we actually find that the
word vâm which occurs in hymn 90, 1, and which
might be taken as a dual, though Sâya*n*a explains
it as a singular, is changed into te*.

In hymn vii. 104, rakshoha*n*au might certainly
be added as an epithet of Indrâ-Somau, and Sha*d*-
guru*s*ishya clearly takes it in that sense. The
Anukrama*n*ikâ says: indrâsomâ pañ*k*âdhikaindrâ-
soma*m* râkshoghna*m* *s*âpâbhisâpaprâyam.

In hymn viii. 67, it has been supposed that the
readings Samada and Sâmada instead of Samma*d*a
and Sâmma*d*a were due to a misprint. This is not
the case. That I was aware of the other spelling of
this name, viz. Sammada and Sâmmada, I had shown
in my History of Ancient Sanskrit Literature (2nd
ed.), p. 39, where I had translated the passage of the
*S*âṅkhâyana-sûtras in which Matsya Sâmmada occurs,
and had also called attention to the Â*s*valâyana-
sûtras x. 7, and the *S*atapatha-brâhma*n*a xiii. 3, 1, 1,
where the same passage is found. I there spelt the

---

* The interpunction of Dr. Haug's edition (p. 128) should be
after te. Sha*d*gurusishya says: ata eva brâhma*n*asûtrayo*h* praüge
vâyavatvâya pra vîrayâ *s*u*k*ayo dadrire vâm iti dviva*k*anasthâne ta
ity eka*k*anapâ*th*a*h* k*r*ita*h*, vâm ity ukta*m* *k*ed aindratva*m* *k*a
syâd iti. Possibly the same change should be made in Â*s*valâyana's
Sûtras, viii. 11, and it has been made by the Râma Nârâya*n*a
Vidyâratna. The remark of the commentator, however, dadrire
ta iti prayogapâ*th*a*h*, looks as if vâm might have been retained in
the text. The MSS. I have collated are in favour of te.

name Sâmmada, because the majority of the MSS.
were in favour of that spelling. In the edition of
the Âsvalâyana-sûtras, which has since been published
by Râma Nârâyana Vidyâranya, the name is spelt
Sâmada. My own opinion is that Sâmmada is the
right spelling, but that does not prove that Sâyana
thought so; and unless I deviated from the principles which I had adopted for a critical restoration
of Sâyana's text, I could not but write Sâmada in
our passage. B 1. and B 4. omit sâmada, but both
give samadâkhyasya; Ca. gives likewise samadâkhyasya, and A. semadâkhyasya. This, I believe,
was meant by the writer for sammadâkhyasya, for
in the passage from the Anukramanî both A. and
Ca. give sâmmado. I then consulted the commentary
of Shadgurusishya, and there again the same MS.
gave twice sâmmada, once sâmada, which is explained
by samadâkhyamahâmînarâgaputrah. A better MS.
of Shadgurusishya, MS. Wilson 379, gives the readings sâmmado, sâmmada, and sammadâkhyasya. The
other commentary gives distinctly sâmanda.

It will be seen from these remarks that many
things have to be considered before one can form
an independent judgment as to the exact view
adopted by Sâyana in places where he differs from
other authorities, or as to the exact words in
which he clothed his meaning. Such cases occur
again and again. Thus in ix. 86, I find that
Professor Aufrecht ascribes the first ten verses to
the Akrishtas, whereas Sâyana calls them Âkrishtas.

It is perfectly true that the best MSS. of the
Anukrama*n*ikâ have Ak*r*ish*t*a, it is equally true that
the name of these Ak*r*ish*t*as is spelt with a short a
in the Harivam*s*a, 11,533, but an editor of Sâya*n*a's
work is not to alter the occasional mistakes of that
learned commentator, and he certainly called these
poets Âk*r*ish*t*as.

Verses 21–30 of the same hymn are ascribed by
Professor Aufrecht to the P*r*isniya*h*. Here, again,
several MSS. support that reading; and in Sha*d*-
guru*s*ishya's commentary, the correction of p*r*isniya*h*
into p*r*isnaya*h* is made by a later hand. But Sâya*n*a
clearly took p*r*isnaya*h* for a nominative plural of
p*r*isni, and in this case he certainly was right. The
Dictionary of Boehtlingk and Roth quotes the Mahâ-
bhârata, vii. 8728, in support of the peculiar reading
of p*r*isniya*h*, but the published text gives p*r*isnaya*h*.
Professor Benfey, in his list of poets (Ind. Stud.
vol. iii. p. 223), gives p*r*isniyo*g*a as one word, not
p*r*isniyogâ, as stated in the Dictionary of Boehtlingk
and Roth, but this is evidently meant for two words,
viz. p*r*isnayo 'yâh. However, whether p*r*isniya*h* or
p*r*isnaya*h* be the real name of these poets, an editor
of Sâya*n*a is bound to give that reading of the
name which Sâya*n*a believed to be the right one,
i. e. p*r*isnaya*h*.

Again, in the same hymn, Professor Aufrecht
ascribes verses 31–40 to the Atris. He evidently
read t*r*itîye 'traya*h*. But Sâya*n*a read t*r*itîye
traya*h*, and ascribes verses 31–40 to the three com-

panies together of the *R*ishis mentioned before. On this point the MSS. admit of no doubt, for we read: *k*aturthasya *k*a dasar*k*asya âk*r*ishtâ mâshâ ityâdi-dvinâmânas trayo ganâ drash*t*âra*h*. I do not say that the other explanation is wrong; I only say that, whether right or wrong, Sâya*n*a certainly read traya*h*, not atraya*h*, and that an editor has no more right to correct the text, supported by the best MSS., in the first and second, than in the third of these passages, all taken from one and the same hymn.

But though I insist so strongly on a strict observance of the rules of diplomatic criticism with regard to the text of the Rig-veda, nay, even of Sâya*n*a, I insist equally strongly on the right of independent criticism, which ought to begin where diplomatic criticism ends. Considering the startling antiquity which we can claim for every letter and accent of our MSS. so far as they are authenticated by the Prâtisâkhya, to say nothing of the passages of the hymns which are quoted verbatim in the Brâhma*n*as, the Kalpa-sûtras, the Nirukta, the B*r*ihaddevatâ, and the Anukrama*n*îs, I should deem it reckless to alter one single letter or one single accent in an edition of the hymns of the Rig-veda. As the text has been handed down to us, so it should remain; and whatever alterations and corrections we, the critical Mle*kkh*as of the nineteenth century, have to propose, should be kept distinct from that time-hallowed inherit-ance. Unlikely as it may sound, it is true never-

theless that we, the scholars of the nineteenth
century, are able to point out mistakes in the
text of the Rig-veda which escaped the attention
of the most learned among the native scholars of
the sixth century B. C.   No doubt, these scholars,
even if they had perceived such mistakes, would
hardly have ventured to correct the text of their
sacred writings.   The authors of the Prâtisâkhya
had before their eyes a text ready made, of which
they registered every peculiarity, nay, in which
they would note and preserve every single irregularity, even though it stood alone amidst hundreds
of analogous cases.   With us the case is different.
Where we see a rule observed in 99 cases, we feel
strongly tempted and sometimes justified in altering
the 100th case in accordance with what we consider to be a general rule.   Yet even then I feel
convinced we ought not to do more than place
our conjectural readings below the *textus receptus*
of the Veda,—a text so ancient and venerable that
no scholar of any historical tact or critical taste
would venture to foist into it a conjectural reading,
however plausible, nay, however undeniable.

There can be no clearer case of corruption in the
traditional text of the Rig-veda than if in i. 70, 4, the
Pada text reads :

várdhân yám púrvî*h* kshap*áh* ví-rûpâ*h* sthâtú*h* *k*a
rátham *r*itá-pravîtam.

All scholars who have touched on this verse,
Professors Benfey, Bollensen, Roth, and others, have

pointed out that instead of *k*a rátham, the original
poet must have said *k*arátham. The phrase sthâtú*h*
*k*arátham, what stands and moves, occurs several
times. It is evidently an ancient phrase, and hence
we can account for the preservation in it of the
old termination of the nom. sing. of neuters in *r*i,
which here, as in the Greek μάρ-τυρ or μάρ-τυς,
masc., appears as ur or us, while in the ordinary
Sanskrit we find *r*i only. This nom. sing. neut. in
us, explains also the common genitives and ablatives,
pitu*h*, mâtu*h*, &c., which stand for pitur-s, mâtur-s.
This phrase sthâtú*h* *k*arátham occurs :

i. 58, 5. sthâtú*h* *k*arátham bhayate patatrí*n*a*h*.

What stands and what moves is afraid of Agni.

i. 68, 1. sthâtú*h* *k*arátham aktű́n ví ûr*n*ot.

He lighted up what stands and what moves during
every night.

i. 72, 6. pa*s*ű́n *k*a sthât*r*í̃n *k*arátham *k*a pâhi.

Protect the cattle, and what stands and moves !

Here it has been proposed to read sthâtú*h* instead
of sthât*r*í̃n, and I confess that this emendation is very
plausible. One does not see how pa*s*ú, cattle, could
be called *immobilia* or fixtures, unless the poet wished
to make a distinction between cattle that are kept
fastened in stables, and cattle that are allowed to roam
about freely in the homestead. This distinction is
alluded to, for instance, in the *S*ata*p*atha-brâhma*n*a,
xi. 8, 3, 2. saurya evaisha pa*s*u*h* syâd iti, tasmâd
etasminn astamite pa*s*avo badhyante ; badhnanty
ekân yathâgosh*th*am, eka upasamâyanti.

i. 70, 2. gárbha*h* *k*a sthâtắm gárbha*h* *k*arâthâm, (read sthâtrắm, and see Bollensen, Orient und Occident, vol. ii. p. 462.)

He who is within all that stands and all that moves.

The word *k*arâtha, if it occurs by itself, means flock, movable property :

iii. 31, 15. ắt ít sákhi-bhya*h* *k*arátham sám airat.

He brought together, for his friends, the flocks.

viii. 33, 8. puru-trắ *k*arâtham dadhe.

He bestowed flocks on many people.

x. 92, 13. prá na*h* pûshắ *k*arátham — avatu.

May Pûshan protect our flock !

Another idiomatic phrase in which sthâtú*h* occurs is sthâtú*h* *g*ágata*h*, and here sthâtú*h* is really a genitive :

iv. 53, 6. *g*ágata*h* sthâtú*h* ubháyasya yá*h* vasĭ.

He who is lord of both, of what is movable and what is immovable.

vi. 50, 7. vísvasya sthâtú*h* *g*ágata*h* *g*ánitrî*h*.

They who created all that stands and moves.

vii. 60, 2. vísvasya sthâtú*h* *g*ágata*h* *k*a gopắ*h*.

The guardians of all that stands and moves. Cf. x. 63, 8.

i. 159, 3. sthâtú*h* *k*a satyám *g*ágata*h* *k*a dhármani*i* putrásya pâtha*h* padám ádvayâvina*h*.

Truly while you uphold all that stands and moves, you protect the home of the guileless son. Cf. ii. 31, 5.

But although I have no doubt that in i. 70, 4,

the original poet said sthâtú*h* *k*arátham, I should be
loath to suppress the evidence of the mistake and
alter the Pada text from *k*a rátham to *k*arátham.
The very mistake is instructive, as showing us the
kind of misapprehension to which the collectors of
the Vedic text were liable, and enabling us to judge
how far the limits of conjectural criticism may safely
be extended.

A still more extraordinary case of misunder-
standing on the part of the original compilers of
the Vedic texts, and likewise of the authors of the
Prâtisâkhyas, the Niruktas, and other Vedic trea-
tises, has been pointed out by Professor Kuhn. In
an article of his, 'Zur ältesten Geschichte der Indo-
germanischen Völker' (Indische Studien, vol. i. p. 351),
he made the following observation : 'The Lithuanian
laukas, Lett. *lauks*, Pruss. *laukas*, all meaning field,
agree exactly with the Sk. *lokas*, world, Lat. *locus*,
Low Germ. (in East-Frisia and Oldenburg) *louch*,
lôch, village. All these words are to be traced
back to the Sk. *uru*, Gr. εὐρύς, broad, wide. The
initial u is lost, as in Goth. *râms*, O. H. G. *râmi*,
râmin (Low Germ. *râme*, an open uncultivated field
in a forest), and the r changed into l. In support
of this derivation it should be observed that in
the Veda loka is frequently preceded by the particle u, which probably was only separated from
it by the Diaskeuastæ, and that the meaning is
that of open space.' Although this derivation has
met with little favour, I confess that I look upon

this remark, excepting only the Latin *locus*, i. e. *stlocus*, as one of the most ingenious of this eminent scholar. The fact is that this particle u before loka is one of the most puzzling occurrences in the Veda. Professor Bollensen says that loka never occurs without a preceding u in the first eight Maṇḍalas, and this is perfectly true with the exception of one passage which he has overlooked, viii. 100, 12. dyaúḥ dehí lokám vágrâya vi-skábhe, Dyu! give room for the lightning to step forth! Professor Bollensen (l. c. p. 603) reads vṛitrâya instead of vágrâya, without authority. He is right in objecting to dyaús as a vocative, but dyaúḥ may be a genitive belonging to vágrâya, in which case we should translate, Make room for the lightning of Dyu to step forth!

But what is even more important, is the fact that the occurrence of this unaccented u at the beginning of a pâda is against the very rules, or, at least, runs counter to the very observations which the authors of the Prâtisâkhya have made on the inadmissibility of an unaccented word in such a place, so that they had to insert a special provision exempting the unaccented u from this general observation: 'anudâttam tu pâdâdau na-uvargam vidyate padam,' 'no unaccented word is found at the beginning of a pâda except u!' Although I have frequently insisted on the fact that such statements of the Prâtisâkhya are not to be considered as rules, but simply as more or less general statistical accumulations of facts actually occurring in the Veda, I have also pointed out that we are at liberty to found on these collected facts inductive observations which may assume the character of real rules. Thus, in our case, we can well understand why there should be none, or, at least, very few instances, where an unaccented word begins a pâda. We should not begin a verse with an enclitic particle in any other language either; and as in Sanskrit a verb at the beginning of a pâda receives *ipso facto* the accent, and as the same applies to vocatives, no chance is left for an un-accented word in that place except it be a particle. But the one particle that offends against this general observation is u, and the very word before which this u causes this metrical offence is loka. Can any argument be more tempting in favour of ad-mitting an old form uloka instead of u loka? Lokám is preceded by u in i. 93, 6; ii. 30, 6; (asmín bhayá-sthe kri*n*utam u lokám, make room for us, grant an escape to us, in this danger!) iv. 17, 17; vi. 23, 3; 7 (with urúm); 47, 8 (urúm na*h* lokám, or ulokám?); 73, 2; vii. 20, 2; 33, 5 (with urúm); 60, 9 (with urúm); 84, 2 (with urúm); 99, 4 (with urúm); ix. 92, 5; x. 13, 2; 16, 4 (suk*r*ítâm u lokám); 30, 7; 104, 10; 180, 3 (with urúm). Loké is preceded by u in iii. 29, 8; v. 1, 6; loka-k*r*ít, ix. 86, 21; x. 133, 1. In all remaining passages u loká is found at the be-ginning of a pâda: lokâ*h*, iii. 37, 11; lokám, iii. 2, 9 (u lokám u dvé (íti) úpa *g*âmím îyatu*h*); v. 4, 11;

loka-kritnúm, viii. 15, 4; ix. 2, 8. The only passages in which loka occurs without being preceded by u, are lokám, vi. 47, 8 (see above); viii. 100, 12 ; x. 14, 9 ; 85, 20 (amrítasya); lokáh, ix. 113, 9 ; lokán, x. 90, 14 ; loké, ix. 113, 7²; x. 85, 24.

Considering all this, I feel as convinced as it is possible to be in such matters, that in all the passages where u loká occurs and where it means space, *carrière ouverte*, freedom, we ought to read uroká ; but in spite of this I could never bring myself to insert this word, of which neither the authors of the Bráhmanas nor the writers of the Prátisákhyas or even later grammarians had any idea, into the text. On the contrary, I should here, too, consider it most useful to leave the traditional reading, and to add the corrections in the margin, in order that, if these conjectural emendations are in time considered as beyond the reach of doubt, they may be used as evidence in support of conjectures which, without such evidence, might seem intolerable in the eyes of timid critics.

There remains one difficulty about this hypothetical word uloká, which it is but fair to mention. If it is derived from uru, or, as Professor Bollensen suggests, from urvak or urvak, the change of va into o would require further support. Neither maghon for maghavan, nor durona for dura-vana are strictly analogous cases, because in each we have an a preceding the va or u. Strictly speaking, uroka presupposes uravaka, as slóka presupposes

sravaka, or óka, house, avaka (from av, not from
u*k*). That, on the other hand, the u of uru is liable
to disappear, is shown by passages such as i. 138, 3;
vii. 39, 3, where the metre requires uru to be treated
as one syllable; and possibly by ix. 96, 15, if the
original reading was urur iva instead of urviva.

The most powerful instrument that has hitherto
been applied to the emendation of Vedic texts, is
the metre. Metre means measure, and uniform
measure, and hence its importance for critical purposes, as second only to that of grammar. If our
knowledge of the metrical system of the Vedic
poets rests on a sound basis, any deviations from
the general rule are rightly objected to ; and if by
a slight alteration they can be removed, and the
metre be restored, we naturally feel inclined to
adopt such emendations. Two safeguards, however, are needed in this kind of conjectural criticism.
We ought to be quite certain that the anomaly is
impossible, and we ought to be able to explain to a
certain extent how the deviation from the original
correct text could have occurred. As this subject
has of late years received considerable attention,
and as emendations of the Vedic texts, supported
by metrical arguments, have been carried on on a
very large scale, it becomes absolutely necessary to
re-examine the grounds on which these emendations
are supposed to rest. There are, in fact, but few
hymns in which some verses or some words have
not been challenged for metrical reasons, and I feel

bound, therefore, at the very beginning of my
translation of the Rig-veda, to express my own
opinion on this subject, and to give my reasons
why in so many cases I allow metrical anomalies
to remain which by some of the most learned and
ingenious among Vedic scholars would be pronounced intolerable.

Even if the theory of the ancient metres had not
been so carefully worked out by the authors of the
Pratisâkhyas and the Anukramanîs, an independent
study of the Veda would have enabled us to discover the general rules by which the Vedic poets
were guided in the composition of their works. Nor
would it have been difficult to show how constantly
these general principles are violated by the introduction of phonetic changes which in the later
Sanskrit are called the euphonic changes of Sandhi,
and according to which final vowels must be joined
with initial vowels, and final consonants adapted
to initial consonants, until at last each sentence becomes a continuous chain of closely linked syllables.
It is far easier, as I remarked before, to discover
the original and natural rhythm of the Vedic hymns
by reading them in the Pada than in the Sanhitâ
text, and after some practice our ear becomes suffi-
ciently schooled to tell us at once how each line
ought to be pronounced. We find, on the one hand,
that the rules of Sandhi, instead of being generally
binding, were treated by the Vedic poets as poetical
licences only ; and, on the other, that a greater

freedom of pronunciation was allowed even in the body of words than would be tolerated in the later Sanskrit. If a syllable was wanted to complete the metre, a semivowel might be pronounced as a vowel, many a long vowel might be protracted so as to count for two syllables, and short vowels might be inserted between certain consonants, of which no trace exists in the ordinary Sanskrit. If, on the contrary, there were too many syllables, then the rules of Sandhi were observed, or two short syllables contracted by rapid pronunciation into one ; nay, in a few cases, a final m or s, it seems, might be omitted. It would be a mistake to suppose that the authors of the Prâtisâkhyas were not aware of this freedom allowed or required in the pronunciation of the Vedic hymns. Though they abstained from introducing into the text changes of pronunciation which even we ourselves would never tolerate, if inserted in the texts of Homer and Plautus, in the Pali verses of Buddha, or even in modern English poetry, the authors of the Prâtisâkhya were clearly aware that in many places one syllable had to be pronounced as two, or two as one. They were clearly aware that certain vowels, generally con- sidered as long, had to be pronounced as short, but they did not change the text. They were clearly aware that in order to satisfy the demands of the metre, certain changes of pronunciation were indis- pensable. They knew it, but they did not change the text. And this shows that the text, as they describe it, enjoyed even in their time a high authority, that they did not make it, but that, such as it is, with all its incongruities, it had been made before their time. In many cases, no doubt, certain syllables in the hymns of the Veda had been actually lengthened or shortened in the Sanhitâ text in accordance with the metre in which they are composed. But this was done by the poets themselves, or, at all events, it was not done by the authors of the Prâtisâkhya. They simply register such changes, but they do not enjoin them, and in this we, too, should follow their example. It is, therefore, a point of some importance in the critical restoration and proper pronunciation of Vedic texts, that in the rules which we have to follow in order to satisfy the demands of the metre, we should carefully distinguish between what is sanctioned by ancient authority, and what is the result of our own observations. This I shall now proceed to do.

First, then, the authors of the Prâtisâkhya distinctly admit that, in order to uphold the rules they have themselves laid down, certain syllables are to be pronounced as two syllables. We read in Sûtra 527: 'In a deficient pâda the right number is to be provided for by protraction of semivowels (which were originally vowels), and of contracted vowels (which were originally two independent vowels).' It is only by this process that the short syllable which has been lengthened in the Sanhitâ, viz. the sixth, or the eighth, or the tenth, can be shown

to have occupied and to occupy that place where
alone, according to a former rule, a short syllable is
liable to be lengthened. Thus we read:

i. 161, 11. ŭdvātsvăsmā ăkṛiṇotānā tṛiṇām.

This would seem to be a verse of eleven syllables,
in which the ninth syllable na has been lengthened.
This, however, is against the system of the Prâtisâkhya. But if we protract the semivowel v in
udvatsv, and change it back into u, which it was
originally, then we gain one syllable, the whole
verse has twelve syllables, na occupies the tenth
place, and it now belongs to that class of cases
which is included in a former Sûtra, 523.

The same applies to x. 103, 13, where we read:

prĕtā gằyătā nằraḥ.

This is a verse of seven syllables, in which the fifth
syllable is lengthened, without any authority. Let
us protract pretâ by bringing it back to its original
component elements pra itâ, and we get a verse of
eight syllables, the sixth syllable now falls under
the general observation, and is lengthened in the
Sanhitâ accordingly.

The same rules are repeated in a later portion
of the Prâtisâkhya. Here rules had been given as
to the number of syllables of which certain metres
consist, and it is added (Sûtras 972, 973) that where
that number is deficient, it should be completed
by protracting contracted vowels, and by separating consonantal groups in which semivowels

(originally vowels) occur, by means of their corresponding vowel.

The rules in both places are given in almost
identically the same words, and the only difference
between the two passages is this, that, according
to the former, semivowels are simply changed back
into their vowels, while, according to the latter, the
semivowel remains, but is separated from the preceding consonant by its corresponding vowel.

These rules therefore show clearly that the authors
of the Prâtisâkhya, though they would have shrunk
from altering one single letter of the authorised
Sanhitâ, recognized the fact that where two vowels
had been contracted into one, they might yet be pronounced as two ; and where a vowel before another
vowel had been changed into a semivowel, it might
either be pronounced as a vowel, or as a semivowel
preceded by its corresponding vowel. More than these
two modifications, however, the Prâtisâkhya does not
allow, or, at least, does not distinctly sanction. The
commentator indeed tries to show that by the wording of the Sûtras in both places, a third modification
is sanctioned, viz. the vocalisation, in the body of a
word, of semivowels which do not owe their origin
to an original vowel. But in both places this interpretation is purely artificial. Some such rule
ought to have been given, but it was not given by
the authors of the Prâtisâkhya. It ought to have
been given, for it is only by observing such a rule
that in i. 61, 12, gŏr nă parva vĭ rădā tirăskă, we get

a verse of eleven syllables, and thus secure for dâ
in radâ the eighth place, where alone the short
a could be lengthened. Yet we look in vain for a
rule sanctioning the change of semivowels into
vowels, except where the semivowels can rightly
be called kshaipra-varna (Sûtra 974), i. e. semivowels
that were originally vowels. The independent (svâbhâvika) semivowels, as e. g. the v in parva, are
not included; and to suppose that in Sûtra 527
these semivowels were indicated by varna is impossible, particularly if we compare the similar wording
of Sûtra 973 *.

We look in vain, too, in the Prâtisâkhya for another
rule according to which long vowels, even if they do
not owe their origin to the coalescence of two vowels,
are liable to be protracted. However, this rule, too,
though never distinctly sanctioned, is observed in
the Prâtisâkhya, for unless its author observed it, he
could not have obtained in the verses quoted by
the Prâtisâkhya the number of syllables which he
ascribes to them. According to Sûtra 937, the verse,
Rv. x. 134, 1, is a Mahâpankti, and consists of six

---

* It will be seen from my edition of the Prâtisâkhya, particularly from the extracts from Uvata, given after Sûtra 973,
that the idea of making two syllables out of goh, never entered
Uvata's mind. M. Regnier was right, Professor Kuhn (Beiträge,
vol. iv. p. 187) was wrong. Uvata, no doubt, wishes to show that
original (svâbhâvika) semivowels are liable to vyûha, or at least
to vyavâya; but though this is true in fact, Uvata does not succeed in his attempt to prove that the rules of the Prâtisâkhya
sanction it.

pâdas, of eight syllables each. In order to obtain
that number, we must read:

samrâgam *k*arshânînâm.

We may therefore say that, without allowing any
actual change in the received text of the Sanhitâ,
the Prâtisâkhya distinctly allows a lengthened pronunciation of certain syllables, which in the Pada
text form two syllables; and we may add that, by
implication, it allows the same even in cases where
the Pada text also gives but one instead of two
syllables. Having this authority in our favour, I
do not think that we use too much liberty if we
extend this modified pronunciation, recognized in so
many cases by the ancient scholars of India themselves, to other cases where it seems to us required
as well, in order to satisfy the metrical rules of the
Veda.

Secondly, I believe it can be proved that, if not
the authors of the Prâtisâkhya, those at least who
constituted the Vedic text which was current in the
ancient schools and which we now have before us,
were fully aware that certain long vowels and diphthongs could be used as short. The authors of the
Prâtisâkhya remark that certain changes which can
take place before a short syllable only, take place
likewise before the word no, although the vowel of
this 'no' is by them supposed to be long. After
having stated in Sûtra 523 that the eighth syllable
of hendecasyllabics and dodecasyllabics, if short, is
lengthened, provided a short syllable follows, they

remark that for this purpose na*h* or no is treated as a short syllable:

x. 59, 4. dyŭ-bhĭ*h* hĭtā*h* gă͞rĭmā sŭ nă̊*h* āstū, (Sanh. sū nŏ āstū.)

. Again, in stating that the tenth syllable of hendeca-syllabics and dodecasyllabics, if short, is lengthened, provided a short syllable follows, the same exception is understood to be made in favour of na*h* or no, as a short syllable :

vii. 48, 4. nŭ devā̄sa*h* vărĭvā*h* kārtănă nā*h*, (Sanh. kārtānā nŏ, bhúta na*h*, &c.)

With regard to e being shortened before a short a, where, according to rule, the a should be elided, we actually find that the Sanhitâ gives a instead of e in Rv. viii. 72, 5. véti stótave ambyãm, Sanh. véti stótava ambyãm. (Prâtis. 177, 5.)

I do not ascribe very much weight to the authority which we may derive from these observations with regard to our own treatment of the diphthongs e and o as either long or short in the Veda, yet in answer to those who are incredulous as to the fact that the vowels e and o could ever be short in Sanskrit, an appeal to the authority of those who constituted our text, and in constituting it clearly treated o as a short vowel, may not be without weight. We may also appeal to the fact that in Pâli and Prâkṛit every final o and e can be treated as either long or short *. Starting from

---

* See Lassen, Inst. Linguæ Pracriticæ, pp. 145, 147, 151; Cowell, Vararuḱi, Introduction, p. xvii.

this we may certainly extend this observation, as it has been extended by Professor Kuhn, but we must not extend it too far. It is quite clear that in the same verse e and o can be used both as long and short. I give the Sanhitâ text:

i. 84, 17. kă îshătē tŭgyătē kō bĭbhāyā
      kō mămsătē săntăm îndrăm kŏ ăntî,
      kās tŏkāyă kă ĭbhāyŏtă răyē
      ădhĭ brăvăt tănvē kō gănăyā.

But although there can be no doubt that e and o, when final, or at the end of the first member of a compound, may be treated in the Veda as anceps, there is no evidence, I believe, to show that the same licence applies to a medial or initial e or o. In iv. 45, 5, we must scan

    ŭsrăh gărāntē prătĭ văstŏh āsvĭnă,

ending the verse with an epitritus tertius instead of the usual dijambus *.

***

* See Professor Weber's pertinent remarks in Kuhn's Beiträge, vol. iii. p. 394. I do not think that in the verses adduced by Professor Kuhn, in which final o is considered by him as an iambus or trochee, this scanning is inevitable. Thus we may scan the Sanhitâ text :

i. 88, 2. rŭkmō nă kĭtrăh svădhĭtîvăn.
i. 141, 8. răthō nă yātăh sĭkvăbhĭh krĭtō.
i. 174, 3. sĭmhō nă dămē ăpāmsĭ văstŏh.
vi. 24, 3. ăkshō nă kăkryŏh sŭră brĭhăn.
x. 3, 1. ĭnō răgănn ărătĭh sămĭddhō.

This leaves but one of Professor Kuhn's examples (Beiträge, vol. iv. p. 192) unexplained: i. 191, 1. kănkăto nă kănkăto, where iva for na would remove the difficulty.

Thirdly, the fact that the initial short a, if following upon a word ending in o or e, is frequently not to be elided, is clearly recognized by the authors of the Prâtisâkhya (see p. xxxv). Nay, that they wished it to be pronounced even in passages where, in accordance with the requirements of the Prâtisâkhya, it had to disappear in the Sanhitâ text, we may conclude from Sûtra 978. It is there stated that no pâda should ever begin with a word that has no accent. The exceptions to this rule are few, and they are discussed in Sûtras 978–987. But if the initial a were not pronounced in i. 1, 9, sáh naḥ pitấ-iva sûnáve ágne su-upâyanáḥ bhava, the second pâda would begin with 'gne, a word which, after the elision of the initial a, would be a word without an accent.

Fourthly, the fact that other long vowels, besides e and o, may under certain circumstances be used as short in the Veda, is not merely a modern theory, but rests on no less an authority than Pâṇini.

Pâṇini says, vi. 1, 127, that i, u, ṛi (see Rv. Bh. iv. 1, 12) at the end of a pada (but not in a compound*)

---

* There are certain compounds in which, according to Professor Kuhn, two vowels have been contracted into one short vowel. This is certainly the opinion of Hindu grammarians, also of the compiler of the Pada text. But most of them would admit of another explanation. Thus dhánvarṇasaḥ, which is divided into dhánva-arṇasaḥ, may be dhánu-arṇasaḥ (Rv. v. 45, 2). Dhánarkam, divided into dhána-arkam, may have been dhána-ṛikam (Rv. x. 46, 5). Satárkasam (Rv. vii. 100, 3) may be taken as satáriḳasam instead of satá-arḳasam.

may remain unchanged, if a different vowel follows,
and that, if long, they may be shortened. He
ascribes this rule, or, more correctly, the first portion of it only, to *S*âkalya, Prâtisâkhya 155 seq.*
Thus *k*akrî atra may become *k*akrĭ atra or *k*akry
atra. Madhû atra may become madhŭ atra or
madhv atra. In vi. 1, 128, Pâ*n*ini adds that a,
i, u, *r*i may remain unchanged before *r*i, and, if
long, may be shortened, and this again according
to the teaching of *S*âkalya, i. e. Prâtisâkhya 136.
Hence brahmâ *r*ishi*h* becomes brahmă *r*ishi*h* or
brahmarshi*h* ; kumârî *r*isya*h* becomes kumârĭ *r*isya*h*
or kumâ*r*y *r*isya*h*. This rule enables us to explain
a number of passages in which the Sanhitâ text
either changes the final long vowel into a semivowel, or leaves it unchanged, when the vowel
is a prag*r*ihya vowel. To the first class belong
such passages as i. 163, 12 ; iv. 38, 10. vâ*g*ï ârvâ,
Sanh. vâ*gy*ârvâ ; vi. 7, 3. vâ*g*ï agne, Sanh. vâ*gy*âgne ;
vi. 20, 13. pakthî arka*íh*, Sanh. pakthyârka*íh* ; iv. 22, 4.
*s*ushmî ä *g*ó*h*, Sanh. *s*ushmyä *g*ó*h*. In these passages î is the termination of a nom. masc. of a
stem ending in in. Secondly, iv. 24, 8. pátnî â*kkh*a,
Sanh. pátnyâ*kkh*a ; iv. 34, 1. devî âhnâm, Sanh. devy-
âhnâm ; v. 75, 4. vâ*n*îkî â-hitâ, Sanh. vâ*n*îkyâhitâ ;
vi. 61, 4. avitrî avatu, Sanh. avitryâvatu. In these

---

* In the Prâtisâkhya the rule which allows vowel before vowel
to remain unchanged, is restricted to special passages, and in some
of them the two vowels are sava*rn*a ; cf. Sûtra 163.

passages the î is the termination of feminines. In
x. 15, 4, ûtî arvằk, Sanh. ûtyằrvằk, the final î of
the instrumental ûtî ought not to have been changed
into a semivowel, for, though not followed by íti,
it is to be treated as pragrihya; (Pràtis. 163, 5.)
It is, however, mentioned as an exception in Sûtra
174, 9. The same applies to ii. 3, 4. védî íti asyằm,
Sanh. védyasyằm. The pragrihya î ought not to
have been changed into a semivowel, but the fact
that it had been changed irregularly, was again duly
registered in Sûtra 174, 5. These two pragrihya
î therefore, which have really to be pronounced
short, were irregularly changed in the Sanhitâ into
the semivowel; and as this semivowel, like all semivowels, may take vyavâya, the same object was
attained as if it had been written by a short vowel.
With regard to pragrihya û, no such indication is
given by the Sanhitâ text; but in such passages
as i. 46, 13. sambhû íti sam-bhû ằ gatam, Sanh.
sambhû ằ gatam; v. 43, 4. bâhû íti ádrim, Sanh.
bâhû ádrim, the pragrihya û of the dual can be
used as short, like the û of madhû atra, given as
an example by the commentators of Pânini.

    To Professor Kuhn, I believe, belongs the merit
of having extended this rule to final â. That the
â of the dual may become short, was mentioned
in the Prâtisâkhya, Sûtra 309, though in none of
the passages there mentioned is there any metrical
necessity for this shortening (see p. xli). This being
the case, it is impossible to deny that where this â

is followed by a vowel, and where Sandhi between the two vowels is impossible, the final â *may* be treated as short. Whether it *must* be so treated, depends on the view which we take of the Vedic metres, and will have to be discussed hereafter. I agree with Professor Kuhn when he scans :

vi. 63, 1. kvă tyă valgŭ pŭru-hŭtă adyā, (Sanh. puruhûtâdya); and not kvā tyā valgū pŭrŭhŭtâdyā, although we might quote other verses as ending with an epitritus primus.

iv. 3, 13. mā vēsāsyă pră-mīnātă*h* mă ăpe*h*, (Sanh. mâpe*h*,) although the dispondeus is possible.

i. 77, 1. kăthă dăsēmă agnăyē kă asmai, (Sanh. kâsmai.)

vi. 24, 5. aryă*h* vāsāsyă pări-etă astĭ.

Even in a compound like tvâ-ûta, I should shorten the first vowel, e. g.

x. 148, 1. tmănă tănă sănŭyămă tvă-ûtă*h*, although the passage is not mentioned by the Prâti-sâkhya among those where a short final vowel in the eighth place is not lengthened when a short syllable follows[*].

But when we come to the second pâda of a Gâyatrî, and find there a long â, and that long â not followed by a vowel, I cannot agree with Professor Kuhn, that the long â, even under such

---

[*] I see that Professor Kuhn, vol. iv. p. 186, has anticipated this observation in esh*t*au, to be read ă-ĭsh*t*au.

circumstances, ought to be shortened. We may scan :

v. 5, 7. vắtāsyă pātmăn ĭ̄ltắ dāivyā hōtā̆iằ mänŭ-shă̄h.

The same choriambic ending occurs even in the last pâda of a Gâyatrî, and is perfectly free from objection at the end of the other pâdas.

So, again, we may admit the shortening of au to o in sâno avye and sâno avyaye, as quoted in the Prâtisâkhya, 174 and 177, but this would not justify the shortening of au to av in Anush*t*ubh verses, such as

v. 86, 5. mārtā̆yă dēvâu ădăbhā̆,

ā*m*sā̆-ivă dēvâu ārvătē,

while, with regard to the Trish*t*ubh and *G*agatî verses, our views on these metres must naturally depend on the difficulties we meet with in carrying them out. On this more by and by.

There is no reason for shortening â in

v. 5, 10. dēvā̆nā̆m gūhyā̆ nā̆mā̆nî.

It is the second pâda of a Gâyatrî here; and we shall see that, even in the third pâda, four long syllables occur again and again.

For the same reason I cannot follow Dr. Kuhn in a number of other passages where, for the sake of the metre, he proposes to change a long â into a short one. Such passages are in the Pada text:

vi. 46, 11. dĭdyă̄vă*h* tĭgmă̆-mūrdhā̆nă*h*, not mūr-dhă̆nă*h*.

i. 15, 6. rĭtŭnă yagñăm ăsâthē, not âsăthē.

v. 66, 2. sămyăk ăsŭryăm ăsâtē, not âsâtē.

v. 67, 1. vărshĭshtŭăm kshâtrăm ăsâthē, not âsâthē. See Beiträge, vol. iii. p. 122.

i. 46, 6. tâm âsmē râsâthăm ĭshăm, not râsâthăm ĭshăm.

iv. 32, 23. băbhrŭ yâmeshŭ sŏbhĕtē, not sŏbhĕtē.

iv. 45, 3. ŭtă prĭyăm mădhŭnē yŭñgâthăm răthăm, not yŭñgâthăm răthăm.

v. 74, 3. kăm ăkkhă yŭñgâthē răthăm, not yŭñgâthē răthăm.

iv. 55, 1. dyâvâbhŭmĭ (ĭti) ădĭtē trâsĭthăm năŭ, not trâsĭthăm năŭ.

v. 41, 1. rĭtâsyă vâ sădăsĭ trâsĭthăm năŭ, not trâsĭthăm năŭ.

I must enter the same protest against shortening other long vowels in the following verses which Professor Kuhn proposes to make metrically correct by this remedy :

i. 42, 6. hĭrăŭyăvâsĭmât-tămâ, not vâsĭmât-tămâ.

Here the short syllable of gaŭasrĭ-bhĭŭ in v. 60, 8, cannot be quoted as a precedent, for the i in gaŭasri, walking in companies, was never long, and could therefore not be shortened. Still less can we quote nâri-bhyaŭ as an instance of a long î being short-ened, for nâri-bhyaŭ is derived from nâriŭ, not from nâri, and occurs with a short i even when the metre requires a long syllable ; i. 43, 6. nrĭ-bhyaŭ nârĭbhyâ*h* gāve. The fact is, that in the Rig-veda the forms nârishu and nâri-bhya*h* never occur, but always nârishu, nâri-bhya*h*; while from vâsî we never find any forms with short i, but always vā́sishu, vā́sî-bhi*h*.

Nor is there any justification for change in i. 25, 16. gâva*h* nā gāvyûti*h* ānū, the second pâda of a Gâyatrî. Nor in v. 56, 3. *rī*kshā*h* nā va*h* mārutā*h* *s*imī́-vân āmā*h*. In most of the passages mentioned by Professor Kuhn on p. 122, this peculiarity may be observed, that the eighth syllable is short, or, at all events, may be short, when the ninth is long :

vi. 44, 21. v*rī*shnē̄ tē̄ indū*h* v*rī*shābhā̆ ́ pī̄pāyā̄.

i. 73, 1. syōnā-*s*ī*h* ătīthī*h* nā ́ prī*n*ânā*h*.

vii. 13, 1. bhārē̄ hăvī*h* nā bārhishī̆ ́ prī*n*ânā*h*.

ii. 28, 7. ēnā*h* k*rī*nvāntām āsūrā ́ bhrī*n*ântī.

Before, however, we can settle the question whether in these and other places certain vowels should be pronounced as either long or short, we must settle the more general question, what authority we have for requiring a long or a short syllable in certain places of the Vedic metres. Now it has generally been supposed that the Prâtisâkhya teaches that there must be a long syllable in the eighth or tenth place of Traish*t*ubha and *G*â-gata, and in the sixth place of Ânush*t*ubha pâdas. This is not the case. The Prâtisâkhya, no doubt, says, that a short final vowel, but not any short syllable, occupying the eighth or tenth place in a Traish*t*ubha and *G*âgata pâda, or the sixth

place in a Gâyatra pâda, is lengthened, but it
never says that it *must* be lengthened; on the
contrary, it gives itself a number of cases where
it is not so lengthened. But, what is even more
important, the Prâtisâkhya distinctly adds a proviso
which shows that the ancient critics of the Veda
did not consider the trochee as the only possible
foot for the sixth and seventh syllables of Gâyatra,
or for the eighth and ninth, or tenth and eleventh
syllables of Traish*t*ubha and *G*âgata pâdas. They
distinctly admit that the seventh and the ninth
and the eleventh syllables in such pâdas may be
long, and that in that case the preceding short
vowel is not lengthened. We thus get the iambus
in the very place which is generally occupied by the
trochee. According to the Prâtisâkhya, the general
scheme for the Gâyatra would be, not only

$$\overset{}{+} \; + \; + \; + \; \Big| \; + \; \overset{6}{-} \; \overset{7}{\cup} \; + \; ,$$

but also

$$+ \; + \; + \; + \; \Big| \; + \; \overset{6}{\cup} \; \overset{7}{-} \; + \; ;$$

and for the Traish*t*ubha and *G*âgata, not only

$$+ \; + \; + \; + \; \Big| \; + \; + \; + \; \overset{8}{-} \; \Big| \; \overset{9}{\cup} \; + \; + \; (+),$$

but also

$$+ \; + \; + \; + \; \Big| \; + \; + \; + \; \overset{8}{\cup} \; \Big| \; \overset{9}{-} \; + \; + \; (+).$$

And again, for the same pâdas, not only

$$+ \; + \; + \; + \; \Big| \; + \; + \; + \; + \; \Big| \; + \; \overset{10}{-} \; \overset{11}{\cup} \; (+),$$

but also

$$+ \; + \; + \; + \; \Big| \; + \; + \; + \; + \; \Big| \; + \; \overset{10}{\cup} \; \overset{11}{-} \; (+).$$

Before appealing, however, to the Prâtisâkhya for the establishment of such a rule as that the sixth syllable of Ânushtubha and the eighth or tenth syllable of Traishtubha and Gâgata pâdas must be lengthened, provided a short syllable follows, it is indispensable that we should have a clear appreciation of the real character of the Prâtisâkhya. If we carefully follow the thread which runs through these books, we shall soon perceive that, even with the proviso that a short syllable follows, the Prâtisâkhya never teaches that certain final vowels *must* be lengthened. The object of the Prâtisâkhya is, as I pointed out on a former occasion, to register all the facts which possess a phonetic interest. In doing this, all kinds of plans are adopted in order to bring as large a number of cases as possible under general categories. These categories are purely technical and external, and they never assume, with the authors of the Prâtisâkhya, the character of general rules. Let us now, after these preliminary remarks, return to the Sûtras 523 to 535, which we discussed before. The Prâtisâkhya simply says that certain syllables which are short in the Pada, if occupying a certain place in a verse, are lengthened in the Sanhitâ, provided a short syllable follows. This looks, no doubt, like a general rule which should be carried out under all circumstances. But this idea never entered the minds of the authors of the Prâtisâkhya. They only give this rule as the most convenient way of registering the lengthening of

certain syllables which have actually been lengthened
in the text of the Sanhitâ, while they remain short
in the Pada; and after having done this, they proceed to give a number of verses where the same
rule might be supposed to apply, but where in the
text of the Sanhitâ the short syllable has not been
lengthened. After having given a long string of
words which are short in the Pada and long in
the Sanhitâ, and where no intelligible reason of
their lengthening can be given, at least not by the
authors of the Prâtisâkhya, the Prâtisâkhya adds in
Sûtra 523, ' The final vowel of the eighth syllable
is lengthened in pâdas of eleven and twelve syllables, provided a syllable follows which is short in
the Sanhitâ.' As instances the commentator gives
(Sanhitâ text):

i. 32, 4. tādī́tnā sátrum nă kī́la vívitse.

i. 94, 1. ágnē sākhyṓ mā́ rĭshāmā̊ váyăm tắvā.

Then follows another rule (Sûtra 525) that 'The
final vowel of the tenth syllable in pâdas of eleven
and twelve syllables is lengthened, provided a syllable follows which is short in the Sanhitâ.' As
instances the commentator gives:

iii. 54, 22. ắhā vīsvā́ sŭmănā́ dīdihī́ naḥ.

ii. 34, 9. ắvă rūdrā́ ăsắsō hāntănā́ vắdhaḥ.

Lastly, a rule is given (Sûtra 526) that ' The final
vowel of the sixth syllable is lengthened in a pâda

of eight syllables, provided a syllable follows which is short:'

i. 5, 10. îsânŏ yăvăyă vădhắm.

If the seventh syllable is long no change takes place :

ix. 67, 30. ă pắvāsvă dēvă sŏmā.

While we ourselves should look upon these rules as founded in the nature of the metre, which, no doubt, to a certain extent they are, the authors of the Prâtisâkhya use them simply as convenient nets for catching as many cases as possible of lengthened syllables actually occurring in the text of the Sanhitâ. For this purpose, and in order to avoid giving a number of special rules, they add in this place an observation, very important to us as throwing light on the real pronunciation of the Vedic hymns at the time when our Sanhitâ text was finally settled, but with them again a mere expedient for enlarging the preceding rules, and thus catching more cases of lengthening at one haul. They say in Sûtra 527, that in order to get the right number of syllables in such verses, we must pronounce sometimes one syllable as two. Thus only can the lengthened syllable be got into one of the places required by the preceding Sûtra, viz. the sixth, the eighth, or the tenth place, and thus only can a large number of lengthened syllables be comprehended under the same general rule of the Prâtisâkhya. In all this we ourselves can easily

recognize a principle which guided the compilers of
the Sanhitâ text, or the very authors of the hymns,
in lengthening syllables which in the Pada text
are short, and which were liable to be lengthened
because they occupied certain places on which the
stress of the metre would naturally fall. We also see
quite clearly that these compilers, or those whose
pronunciation they tried to perpetuate, must have
pronounced certain syllables as two syllables, and
we naturally consider that we have a right to try
the same expedient in other cases where to us,
though not to them, the metre seems deficient, and
where it could be rendered perfect by pronouncing
one syllable as two. Such thoughts, however, never
entered the minds of the authors of the Prâtisâkhyas,
who are satisfied with explaining what is, according
to the authority of the Sanhitâ, and who never
attempt to say what ought to be, even against the
authority of the Sanhitâ. While in some cases they
have ears to hear and to appreciate the natural flow
of the poetical language of the *R*ishis, they seem
at other times as deaf as the adder to the voice of
the charmer.

A general rule, therefore, in our sense of the word,
that the eighth syllable in hendecasyllabics and dodecasyllabics, the tenth syllable in hendecasyllabics
and dodecasyllabics, and the sixth syllable in octo-
syllabics should be lengthened, rests in no sense on
the authority of ancient grammarians. Even as a
mere observation, they restrict it by the condition

that the next syllable must be short, in order to provoke the lengthening of the preceding syllable, thereby sanctioning, of course, many exceptions; and they then proceed to quote a number of cases where, in spite of all, the short syllable remains short*. In some of these quotations they are no doubt wrong, but in most of them their statement cannot be disputed.

As to the eighth syllable being short in hendecasyllabics and dodecasyllabics, they quote such verses as,

vi. 66, 4. āntār (íti) sāntă*h* āvādyānĭ pūnānā*h*.

Thus we see that in vi. 44, 9, varshīya*h* vāya*h* kr*i*nŭhĭ sa*k*ībhĭ*h*, hi remains short; while in vi. 25, 3, *g*āhĭ vr*i*sh*n*yānĭ kr*i*nŭhĭ pārā*k*ā*h*, it is lengthened in the Sanhitâ, the only difference being that in the second passage the accent is on hí.

As to the tenth syllable being short in a dodecasyllabic, they quote

ii. 27, 14. ădītē mĭtrā vărŭnă ŭtă mr*i*la.

---

* 'Wo die achtsilbigen Reihen mit herbeigezogen sind, ist es in der Regel bei solchen Liedern geschehen, die im Ganzen von der regelmässigen Form weniger abweichen, und für solche Fälle, wo auch das Prâtisâkhya die Längung der sechsten Silbe in achtsilbigen Reihen vorschreibt, nämlich wo die siebente von Natur kurz ist. Die achtsilbigen Reihen bedürfen einer erneuten Durchforschung, da es mehrfach schwer fällt, den Sanhitâtext mit der Vorschrift der Prâtisâkhya in Übereinstimmung zu bringen.' Kuhn, Beiträge, vol. iii. p. 450 ; and still more strongly, p. 458.

As to the tenth syllable being short in a hendecasyllabic, they quote

ii. 20, 1. vayām tē vayă*h* īndră vĭddhĭ sŭ nă*h*.

As to the sixth syllable being short in an octosyllabic, they quote

viii. 23, 26. măhā*h* vĭsvân ăbhĭ sătă*h*.

A large number of similar exceptions are collected
from 528, 3 to 534, 94, and this does not include any
cases where the ninth, the eleventh, or the seventh
syllable is long, instead of being short, while it
does include cases where the eighth syllable is
long, though the ninth is not short, or, at least, is
not short according to the views of the collectors of
these passages. See Sûtra 522, 6.

Besides the cases mentioned by the Prâtisâkhya
itself, where a short syllable, though occupying a
place which would seem to require lengthening,
remains short, there are many others which the
Prâtisâkhya does not mention, because, from its
point of view, there was no necessity for doing so.
The Prâtisâkhya has been blamed* for omitting
such cases as i. 93, 6. uru*m* ya*gñ*âya *k*akrathŭr u
lokam; or i. 96, 1. devâ agnim dhârayan drăvi*n*odâm.
But though occupying the eighth place, and though
followed by a short syllable, these syllables could

---

* ' Dazu kommt, dass der uns vorliegende Sanhitâtext vielfä!tig
gar nicht mit *S*aunaka's allgemeinen Regel übereinstimmt, in dem
die Verlängerung *kurzer Silben* nicht unter den Bedingungen ein-
getreten ist, die er vorschreibt.' Kuhn, Beiträge, vol. iii. p. 459.

never fall under the general observation of the Prâtisâkhya, because that general observation refers to *final vowels* only, but not to short syllables in general. Similar cases are i. 107, 1^a; 122, 9; 130, 10; 152, 6; 154, 1; 158, 5^a; 163, 2; 167, 10^a; 171, 4; 173, 6; 179, 1^a; 182, 8^a; 186, 6, &c.

If, therefore, we say that, happen what may, these metrical rules must be observed, and the text of the Veda altered in order to satisfy the requirements of these rules, we ought to know at all events that we do this on our own responsibility, and that we cannot shield ourselves behind the authority of Saunaka or Kâtyâyana. Now it is well known that Professor Kuhn[*] has laid down the rule that the Traishtubha pâdas must end in a bacchius or amphi-brachys ◡ – ⌣, and the Gâgata pâdas in a dijambus or pæon secundus ◡ – ◡ ⌣. With regard to Ânush-tubha pâdas, he requires the dijambus or pæon secundus ◡ – ◡ ⌣ at the end of a whole verse only, allowing greater freedom in the formation of the preceding pâdas. In a later article, however, the final pâda, too, in Ânushtubha metre is allowed greater freedom, and the rule, as above given, is strictly maintained with regard to the Traishtubha and Gâgata pâdas only.

This subject is so important, and affects so large a number of passages in the Veda, that it requires the most careful examination. The Vedic metres,

[*] Beiträge zur Vergleichenden Sprachforschung, vol. iii. p. 118.

g 2

though at first sight very perplexing, are very
simple, if reduced to their primary elements. The
authors of the Prâtisâkhyas have elaborated a most
complicated system. Counting the syllables in the
most mechanical manner, they have assigned nearly
a hundred names to every variety which they discovered in the hymns of the Rig-veda*. But they also
observed that the constituent elements of all these
metres were really but four, (Sûtras 988, 989):

1. The Gâyatra pâda, of eight syllables, ending in ∪ –.
2. The Vairâga pâda, of ten syllables, ending in – –.
3. The Traishtubha pâda, of eleven syllables, ending
   in – –.
4. The Gâgata pâda, of twelve syllables, ending in ∪ –.

Then follows an important rule, Sûtra 990: 'The
penultimate syllable,' he says, 'in a Gâyatra and
Gâgata pâda is light (laghu), in a Vairâga and
Traishtubha pâda heavy (guru).' This is called
their vritta.

This word vritta, which is generally translated
by metre, had evidently originally a more special
meaning. It meant the final rhythm, or if we
take it literally, the turn of a line, for it is derived
from vrit, to turn. Hence vritta is the same word
as the Latin *versus*, verse; but I do not wish to
decide whether the connection between the two
words is historical, or simply etymological. In
Latin, *versus* is always supposed to have meant

---

* See Appendix to my edition of the Prâtisâkhya, p. ccclvi.

originally a furrow, then a line, then a verse. In Sanskrit the metaphor that led to the formation of v*r*itta, in the sense of final rhythm, has nothing to do with ploughing. If, as I have tried to prove (Chips from a German Workshop, vol. i. p. 84), the names assigned to metres and metrical language were derived from words originally referring to choregic movements, v*r*itta must have meant the turn, i. e. the last step of any given movement; and this turn, as determining the general character of the whole movement, would naturally be regulated by more severe rules, while greater freedom would be allowed for the rest.

Having touched on this subject, I may add another fact in support of my view. The words Trish*t*ubh and Anush*t*ubh, names for the most common metres, are generally derived from a root stubh, to praise. I believe they should be derived from a root stubh, which is preserved in Greek, not only in στυφελός, hard, στυφελίζω, to strike hard, but . in the root στεμφ, from which στέμφυλον, stamped or pressed olives or grapes, and ἀστεμφής, untrodden (grapes), then unshaken; and in στέμβω, to shake, στοβέω, to scold, &c. In Sanskrit this root exists in a parallel form as stambh, lit. to stamp down, then to fix, to make firm, with which Bopp has compared the German *stampfen*, to stamp; (Glossarium, s. v. stambh.) I therefore look upon Trish*t*ubh as meaning originally *tripudium*, (supposing this word to be derived from *tri* and *pes*, according to

the expression in Horace, pepulisse ter pede terram,
Hor. Od. iii. 18,) and I explain its name ' Three-
step,' by the fact that the three last syllables ∪ – ∪,
which form the characteristic feature of that metre,
and may be called its real vritta or turn, were
audibly stamped at the end of each turn or strophe.
I explain Anushtubh, which consists of four equal
pâdas, each of eight syllables, as the ' After-step,'
because each line was stamped regularly after the
other, possibly by two choruses, each side taking
its turn. There is one passage in the Veda where
Anushtubh seems to have preserved this meaning :

x. 124, 9. anu-stúbham ánu karkúryámânam índram
ní kikyuh kaváyah manîshâ.

Poets by their wisdom discovered Indra dancing
to an Anushtubh.

Other names of metres which point to a similar
origin, i. e. to their original connection with dances,
are Padapankti, ' Step-row ;' Nyanku-sârinî, ' Roe-
step ;' Abhisârinî, ' Contre-danse,' &c.

If now we return to the statement of the Prâtisâkhya in reference to the vrittas, we should observe
how careful its author is in his language. He does
not say that the penultimate is long or short, but
he simply states, that, from a metrical point of
view, it must be considered as light or heavy,
which need not mean more than that it must be
pronounced with or without stress. The fact that
the author of the Prâtisâkhya uses these terms, laghu
and guru, instead of hrasva, short, and dîrgha, long,

shows in fact that he was aware that the penultimate in these pâdas is not invariably long or short, though, from a metrical point of view, it is always heavy or light.

It is perfectly true that if we keep to these four pâdas, (to which one more pâda, viz. the half Vairâga, consisting of five syllables, might be added,) we can reduce nearly all the hymns of the Rig-veda to their simple elements which the ancient poets combined together, in general in a very simple way, but occasionally with greater freedom. The most important strophes, formed out of these pâdas, are,

1. Three Gâyatra pâdas = the Gâyatrî, (24 syllables.)
2. Four Gâyatra pâdas = the Anushtubh, (32 syllables.)
3. Four Vairâga pâdas = the Virâg, (40 syllables.)
4. Four Traishtubha pâdas = the Trishtubh, (44 syllables.)
5. Four Gâgata pâdas = the Gagatî, (48 syllables.)

Between the Gâyatrî and Anushtubh strophes, another strophe may be formed, by mixture of Gâyatra and Gâgata pâdas, consisting of 28 syllables, and commonly called Ushnih; likewise between the Anushtubh and the Virâg, a strophe may be formed, consisting of 36 syllables, and commonly called Brihatî.

In a collection of hymns, however, like that of the Rig-veda, where poems of different ages, different places, and different families have been put together, we must be prepared for exceptions to many rules. Thus, although the final turn of the hendecasyllabic Traishtubha is, as a rule, the bacchius, ⏑ – –, yet if we take, for instance, the 77th hymn of the tenth Mandala, we clearly perceive another hendecasyllabic pâda of a totally different structure, and worked up into one of the most beautiful strophes by an ancient poet. Each line is divided into two halves, the first consisting of seven syllables, being an exact counterpart of the first member of a Saturnian verse (fato Romæ Metelli); the second a dijambus, answering boldly to the broken rhythm of the first member*. We have, in fact, a Trishtubh where the turn or the three-step, ⏑ – –, instead of being at the end, stands in the middle of the line.

x. 77, 1–5, in the Pada text:

1. ābhrā-prŭshāh nă vâkâ prŭshā vāsū,
havĭshmāntāh nă yăgñāh vĭ-gânŭshāh ı

* Professor Kuhn (vol. iii. p. 450) is inclined to admit the same metre as varying in certain hymns with ordinary Traishtubha pâdas, but the evidence he brings forward is hardly sufficient. Even if we object to the endings ⏑ – ⏑ – and – – ⏑ –, v. 33, 4, may be a *G*âgata, with vyûha of dâsa, the remark quoted from the Prâtisâkhya being of no consequence on such points; and the same remedy would apply to v. 41, 5, with vyûha of eshe. In vi. 47, 31, vyûha of asvaparnaih; in i. 33, 9, vyûha of indra and rodasî; in ii. 24, 5, vyûha of mâdbhih would produce the same effect; while in i. 121, 8, we must either admit the Traishtubha vritta – ⏑ – or scan dhŭkshăn. In iii. 58, 6, I should admit vyûha for nărâ; in iv. 26, 6, for māndrăm; in i. 100, 8, for gyŏtih, always supposing that we consider the ending – – ⏑ – incompatible with a Trishtubh verse.

sŭ-mărŭtăm nă brāhmā́nam ārhāse,
gánăm āstōshī ēshā́m nă sŏbhāse ॥

2. sriyē māryāsăh āṅgīn ăkrĭnvātā,
sŭ-mărŭtăm nă pūrvĭh ātī kshāpăh ।
dĭvăh pūtrāsăh ētăh nă yetĭre,
ādĭtyāsăh tĕ ākrăh nă vāvrĭdhŭh ॥

3. pră yĕ dĭvăh prĭthīvyăh nă bārhănā,
tmănā rĭrĭkrĕ ābhrăt nă sŭryăh ।
pāgāsvāntăh nă vīrăh pănāsyăvăh,
rĭsădāsăh nă māryăh ābhī-dyăvăh ॥

4. yŭshmākăm būdhnĕ āpām nă yămānī,
vĭthūryătĭ nă măhī srāthāryătī ।
vīsvā-psŭh yăgñăh ārvăk āyăm sŭ văh,
prāyāsvāntăh nă sātrăkăh ā gātā ॥

5. yŭyăm dhŭh-sŭ pră-yŭgăh nă rāsmĭ-bhĭh,
gyōtĭshmāntăh nă bhāsā vĭ-ūshtĭshū ।
syenāsăh nă svă-yăsasăh rĭsădāsăh,
prăvăsăh nă pră-sĭtăsăh pări-prŭshăh ॥

Another strophe, the nature of which has been totally misapprehended by native metricians, occurs in iv. 10. It is there called Padapaṅkti and Mahâpadapaṅkti; nay, attempts have been made to treat it even as an Ushnih, or as a kind of Gâyatrî. The real character of that strophe is so palpable that it is difficult to understand how it could have been mistaken. It consists of two lines, the first

embracing three or four feet of five syllables each,
having the ictus on the first and the fourth syllables, and resembling the last line of a Sapphic
verse. The second line is simply a Trishtubh. It
is what we should call an asynartete strophe, and
the contrast of the rhythm in the first and second
lines is very effective. I am not certain whether
Professor Bollensen, who has touched on this metre
in an article just published (Zeitschrift der D. M. G.,
vol. xxii. p. 572), shares this opinion. He has clearly
seen that the division of the lines, as given in the
MSS. of the Sanhitâ text, is wrong; but he seems
inclined to admit the same rhythm throughout, and
to treat the strophe as consisting of four lines of
five syllables each, and one of six syllables, which
last line is to submit to the prevailing rhythm
of the preceding lines. If we differ, however, as
to the internal architecture of this strophe, we
agree in condemning the interpretation proposed
by the Prâtisâkhya; and I should, in connection
with this, like to call attention to two important
facts: first, that the Sanhitâ text, in not changing,
for instance, the final t of martât, betrays itself as
clearly later than the elaboration of the ancient
theory of metres, later than the invention of such
a metre as the Padapankti; and secondly, that
the accentuation, too, of the Sanhitâ is thus
proved to be posterior to the establishment of
these fanciful metrical divisions, and hence cannot
throughout claim so irrefragable an authority as

certainly belongs to it in many cases. I give the Sanhitâ text :

1. Āgnē tắm ādyā ı aśvằm nằ stōmaĭ/ ı krắtŭ*m* nằ bhằdrằm,
   h*r*idisp*r*ĭśằm *r*idhy̆ằmằ tằ ōhaĭ/.

2. Ādhằ hy̆ ằgnē ı krắtōr bhằdrăsyằ ı dằkshằsyằ sằdh/ŏ/,
   rằthĭr *r*ĭtằsyằ b*r*ĭhằtō bằbh/ằthằ.

3. Ēbhĭr nŏ ằrkaĭr ı bhằvằ nŏ ằrvằ/i ı svằr nằ *gy*ōtĭ/,
   ằgnē vĭśvēbhĭ/ sŭmằnằ ằnĭkaĭ/.

4. Ābhĭsh *t*ē ằdyā ı gĭrbhĭr g*r*ĭ*n*ằntō ı ằgnē dằsēmằ,
   prắ tē dĭvō nằ stằnằyằntĭ śŭshmằ/.

5. Tắvă svằdĭsh*t/*ằ ı ằgnē sằ*m*d*r*ĭsh*t*ĭr,
   ĭdằ k/ĭd ằlmằ ı ĭdằ k/ĭd ằktŏ/,
   śrĭyē rŭkmō nắ rŏk/ắtă ŭpằkē.

6. Ghrĭtắ*m* nằ pŭtắ*m* ı tắnŭr ằrēpằ/ ı śŭk/ĭ hĭra*n*yằm,
   tắt tē rŭkmō nằ rŏk/ắtằ svằdhằvă/.

7. K*r*ĭtằ*m* k/ĭd dhĭ shmằ ı sằnēmĭ dvēshō ı ằgnắ ĭnōshĭ,
   mằrtằd ĭtthằ yắ*g*ằmằnằd *r*ĭtằvă/.

8. Śĭvằ nă/ sằkhyằ ı sằntŭ bhrằtrằgnē ı dēvēshŭ yŭshmē,
   sằ nō nằbhĭ/ sắdằnē sằsmĭn ŭdhằn.

Now it is perfectly true that, as a general rule, the syllables composing the v*r*itta or turn of the different metres, and described by the Prâtisâkhya as heavy or light, are in reality long or short. The question, however, is this, have we a right, or are we obliged, in cases where that syllable is not either long or short, as it ought to be, so to alter the text, or so to change the rules of pronunciation, that the penultimate may again be what we wish it to be ?

If we begin with the Gâyatra pâda, we have not to read long before we find that it would be hopeless to try to crush the Gâyatrî verses of the Vedic *Ri*shis on this Procrustean bed. Even Professor Kuhn very soon perceived that this was impossible. He had to admit that in the Gâyatrî the two first pâdas, at all events, were free from this rule, and though he tried to retain it for the third or final pâda, he was obliged after a time to give it up even there. Again, it is perfectly true, that in the third pâda of the Gâyatrî, and in the second and fourth pâdas of the Anush*t*ubh strophe, greater care is taken by the poets to secure a short syllable for the penultimate, but here, too, exceptions cannot be entirely removed. We have only to take such a single hymn as i. 27, and we shall see that it would be impossible to reduce it to the uniform standard of Gâyatrî pâdas, all ending in a dijambus. But what confirms me even more in my view that such strict uniformity must not be looked for in the ancient hymns of the *Ri*shis, is the fact that in many cases it would be so very easy to replace the irregular by a regular dipodia. Supposing that the original poets had restricted themselves to the dijambus, who could have put in the place of that regular dijambus an irregular dipodia ? Certainly not the authors of the Prâti-sâkhya, for their ears had clearly discovered the

general rhythm of the ancient metres; nor their
predecessors, for they had in many instances preserved the tradition of syllables lengthened in
accordance with the requirements of the metre.
I do not mean to insist too strongly on this argument, or to represent those who handed down the
tradition of the Veda as endowed with anything like
apaurusheyatva. Strange accidents have happened
in the text of the Veda, but they have generally
happened when the sense of the hymns had ceased
to be understood; and if anything helped to preserve the Veda from greater accidents, it was due,
I believe, to the very fact that the metre continued
to be understood, and that oral tradition, however
much it might fail in other respects, had at all
events to satisfy the ears of the hearers. I should
have been much less surprised if all irregularities
in the metre had been smoothed down by the flux
and reflux of oral tradition, a fact which is so
apparent in the text of Homer, where the gaps
occasioned by the loss of the digamma, were made
good by the insertion of unmeaning particles; but
I find it difficult to imagine by what class of men,
who must have lived between the original poets
and the age of the Prâtisâkhyas, the simple rhythm
of the Vedic metres should have been disregarded,
and the sense of rhythm, which ancient people
possess in a far higher degree than we ourselves,
been violated through crude and purposeless alterations. I shall give a few specimens only. What

but a regard for real antiquity could have induced
people in viii. 2, 8, to preserve the defective foot
of a Gâyatrî verse, sămâne ădhĭ bhârman? Any
one acquainted with Sanskrit would naturally read
sămâne ădhĭ bhârmăni. But who would have
changed bhârmani, if that had been there originally,
to bhârman? I believe we must scan sămâne ădhĭ
bhârman, or sămâne ădhĭ bhârman, the pæon tertius being a perfectly legitimate foot at the end
of a Gâyatrî verse. In x. 158, 1, we can understand how an accident happened. The original
poet may have said: Sŭryŏ nŏ dĭvâs pâtŭ pâtŭ
vâtŏ ântărĭkshât, âgnĭr nah pârthĭvêbhyah. Here
one of the two pâtu was lost. But if in the same
hymn we find in the second verse two feet of nine
instead of eight syllables each, I should not venture
to alter this except in pronunciation, because no
reason can be imagined why any one should have
put these irregular lines in the place of regular
ones.

In v. 41, 10, grĭnîtê âgnĭr êtărî nă sŭshaih, sŏkĭ-
shkêsŏ nĭ rĭnâtĭ vânâ, every modern Pandit would
naturally read vanâni instead of vanâ, in order to
get the regular Trishtubh metre. But this being
the case, how can we imagine that even the most
ignorant member of an ancient Parishad should
wilfully have altered vanâni into vanâ? What
surprises one is, that vanâ should have been spared,
in spite of every temptation to change it into
vanâni: for I cannot doubt for one moment that

vanâ is the right reading, only that the ancient
poets pronounced it vănă̄. Wherever we alter the
text of the Rig-veda by conjecture, we ought to
be able, if possible, to give some explanation how
the mistake which we wish to remove came to be
committed. If a passage is obscure, difficult to
construe, if it contains words which occur in no
other place, then we can understand how, during
a long process of oral tradition, accidents may have
happened. But when everything is smooth and
easy, when the intention of the poet is not to be
mistaken, when the same phrase has occurred many
times before, then to suppose that a simple and
perspicuous sentence was changed into a complicated and obscure string of words is more difficult
to understand. I know there are passages where
we cannot as yet account for the manner in which
an evidently faulty reading found its way into
both the Pada and Sanhitâ texts, but in those very
passages we cannot be too circumspect. If we read
viii. 40, 9, pûrvîsh tă̄ indropămătăyă̄h pûrvîr ŭtă̄
prăsăstăyăh, nothing seems more tempting than to
omit indra, and to read pûrvîsh tă̄ ŭpămătăyăh.
Nor would it be difficult to account for the insertion of indra; for though one would hardly venture
to call it a marginal gloss that crept into the text—
a case which, as far as I can see, has never happened in the hymns of the Rig-veda—it might be
taken for an explanation given by an Âkârya to his
pupils, in order to inform them that the ninth verse,

different from the eighth, was addressed to Indra.
But however plausible this may sound, the question
remains whether the traditional reading could not
be maintained, by admitting synizesis of ọpa, and
reading pûrvîsh tă îndrŏpămătăyăh. For a similar
synizesis of ‿ ‿, see iii. 6, 10. prăĺî ădhvărĕvă tă-
sthătŭh, unless we read prăḱy ădhvărĕvă.

Another and more difficult case of synizesis
occurs in

vii. 86, 4. ăvă tvănĕnă nămăsă tŭra(h) ĭyăm.
It would be easy to conjecture tvareyâm instead
of tura iyâm, but tvareyâm, in the sense of 'let
me hasten,' is not Vedic. The choriambic ending,
however, of Trishtubha can be proved to be legitimate, and if that is the case, then even the
synizesis of tŭră, though hard, ought not to be
regarded as impossible.

In ii. 18, 5, â vīmsătyă trîmsătă yăhў ărvăn̊,

â ḱatvărĭmsătă harĭbhĭr yŭgănăh,

â pănḱăsătă sŭrăthĕbhĭr ĭndră,

â shăshtўă săptătyă sŏmăpĕyăm,   .

Professor Kuhn proposes to omit the â at the
beginning of the second line, in order to have
eleven instead of twelve syllables. By doing so
he loses the uniformity of the four pâdas, which
all begin with â, while by admitting synizesis of
harĭbhĭh all necessity for conjectural emendation
disappears.

If the poets of the Veda had objected to a pæon

quartus (◡◡◡–) at the end of a Gâyatrî, what could have been easier than to change iv. 52, 1, divo adarsi dŭhĭtā, into adarsi duhĭtā dĭvaḥ? or x. 118, 6, ădā-bhyăm gṛĭhăpătĭm, into gṛĭhăpătĭm ădābhyăm?

If an epitritus secundus (–◡––).had been objectionable in the same place, why not say vi. 61, 10, stŏmyă bhŭt sărāsvătī, instead of sărāsvătī stŏmyă bhŭt? Why not viii. 2, 11, revāntăm hĭ sṛĭnŏmĭ tvā, instead of revāntăm hĭ tvā sṛĭnŏmĭ?

If an ionicus a minore (◡◡––) had been excluded from that place, why not say i. 30, 10, gărĭtṛĭbhyaḥ săkhē văsō, instead of săkhē văsō gărĭtṛĭbhyaḥ? or i. 41, 7, vărŭnăsyă măhī psăraḥ, instead of măhī psărō vărŭnăsyā?

If a dispondeus (––––) was to be avoided, then v. 68, 3, măhĭ văm kshătrăm dēvĕshŭ, might easily have been replaced by deveshu văm kshătrăm măhĭ, and viii. 2, 10, sukrâ âsirăm yăƙāntē, by sukrâ yăƙantă âsirăm.

If no epitritus primus (◡–––) was allowed, why not say vi. 61, 11, nĭdās pătŭ sărāsvătĭ, instead of sărāsvătĭ nĭdās pătŭ, or viii. 79, 4, dvĕshō yăvĭr ăghāsyă ƙit, instead of yăvĭr ăghāsyă ƙid dvĕshaḥ?

Even the epitritus tertius (––◡–) might easily have been avoided by dropping the augment of apâm in x. 119, 1–13, kuvit somasyăpăm ĭtĭ. It is, in fact, a variety of less frequent occurrence than the rest, and might possibly be eliminated with some chance of success.

Lastly, the choriambus (–◡◡–) could have been

removed in iii. 24, 5, *sisîhî* na*h* sûnumâta*h*, by reading
sûnumâta*h* *sisîhî* na*h*, and in viii. 2, 31, sânâd am*r*iktô
dâyâtê, by reading ăm*r*iktô dâyâtê sânât.

But I am afraid the idea that regularity is better
than irregularity, and that in the Veda, where there
is a possibility, the regular metre is to be restored by
means of conjectural emendations, has been so ably
advocated by some of the most eminent scholars,
that a merely general argument would now be of
no avail. I must therefore give as much evidence
as I can bring together in support of the contrary
opinion; and though the process is a tedious one,
the importance of the consequences with regard to
Vedic criticism leaves me no alternative. With
regard, then, to the final dipodia of Gâyatrî verses,
I still hold and maintain, that, although the dijambus is by far the most general metre, the following
seven varieties have to be recognized in the poetry
of the Veda :

1. ∪ − ∪ −, 2. ∪ ∪ ∪ −, 3. − ∪ − −, 4. ∪ ∪ − −, 5. − − − −,
6. ∪ − − −, 7. − − ∪ −, 8. − ∪ ∪ −.

I do not pretend to give every passage in which
these varieties occur, but I hope I shall give a
sufficient number in support of every one of them.
I have confined myself almost entirely to the final
dipodia of Gâyatrî verses, as the Ânush*t*ubha verses
would have swelled the lists too much; and in
order to avoid every possible objection, I have
given the verses, not in their Pada, but in their
Sanhitâ form.

§ 2. ⏑ ⏑ ⏑ –.

i. 12, 9. tasmai pâvakă mṛil̆ayā. (Instead of mṛilaya, it has been proposed to read mardaya.)

i. 18, 9. divo na sadmămăkhăsām.

i. 42, 4. padâbhi tishṭhă tăpŭshĭm.

i. 46, 2. dhiyâ devâ văsŭvĭdā. (It would have been easy to read vasûvidâ.)

i. 97, 1–8. apa naḥ soṣŭḱăt ăghām.

iii. 11, 3. artham hy asyă tărăṇī.

iii. 27, 10. agne sudîtĭm ŭṣĭgăm.

iv. 15, 7. akkhâ na hûtă ŭd ărăm.

iv. 32, 4. asmâñ-asmâñ̆ ĭd ŭd ăvā.

iv. 52, 1. divo adarṣĭ dŭhĭtā.

v. 5, 9. yagñe-yagñe nă ŭd ăvā.

v. 7, 4. pra smâ minâty̆ ăgărāḥ.

v. 7, 5. bhûmâ pṛishṭhevă rŭrŭhŭḥ.

v. 7, 7. anibhṛishṭătăvĭshĭḥ.

v. 9, 4. agne paṣur nă yăvāse.

v. 53, 12. enâ yâmenă mărŭtāḥ.

v. 61, 3. putrakṛithe nă gănăyāḥ.

v. 61, 11. atra ṣravâṁsĭ dădhĭre.

v. 64, 5. săkhĭnấm ḱă vṛidhāse.

v. 65, 4. sumatir astĭ vĭdhātāḥ.

v. 82, 9. pra ḱa suvâtĭ săvĭtā.

vi. 16, 17. tatrâ sadaḥ kṛĭnăvăse.

vi. 16, 18. athâ duvo vănăvăse.

h 2

vi. 16, 45. soḱâ vi bhâhy̆ ăgărā.

vi. 45, 17. sa tvaṃ na indră mṛĭlāyā.

vi. 61, 4. dhĭnâm ăvītry̆ ăvātū.

vii. 15, 14. p̆ūr bhăvā sătăbhŭgĭh.

vii. 66, 2. asuryâya prămăhăsâ.

viii. 6, 35. anuttamany̆um ăgărām.

viii. 6, 42. satam vahantŭ hărăyăh.

viii. 32, 10. sâdhu kṛĭṅvantăm ăvăsē.

viii. 44, 28. tasmai pâvakă mṛĭlāyā.

viii. 45, 31. mâ tat kar indră mṛĭlāyā.

viii. 72, 6. dâmâ rathasy̆ă dădṛĭsē.

viii. 72, 13. rasâ dadhītă vṛĭshăbhām.

viii. 80, 1 and 2. tvaṃ na indră mṛĭlāyă.

viii. 83, 3. yûyam ṛitasy̆ă răthy̆ăh.

viii. 93, 27. stotṛibhy̆a indră mṛĭlāyā.

ix. 61, 5. tebhir naḥ somă mṛĭlāyă.

ix. 64, 1. vṛishâ dharmăṅĭ dădhĭshē.

x. 118, 6. adâbhyaṃ gṛĭhăpătĭm.

§ 3. – ᴗ – –.

i. 22, 11. aḱḱhinnapatrāḥ săḱāntâm.

i. 30, 13. kshumanto y̆âbhĭr mădēmā.

i. 41, 8. sumnair id va ā vĭvâsē.

i. 90, 1. aryamâ devaïḥ săgōshăḥ.

i. 90, 4. pûshâ bhago vândy̆âsaḥ.

i. 120, 1. kathâ vidhâty āprăḱētăḥ.

v. 19, 1. upasthe mâtūr vĭ ḱăshḱe.

v. 70, 3. turyâma dasyûn tănûbhĭ*h*.

vi. 61, 10. sarasvatî stōmyắ bhût.

viii. 2, 2. asvo na niktō nădîshû.

viii. 2, 4. antar devân mártyǎ*m*s *k*â.

viii. 2, 5. apasp*r*invatē sŭhấrdām.

viii. 2, 11. revanta*m* hi tvắ s*r*inōmî.

viii. 2, 12. ûdhar na nagnắ *g*ărántē.

viii. 2, 13. pred u harivă*h* srútāsyâ.

viii. 2, 14. na gâyatra*m* gĭyắmânâm.

viii. 2, 15. sikshâ sa*k*îvă*h* să*k*ĭbhĭ*h*.

viii. 2, 16. ka*n*vâ ukthebhĭr *g*ărántē.

viii. 2, 17. taved u stomā*m* *k*ĭkētâ.

viii. 2, 29. indra kâri*n*ā*m* v*r*ĭdhāntă*h*.

viii. 2, 30. satrâ dadhirē săvǎ*m*sî.

viii. 2, 32. mahân mahîbhĭ*h* să*k*ĭbhĭ*h*.

viii. 2, 33. anu ghen mandĭ́ măghōnă*h*.

viii. 2, 36. sātyō ʾvîtắ vĭdhāntām.

viii. 2, 37. yo bhût somai*h* sátyămādvắ.

viii. 7, 30. mâr*d*îkebhir nắdhămấnām.

viii. 7, 33. vâv*r*ĭtyǎ*m* *k*ĭtrāvắ*g*ân.

viii. 11, 2. agne rathîr ādhvarắ*n*ắm.

viii. 11, 3. adevîr agnē ắrắtĭ*h* (or § 4).

viii. 11, 4. nopa veshi *g*ấtāvēdă*h*.

viii. 16, 3. maho vâ*g*inā*m* sănĭbhyă*h*.

viii. 16, 4. harshumanta*h* sûrăsâtāu.

viii. 16, 5. yeshâm indras tē *g*ấyāntî.

viii. 16, 7. mahân mahîbhĭ*h* să*k*ĭbhĭ*h*. Cf. viii. 2, 32.

viii. 46, 2. vidma dâtâram rayīnām.

viii. 71, 2. tvăm ĭd ăsī kshăpăvăn (or § 4).

viii. 81, 1. mahâhastî dăkshĭnēnā.

viii. 81, 3. bhîmam na gâm vărăyântē.

viii. 81, 4. na râdhasâ mârdhĭshăn nă/.

viii. 81, 7. adâsûsh/arāsyā vēdā/.

viii. 81, 9. vasais /a makshû ğărānte.

viii. 94, 2. sŭryâmăsâ d/ĭse kām.

ix. 62, 5. svadanti gâva/ păyōbhĭ/.

x. 20, 4. kavir abhram dĭdyănă/.

x. 20, 7. adre/ sûnum âyŭm âhŭ/.

§ 4. ◡ ◡ – – .

i. 3, 8. usrâ iva svăsărănī.

i. 27, 4. agne deveshŭ pr
ă vō/ă/.

i. 30, 10. sakhe vaso gărĭt/ĭbhyă/.

i. 30, 15. /ĭnor aksham nă să/ĭbhī/.

i. 38, 7. miham k/ĭnvanty ăvātăm.

i. 38, 8. yad eshâm vrishtĭr ăsărğī.

i. 41, 7. mahi psaro vărŭnāsyā.

i. 43, 7. mahi sravas tŭvĭm/ĭm/ăm.

ii. 6, 2. enâ sûktenâ sŭ/ătă.

iii. 27, 3. ăti dveshâmsĭ tărēmā.

v. 82, 7. satyasavam săvĭtărăm.

vi. 16, 25. ûrğo napâd ăm/ĭtāsyā.

vi. 16, 26. marta ânâsă sŭv/ĭktĭm.

vi. 61, 12. vâğe-vâğe hăvyâ bhŭt.

viii. 2, 1. anâbhayin rărĭmä̃ te̅.

viii. 2, 3. indra tvâsmint sădhămä̃de̅.

viii. 2, 8. sămä̃ne̅ ădhĭ bhä̃rmän (see page cx).

viii. 2, 18. yanti pramâdä̃m ătä̃ndrä̃h.

viii. 2, 19. mahâñ iva yŭvä̃gänĭh.

viii. 2, 21. trishu gâtasyä̃ mänä̃msi̅.

viii. 2, 22. yasastaram sätämä̃teh.

viii. 2, 23. bharâ piban näryä̃yä̃.

viii. 2, 26. ni yamate sätämä̃tĭh.

viii. 2, 35. ino vasu sä̆ hĭ vo̅llhä̃.

viii. 16, 2. apâm avo nä̆ sämŭdre̅.

viii. 16, 6. esha indro vărĭvä̃skrĭt.

viii. 16, 8. ekas kit sann ăbhĭbhŭtĭh.

viii. 71, 9. sakhe vaso gărĭtrĭbhyah. Cf. i. 30, 10.

viii. 79, 3. uru yantâsi̅ vărŭthä̃m.

ix. 21, 5. yo asmabhyäm ărä̃vä̃ (or ărä̃vä̆).

ix. 62, 6. madhvo rasam sädhämä̃de̅.

ix. 66, 21. dadhad rayim mä̆yĭ po̅shäm.

x. 20, 5. minvant sadına pŭrä̃ e̅ti̅.

x. 185, 1. durâdharsham värŭnasyä̃.

x. 185, 2. î̵e ripur ăghä̃sämsäh.

x. 185, 3. gyotir yakkhantй̆ ăgäsräm.

§ 5. – – – –.

i. 2, 7. dhiyam ghritâkĭm sädhäntä̃.

i. 3, 4. anvibhis tanä̃ pŭtä̃sah.

i. 27, 3. pâhi sadam ĭd vĭsvä̃yüh.

i. 90, 2. vratâ rakshantē vīsvâhā (or § 6).

ii. 6, 4. yuyodhy asmād dvēshāmsī.

iii. 41, 8. indra svadhâvō mātsvēhā (or § 6).

v. 68, 3. mahi vâm kshatrām dēvēshū.

v. 68, 4. adruhâ devau vârdhētē.

viii. 2, 10. sukrâ âsirām yâkântē.

viii. 2, 24. vâgam stotribhyō gōmāntām (or § 6).

viii. 16, 1. naram nrishâhām māmhishthām.

viii. 16, 12. akkhâ ka nah sumnām nēshī.

viii. 79, 2. prem andhah khyan nīh srōnō bhût.

ix. 66, 17. bhûridâbhyas kīn māmhīyân.

x. 20, 6. agnim devâ vâsīmāntâm.

x. 20, 8. agnim havishâ vārdhāntah.

§ 6. ⏑ – – –.

i. 15, 6. ritunâ yagñam âsâthē.

i. 38, 2. kva vo gâvo nă rănyāntī (see page 70).

i. 38, 9. yat prithivîm vyūndāntī.

i. 86, 9. vidhyatâ vidyûtâ rākshah.

iii. 27, 2. srushtîvânam dhîtâvânām.

iii. 41, 3. vîhi sûra purolâsām.

iv. 32, 23. babhrû yâmeshû sobhctē.

v. 68, 5. brihantam gartām âsâtē.

v. 70, 2. vayam te rudrâ syâmā.

vi. 61, 11. sarasvatî nidās pâtū.

viii. 2, 20. asrira ivă gâmâtâ.

viii. 2, 25. somam vîrâyă sûrâyâ.

viii. 7, 32. stushe hira*n*yavāsībhi*h*.

viii. 26, 19. vahethe *s*ubhrāyāvānā.

viii. 79, 4. yâvîr aghasyā *k*id dveshā*h*.

viii. 79, 5. vav*r*igyus trishyātā*h* kāmam.

viii. 81, 6. indra mâ no vāsŏr nīr bhāk.

x. 158, 4. sa*m* *k*edam vi *k*ā pāsyemā.

§ 7. – ‿ ‿ –.

i. 10, 8. sa*m* gā̆ āsmābhya*m* dhūnŭhī.

i. 12, 5. āgnē tvă̄m rākshāsvīnā*h*.

i. 37, 15. visva*m* *k*id âyūr *g*īvāsĕ.

i. 43, 8. â na indo vā*g*ē bhā*g*ā.

i. 46, 6. tâm asme rāsā̆thā̆m īshām.

iii. 62, 7. asmā́bhis tubhyā̄m sāsyă̄tē.

iv. 30, 21. dâsânâm indrŏ̎ mā̆yāyā̆.

v. 86, 5. a*m*seva devā̆v ārvă̄tē.

viii. 5, 32. pū̆rū*s*kāndrā̆ nā̆sātyā̆ (or nā̆sātyā̆, § 8).

viii. 5, 35. dhī*g*āvānā̆ nā̆sātyā̆.

x. 119, 1–13. kuvit somasyā́pā́m ĭtī̄.

x. 144, 4. *s*ătă*k*ākrā*m* yŏ̄ 'hyŏ̄ vārtānī*h*.

§ 8. – ‿ ‿ –.

i. 2, 9. daksha*m* dadhātē̄ ă̆pāsām (or § 2).

i. 6, 10. indra*m* maho vā̆ ra*g*āsa*h*.

i. 27, 6. sadyo dâsushē̄ kshă̄rāsī̄.

i. 30, 21. asve na *k*itrē̄ ārŭshī̄ (or § 2).

i. 41, 9. na duruktâyā sp*r*ĭhāyēt (or § 2).

i. 90, 5. kā̄rtā̆ nā*h* svā̄stĭmātā*h*.

iii. 24, 5. sisîhi na*h* sŭnŭmătā*h.*

v. 19, 2. â d*r*il*h*âm pura̅m vĭvĭsū*h.*

v. 70, 1. mitra va̅msi vām sŭmātīm.

v. 70, 4. mâ seshasâ mā tănāsā.

v. 82, 8. svādhīr devā*h* săvĭtā.

viii. 2, 27. gîrbhi*h* srutam gĭrvănăsăm.

viii. 2, 31. sanâd am*r*iktō dăyăte (or § 2).

viii. 16, 9. indra*m* vardhantī kshĭtāyā*h* (or § 2).

viii. 55, 4. asvâso na *k*ańkrămătā.

viii. 67, 19. yûyam asmabhyā*m* m*r*ĭ*l*ătā.

viii. 81, 5. abhi râdhasā *g*ŭgŭrăt.

viii. 81, 8. asmâbhi*h* su tā*m* sănŭhī.

ix. 47, 2. *r*inâ *k*a dh*r*ishnūs *k*ăyăte.

But although with regard to the Gâyatra, and
I may add, the Ânush*t*ubha pâdas, the evidence
as to the variety of their v*r*ittas is such that it
can hardly be resisted, a much more determined
stand has been made in defence of the v*r*itta of
the Traish*t*ubha and *G*âgata pâdas. Here Professor
Kuhn and those who follow him maintain that the
rule is absolute, that the former must end in ᴗ – ᴗ,
the latter in ᴗ – ᴗ –, and that the eighth syllable,
immediately preceding these syllables, ought, if possible, to be long. Nor can I deny that Professor
Kuhn has brought forward powerful arguments in
support of his theory, and that his emendations of
the Vedic text recommend themselves by their great
ingenuity and simplicity. If his theory could be

carried out, I should readily admit that we should gain something. We should have throughout the Veda a perfectly uniform metre, and wherever we found any violation of it, we should be justified in resorting to conjectural criticism.

The only question is at what price this strict uniformity can be obtained. If, for instance, in order to have the regular vrittas at the end of Traishtubha and Gâgata lines, we were obliged to repeal all rules of prosody, to allow almost every short vowel to be used as long, and every long vowel to be used as short, whether long by nature or by position, we should have gained very little, we should have robbed Peter to pay Paul, we should have removed no difficulty, but only ignored the causes which created it. Now, if we examine the process by which Professor Kuhn establishes the regularity of the vrittas or final syllables of Traishtubha and Gâgata pâdas, we find, in addition to the rules laid down before, and in which he is supported, as we saw, to a great extent by the Prâtisâkhya and Pânini, viz. the anceps nature of e and o, and of a long final vowel before a vowel, the following exceptions or metrical licences, without which that metrical uniformity at which he aims, could not be obtained :

i. The vowel o in the body of a word is to be treated as optionally short :

ii. 39, 3. prăti văstŏr ūsrā (see Trisht. § 5).

Here the o of vastoh is supposed to be short, although it is the Guna of u, and therefore very different from the final e of sarve or âste, or the final o of sarvo for sarvas or mano for manas*. It should be remarked that in Greek, too, the final diphthongs corresponding to the e of sarve and âste are treated as short, as far as the accent is concerned. Hence ἄποικοι, τύπτεται, and even γνῶμαι, nom. plur. In Latin, too, the old terminations of the nom. sing. o and u, instead of the later us, are short. (Neue, Formenlehre, § 23 seq.)

vi. 51, 15. gŏpâ ămâ.

Here the o of gopâ is treated as short, in order to get ⏑–⏑– instead of ––⏑–, which is perfectly legitimate at the end of an Ushnih.

2. The long î and û are treated as short, not only before vowels, which is legitimate, but also before consonants :

vii. 62, 4. dyâvâbhûmî ădĭtē trâsîthâm naḥ (see Trisht. § 5).

The forms îsîyâ and râsîyâ in vii. 32, 18, occur at the end of octosyllabic or Gâyatra pâdas, and are therefore perfectly legitimate, yet Professor Kuhn would change them too, into îsĭyâ and râsĭyâ. In vii. 28, 4, even mâyî is treated as mâyĭ (see Trisht. § 5); and in vii. 68, 1, vîtam as vĭtam. If, in explanation

* A very strong divergence of opinion is expressed on this point by Professor Bollensen. He says : 'O und E erst später in die Schrifttafel aufgenommen, bewahren ihre Länge durch das ganze indische Schriftenthum bis ins Apabhramsa hinab. Selbstverständlich kann kurz o und e im Veda erst recht nicht zugelassen werden.' Zeitschrift der D. M. G., vol. xxii. p. 574.

of this shortening of vîtam, vîhi is quoted, which
is identified with vîhi, this can hardly be considered
as an argument, for vĭhĭ occurs where no short
syllable is required, iv. 48, 1; ii. 26, 2; and where,
therefore, the shortening of the vowel cannot be
attributed to metrical reasons.

3. Final m followed by an initial consonant is
allowed to make no position, and even in the
middle of a word a nasal followed by a liquid is
supposed to make positio debilis. Several of the instances, however, given in support, are from Gâyatra
pâdas, where Professor Kuhn, in some of his later
articles, has himself allowed greater latitude; others
admit of different scanning, as for instance,

i. 117, 8. māhaḥ kshōṇāsyā āsvinā kānvāyā.

Here, even if we considered the dispondeus as ille-
gitimate, we might scan kă̄nvāyā, for this scanning
occurs in other places, while to treat the first a as
short before ṇo seems tantamount to surrendering
all rules of prosody.

4. Final n before semivowels, mutes, and double
n before vowels make no position*. Ex. iii. 49, 1.
yāsmĭn vĭsvā̆ (Trisht. § 5); i. 174, 5. yāsmĭñ ḱā̆kān;
i. 186, 4. sāsmĭn(n) ūdhān†.

---

* Professor Kuhn has afterwards (Beiträge, vol. iv. p. 207)
modified this view, and instead of allowing a final nasal followed
by a mute to make positio debilis, he thinks that the nasal should
in most cases be omitted altogether.

† Here a distinction should be made, I think, between an n
before a consonant, and a final n following a short vowel, which,

5. Final Visarga before sibilants makes no position *. Ex. iv. 21, 10. satyă̄h̆ sāmrā̆t (Trishṭ. § 5). Even in i. 63, 4. ḱodī̆h sākhā̆ (probably a G̈âgata), and v. 82, 4. sāvı̆h saūbhăgām (a Gây. § 7), the long i is treated as short, and the short a of sakhâ is lengthened, because an aspirate follows.

6. S before mutes makes no position. Ex. vi. 66, 11. ūgrā̆ ăspṛidhrān (Trishṭ. § 3).

7. S before k makes no position. Ex. vĭsvā̆-sḱāndṛăh; &c.

8. Mutes before s make no position. Ex. rắkshās, according to Professor Kuhn, in the seventh Maṇḍala only, but see i. 12, 5; kŭtsa, &c.

9. Mutes before r or v make no position. Ex. sŭsı̆prā̆, dīrgḧăsrūt.

10. Sibilants before y make no position. Ex. dăsyŭn.

11. R followed by mutes or sibilants makes no position. Ex. ā̆yūr ǵı̆vāsē, kḧārdı̆h, vărshishṭḧām.

12. Words like smă̄ddishṭı̆m &c. retain their vowel short before two following consonants.

We now proceed to consider a number of pro-

according to the rules of Sandhi, is doubled, if a vowel follows. In the latter case, the vowel before the n remains, no doubt, short in many cases, or, more correctly, the doubling of the n does not take place, e. g. i. 63, 4; 186, 4. In other places, the doubling seems preferable, e. g. i. 33, 11, though Professor Kuhn would remove it altogether. Kuhn, Beiträge, vol. iii. p. 125.

* Here, too, according to later researches, Professor Kuhn would rather omit the final sibilant altogether, loc. cit. vol. iv. p. 207.

sodial rules which Professor Kuhn proposes to repeal in order to have a long syllable where the MSS. supply a short:

1. The vowel *ri* is to be pronounced as long, or rather as ar. Ex. i. 12, 9. tásmaĭ pāvākă mri̯ĭ̆/āyă is to be read mārdā̆yā; v. 33, 10. sămvărăṅasyă *ri*shĕ/ is to be read arshĕ/. But why not sămvărăṅasyă *ri*shĕ/ (i. e. siarshĕ/)?

2. The *a* privativum may be lengthened. Ex. ağărā/, ămrĭ̯tā/.

3. Short vowels before liquids may be long. Ex. nără/, tărutâ, tărati, mărutâm, hărivă/, ărushi, dadhŭr iha, sŭvitâ (p. 471).

4. Short vowels before nasals may be lengthened. Ex. ğanân, sănitar, tănŭ/, ŭpă nă/.

5. Short vowels before the *ma* of the superlative may be lengthened. Ex. nri̯tăma.

6. The short *a* in the roots *sam* and *yam*, and in *am* (the termination of the accusative) may be lengthened.

7. The group ăvă is to be pronounced aŭă. Ex. ăvăsĕ becomes aŭăsĕ; săvitâ becomes saŭitâ; năvă becomes naŭă.

8. The group ăyă is to be changed into aĭă or ĕă. Ex. năyăsĭ becomes nāĭăsĭ.

9. The group vă is to be changed into ua, and this ua to be treated as a kind of diphthong and therefore long. Ex. kănvătămă/ becomes kănŭâtă-mā/; vărŭṅā/ becomes ŭārŭṅă/.

10. The short vowel in the reduplicated syllable of perfects is to be lengthened. Ex. tătănā/, dădhĭrĕ.

11. Short vowels before all aspirates may be lengthened. Ex. ráthâ*h* becomes rāthâ*h;* sắkhâ becomes sâkhâ.

12. Short vowels before h and all sibilants may be lengthened. Ex. măhĭnĭ becomes māhĭnĭ; ŭsĭgâm becomes ūsĭgâm; rĭshătē becomes rĭshătē; dăsăt becomes dāsăt.

13. The short vowel before t may be lengthened. Ex. vâgavătă*h* becomes vâgavătă*h;* ătithĭ*h* becomes ātithĭ*h*.

14. The short vowel before d may be lengthened. Ex. ŭdaram becomes ūdaram; ŭd ava becomes ūd ava.

15. The short vowel before p may be lengthened. Ex. ăpâm becomes āpâm; tăpushim becomes tāpushim; g*ʳ*ihăpatim becomes g*ʳ*ihāpatim.

16. The short vowel before g and *g* may be lengthened. Ex. sânushăg asat becomes sânushāg asat; yunăgan becomes yunāgan.

Let us now turn back for one moment to look at the slaughter which has been committed! Is there one single rule that has been spared? Is there one single short syllable that must always remain short, or a long syllable that must always remain long? If all restrictions of prosody are thus removed, our metres, no doubt, become perfectly regular. But it should be remembered that these metrical rules, for which all this carnage has been committed, are not founded upon any *à priori* principles, but deduced by ancient or modern metricians from those very hymns which seem so constantly to violate them. Neither ancient nor modern metricians had, as far as we know, any evidence to go upon besides the hymns of the Rig-veda; and the philosophical speculations as to the origin of metres in which some of them indulge, and from which they would fain derive some of their unbending rules, are, as need hardly be said, of no consequence whatever. I cannot understand what definite idea even modern writers connect with such statements as that, for instance, the Trish*t*ubh metre sprang from the *G*agatî metre, that the eleven syllables of the former are an abbreviation of the twelve syllables of the latter. Surely, metres are not made artificially, and by addition or subtraction. Metres have a natural origin in the rhythmic sentiment of different people, and they become artificial and arithmetical in the same way as language with its innate principles of law and analogy becomes in course of time grammatical and artificial. To derive one metre from another is like deriving a genitive from a nominative, which we may do indeed for grammatical purposes, but which no one would venture to do who is at all acquainted with the natural and independent production of grammatical forms. Were we to arrange the Trish*t*ubh and *G*agatî metres in chronological order, I should decidedly place the Trish*t*ubh first, for we see, as it were before our eyes, how sometimes one foot, sometimes two and three feet in a Trish*t*ubh verse admit an additional syllable at the end, particularly in set phrases which would not submit to a Trish*t*ubh ending. The phrase *sam* no bhava dvipade *sam* *k*atushpade is evidently a solemn phrase, and we see it brought in without hesitation, even though every other line of the same strophe or hymn is Trish*t*ubh, i. e. hendecasyllabic, not dodecasyllabic. See, for instance, vi. 74, 1; vii. 54, 1; x. 85, 44; 165, 1. However, I maintain by no means that this was the actual origin of *G*agatî metres; I only refer to it in order to show the groundlessness of metrical theories which represent the component elements, a foot of one or two or four syllables as given first, and as afterwards compounded into systems of two, three or four such feet, and who therefore would wish us to look upon the hendecasyllabic Trish*t*ubh as originally a dodecasyllabic *G*agatî, only deprived of its tail. If my explanation of the name of Trish*t*ubh, i. e. Three-step, is right, its origin must be ascribed to a far more natural process than that of artificial amputation. It was to accompany a choros, i. e. a dance, which after advancing freely for eight steps in one direction, turned back (v*r*itta) with three steps, the second of which was strongly marked, and would therefore, whether in song or recitation, be naturally accompanied by a long syllable. It certainly is so in the vast majority of Trish*t*ubhs which have been handed down to us. But if among these verses we find a small number in which this simple and palpable rhythm is violated, and which nevertheless were preserved from the first in that imperfect form, although the temptation to set them right must have been as great to the ancient as it has proved to be to the modern students of the Veda, are we to say that nearly all, if not all, the rules that determine the length and shortness of syllables, and which alone give character to every verse, are to be suspended? Or, ought we not rather to consider, whether the ancient choregic poets may not have indulged occasionally in an irregular movement? We see that this was so with regard to Gâyatrî verses. We see the greater freedom of the first and second pâdas occasionally extend to the third; and it will be impossible, without intolerable violence, to remove all the varieties of the last pâda of a Gâyatrî of which I have given examples above, pages cxv seq.

It is, of course, impossible to give here all the evidence that might be brought forward in support of similar freedom in Trishtubh verses, and I admit that the number of real varieties with them is smaller than with the Gâyatrîs. In order to make the evidence which I have to bring forward in support of these varieties as unassailable as possible, I have excluded nearly every pâda that occurs only in the first, second, or third line of a strophe, and have restricted myself, with few exceptions, and those chiefly referring to pâdas that had been quoted by other scholars in support of their own theories, to the final pâdas of Trishtubh verses. Yet even with this limited evidence, I think I shall be able to establish at least three varieties of Trishtubh.

i 2

Preserving the same classification which I adopted
before for the Gâyatrîs, so as to include the important eighth syllable of the Trish*tubh*, which
does not properly belong to the v*ri*tta, I maintain
that class 4. ᴜ ᴜ – –, class 5. – – – –, and class
8. – ᴜ ᴜ – must be recognized as legitimate endings
in the hymns of the Veda, and that by recognizing
them we are relieved from nearly all, if not all, the
most violent prosodial licences which Professor Kuhn
felt himself obliged to admit in his theory of Vedic
metres.

§ 4. ᴜ ᴜ – –.

The verses which fall under § 4 are so numerous
that after those of the first Ma*n*dala, mentioned
above, they need not be given here in full. They
are simply cases where the eighth syllable is not
lengthened, and they cannot be supposed to run
counter to any rule of the Prâtisâkhya, for the
simple reason that the Prâtisâkhya never gave such
a rule as that the eighth syllable must be lengthened
if the ninth is short. Examples will be found in the
final pâda of Trish*tu*bhs : ii. 30, 6; iii. 36, 4; 53, 15;
54, 12; iv. 1, 16; 2, 7; 9; 11; 4, 12; 6, 1; 2; 4; 7, 7;
11, 5; 17, 3; 23, 6; 24, 2; 27, 1; 28, 5; 55, 5; 57, 2;
v. 1, 2; vi. 17, 10; 21, 8; 23, 7; 25, 5; 29, 6; 33, 1;
62, 1; 63, 7; vii. 21, 5; 28, 3; 42, 4; 56, 15; 60, 10;
84, 2; 92, 4; viii. 1, 33; 96, 9; ix. 92, 5; x. 61, 12;
13; 74, 3; 117, 7.

In support of § 5. – – – –, the number of cases is
smaller, but it should be remembered that it might

be considerably increased if I had not restricted myself to the final pâda of each Trish*t*ubh, while the first, second, and third pâdas would have yielded a much larger harvest:

§ 5. – – – –.

i. 89, 9. mâ no madhyâ rîrishatâyŭr gāntŏ*h*.

i. 92, 6. supratîkâ saumanasâyā*g*î̄ga*h*.

i. 114, 5. *s*arma varma *kh*ardir asmābhyā*m* yā*m*sat.

i. 117, 2. tena narâ vartir asmābhyā*m* yātām.

i. 122, 1. ĭshŭdhyĕvă mărŭtŏ rŏdāsyŏ*h* (or rŏdāsyŏ*h*).

i. 122, 8. asvâvato rathino māhya*m* sŭrī*h*.

i. 186, 3. ishas *k*a parshad arigŭrtā*h* sŭrī*h*.

ii. 4, 2. devânâm agnir aratĭr *g*ĭrāsvā*h*.

iii. 49, 2. p*r*ithu*g*rayâ aminâd âyŭr dāsyŏ*h*.

iv. 3, 9. *g*âmaryena payasā pī̄pāyă.

iv. 26, 6. divo amushmâd uttarâd âdâyā.

v. 41, 14. udâ vardhantâm abhishâtā(*h*) ārnâ*h*.

vi. 25, 2. âryâya vi*s*o (a)va târĭr dâsî*h*.

vi. 66, 11. girayo nâpa ugrā asp*r*idhran.

vii. 8, 6. dyumad amîva*k*âtanām rākshŏhā.

vii. 28, 4. ava dvitâ varu*n*o māyĭ na*h* sât.

vii. 68, 1. havyâni *k*a pratibh*r*itā vĭtā*m* na*h*.

vii. 71, 2. divâ naktam mâdhvî trāsĭthâ*m* na*h*.

vii. 78, 1. *g*yotishmatâ vâmam asmābhyā*m* vākshī.

vii. 93, 7[b]. a*kkh*â mitra*m* varu*n*am ĭndrām vŏ*kč*h.

ix. 90, 4. sa*m* *k*ikrado maho asmābhyā*m* vā*g*ân.

x. 11, 8. bhâga*m* no atra vasumāntā*m* vĭtât.

I do not wish to deny that in several of these
lines it would be possible to remove the long
syllable from the ninth place by conjectural emendation. Instead of âyur in i. 89, 9, we might read
âyu ; in i. 92, 6, we might drop the augment of
aǵigar ; in ii. 4, 2, we might admit synizesis in
ârâtir, and then read ǵirâ-asvaḥ, as in i. 141, 12.
In vi. 25, 2, after eliding the a of ava, we might
read dâsiḥ. But even if, in addition to all this,
we were to admit the possible suppression of final
m in asmabhyam, mahyam, and in the accusative
singular, or the suppression of s in the nominative
singular, both of which would be extreme measures,
we should still have a number of cases which could
not be righted without even more violent remedies.
Why then should we not rather admit the occasional appearance of a metrical variation which
certainly has a powerful precedent in the dispondeus of Gâyatrîs ? I am not now acquainted with
the last results of metrical criticism in Virgil, but,
unless some new theories now prevail, I well recollect that spondaic hexameters, though small in
number, much smaller than in the Veda, were
recognized by the best scholars, and no emendations
attempted to remove them. If then in Virgil we
read, 'Cum patribus populoque, penatibusque et
magnis dis,' why not follow the authority of the
best MSS. and the tradition of the Prâtisâkhyas
and admit a dispondeus at the end of a Trishṭubh
rather than suspend, in order to meet this single

difficulty, some of the most fundamental rules of prosody ?

I now proceed to give a more numerous list of Traishṭubha pâdas ending in a choriambus, – ◡ ◡ –, again confining myself, with few exceptions, to final pâdas :

§ 8. – ◡ ◡ –.

i. 62, 3. sam usriyâbhir vâvasāntă nărăh.

i. 103, 4. yad dha sûnuh sravase nāmă dădhē.

i. 121, 9. sushṇam anantaih pariyāsi vādhaih.

i. 122, 10ᵇ. sārdhāstărō nārăm gŭrtăsrăvăh.

i. 173, 8. sûrîms kid yadi dhishâ vēshî gănăn.

i. 186, 2. karant sushâhâ vithurăm nă săvăh.

ii. 4, 3. dakshâyyo yo dâsvatē dămă ā (not dămē ā).

ii. 19, 1. oko dadhe brahmaṇyantās kă nărăh.

ii. 33, 14. mîdhvas tokâya tanayāyă mṛĭlă.

iv. 1, 19ᶜ. sŭky ŭdhō ătṛĭnān nă găvăm*.

iv. 25, 4. nare naryâya nṛitamāyă nṛĭnăm.

iv. 39, 2. dadathur mitrâvaruṇā tătŭrîm.

v. 30, 12. prăty āgrābhîshṇă nṛitămasyă nṛĭnăm.

v. 41, 4. ăgĭm nă găgmŭr âsvăsvătămăh.

v. 41, 15. smāt sŭrĭbhir ṛigŭhāstā ṛigŭvănĭh.

vi. 4, 7. vâyūm pṛĭṇāntī rădhāsā nṛitămăh.

vi. 10, 5. sŭvĭryĕbhĭs kăbhĭ sāntĭ gănăn.

---

* 'Nur eine Stelle habe ich mir angemerkt, wo das Metrum âam verlangt.' Kuhn, Beiträge, vol. iv. p. 180 ; Bollensen, Zeitschrift der D. M. G., vol. xxii. p. 587.

vi. 11, 4. añganti suprayasam pañḱa gănā̆ḣ.

vi. 13, 1ᵇ. agne vi yanti vaninō nă vāyā̆ḣ.

vi. 13, 1ᵈ. divo vrishṭir ī́dyō rī̆tir āpām.

vi. 20, 1ᵇ. tasthaú rayíḣ savasâ prĭtsŭ gănā̆n.

vi. 20, 1ᵈ. daddhi sûno sahaso vrĭtrátŭrām.

vi. 29, 4. ukthâ saṃsanto devavā̆tătămā̆ḣ.

vi. 33, 3. ā́ prĭtsŭ dărshĭ nrĭñā̆m nrĭtāmā.

vi. 33, 5. dĭvĭ shyā̆mă pā̆ryē gōshătămā̆ḣ.

vi. 44, 11. găhy̆ ăsŭshvĭn pră vrĭhā̆prĭñātăḣ.

vi. 49, 12. strĭbhĭr nă nā̆kăm văḱănāsyă vĭpăḣ.

vi. 68, 5. vaṃsad rayiṃ rayivată̄s ḱă gănā̆n.

vi. 68, 7. pra sadyo dyumnâ tiratē tă̄tŭrĭḣ.

vii. 19, 10. săkhâ ḱ̆ă sŭ́ro 'vĭtā̆ ḱă nrĭñā̆m.

vii. 62, 4. mă̄ mĭtrāsyă̄ prĭyă̄tă̄măsyă̄ nrĭñā̆m.

ix. 97, 26. hōtā̆ro nă̄ dĭvĭyă̄gō mă̄ndrătă̄mă̄ḣ (?).

x. 55, 8. sŭ́rō nĭr yŭdhā̆dhămăd dăsyŭ̆n (?).

x. 99, 9. atkam yo asya sanĭtōtă̄ nrĭñă̄m.

x. 108, 6. brĭhaspatir va ubhayă̄ nă̄ mrĭḷă̄t.

x. 169, 1. ă̆vā̆să̄yă̄ pă̄dvăte rŭdră̄ mrĭḷă̄.

It is perfectly true that this sudden change in
the rhythm of Trishṭubh verses, making their ending
iambic instead of trochaic, grates on our ears. But,
I believe, that if we admit a short stop after the
seventh syllable, the intended rhythm of these verses
will become intelligible. We remarked a similar
break in the verses of hymn x. 77, where the sudden
transition to an iambic metre was used with great

effect, and the choriambic ending, though less
effective, is by no means offensive. It should be
remarked also, that in many, though not in all cases,
a cæsura takes place after the seventh syllable, and
this is, no doubt, a great help towards a better
delivery of these choriambic Trish*t*ubhs.

While, however, I contend for the recognition of
these three varieties of the normal Trish*t*ubh metre,
I am quite willing to admit that other variations
besides these, which occur from time to time in
the Veda, form a legitimate subject of critical
discussion.

$$\S\ 2.\quad \cup\ \cup\ \cup\ -.$$

Trish*t*ubh verses the final pâda of which ends in
$\cup\ \cup\ \cup\ -$, I should generally prefer to treat as ending
in a *G*âgata pâda, in which this ending is more
legitimate. Thus I should propose to scan :

i. 122, 11. pra̅sa̅stăye̅ măhĭna̅ 'ra̅thăva̅te̅.

iii. 20, 5. va̅sŭn ru̅dra̅n̊ a̅di̅tya̅n̊ ĭhă hŭve̅.

v. 2, 1. pu̅ra*h* pa̅sya̅ntĭ nĭhĭta̅m (ta̅m) ăra̅ta̅u.

vi. 13, 5. va̅yo̅ vr̊ika̅yăra̅ye̅ *g*a̅sŭra̅ye̅.

$$\S\ 3.\quad \cup\ -\ \cup\ -.$$

I should propose the same medela for some final
pâdas of Trish*t*ubhs apparently ending in $\cup\ -\ \cup\ -$.
We might indeed, as has been suggested, treat
these verses as single instances of that peculiar

metre which we saw carried out in the whole of
hymn x. 77, but at the end of a verse the admission of an occasional *Gâgata* pâda is more in accordance with the habit of the Vedic poets.   Thus I
should scan :

v. 33, 4. vrishâ sâmatsŭ dăsâsyă nâmă *kit* *.

v. 41, 5ᵇ. râyă eshē 'vāse 'dadhîtă dhī*h*.

After what I have said before on the real character of the teaching of the Prâtisâkhya, I need
not show again that the fact of U*v*a*t*a's counting
ta of dadhîta as the tenth syllable is of no importance in determining the real nature of these hymns,
though it is of importance, as Professor Kuhn remarks (Beiträge, vol. iii. p. 451), in showing that
U*v*a*t*a considered himself at perfect liberty in
counting or not counting, for his own purposes,
the elided syllable of avase.

vii. 4, 6. măpsăvă*h* părĭ shădâmă mădŭvă*h*.

§ 6. ᵕ − − −.

Final pâdas of Trish*t*ubhs ending in ᵕ − − − are
very scarce.   In vi. 1, 4,

bhadrâyâm te ra*n*ayantă sămdr*i*sh*t*aū,

it would be very easy to read bhadrâyâ*m* te sam-
dr*i*sh*t*au ră*n*āyāntā ; and in x. 74, 2,

---

* Professor Kuhn has finally adopted the same scanning,
Beiträge, vol. iv. p. 184.

dyāur nā vārĕbhīh krĭnāvāntă svāih,
we may either recognize a *Gā*gata pāda, or read
dyāur nā vārĕbhīh krĭnāvāntă svāih,
which would agree with the metre of hymn x. 77.

§ 7. $-\ -\ \cup\ -$.

Pādas ending in $-\ -\ \cup\ -$ do not occur as final in
any Traish*t*ubha hymn, but as many *Gā*gata pādas
occur in the body of Traish*t*ubha hymns, we have
to scan them as dodecasyllabic :

i. 63, 4[a]. tvām hā tyād īndrā *k*odīh sākhā.

iv. 26, 6[b]. pārāvātah sākūnō māndrām mādām.

The adjective pâvaka which frequently occurs at
the end of final and internal pâdas of Trish*t*ubh
hymns has always to be scanned pāvākā. Cf. iv.
51, 2; vi. 5, 2; 10, 4; 51, 3; vii. 3, 1; 9; 9, 1[b]; 56, 12;
x. 46, 7[b].

I must reserve what I have to say about other
metres of the Veda for another opportunity, but
I cannot leave this subject without referring once
more to a metrical licence which has been strongly
advocated by Professor Kuhn and others, and by
the admission of which there is no doubt that
many difficulties might be removed, I mean the
occasional omission of a final m and s, and the
subsequent contraction of the final and initial
vowels. The arguments that have been brought
forward in support of this are very powerful.
There is the general argument that final s and m

are liable to be dropt in other Aryan languages,
and particularly for metrical purposes. There is
the stronger argument that in some cases final s
and m in Sanskrit may or may not be omitted,
even apart from any metrical stress. In Sanskrit
we find that the demonstrative pronoun sas appears
most frequently as sa (sa dadâti), and if followed
by liquid vowels, it may coalesce with them even
in later Sanskrit. Thus we see saisha for sa esha,
sendra*h* for sa indra*h* sanctioned for metrical purposes even by Pâ*n*ini, vi. i, 134. We might refer
also to feminines which have s in the nominative
singular after bases in û, but drop it after bases
in î. We find in the Sanhitâ text, v. 7, 8, svâdhitîva,
instead of svâdhiti*h*-iva in the Pada text, sanctioned
by the Prâtisâkhya 259; likewise ix. 61, 10, Sanhitâ,
bhûmy â dade, instead of Pada, bhûmi*h* â dade. But
before we draw any general conclusions from such
instances, we should consider whether they do not
admit of a grammatical instead of a metrical explanation. The nominative singular of the demonstrative pronoun was sa before it was sas; by the
side of bhûmi*h* we have a secondary form bhûmî;
and we may conclude from svâdhitî-vân, i. 88, 2,
that the Vedic poets knew of a form svâdhitî,
by the side of svâdhiti*h*.

As to the suppression of final m, however, we
see it admitted by the best authorities, or we see
at least alternate forms with or without m, in
túbhya, which occurs frequently instead of tú-

bhyam*, and twice, at least, without apparently
any metrical reason †. We find asmâka instead of
asmâkam (i. 173, 10), yushmâka instead of yushmâ-
kam (vii. 59, 9–10), yágadhva instead of yágadhvam
(viii. 2, 37) sanctioned both by the Sanhitâ and Pada
texts ‡.

If then we have such precedents, it may well
be asked why we should hesitate to adopt the
same expedient, the omission of final m and s,
whenever the Vedic metres seem to require it.
Professor Bollensen's remark, that Vedic verses cannot be treated to all the licences of Latin scanning§,
is hardly a sufficient answer ; and he himself, though
under a slightly different form, would admit as
much, if not more, than has been admitted on
this point by Professors Kuhn and Roth. On à
priori grounds I should by no means feel opposed
to the admission of a possible elision of final s or
m, or even n ; and my only doubt is whether it is
really necessary for the proper scanning of Vedic
metres. My own opinion has always been, that
if we admit on a larger scale what in single
words can hardly be doubted by anybody, viz. the
pronunciation of two syllables as one, we need

---

* i. 54, 9; 135, 2 ; iii. 42, 8 ; v. 11, 5 ; vii. 22, 7; viii. 51, 9;
76, 8; 82, 5; ix. 62, 27; 86, 30; x. 167, 1.

† ii. 11, 3; v. 30, 6.

‡ See Bollensen, Orient und Occident, vol. iii. p. 459; Kuhn,
Beiträge, vol. iv. p. 199.

§ Orient und Occident, vol. iv. p. 449.

not fall back on the elision of final consonants in order to arrive at a proper scanning of Vedic metres. On this point I shall have to say a few words in conclusion, because I shall frequently avail myself of this licence, for the purpose of righting apparently corrupt verses in the hymns of the Rig-veda; and I feel bound to explain, once for all, why I avail myself of it in preference to other emendations which have been proposed by scholars such as Professors Benfey, Kuhn, Roth, Bollensen, and others.

The merit of having first pointed out some cases where two syllables must be treated as one, belongs, I believe, to Professor Bollensen in his article, 'Zur Herstellung des Veda,' published in Benfey's Orient und Occident, vol. ii. p. 461. He proposed, for instance, to write hyânấ instead of hiyânấ, ix. 13, 6; dhyânó instead of dhiyânó, viii. 49, 5; sâhyase instead of sâhîyase, i. 71, 4; yânó instead of iyânó, viii. 50, 5, &c. The actual alteration of these words seems to me unnecessary; nor should we think of resorting to such violent measures in Greek where, as far as metrical purposes are concerned, two vowels have not unfrequently to be treated as one.

That iva counts in many passages as one syllable is admitted by everybody. The only point on which I differ is that I do not see why iva, when mono-syllabic, should be changed to va, instead of being pronounced quickly, or, to adopt the terminology of Greek grammarians, by synizesis *. Synizesis is well explained by Greek scholars as a quick pronunciation of two vowels so that neither should be lost, and as different thereby from synalœphe, which means the contraction of two vowels into one †. This synizesis is by no means restricted to iva and a few other words, but seems to me a very frequent expedient resorted to by the ancient *R*ishis.

Originally it may have arisen from the fact that language allows in many cases alternate forms of one or two syllables. As in Greek we have double forms like ἀλεγεινός and ἀλγεινός, γαλακτοφάγος and γλακτοφάγος, πετηνός and πτηνός, πυκινός and πυκνός ‡, and as in Latin we have the shortening or suppression of vowels carried out on the largest scale §,

---

* Synizesis in Greek applies only to the quick pronunciation of two vowels, if in immediate contact; and not, if separated by consonants. Samprasâra*n*a might seem a more appropriate term, but though the grammatical process designated in Sanskrit by Samprasârana offers some analogies, it could only by a new definition be applied to the metrical process here intended.

† A. B. p. 835, 30. ἐστὶ δὲ ἐν τοῖς κοινοῖς μέτροις καὶ ἡ καλουμένη συνεκφώνησις ἢ καὶ συνίζησις λέγεται. Ὅταν γὰρ φωνηέντων ἐπάλληλος γένηται ἡ προφορά, τότε γίνεται ἡ συνίζησις εἰς μίαν συλλαβήν. Διαφέρει δὲ συναλοιφῆς· ἡ μὲν γὰρ γραμμάτων ἐστὶ κλοπή, ἡ δὲ χρόνων· καὶ ἡ μὲν συναλοιφή, ὡς λέγεται, φαίνεται, ἡ δὲ οὔ. Mehlhorn, Griechische Grammatik, § 101. Thus in Νεοπτόλεμος we have synizesis, in Νουπτόλεμος synæresis.

‡ Cf. Mehlhorn, Griechische Grammatik, § 57.

§ See the important chapters on ' Kürzung der Vokale ' and

we find in Sanskrit, too, such double forms as prithvî or prithivî, adhi and dhi, api and pi, ava and va. The occurrence of such forms which have nothing to do with metrical considerations, but are perfectly legitimate from a grammatical point of view, would encourage a tendency to treat two syllables—and particularly two short syllables—as one, whenever an occasion arose. There are, besides, in the Vedic Sanskrit a number of forms where, as we saw, long syllables have to be pronounced as two. In some of these cases this pronunciation is legitimate, i. e. it preserves an original dissyllabic form which in course of time had become mono-syllabic. In other cases the same process takes place through a mistaken sense of analogy, where we cannot prove that an original dissyllabic form had any existence even in a prehistoric state of language. The occurrence of a number of such alternate forms would naturally leave a general impression in the mind of poets that two short syllables and one long syllable were under cer-tain circumstances interchangeable. So consider-able a number of words in which a long syllable has to be pronounced as two syllables has been collected by Professors Kuhn, Bollensen, and

'Tilgung der Vokale' in Corssen's 'Aussprache des Lateinischen;' and more especially his remarks on the so-called irrational vowels in Plautus, ibid. vol. ii. p. 70.

others, that no doubt can remain on this subject.
Vedic poets, being allowed to change a semivowel
into a vowel, were free to say nâsatyâ and nâsatyâ,
viii. 5, 32; prithivyâs and prithivyâh; pitroh and
pitroh, i. 31, 4. They could separate compound
words, and pronounce ghritânnah or ghrita-ânnah,
vii. 3, 1. They could insert a kind of shewa or
svarabhakti in words like sâmne or sâmne, viii. 6, 47;
dhâmne or dhâmne, viii. 92, 25; arâvnah and arâvnah,
ix. 63, 5. They might vary between pânti and
pânti, i. 41, 2; yâthana and yâthana, i. 39, 3; nidhâtoh and nidhâtoh, i. 41, 9; tredhâ and tredhâ,
i. 34, 8; devâh and devâh (besides devâsah), i. 23, 24;
rodasî and rodasî, i. 33, 9; 59, 4; 64, 9; and rodasyoh,
i. 33, 5; 59, 2; 117, 10; vi. 24, 3; vii. 6, 2; x. 74, 1*.
Need we wonder then if we find that, on the other
hand, they allowed themselves to pronounce prithivî
as prithivî, i. 191, 6; vii. 34, 7; 99, 3; dhrishnavâ
as dhrishnava, v. 52, 14; suvânâ as suvâna? There
is no reason why we should change the spelling of
suvâna into svâna. The metre itself tells us at
once where suvâna is to be pronounced as two or
as three syllables. Nor is it possible to believe
that those who first handed down and afterwards
wrote down the text of the Vedic hymns, should

---

* Professor Bollensen in some of these passages proposes to read
rodasîos. In i. 96, 4, no change is necessary if we read visâm.
Zeitschrift der D. M. G., vol. xxii. p. 587.

have been ignorant of that freedom of pronunciation. Why, there is not one single passage in the
whole of the ninth Maṇḍala, where, as far as I know,
suvâna should not be pronounced as dissyllabic,
i. e. as suvâ̄nā; and to suppose that the scholars
of India did not know how that superfluous syllable
should be removed, is really taking too low an
estimate of men like Vyâḻi or Śaunaka.

But if we once admit that in these cases two
syllables separated by a single consonant were pronounced as one and were metrically counted as
one, we can hardly resist the evidence in favour
of a similar pronunciation in a large number of
other words, and we shall find that by the admission of this rapid pronunciation, or of what in
Plautus we should call irrational vowels, many
verses assume at once their regular form without
the necessity of admitting the suppression of final
s, m, n, or the introduction of other prosodial
licences. To my mind the most convincing passages are those where, as in the Atyashṭi and
similar hymns, a poet repeats the same phrase
twice, altering only one or two words, but without
endeavouring to avoid an excess of syllables which,
to our mind, unless we resort to synizesis, would
completely destroy the uniformity of the metre.
Thus we read :

i. 133, 6. ăpŭrŭshăghnŏ 'prătītă sŭră sātvăbhih̤,

                    trĭsāptaih̤ sŭră sātvăbhih̤.

Here no 'pra must be pronounced with one ictus

only, in order to get a complete agreement between the two iambic diameters.

i. 134, 5. ūgrā́ ĭshăŭ̆antă bhūrvắṇ̆i,
ăpā́m ĭshăntă bhūrvắṇī.

As ishanta never occurs again, I suspect that the original reading was ishaṇanta in both lines, and that in the second line ishaṇanta, pronounced rapidly, was mistaken for ishanta. Is not bhurvá́ṇi a locative, corresponding to the dativ̆s in vá́ne which are so frequently used in the sense of infinitives? See note to i. 6, 8, page 34. In i. 138, 3, we must read:

ăhĕ́l̄amā́nă ūrŭsắṃsă sărī́ bhă̆vā̄,
vā́ğe-vā́ğe sărī́ bhă̆vā̄.

In i. 129, 11,

ăd̆hā̆́ hĭ tvā̆́ ğănī́tā ğī́ğănā̄d vă̆sō̄,
rākshōhắṇam tvā̄́ ğī́ğănā̄d vă̆sō̄,

we might try to remove the difficulty by omitting vaso at the end of the refrain, but this would be against the general character of these hymns. We want the last word vaso, if possible, at the end of both lines. But, if so, we must admit two cases of synizesis, or, if this seems too clumsy, we must omit tvâ.

I shall now proceed to give a number of other examples in which the same consonantal synizesis seems necessary in order to make the rhythm of the verses perceptible to our ears as it was to the ears of the ancient *R*ishis.

The preposition anu takes synizesis in

i. 127, 1. ghṛitāsyă vĭbhrāshṭĭm anŭ vāshṭĭ soḱishā.
Cf. x. 14, 1.

The preposition abhi:

i. 91, 23. rắyŏ bhāgăm săhăsắvănn abhĭ yūdhyā.
Here Professor Kuhn changes sahasâvan into sahasvaḥ, which, no doubt, is a very simple and very
plausible emendation. But in altering the text of
the Veda many things have to be considered, and
in our case it might be objected that sahasvaḥ
never occurs again as an epithet of Soma. As an
invocation sahasvaḥ refers to no deity but Agni,
and even in its other cases it is applied to Agni
and Indra only. However, I do not by any means
maintain that sahasvaḥ could not be applied to
Soma, for nearly the same arguments could be
used against sahasâvan, if conjecturally put in the
place of sahasvaḥ; I only wish to point out how
everything ought to be tried first, before we resort
in the Veda to conjectural emendations. Therefore,
if in our passage there should be any objection
to admitting the synizesis in abhi, I should much
rather propose synizesis of sahasâvan, than change
it into sahasvaḥ. There is synizesis in maha, e. g.
i. 133, 6. ăvăr mălă ĭndră dādṛĭhĭ srŭdhī nắḥ.
Although this verse is quoted by the Prâtisâkhya,
Sûtra 522, as one in which the lengthened syllable
dhī of srudhī does not occupy the tenth place, and
which therefore required special mention, the original
poet evidently thought otherwise, and lengthened

the syllable, being a syllable liable to be lengthened, because it occupied the tenth place, and therefore received a peculiar stress.

The preposition pari :

vi. 52, 14. mā vō vākā̆msĭ parĭkākshyā̆nĭ vŏkam, sŭmnēshv ĭd vŏ āntămā̆ mādēmā.

Here Professor Kuhn (Beiträge, vol. iv. p. 197) begins the last pâda with vokam, but this is impossible unless we change the accent of vokam, though even then the separation of the verb from mâ and the accumulation of two verbs in the last line would be objectionable.

Hărĭ is pronounced as hărĭ :

vii. 32, 12. yă ĭndrō harĭvā̆n nă dăbhāntĭ tăm rĭpăh.

ii. 18, 5. ā̆ kătvā̆rĭmsătā harĭbhĭr yŭgā̆nah.

Hence I propose to scan the difficult verse i. 167, 1, as follows :

săhāsrăm tă ĭndră-ūtāyō năh,

săhāsrăm ĭshō harĭvō gūrtătămă̆h*,

săhāsrăm răyō mādāyādhyāi,

săhāsrĭnă ŭpă nō yāntŭ vă̆găh.

That the final o instead of as is treated as a short syllable we saw before, and in i. 133, 6, we observed that it was liable to synizesis. We see the same in

i. 175, 6. māyă ĭvāpō nă trĭshyātē bābhūthā.

v. 61, 16. ā̆ yāgñĭyāsō vāvrĭttānă.

---

* As to the scanning of the second line see page cxxxv.

The pragrihya î of the dual is known in the
Veda to be liable in certain cases to Sandhi. If
we extend this licence beyond the limits recognized
by the Prâtisâkhya, we might scan

vi. 52, 14. ûbhē rōdāsy āpā́m nāpā́k ka̋ mānmā, or
we might shorten the î before the a, and admitting
synizesis, scan:

ûbhē rōdāsî āpā́m nāpā́k ka̋ mānmā.

In iii. 6, 10, we must either admit Sandhi between
prắkî and adhvaréva, or contract the first two syllables of adhvaréva.

The o and e of vocatives before vowels, when
changed into av or a(y), are liable to synizesis:

iv. 48, 1. vāyav ā̀ kandrēṇa rāthēnā (Anushṭubh, c.)

iv. 1, 2. sā bhrā́tāram vāruṇ̆am āgnā ā̀ vāvrītsvā.

The termination avaḥ also, before vowels, seems
to count as one syllable in v. 52, 14, dīvō vā̀
dhrishṇávā ōǵāsâ, which would render Professor
Bollensen's correction (Orient und Occident, vol. ii.
p. 480), dhrishṇúoǵasâ, unnecessary.

Like ava and iva, we find aya and iya, too, in
several words liable to be contracted in pronunciation; e. g. vayam, vi. 23, 5; ayam, i. 177, 4; iyam,
vii. 66, 8[2]; i. 186, 11 (unless we read vo 'sme);
x. 129, 6. Professor Bollensen's proposal to change
iyam to îm, and ayam to âm (Orient und Occident,
vol. ii. p. 461), would only cause obscurity, without any
adequate gain, while other words would by a similar
suppression of vowels or consonants become simply

irrecognizable. In i. 169, 6, for instance, ádha has to be pronounced with one ictus; in vi. 26, 7, sádhavîra is trisyllabic. In vi. 10, 1, we must admit synizesis in adhvaré; in i. 161, 8, either in udakám or in abravîtana; i. 110, 9, in *ri*bhumán; viii. 79, 4, in divá*h*; v. 4, 6, in n*ri*tama (unless we read so 'gne); i. 164, 17, in pará*h*; vi. 15, 14, in pâvaka; i. 191, 6; vii. 34, 7; 99, 3, in p*ri*thivî; ii. 20, 8, in púra*h*; vi. 10, 1, in prayatí; vi. 17, 7, in b*ri*hát; ix. 19, 6, in bhiyásam; i. 133, 6, in mahá*h*; ii. 28, 6; iv. 1, 2; vi. 75, 18, in varu*n*a; iii. 30, 21, in v*ri*shabha; vii. 41, 6, in vâ*g*ína*h*; ii. 43, 2, in sísumatí*h*; vi. 51, 2, in sanutár; vi. 18, 12, in sthávirasya, &c.

These remarks will, I hope, suffice in order to justify the principles by which I have been guided in my treatment of the text and in my translation of the Rig-veda. I know I shall seem to some to have been too timid in retaining whatever can possibly be retained in the traditional text of these ancient hymns, while others will look upon the emendations which I have suggested as unpardonable temerity. Let everything be weighed in the just scales of argument. Those who argue for victory, and not for truth, can have no hearing in our court. There is too much serious work to be done to allow time for wrangling or abuse. Any dictionary will supply strong words to those who condescend to such warfare, but strong arguments require honest labour, sound judgment, and, above all, a genuine love of truth.

The second volume, which I am now preparing for Press, will contain the remaining hymns addressed to the Maruts. The notes will necessarily have to be reduced to smaller dimensions, but they must always constitute the more important part in a translation or, more truly, in a deciphering of Vedic hymns.

F. MAX MÜLLER.

Parks End, Oxford :
March, 1869.

FIRST BOOK.

HYMNS TO THE MARUTS.

Mandala I, Sûkta 6.
Ashtaka I, Adhyâya 1, Varga 11–12.

1. Yuñgánti bradhnám arushám kárantam pári tasthúshaḥ, rókante rokaná diví.

2. Yuñgánti asya kâmyâ hárî (íti) ví-pakshasâ ráthe, sóná dhrishnû (íti) nri-vâhasâ. ·

3. Ketúm krinván aketáve pésaḥ maryâḥ apesáse, sám ushát-bhiḥ agâyathâḥ.

4. Ất áha svadhấm ánu púnaḥ garbha-tvám â-îriré, dádhânâḥ nấma yagñíyam.

---

1. Wilson: The circumstationed (inhabitants of the three worlds) associate with (Indra), the mighty (Sun), the inde-structive (fire), the moving (wind), and the lights that shine in the sky.

Benfey: Die rothe Sonne schirr'n sie an, die wandelt um die stehenden, Strahlen strahlen am Himmel auf.

Langlois: Placés autour du (foyer, les hommes) préparent le char (du dieu) brillant, pur et rapide; (cependant) brillent dans le ciel les feux (du matin).

2. Wilson: They (the charioteers) harness to his car his two desirable coursers, placed on either hand, bay-coloured, high-spirited, chief-bearing.

Benfey: Die lieben Falben schirren sie zu beiden Seiten des Wagens an, braune, kühne, held-tragende.

Langlois: A ce char sont attelés ses deux coursiers, beaux, brillants, impétueux, rougeâtres, et dignes de porter un héros.

3. Wilson: Mortals, you owe your (daily) birth (to such

HYMN TO INDRA AND THE MARUTS (THE STORM-GODS).

1. Those who stand around him while he moves on, harness the bright red steed;[1] the lights in heaven shine forth.[2]

2. They harness to the chariot on each side his (Indra's)[1] two favourite bays, the brown, the bold, who can carry the hero.

3. Thou who createst light where there was no light, and form, O men![1] where there was no form, hast been born together with the dawns.[2]

4. Thereafter[1] they (the Maruts), according to their wont,[2] assumed again the form of new-born babes,[3] taking their sacred name.

---

an Indra), who with the rays of the morning, gives sense to the senseless, and to the formless, form.

BENFEY: Licht machend—Männer!—das Dunkele und kenntlich das Unkenntliche, entsprangst du mit dem Morgenroth.

LANGLOIS: O mortels, (voyez-le) mettant l'ordre dans la confusion, donnant la forme au chaos. O Indra, avec les rayons du jour tu viens de naître.

4. WILSON: Thereafter, verily, those who bear names invoked in holy rites, (the Maruts,) having seen the rain about to be engendered, instigated him to resume his embryo condition (in the clouds).

BENFEY: Sodann von freien Stücken gleich erregen wieder Schwangerschaft die heilgen Namen tragenden.

LANGLOIS: A peine la formule de l'offrande a-t-elle été prononcée, que les (Marouts), dont le nom mérite d'être invoqué dans les sacrifices, viennent exciter (de leur souffle) le feu à peine sorti du sein (de l'arani).

5. Vílú *k*it âru*g*atnú-bhi*h* gúhâ *k*it indra váhni-bhi*h*, ávinda*h* usríyâ*h* ánu.

6. Deva-yántu*h* yáthâ matím á*kkh*a vidát-vasum gíra*h*, mahấm anûshata *s*rutám.

7. Índre*n*a sám hí d*ri*kshase sam-*g*agmânâ*h* ábi-bhyushâ, mandû (íti) samânâ-var*k*asâ.

8. Anavadya*íh* abhídyu-bhi*h* makhâ*h* sáhasvat ar-*k*ati, ga*n*a*íh* índrasya kâmyai*h*.

9. Áta*h* pari-*g*man â gahi divâ*h* vâ ro*k*anât ádhi, sám asmin *r*iñ*g*ate gíra*h*.

---

5. WILSON: Associated with the conveying Maruts, the traversers of places difficult of access, thou, Indra, hast discovered the cows hidden in the cave.

BENFEY: Mit den die Festen brechenden, den Stürmenden fandst, Indra, du die Kühe in der Grotte gar.

LANGLOIS: Avec ces (Marouts), qui brisent tout rempart et supportent (la nue) Indra, tu vas, du sein de la caverne, délivrer les vaches (célestes).

6. WILSON: The reciters of praises praise the mighty (troop of Maruts), who are celebrated, and conscious of the power of bestowing wealth in like manner as they (glorify) the counsellor (Indra).

BENFEY: Nach ihrer Einsicht verherrlichend besingen Sänger den Schätzeherrn, den berühmten, gewaltigen.

LANGLOIS: Voilà pourquoi l'hymne qui chante les dieux célèbre aussi le grand (dieu des vents), qui assiste (Indra) de ses conseils, et découvre les heureux trésors.

7. WILSON: May you be seen, Maruts, accompanied by the undaunted (Indra); both rejoicing, and of equal splendour.

5. Thou, O Indra, with the swift Maruts[1] who break even through the stronghold,[2] hast found even in their hiding-place the bright cows[3] (the days).

6. The pious singers[1] (the Maruts) have, after their own mind,[2] shouted towards the giver of wealth, the great, the glorious (Indra).

7. Mayest thou[1] (host of the Maruts) be verily seen[2] coming together with Indra, the fearless: you are both happy-making, and of equal splendour.

8. With the beloved hosts of Indra, with the blameless, heavenward-tending (Maruts), the sacrificer[1] cries aloud.

9. From yonder, O traveller (Indra), come hither, or down from the light of heaven;[1] the singers all yearn for it;—

BENFEY: So lass mit Indra denn vereint, dem furchtlosen, erblicken dich, beide erfreu'nd und glanzesgleich.

LANGLOIS: Avec l'intrépide Indra, (ô dieu,) on te voit accourir; tous deux pleins de bonheur, tous deux également resplendissants.

8. WILSON: This rite is performed in adoration of the powerful Indra, along with the irreproachable, heavenward-tending, and amiable bands (of the Maruts).

BENFEY: Durch Indra's liebe Schaaren, die untadligen, himmelstürmenden, strahlet das Opfer mächtiglich.

LANGLOIS: Notre sacrifice confond, dans un homage aussi empressé, Indra et la troupe (des Marouts) bienfaisante, irréprochable, et brillante des feux (du matin).

9. WILSON: Therefore circumambient (troop of Maruts), come hither, whether from the region of the sky, or from the solar sphere; for, in this rite, (the priest) fully recites your praises.

BENFEY: Von hier, oder vom Himmel komm ob dem Æther, Umkreisender! zu dir streben die Lieder all.

10. Itá*h* vâ sâtím ímahe divá*h* vâ pắrthivât ádhi, índram mahá*h* vâ rá*g*asa*h*.

LANGLOIS : (Dieu des vents), qui parcours le monde, viens vers nous, ou de ton séjour habituel, ou de la demeure céleste de la lumière ; notre voix aujourd'hui t'appelle.

10. WILSON : We invoke Indra,—whether he come from this earthly region, or from the heaven above, or from the vast firmament,—that he may give (us) wealth.

COMMENTARY.

This hymn is ascribed to Ka*n*va, the son of Ghora. The metre is Gâyatrî throughout.

Verse 1, note [1]. The poet begins with a somewhat abrupt description of a sunrise. Indra is taken as the god of the bright day, whose steed is the sun, and whose companions the Maruts, or the storm-gods. Arushá, meaning originally red, is used as a proper name of the horse or of the rising sun, though it occurs more frequently as the name of the red horses or flames of Agni, the god of fire, and also of the morning light. In our passage, Arushá, a substantive, meaning the red of the morning, has taken bradhná as an adjective,—bradhná meaning, as far as can be made out, bright in general, though, as it is especially applied to the Soma-juice, perhaps bright-brown or yellow. Names of colour are difficult to translate from one language into another, for their shades vary, and withdraw themselves from sharp definition. We shall meet with this difficulty again and again in the Veda.

The following passages will illustrate the principal meaning of arushá, and justify the translation here adopted.

Arushá as an Adjective.

Arushá is used as an adjective in the sense of red :

vii. 97, 6. tám *s*agmãsa*h* arushãsa*h* ásvâ*h* bríhaspátim saha-vâha*h* vahanti,—nábha*h* ná rûpám arushám vásânâ*h*.

10. Or we ask Indra for help from here, or from heaven, above the earth, or from the great sky.

BENFEY: Von hier, oder vom Himmel ob der Erde begehren Spende wir, oder, Indra! aus weiter Luft.

LANGLOIS: Nous invoquons aussi la libéralité d'Indra; (qu'il nous entende), soit d'ici-bas, soit de l'air qui enveloppe la terre, soit du vaste séjour de la lumière.

Powerful red horses, drawing together draw him, Brihas-pati: horses clothed in red colour like the sky.

iii. 1, 4. svetám gagñânám arushám mahi-tvã.
Agni, the white, when born; the red, by growth.

iii. 15, 3. krishnâsu agne arusháh ví bhâhi.
Shine, O Agni, red among the dark ones.

iii. 31, 21. antár (íti) krishnân arushaíh dhâma-bhih gât.
He (Indra) went among the dark ones with his red companions.

vi. 27, 7. yásya gâvau arushâ.
He (Indra) whose two cows are red.

vii. 75, 6. práti dyutânâm arushâsah ásvâh kitrâh adrisran ushâsam váhantah.
The red horses, the beautiful, were seen bringing to us the bright dawn.

v. 43, 12. híranya-varnam arushám sapema.
Let us worship the gold-coloured, the red, i.e. Brihaspati (the fire).

i. 118, 5. pári vâm ásvâh vápushah patangâh váyah vahantu arushâh abhíke.
May the winged beautiful horses, may the red birds bring you (the Asvins) back near to us.

iv. 43, 6. ghrinâ váyah arushâsah pári gman.
The red birds (of the Asvins) came back by day.

v. 73, 5. pári vâm arushâh váyah ghrinâ varante â-tápah.
The red birds shield you (the Asvins) around by day from the heat.

i. 36, 9. ví dhûmám agne arushám miyedhya *sr*igá.

Send off, O Agni, the red smoke, thou who art worthy of sacrificial food.

vii. 3, 3. á*kkh*a dyấm arushá*h* dhûmấ*h* eti.

The red smoke goes up to the sky.

vii. 16, 3. út dhûmấsa*h* arushấsa*h* divi-sp*r*ísa*h*.

The clouds of red smoke went up touching the sky.

x. 45, 7. íyarti dhûmám arushám.

He (Agni) rouses the red smoke.

i. 141, 8. dyấm ángebhi*h* arushébhi*h* îyate.

He (Agni) goes to the sky with his red limbs.

ii. 2, 8. sá*h* idhâná*h* ushása*h* rấmyâ*h* ánu svâ*h* ná dîdet arushé*n*a bhânúnâ.

He (Agni), lit after the lovely dawns, shone like the sky with his red splendour.

iii. 29, 6. á*s*va*h* ná vâ*g*î arushá*h* váneshu ấ.

Like a stallion, the red one (Agni) appears in the wood.

iv. 58, 7. arushá*h* ná vâ*g*î kâsh*th*â*h* bhindán.

Like a red stallion, breaking the bounds.

i. 114, 5. divấ*h* varâhám arushám.

Him (Rudra), the boar of the sky, the red.

v. 59, 5. á*s*vâ*h*-iva ít arushấsa*h*.

Like red horses, (O Maruts.)

v. 12, 2. *r*itám sapâm*r*urushásya v*r*ísh*n*a*h*.

I follow the rite of the red hero (Agni).   The meaning here assigned to v*r*íshan will be explained hereafter, see note to i. 85, 12.

v. 12, 6. *r*itám sá*h* pâti arushásya v*r*ísh*n*a*h*.

He observes the rite of the red hero (Agni).

vi. 8, 1. p*r*ikshásya v*r*ísh*n*a*h* arushásya nú sáha*h* prá nú vo*k*am.

I celebrate the power of the quick red hero (Agni Vaisvâ-nara).

vi. 48, 6. *s*yâvâsu arushá*h* v*r*íshâ.

In the dark (nights) the red hero (Agni).

iii. 7, 5. *g*ânánti v*r*ísh*n*a*h* arushásya sévam.

They know the treasure of the red hero (of Agni).

In one passage v*r*íshan arushá is intended for fire in the shape of lightning.

x. 89, 9. ní amítreshu vadhám indra túmram vríshan vríshânam arushám sisîhi.

Whet, O strong Indra, the heavy strong red weapon, against the enemies.

x. 43, 9. út gâyatâm parasúh gyótishâ sahá—ví rokatâm arusháh bhânúnâ súkih.

May the axe (the thunderbolt) appear with the light—may the red one blaze forth, bright with splendour.

x. 1, 6. arusháh gátáh padé ílâyâh.

Agni, born red in the place of the altar.

vi. 3, 6. náktam yáh îm arusháh yáh dívâ.

He (Agni) being red by night and by day.

x. 20, 9. krishnáh svetáh arusháh yâmah asya bradhnáh rigráh utá sónah.

His (Agni's) path is black, white, red, bright, reddish, and yellow.

Here it is extremely difficult to keep all the colours distinct.

Arushá is frequently applied to Soma, particularly in the 9th Mandala. There we read:

ix. 8, 6. arusháh hárih.

ix. 71, 7. arusháh diváh kavíh vríshâ.

ix. 74, 1. vâgí arusháh.

ix. 82, 1. arusháh vríshâ hárih.

ix. 89, 3. hárim arushám.

ix. 111, 1. arusháh hárih. See also ix. 25, 5; 61, 21. In ix. 72, 1, arushá seems used as a substantive in the sense of red-horse.

Arushá as an Appellative.

Arushá is used as an appellative, and in the following senses :

1. The one red-horse of the Sun, the two or more red-horses of Agni.

i. 6, 1. yuñgánti bradhnám arushám.

They yoke the bright red-horse (the Sun).

i. 94, 10. yát áyukthâh arushâ róhitâ râthe.

When thou (Agni) hast yoked the two red-horses and the two ruddy horses to the chariot.

i. 146, 2. rihánti údha*h* arushása*h* asya.

His (Agni's) red-horses lick the udder.

ii. 10, 2. sruyâ*h* agní*h*—hávam me—syâvâ rátham vahata*h* róhitâ vâ utá arushâ.

Mayest thou, Agni, hear my call, whether the two black,
or the two ruddy, or the two red-horses carry you.

Here three kinds of colours are clearly distinguished,
and an intentional difference is made between róhita and
arushá.

iv. 2, 3. arushâ yugânâ*h*.

Agni having yoked the two red-horses.

iv. 6, 9. táva tyé agne haríta*h*—róhitâsa*h*—arushâsa*h*
vrishana*h*.

To thee (Agni) belong these bays, these ruddy, these red-
horses, the stallions.

Here, again, three kinds of horses are distinguished—
Haríts, Róhitas, and Arushás.

viii. 34, 17. yé rigrâ*h* vâta-ramhasa*h* arushâsa*h* raghu-
syâda*h*.

Here arushá may be the subject and the rest adjectives;
but it is also possible to take all the words as adjectives,
referring them to âsú in the next verse. The fact that rigrá
likewise expresses a peculiar red colour is no objection, as
may be seen from i. 6, 1; 94, 10.

vii. 16, 2. sá*h* yogate arushâ vievá-bhogasâ.

May he (Agni) yoke the two all-nourishing red-horses.

vii. 42, 2. yuṅkshvá—haríta*h* rohíta*h* *k*a yé vâ sâdman
arushâ*h*.

Yoke (O Agni) the bays, and the ruddy horses, or the
red-horses which are in thy stable.

2. The cloud, represented as the enemy of Indra, as retaining, like Vritra, the waters which Indra and the Maruts
wish to liberate.

i. 85, 5. utá arushásya ví syanti dhârâ*h*.

(When you go to the battle, O Maruts), the streams of
the red enemy flow off.

v. 56, 7. utá syâ*h* vâgí arushâ*h*.

This strong red-horse,—meant for the cloud, as it would
seem; but possibly, too, for one of the horses of the
Maruts.

Besides the passages in which arushá is used either as an adjective, in the sense of red, or as an appellative, meaning some kind of horse, there are others in which, as I pointed out in my Essay on Comparative Mythology*, Arushá occurs as a proper name, as the name of a solar deity, as the bright deity of the morning (*Morgenroth*). My interpretation of some of these passages has been contested, nor shall I deny that in some of them a different interpretation is possible, and that in looking for traces of Arushá, as a Vedic deity, representing the morning or the rising sun, and containing, as I endeavoured to show, the first germs of the Greek name of Eros, I may have seen more indications of the presence of that deity in the Veda than others would feel inclined to acknowledge. Yet in going over the same evidence again, I think that even verses which for a time I felt inclined to surrender, yield a better sense if we take the word arushá which occurs in them as a substantive, as the name of a matutinal deity, than if we look upon it as an adjective or a mere appellative. It might be said that wherever this arushá occurs, apparently as the name of a deity, we ought to supply Agni or Indra or Sûrya. This is true to a certain extent, for the sun, or the light of the morning, or the bright sky are no doubt the substance and subject-matter of this deity. But the same applies to many other names originally intended for these conceptions, but which, nevertheless, in the course of time, became independent names of independent deities. In our passage i. 6, 1, yuñgánti bradhnám arushám, we may retain for arushá the appellative power of steed or red-steed, but if we could ask the poet what he meant by this red-steed, or if we ask ourselves what we can possibly understand by it, the answer would be, the morning sun, or the light of the morning. In other passages, however, this meaning of red-steed is no longer applicable, and we can only translate Arushá by the Red, understanding by this name the deity of the morning or of the morning sun.

---

* Chips from a German Workshop, 2nd ed., vol. ii. p. 137 seq.

vii. 71, 1. ápa svásu*h* ushása*h* nák *g*ihîte ri*n*ákti krishn*î*h
arushâya pánthâm.

The Night retires from her sister, the Dawn; the Dark one
yields the path to the Red one, i. e. the red morning.

Here Arushá shares the same half-mythological character
as Ushas, and where we should speak of dawn and morning
as mere periods of time, the Vedic poet speaks of them as
living and intelligent beings, half human, half divine, as
powers of nature capable of understanding his prayers, and
powerful enough to reward his praises. I do not think
therefore that we need hesitate to take Arushá in this
passage as a proper name of the morning, or of the morning
sun, to whom the dark goddess, the Night, yields the path
when he rises in the East.

vi. 49, 2. divá*h* si*s*um sáhasa*h* sûnúm agním ya*g*ñásya
ketúm arushám yá*g*adhyai.

To worship the child of Dyu, the son of strength, Agni,
the light of the sacrifice, the Red one (Arushá).

In this verse, where the name of Agni actually occurs, it
would be easier than in the preceding verse to translate
arushá as an adjective, referring it either to Agni, the god
of fire, or to ya*g*ñásya ketúm, the light of the sacrifice.
I had myself yielded* so far to these considerations that I
gave up my former translation, and rendered this verse by
'to worship Agni, the child of the sky, the son of strength,
the red light of the sacrifice†.' But I return to my original
translation, and I see in Arushá an independent name, intended, no doubt, for Agni, as the representative of the rising
sun and, at the same time, of the sacrificial fire of the
morning, but nevertheless as having in the mind of the poet
a personality of its own. He is the child of Dyu, originally
the offspring of heaven. He is the son of strength, originally generated by the strong rubbing of the ara*n*is, i. e. the
wood for kindling fire. He is the light of the sacrifice,
whether as reminding man that the time for the morning
sacrifice has come, or as himself lighting the sacrifice on the
Eastern altar of the sky. He is Arushá, originally as

---

* Chips from a German Workshop, vol. ii. p. 139.
† Journal of the Royal Asiatic Society, 1867, p. 204.

clothed in bright red colour, but gradually changed into the representative of the morning. We see at once, if examining these various expressions, how some of them, like the child of Dyu, are easily carried away into mythology, while others, such as the son of strength, or the light of the sacrifice, resist that unconscious metamorphosis. That Arushá was infected by mythology, that it had approached at least that point where *nomina* become changed into *numina*, we see by the verse immediately following:

vi. 49, 3. arushásya duhitárâ vírûpe (íti ví-rûpe) strí-bhi*h* anyấ pipisé súra*h* anyấ.

There are two different daughters of Arushá; the one is clad in stars, the other belongs to the sun, or is the wife of Svar.

Here Arushá is clearly a mythological being, like Agni or Savitar or Vaisvânara; and if Day and Night are called his daughters, he, too, can hardly have been conceived otherwise than as endowed with human attributes, as the child of Dyu, as the father of Day and Night, and not as a mere period of time, not as a mere cause or effect.

iv. 15, 6. tám árvantam ná sânasím arushám ná divá*h* sísum marmr*i*gyánte divé-dive.

They trim the fire day by day, like a strong horse, like Arushá, the child of Dyu.

Here, too, Arushá, the child of Dyu, has to be taken as a personal character, and, if the ná after arushám is right, a distinction is clearly made between Agni, the sacrificial fire, to whom the hymn is addressed, and Arushá, the child of heaven, the pure and bright morning, here used as a simile for the cleaning or trimming of the fire on the altar.

v. 47, 3. arushá*h* su-par*n*á*h*.

Arushá, the morning sun, with beautiful wings.

The feminine Árushî as an Adjective.

Árushî, like arushá, is used as an adjective, in the same sense as arushá, i. e. red:

iii. 55, 11. syávî *k*a yát árushî *k*a svásârau.

As the dark and the red are sisters.

i. 92, 1 and 2. gávah árushî*h* and árushî*h* gá*h*.

The red cows of the dawn.

i. 92, 2. rúsantam bhânúm árushîh asisrayuh.

The red dawns obtained bright splendour.

Here ushásah, the dawns, occur in the same line, so that we may take árushîh either as an adjective, referring to the dawns, or as a substantive, as a name of the dawn or of her cows.

i. 30, 21. ásve ná kitre arushi.

Thou bright, red dawn, thou, like a mare.

Here, too, the vocative arushi is probably to be taken as an adjective, particularly if we consider the next following verse :

iv. 52, 2. ásvâ-iva kitrá árushî mâtá gávâm rítá-varî sákhâ abhût asvínoh ushâh.

The dawn, bright and red, like a mare, the mother of the cows (days), the never-failing, she became the friend of the Asvins.

x. 5, 5. saptá svásrîh árushîh.

The seven red sisters.

The feminine Árushî as a Substantive.

If used as a substantive, árushî seems to mean the dawn. It is likewise used as a name of the horses of Agni, Indra, and Soma; also as a name for mare in general.

It means dawn in x. 8, 3, though the text points here so clearly to the dawn, and the very name of dawn is mentioned so immediately after, that this one passage seems hardly sufficient to establish the use of árushî as a recognized name of the dawn. Other passages, however, would likewise gain in perspicuity, if we took árushî by itself as a name of the dawn, just as we had to admit in several passages arushá by itself as a name of the morning. Cf. i. 71, 1.

Árushî means the horses of Agni, in i. 14, 12 :

yukshvá hí árushîh ráthe harítah deva rohítah.

Yoke, O god (Agni), the red-horses to the chariot, the bays, the ruddy.

i. 72, 10. prá níkíh agne árushîh agânan.

They knew the red-horses, Agni, coming down.

In viii. 69, 5, árushî refers to the horses of Indra, whether as a noun or an adjective, is somewhat doubtful :

ā́ hárayaḥ sasṛigrire árushīḥ.
The bay horses were let loose, the red-horses ; or, possibly,
thy bright red-horses were let loose.
Soma, as we saw, was frequently spoken of as arushā́ḥ
háriḥ.
In ix. 111, 2, tridhā́tu-bhiḥ árushíbhiḥ seems to refer to the
same red-horses of Soma, though this is not quite clear.
The passages where árushī means simply a mare, without
any reference to colour, are viii. 68, 18, and viii. 55, 3.
It is curious that Arushá, which in the Veda means red,
should in its Zendic form aurusha, mean white. That in
the Veda it means red and not white is shown, for instance,
by x. 20, 9, where sveta, the name for white, is mentioned by
the side of arushá. Most likely arushá meant originally brilliant, and became fixed with different shades of brilliancy in
Sanskrit and Persian. Arushá presupposes a form ar-vas, and
is derived from a root ar in the sense of running or rushing.
See Chips from a German Workshop, vol. ii. pp. 135, 137.

Having thus explained the different meanings of arushá
and árushī in the Rig-veda, I feel it incumbent, at least for
once, to explain the reasons why I differ from the classification of Vedic passages as given in the Dictionary published by Messrs. Boehtlingk and Roth. Here, too, the
passages in which arushá is used as an adjective are very
properly separated from those in which it appears as a
substantive. To begin with the first, it is said that 'arushá
means ruddy, the colour of Agni and his horses ; he (Agni)
himself appears as a red-horse.' In support of this, the
following passages are quoted :
iii. 1, 4. ávardhayan su-bhágam saptá yahvī́ḥ svetám
gagñā́nám arushám mahi-tvā́, sísum ná gātám abhí áruḥ
ásvāḥ. Here, however, it is only said that Agni was born
brilliant-white*, and grew red, that the horses came to him
as they come to a new-born foal. Agni himself is not called
a red-horse.
iii. 7, 5. Here, again, vríshṇaḥ arushásya is no doubt

---

* See v. 1, 4. svetā́ḥ vā́gī gāyate ā́gre áhnām. x. 1, 6. arushā́ḥ gā́tā́ḥ
padé íḷāyā́ḥ.

meant for Agni. But *vrishan* by itself does not mean
horse, though it is added to different names of horses to
qualify them as male horses; cf. vii. 69, 1. ấ vâm ráth*h*
vr*í*sha-bhi*h* y*â*tu *á*svai*h*, may your chariot come near with
powerful horses, i. e. with stallions. See note to i. 85, 12.
We are therefore not justified in translating arushá vr*í*shan
by red-horse, but only by the red male, or the red hero.

In iii. 31, 3, agn*í*h *g*a*g*ñe *g*uhvấ ré*g*amâna*h* mahấ*h* putr*â*n
arushásya pra-yáksha, I do not venture to say who is
meant by the mahấ*h* putr*â*n arushásya, whether Ádityas or
Maruts, but hardly the sons of Agni, as Agni himself is
mentioned as only born. But, even if it were so, the father
of these sons (putra) could hardly be intended here for
a horse.

iv. 6, 9. táva tyé agne haríta*h* ghrita-snấ*h* róhitấsa*h* *ri*gu-
ấñka*h* su-áñka*h*, arushấsa*h* vr*í*shana*h* *ri*gu-mushkấ*h*. Here,
so far from Agni being represented as a red-horse, his
different horses, the Harits or bays, the Róhitas or ruddy,
and the arushấsa*h* vr*í*shana*h*, the red stallions, are distinctly
mentioned. Here vr*í*shan may be translated by stallion,
instead of simply by male, because arushá is here a substantive, the name of a horse.

v. 1, 5. *g*ánish*t*a hí *g*ényah ágre áhnâm hitấ*h* hitéshu
arushấ*h* váneshu. Here arushấ*h* is simply an adjective, red,
referring to Agni who is understood throughout the hymn
to be the object of praise. He is said to be kind to those
who are kind to him, and to be red in the woods, i. e.
brilliant in the wood which he consumes; cf. iii. 29, 6.
Nothing is said about his equine nature.

In v. 12, 2 and 6, vi. 48, 6, we have again simply
arushá vr*í*shan, which does not mean the red-horse, but
the red male, the red hero, i. e. Agni.

In vi. 49, 2, divấ*h* *s*ísum sáhasa*h* sûnúm agním ya*g*ñásya
ketûm arushám y*á*gadhyai, there is no trace of Agni being
conceived as a horse. He is called the child of the sky or
of Dyu, the son of strength (who is produced by strong
rubbing of wood), the light or the beacon of the sacrifice,
and lastly Arushá, which, for reasons stated above, I take to
be used here as a name.

Next follow the passages in which, according to Professor

Roth, arushá is an adjective, is said to be applied to the horses, cows, and other teams of the gods, particularly of the dawn, the Asvins, and Brihaspati.

i. 118, 5. pári vâm ásvâ*h* vápusha*h* pataṅgâ*h*, váya*h* vahantu arushấ*h* abhîke. Here we find the váya*h* arushấ*h* of the Asvins, which it is better to translate by red birds, as immediately before the winged horses are mentioned. In fact, whenever arushá is applied to the vehicle of the Asvins, it is to be understood of these red birds, iv. 43, 6.

In i. 92, 1 and 2 (not 20), árushî occurs three times, referring twice to the cows of the dawn, once to the dawn herself.

In iv. 15, 6, tám árvantam ná sânasím arushám ná divấ*h* *s*ísum marm*rig*yánte divé-dive, arushá does not refer to the horse or any other animal of Agni. The verse speaks of a horse by way of comparison only, and says that the sacrificers clean or trim Agni, the fire, as people clean a horse. We cannot join arushám in the next pâda with árvantam in the preceding pâda, for the second ná would then be without any construction. The construction is certainly not easy, but I think it is safer to translate: they trim him (Agni), day by day, as they clean a strong horse, as they clean Arushá, the child of Dyu. In fact, as far as I know, arushá is never used as the name of the one single horse belonging to Agni, but always of two or more.

In iii. 31, 21, antár (íti) krish*n*ân arushaí*h* dhấma-bhi*h* gât, dhấma-bhi*h* is said to mean flames of lightning. But dhấman in the Rig-veda does not mean flames, and it seems better to translate, with thy red companions, scil. the Maruts.

That arushá in one or two passages means the red cloud, is true. But in x. 43, 9, arushá refers to the thunderbolt mentioned in the same verse; and in i. 114, 5, everything refers to Rudra, and not to a red cloud, in the proper sense of the word.

Further on, where the meanings attributable to árushî in the Veda are collected, it is said that árushî means a red mare, also the teams of Agni and Ushas. Now, here, surely, a distinction should have been made between those passages in which árushî means a real horse, and those where it expresses the imaginary steeds of Agni. The former, it should be observed, occur in one Ma*n*dala only, and in places of somewhat doubtful authority, in viii. 55, 3, a Vâlakhilya hymn, and in viii. 68, 18, a dâna-stuti or panegyric. Besides, no passage is given where árushî means the horses of the dawn, and I doubt whether such a passage exists, while the verse where árushî is really used for the horses of Indra, is not mentioned at all. Lastly, two passages are set apart where árushî is supposed to mean flames. Now, it may be perfectly true that the red-horses of Agni are meant for flames, just as the red-horses of Indra may be the rays of the sun. But, in that case, the red-horses of Agni should always have been thus translated, or rather interpreted, and not in one passage only. In ix. 111, 2, árushî is said to mean flames, but no further light is thrown upon that very difficult passage.

Verse 1, note[2]. A similar expression occurs iii. 61, 5, where it is said of Ushas, the dawn, that she lighted the lights in the sky, prá ro*k*anấ ruru*k*e ra*n*vá-sand*r*ik.

Verse 2, note[1]. Although no name is given, the pronoun asya clearly refers to Indra, for it is he to whom the two bays belong. The next verse, therefore, must likewise be taken as addressed to Indra, and not to the sun or the morning-red, spoken of as a horse in the first verse.

Verse 3, note[1]. The vocative maryâ*h*, which I have trans-lated by O men, had evidently become a mere exclamation at a very early time. Even in our passage it is clear that the poet does not address any men in particular, for he addresses Indra, nor is marya used in the general sense of men. It means males, or male offspring. It sounds more like some kind of asseveration or oath, like the Latin mehercle, or like the English O ye powers, and it is there-fore quoted as a nipâta or particle in the Vâ*g*asan. Prâtis. ii. 16. It certainly cannot be taken as addressed to the Maruts, though the Maruts are the subject of the next verse.

Verse 3, note [2]. Ushádbhi*h*, an instrumental plural which attracted the attention of the author of the Vârttika to Pân. vii. 4, 48. It occurs but once, but the regular form, ushobhi*h*, does not occur at all in the Rig-veda. The same grammarian mentions mâs, month, as changing the final s of its base into d before bhis. This, too, is confirmed by Rv. ii. 24, 5, where mâdbhí*h* occurs. Two other words, svavas, offering good protection, and svatavas, of independent strength, mentioned together as liable to the same change, do not occur with bhi*h* in the Rig-veda, but the forms svavadbhi*h* and svatavadbhi*h* probably occurred in some other Vedic writings. Svatavadbhya*h* has been pointed out by Professor Aufrecht in the Vâ*g*asan. Sanhitâ xxiv. 16, and svatavobhya*h* in *S*atap. Br. ii. 5, 1, 14. That the nom. svavân, which is always trisyllabic, is not to be divided into sva-vân, as proposed by *S*âkalya, but into su-avân, is implied by Vârttika to Pân. viii. 4, 48, and distinctly stated in the Siddhânta-Kaumudî. That the final n of the nom. su-avân disappeared before semi-vowels is confirmed by the *S*âkala-prâti*s*âkhya, Sûtra 287; see also Vâ*g*asan. Prâti*s*. iii. Sûtra 135 (Weber, Ind. Stud. vol. iv. p. 206). On the proper division of su-avas, see Aufrecht, Zeitschrift der Deutschen Morgen-ländischen Gesellschaft, vol. xiii. p. 499.

Verse 4, note [1]. Ât must here take vyûha and be pronounced as an iambus. This is exceptional with ât, but there are at least two other passages where the same pronunciation is necessary. i. 148, 4. a͂t ro*k*ate vâne a͂ vi-bha͂-vâ, though in the line immediately following it is monosyllabic. Also in v. 7, 10. a͂t agne ápri*n*ata*h*.

Verse 4, note [2]. Svadhá͂, literally one's own place, afterwards, one's own nature. It was a great triumph for the science of Comparative Philology that, long before the existence of such a word as svadhâ in Sanskrit was known, it should have been postulated by Professor Benfey in his Griechische Wurzel-lexicon, published in 1839, and in the appendix of 1842. Svadhá͂ was known, it is true, in the ordinary Sanskrit, but there it only occurred as an exclamation used on presenting an oblation to the manes. It

was also explained to mean food offered to deceased ances-
tors, or to be the name of a personification of Mâyâ or
worldly illusion, or of a nymph. But Professor Benfey,
with great ingenuity, postulated for Sanskrit a noun svadhấ,
as corresponding to the Greek ἔθος and the German sitte,
O. H. G. sit-u, Gothic sid-u. The noun svadhấ has since
been discovered in the Veda, where it occurs very frequently; and its true meaning in many passages where
native tradition had entirely misunderstood it, has really
been restored by means of its etymological identification
with the Greek ἔθος or ἦθος. See Kuhn's Zeitschrift, vol. ii.
p. 134, vol. xii. p. 158.

The expressions ánu svadhẩm and svadhẩm ánu are of
frequent occurrence. They mean, according to the nature
or character of the persons spoken of, and may be translated
by as usual, or according to a person's wont. Thus in our
passage we may translate, The Maruts are born again, i. e.
as soon as Indra appeared with the dawn, according to their
wont; they are always born as soon as Indra appears, for
such is their nature.

i. 165, 5. índra svadhẩm ánu hí naḥ babhútha.

For, Indra, according to thy wont, thou art ours.

viii. 20, 7. svadhẩm ánu sríyam náraḥ—váhante.

According to their wont, the men (the Maruts) carry
splendour.

viii. 88, 5. ánu svadhẩm vavakshitha.

Thou hast grown (Indra) according to thy nature.

iv. 33, 6. ánu svadhẩm ríbhávaḥ gagmuḥ etẩm.

According to their nature, the Ribhus went to her, scil.
the cow; or, according to this their nature, they came.

iv. 52, 6. úshaḥ ánu svadhẩm ava.

Dawn, help! as thou art wont.

i. 33, 11. ánu svadhẩm aksharan ẩpaḥ asya.

As usual, or according to his nature, i. e. his strength, the
waters flowed.

i. 88, 6. âsẩm ánu svadhẩm.

According to the nature of these libations.

vii. 56, 13. ánu svadhẩm ẩyudhaiḥ yákkhamânâḥ.

According to their nature, stretching forth with their
weapons.

iii. 51, 11. yáh te ánu svadhâm ásat suté ní yakkha tanvâm.

Direct thy body to that libation which is according to thy nature, or better, according to thy taste.

In all these passages svadhâ may be rendered by manner, habit, usage, and ánu svadhâm would seem to correspond to the Greek ἐξ ἔθους. Yet the history of these words in Sanskrit and Greek has not been exactly the same. First of all we observe in Greek a division between ἔθος and ἦθος, and whereas the former comes very near in meaning to the Sanskrit svadhâ, the latter shows in Homer a much more primitive and material sense. It means in Homer, not a person's own nature, but the own place, for instance, of animals, the haunts of horses, lions, fish ; in Hesiod, also of men. Svadhâ in the Veda does not occur in that sense, although etymologically it might take the meaning of one's own place : cf. dhâ-man, *familia*, etc. Whether in Greek ἦθος, from meaning lair, haunt, home, came, like ιομός and νόμος, to mean habit, manner, character, which would be quite possible, or whether ἦθος in that meaning represents a second start from the same point, which in Sanskrit was fixed in svadhâ, is impossible to determine. In Sanskrit svadhâ clearly shows the meaning of one's own nature, power, disposition. It does not mean power or nature in general, but always the power of some one, the peculiarity, the individuality of a person. This will appear from the following passages :

ii. 3, 8. tisráh devîh svadhâyâ barhíh â idám ákkhidram pântu.

May the three goddesses protect by their power the sacred pile unbroken.

iv. 13, 5. káyâ yâti svadhâyâ.

By what inherent power does he (the Sun) move on ?

iv. 26, 4. akakráyâ svadhâyâ.

By a power which requires no chariot, i. e. by himself without a chariot.

The same expression occurs again x. 27, 19.

In some places ' mad,' to delight, joined with svadhâyâ, seems to mean to revel in his strength, proud of his might.

v. 32, 4. svadháyâ mádantam.

Vritra who delights in his strength.

vii. 47, 3. svadháyâ mádantî*h*.

The waters who delight in their strength. See x. 124, 8.

In other passages, however, as we shall see, the same phrase (and this is rather unusual) requires to be taken in a different sense, so as to mean to rejoice in food.

i. 164, 38. svadháyâ gribhîtá*h*.

Held or grasped by his own strength.

iii. 17, 5. svadháyâ *k*a *s*ambhú*h*.

He who blesses by his own strength.

iii. 35, 10. índra píba svadháyâ *k*it sutásya agné*h* vâ pâhi *g*ihváyâ ya*g*atra.

Indra drink of the libation by thyself (by thy own power), or with the tongue of Agni, O worshipful.

To drink with the tongue of Agni is a bold but not unusual expression. v. 51, 2. agné*h* pibata *g*ihváyâ.

x. 15, 3. yé svadháyâ sutásya bhá*g*anta pitvá*h*.

Those who by themselves share in the offered draught.

i. 165, 6. kvã syã va*h* maruta*h* svadhã âsît yát mãm ékam sam-âdhatta ahi-hátye.

Where was that custom of yours, O Maruts, that ye should have joined me who stand alone in the fight with Ahi?

vii. 8, 3. káyâ na*h* agne ví vasa*h* su-v*r*iktím kãm ûm (íti) svadhãm ri*n*ava*h* *s*asyámâna*h*.

In what character dost thou light up our altar, and what character dost thou assume when thou art praised?

iv. 58, 4. venãt ékam svadháyâ ní*h* tatakshu*h*.

They (the gods) made one out of the sun, by their own power.

iv. 45, 6. ví*s*vân ánu svadháyâ *k*etatha*h* pathá*h*.

You (Asvins) look after all the paths by your own strength.

i. 64, 4. sâkám ga*g*ñire svadháyâ.

They (the Maruts) were born together according to their nature; very much like ánu svadhãm, i. 6, 4. One can hardly render it here by 'they were born by their own strength,' or 'by spontaneous generation.'

In other passages, however, svadháyâ, meaning originally by its own power, or nature, comes to mean, by itself, *sponte suâ.*

vii. 78, 4. ā́ asthât rátham svadháyâ yu*ɡ*yámânam.

She, the dawn, mounted the chariot which was harnessed by itself, by its own power, without requiring the assistance of people to put the horses to.

x. 129, 2. ā́nît avâtám svadháyû tát ékam.

That only One breathed breathlessly, by its own strength, i. e. by itself.

In the same sense svadhā́bhi*h* is used in several passages: i. 113, 13. amr*í*tâ *k*arati svadhā́bhi*h*.

The immortal Dawn moves along by her own strength, i. e. by herself.

viii. 10, 6. yát vâ svadhā́bhi*h* adhi-tíshth*h*atha*h* rátham.

Or whether ye mount your chariot by your own strength, ye Asvins.

i. 164, 30. *ɡ*îvá*h* mr*í*tásya *k*arati svadhā́bhi*h* ámartya*h* mártyena sá-yoni*h*.

The living moves by the powers of the dead, the immortal is the brother of the mortal.

iii. 26, 8. várshishth*h*am rátnam akr*i*ta svadhā́bhi*h*.

He (Agni) made the best jewel by his own powers, i. e. by himself.

v. 60, 4. varā́h-iva ít raivatása*h* híra*n*yai*h* abhí svadhā́bhi*h* tanvā́*h* pipi*s*re.

Like rich suitors, they (the Maruts) by their own strength, i. e. themselves, adorn their bodies with gold ornaments.

There are doubtful passages in which the meaning of svadhā́bhi*h*, too, is doubtful. Thus, i. 180, 6. In vi. 2, 8, svadhā́ looks like an adverb, instead of svadháyâ, and would then refer to párí*ɡ*mâ. The same applies to viii. 32, 6.

But svadhā́ means also food, lit. one's own portion, the sacrificial offering due to each god, and lastly, food in general.

i. 108, 12. yát indrâgnî (íti) út-itâ sû́ryasya mádhye divá*h* svadháyâ mâdáyethe (íti).

Whether you, Indra and Agni, delight in your food at the rising of the sun or at midday.

x. 15, 12. tvám agne î*l*itá*h* *ɡ*âta-veda*h* ávâ*t* havyấni su-rabhî́*n*i kr*i*tvî́, prá adâ*h* pit*r*í-bhya*h* svadháyâ té akshan addhí tvám deva prá-yatâ haví*m*shi. 13. yé *k*a ihá pitára*h* yé *k*a ná ihá yā́n *k*a vidmá yā́n û*m* (íti) *k*a ná pra-vidmá, tvám vettha

yáti té gáta-veda*h* svadhábhi*h* ya*gñ*ám sú-k*r*itam *g*ushasva.
14. yé agni-dagdhá*h* yé ánagni-dagdhá*h* mádhye divá*h* svadháyâ mâdáyante, tébhi*h* sva-râ*t* ásu-nîtim etâm yathâ-va-
*s*âm tanvâm kalpayasva.

12. Thou, O Agni *G*âtavedas, hast carried, when implored,
the offerings which thou hast rendered sweet: thou hast given
them to the fathers, they fed on their share. Eat thou, O
god, the proffered oblations. 13. Our fathers who are here,
and those who are not here, our fathers whom we know and
those whom we do not know, thou knowest how many they
are, O *G*âtavedas, accept the well-made sacrifice with the
sacrificial portions. 14. They who, whether burnt by fire
or not burnt by fire, rejoice in their offering in the midst
of heaven, give to them, O king, that life, and thy (their)
own body, according to thy will.

iii. 4, 7. saptá *pr*ikshâsa*h* svadháyâ madanti.

The seven horses delight in their food.

x. 14, 7. ubhá râ*g*ânâ svadháyâ mádantâ.

The two kings delighting in their food.

ix. 113, 10. yátra kâmâ*h* ni-kâmâ*h* *k*a, yátra bradhnásya
vish*t*ápam, svadhá *k*a yátra t*r*ípti*h* *k*a tátra mâm am*r*ítam
k*r*idhí.

Where wishes and desires are, where the cup of the bright
Soma is, where there is food and rejoicing, there make me
immortal.

i. 154, 4. yásya trî́ pû́r*n*â mádhunâ padấni âkshîyamâ*n*â
svadháyâ mádanti.

He (Vish*n*u) whose three places, full of sweet, imperish-
able, delight or abound in food.

v. 34, 1. svadhá ámitâ.

His unlimited portion or offering.

ii. 35, 7. dhenú*h* svadhấm pîpâya.

The cow yields her food, her portion, her milk.

i. 168, 9. ất ít svadhấm ishirấm pári apa*s*yan.

Thereafter (the Maruts) saw the vigorous food.

i. 176, 2. ánu svadhá yâm upyáte.

After whom, or for whom, his food is scattered.

In the tenth book svadhá is used very much as it occurs
in the later Sanskrit, as the name of a peculiar sacrificial
rite.

x. 14, 3. yấn ka devấh vav*r*idhúh yé ka devấn svấhấ anyé svadháyấ anyé madanti.

Those whom the gods cherish, and those who cherish the gods, the one delight in Svâhâ, the others in Svadhâ; or, in praise and food.

Verse 4, note [3]. The expression garbha-tvám â-îriré is matched by that of iii. 60, 3. saudhanvanấsah am*r*ita-tvám ấ îrire, the Saudhanvanas (the *R*ibhus) obtained immortality. The idea that the Maruts assumed the form of a garbha, lit. of an embryo or a new-born child, is only meant to express that the storms burst forth from the womb of the sky as soon as Indra arises to do battle against the demon of darkness. As assisting Indra in this battle, the Maruts, whose name retained for a long time its purely appellative meaning of storms, attained their rank as deities by the side of Indra, or, as the poet expresses it, they assumed their sacred name. This seems to be the whole meaning of the later legend that the Maruts, like the *R*ibhus, were not originally gods, but became deified for their works.

Vấhni.

Verse 5, note [1]. Sâya*n*a explains vấhnibhih in the sense of Marúdbhih, and he tells the oft-repeated story how the cows were carried off by the Pa*n*is from the world of the gods, and thrown into darkness, and how Indra with the Maruts conquered them and brought them back. Everybody seems to have accepted this explanation of Sâya*n*a, and I myself do not venture to depart from it. Yet it should be stated that the use of vấhni as a name of the Maruts is by no means well established. Vấhni is in fact a most difficult word in the Veda. In later Sanskrit it means fire, and is quoted also as a name of Agni, the god of fire, but we do not learn why a word which etymologically means carrier, from vah, to carry, should have assumed the meaning of fire. It may be that vah, which in Sanskrit, Greek, and Latin means chiefly to carry, expressed originally the idea of moving about (the German *be-wegen*), in which case vấh-ni, fire, would have been formed with the same purpose as

ag-ní, *ig-nis*, fire, from Sk. a*g*, *ἀγ-ω*, *ag-o*.   But in Sanskrit
Agni is so constantly represented as the carrier of the
sacrificial oblation, that something may be said in favour
of the Indian scholastic interpreters who take váhni, as
applied to Agni, in the sense of carrier.   However that
may be, it admits of no doubt that váhni, in the Veda also,
is distinctly applied to the bright fire or light.   In some
passages it looks very much like a proper name of Agni,
in his various characters of terrestrial and celestial light.
It is used for the sacrificial fire :

v. 50, 4. yátra váhni*h* abhí-hita*h*.

Where the sacrificial fire is placed.

It is applied to Agni :

vii. 7, 5. ásâdi vritá*h* váhni*h* â-*g*aganvấn agní*h* brahmấ.

The chosen light came nigh, and sat down, Agni, the priest.

Here Agni is, as usual, represented as a priest, chosen
like a priest, for the performance of the sacrifice.   But, for
that very reason, váhni may here have the meaning of priest,
which, as we shall see, it has in many places, and the translation would then be more natural : He, the chosen minister,
came near and sat down, Agni, the priest.

viii. 23, 3. váhni*h* vindate vásu.

Agni finds wealth (for those who offer sacrifices ?).

More frequently váhni is applied to the celestial Agni, or
other solar deities, where it is difficult to translate it in
English except by an adjective :

iii. 5, 1. ápa dvẫrâ támasa*h* váhni*h* âvar (íty âva*h*).

Agni opened the two doors of darkness.

i. 160, 3. sá*h* váhni*h* putrá*h* pitró*h* pavítra-ván punấti
dhĩra*h* bhúvanâni mâyấyâ.

That light, the son of the two parents, full of brightness,
the wise, brightens the world by his power.

Agni is even called váhni-tama (iv. 1, 4), which hardly
means more than the brightest.

ii. 17, 4. ẫt ródasî (íti) *g*yótishâ váhni*h* ẫ atanot.

Then the luminous (Indra) stretched out or filled heaven
and earth with his light.

ii. 38, 1. út û*m* (íti) syá*h* devá*h* savitấ—váhni*h* asthât.

The bright Savitar, the luminous, arose.

Besides this meaning of light or fire, however, there are

clearly two other meanings of váhni which must be admitted
in the Veda, first that of a carrier, vehicle, and, it may be,
horse; secondly that of minister or priest.

vi. 57, 3. *agāh* anyásya váhnayah hárî (íti) anyásya sám-
bhritâ.

The bearers of the one (Púshan) are goats, the bays are
yoked for the other (Indra).

i. 14, 6. ghritá-prish*thâh* mana*h*-yúgah yé tvâ váhanti
váhnayah.

The horses with shining backs, obedient to thy will, which
carry thee (Agni).

viii. 3, 23. yásmai anyé dása práti dhúram váhanti váhnayah.

A horse against whom other ten horses carry a weight;
i. e. it requires ten horses to carry the weight which this
one horse carries. (See x. 11, 7. váhamánah ásvaih.)

ii. 37, 3. médyantu te váhnayah yébhih ȳyase.

May thy horses be fat on which thou goest.

ii. 24, 13. utá ásish*thâh* ánu srinvanti váhnayah.

The very quick horses (of Brahmanaspati) listen. These
may be the flames, but they are conceived as carriers or
horses.

i. 44, 13. srudhí srut-karna váhni-bhih.

Agni, who hast ears to hear, hear, on thy horses. Unless
váhni-bhih is joined with the words that follow, devaíh
sayáva-bhih.

ñi. 6, 2. va*k*yántâm te váhnayah saptá-*gih*vâh*.

May thy seven-tongued horses be called. Here váhnayah
is clearly meant for the flames of Agni, yet I doubt whether
we should be justified in dropping the simile, as the plural
of váhni is nowhere used in the bald sense of flames.

In one passage váhni is used as a feminine, or at all
events applied to a feminine subject:

viii. 94, 1. yuktá váhnih ráthânâm.

She is yoked as the drawer of the chariots.

The passages in which váhni is applied to Soma in the
9th and 10th Mandalas throw little light on the subject.
(ix. 9, 6; 20, 5; 6; 36, 2; 64, 19; 89, 1; x. 101, 10.)

Instead of visám vispátih, lord of men (vii. 7, 4), we find

---

* Cf. i. 58, 7. saptá guhvâh.

ix. 108, 10. visâm váhni*h* ná vispáti*h*. One feels inclined to translate here váhni*h* by leader, but it is more likely that váhni is here again the common name of Soma, and that it is inserted between visâm ná vispáti*h*, which is meant to form one phrase.

In ix. 97, 34, tisrá*h* vá*k*a*h* îrayati prá váhni*h*, we may take váhni as the common appellation of Soma. But it may also mean minister or priest, as in the passages which we have now to examine. Cf. x. 11, 6.

For besides these passages in which váhni clearly means vector, carrier, drawer, horse, there is a large class of verses in which it can only be translated by minister, i. e. officiating minister, and, as it would seem, chiefly singer or reciter. The verb vah was used in Sanskrit in the sense of carrying out (ud-vah, *ausführen*), or performing a rite, particularly as applied to the reciting of hymns. Hence such compounds as ukthá-váhas or stóma-váhas, offering hymns of praise. Thus we read:

v. 79, 4. abhí yé tvâ vibhâ-vari stómai*h* gri*n*ánti váhnaya*h*.

The ministers who praise thee, splendid Dawn, with hymns.

i. 48, 11. yé tvâ gri*n*ánti váhnaya*h*.

The ministers who praise thee.

vii. 75, 5. ushá*h* u*kkh*ati váhni-bhi*h* gri*n*ânâ.

The dawn lights up, praised by the ministers.

vi. 39, 1. mandrásya kavé*h* divyásya váhne*h*.

Of the sweet poet, of the heavenly priest . . . .

vii. 82, 4. yuvâm ít yut-sú prítanâsu váhnaya*h* yuvâm kshémasya pra-savé mitá-*g*ñava*h* îsânâ vásva*h* ubháyasya kárává*h* índrâvaru*n*â su-hávâ havâmahe.

We, as ministers, invoke you only in fights and battles; we, as supplicants, (invoke) you for the granting of treasure; we, as poets, (invoke) you, the lords of twofold wealth, you, Indra and Varu*n*a, who listen to our call.

vi. 32, 3. sá*h* váhni-bhi*h* ríkva-bhi*h* góshu sásvat mitá*g*ñu-bhi*h* puru-k*rí*tvâ *g*igâya.

He (Indra) was victorious often among the cows, always with celebrating and suppliant ministers.

I have placed these two passages together because they

seem to me to illustrate each other, and to show that although in the second passage the celebrating and suppliant ministers may be intended for the Maruts, yet no argument could be drawn from this verse in favour of váhni by itself meaning the Maruts. See also viii. 6, 2 ; 12, 15 ; x. 114, 2.

iv. 21, 6. hótâ yáh nah mahân sam-váraneshu váhnih.
The Hotar who is our great priest in the sanctuaries.
i. 128, 4. váhnih vedhâh ágâyata.
Because the wise priest (Agni) was born.

The same name which in these passages is applied to Agni, is in others, and, as it will be seen, in the same sense, applied to Indra.

ii. 21, 2. tuvi-gráye váhnaye.
To the strong-voiced priest or leader.

The fact that váhni is followed in several passages by ukthaíh would seem to show that the office of the váhni was chiefly that of recitation or of addressing prayers to the gods.

iii. 20, 1. agním ushásam asvínâ dadhi-krâm ví-ushtishu havate váhnih ukthaíh.
The priest at the break of day calls with his hymns Agni, Ushas, the Asvins, and Dadhikrâ.

i. 184, 1. tâ vâm adyá taú aparám huvema ukkhántyâm ushási váhnih ukthaíh.
Let us invoke the two Asvins to-day and to-morrow, the priest with his hymns is there when the dawn appears.

In a similar sense, it would seem, as váhnih ukthaíh, the Vedic poets frequently use the words váhnih âsâ. This âsâ is the instrumental singular of âs, mouth, and it is used in other phrases also of the mouth as the instrument of praise.

vi. 32, 1. vagríne sám-tamâni vákâmsi âsâ sthávirâya taksham.
I have shaped with my mouth blessed words to the wielder of the thunderbolt, the strong Indra.

x. 115, 3. âsâ váhnim ná sokíshâ vi-rapsínam.
He who sings with his flame as the poet with his mouth. See also i. 38, 14. mimíhí slókam âsyè, make a song in thy mouth.

Thus we find váhnih âsâ in the same place in the sixth

and seventh Man*d*alas (vi. 16, 9; vii. 16, 9), in the phrase váhni*h* ásá vidú*h*-tara*h*, applied to Agni in the sense of the priest wise with his mouth, or taking váhni*h* ásá as it were one word, the wise poet.

i. 129, 5. váhni*h* ásá, váhni*h* na*h* ákk*h*a.

Indra, as a priest by his lips, as a priest coming towards us.

From the parallelism of this passage it would seem that Professor Roth concluded the meaning of ásá* to be near, or *coram*.

i. 76, 4. pra*gá*-vatá vá*k*asá váhni*h* ásá á *k*a huvé ní *k*a satsi ihá devai*h*.

With words in which my people join, I, the poet, invoke, and thou (Agni) sittest down with the gods.

vi. 11, 2. pávaká*y*á *g*uhvá váhni*h* ásá.

Thou, a poet with a bright tongue, O Agni!

The question now arises in what sense váhni is used when applied without further definition to certain deities. Most deities in the Veda are represented as driving or driven, and many as poets or priests. When the Asvins are called váhní, viii. 8, 12; vii. 73, 4, it may mean riders. But when the Visve Devas are so called, i. 3, 9, or the *R*ibhus, the exact

---

* Âs, mouth, the Latin *os, oris*, has been derived from a root as, to breathe, preserved in the Sanskrit as-u, spirit, asu-ra, endowed with spirit, living, the living god. Though I agree with Curtius in admitting a primitive root as, to breathe, from which as-u, breath, must have sprung, I have always hesitated about the derivation of âs and âsya, mouth, from the same root. I do not think, however, that the lengthening of the vowel in âs is so great a difficulty as has been supposed (Kuhn, Zeitschrift, vol. xvii. p. 145). Several roots lengthen their vowel a, when used as substantives without derivative suffixes. In some cases this lengthening is restricted to the Anga base, as in ana*d*vâh; in others to the Anga and Pada base, as in visvavât, visvavâ*d*bhi*h*, &c.; in others again it pervades the whole declension, as in turâshât: (see Sanskrit Grammar, §§ 210, 208, 175.) Among ordinary words vâ*k* offers a clear instance of a lengthened vowel. In the Veda we find ritishá*h*am, vi. 14, 4, and ritishá*h*am (Sanhitâ), i. 64, 15. We find vâh in apsu-vâh (Sâm. Ved.), indra-vâh, havya-vâh. Sah at the end of compounds, such as nri-sah, pritaná-sah, bhúri-sah, satrâ-sah, vibhá-sah, sadá-sah, varies between a long and short â: (see Regnier, Étude sur l'idiome du Védas, p. 111.) At all events no instance has yet been pointed out in Sanskrit, showing the same contraction which we should have to admit if, as has been proposed, we derived âs from av-as, or from an-as. From an we have in the Veda áná, mouth or face, i. 52, 15. From as, to breathe, the Latin *omen*, originally *os-men*, a whisper, might likewise be derived.

meaning is more doubtful. The Maruts are certainly riders, and we can even prove that they were supposed to sit on horseback and to have the bridle through the horse's nostrils (v. 61, 2). But if in our verse i. 6, 5, we translate váhni as an epithet, rider, and not only as an epithet, but as a name of the Maruts, we cannot support our translation by independent evidence, but must rely partly on the authority of Sâyaṇa, partly on the general tenour of the text before us, where the Maruts are mentioned in the preceding verse, and, if I am right, in the verse following also. On the other hand, if váhni can thus be used as a name of the Maruts, there is at least one other passage which would gain in clearness by the admission of that meaning, viz.

x. 138, 1. táva tyé indra sakhyéshu váhnayaḥ—ví adar-diruḥ valám.

In thy friendship, Indra, these Maruts tore asunder the cloud.

Verse 5, note [2]. I have translated vîḷú by stronghold, though it is only an adjective meaning firm. Dr. Oscar Meyer, in his very able essay Quæstiones Homericæ, specimen prius, Bonnæ, 1867, has tried to show that this vîḷú is the original form of Ἴλιος, and he has brought some further evidence to show that the siege and conquest of Troy, as I pointed out in my Lectures on the Science of Language, vol. ii. p. 470, was originally described in language borrowed from the siege and conquest of the dark night by the powers of light, or from the destruction of the cloud by the weapons of Indra. It ought to be considered, however, that vîḷú in the Veda has not dwindled down as yet to a mere name, and that therefore it may have originally retained its purely appellative power in Greek as well as in Sanskrit, and from meaning a stronghold in general, have come to mean the stronghold of Troy.

Verse 5, note [3]. The bright cows are here the cows of the morning, the dawns, or the days themselves, which are represented as rescued at the end of each night by the power of Indra, or similar solar gods. Indra's companions in that daily rescue are the Maruts, the storms, or the

breezes of the morning, the same companions who act even
a more prominent part in the battle of Indra against the
dark clouds; two battles often mixed up together.

Verse 6, note [1]. The reasons why I take gírah as a masculine in the sense of singer or praiser, may be seen in a
note to i. 37, 10.

Verse 6, note [2]. yáthá matím, lit. according to their mind,
according to their heart's desire. Cf. ii. 24, 13.

Verse 7, note [1]. The sudden transition from the plural
to the singular is strange, but the host of the Maruts is
frequently spoken of in the singular, and nothing else can
here be intended. It may be true, as Professor Benfey
suggests, that the verses here put together stood originally
in a different order, or that they were taken from different
sources. Yet though the Sâma-veda would seem to sanction
a small alteration in the order of the verses, the alteration
of verses 7, 4, 5, as following each other, would not help us
much. The Atharva-veda sanctions no change in the order
of these verses.

The transition to the dual at the end of the verse is
likewise abrupt, not more so, however, than we are prepared
for in the Veda. The suggestion of the Nirukta (iv. 12)
that these duals might be taken as instrumentals of the
singular, is of no real value.

Verse 7, note [2]. Dríkshase, a very valuable form, a second
person singular conjunctive of the First Aorist Âtmanepada,
the termination 'sase' corresponding to Greek ση, as the
conjunctive takes the personal terminations of the present
in both languages. Similar forms, viz. prikshase, x. 22, 7,
mamsase, x. 27, 10; Ath. Veda vii. 20, 2—6, and possibly
vívakshase, x. 21, 1—8, 24, 1—3, 25, 1—11, will have to be
considered hereafter. (Nirukta, ed. Roth, p. 30, Notes.)

Verse 8, note [1]. Arkati, which I have here translated by
he cries aloud, means literally, he celebrates. I do not
know of any passage where · arkati, when used, as here,

without an object, means to shine, as Professor Benfey translates it. The real difficulty, however, lies in makhá, which Sâya*n*a explains by sacrifice, and which I have ventured to translate by priest or sacrificer. Makhá, as an adjective, means, as far as we can judge, strong or vigorous, and is applied to various deities, such as Pûshan i. 138, 1, Savitar vi. 71, 1, Soma xi. 20, 7, Indra iii. 34, 2, the Maruts i. 64, 11; vi. 66, 9. By itself, makhá is never used as the name of any deity, and it cannot therefore, as Professor Roth proposes, be used in our passage as a name of Indra, or be referred to Indra as a significant adjective. In i. 119, 3, makhá is applied to men or warriors, but it does not follow that makhá by itself means warrior, though it may be connected with the Greek μαχος in σύμμαχος. See Curtius, Grundzüge, p. 293; Grassmann, in Kuhn's Zeitschrift, vol. xvi. p. 164.

There are two passages where makhá refers to an enemy of the gods, ix. 101, 13; x. 171, 2.

Among the remaining passages there is one where makhá is used in parallelism with váhni, x. 11, 6. vívakti váhni*h*, su-apasyáte makhá*h*. Here I propose to translate, The poet speaks out, the priest works well. The same meaning seems to me applicable likewise to the phrase makhásya dâváne, to the offering of the priest.

i. 134, 1. â yâhi dâváne, vâyo (íti), makhásya dâváne.
Come, Vâyu, to the offering, to the offering of the priest.
viii. 7, 27. â na*h* makhásya dâváne—dévâsa*h* úpa gantana.
Come, gods, to the offering of our priest.

Professor Roth proposes to render makhá in these passages by 'attestation of joy, celebration, praise,' and he takes dâváne, as I have done, as a dative of dâván, a *nomen actionis*, meaning, the giving. There are some passages where one feels inclined to admit a noun dâvána, and to take dâváne as a locative sing.

vi. 71, 2. devásya vayám savitú*h* sávîmani
srésh*th*e syâma vásuna*h* ka dâváne.
May we be in the favour of the god Savitar, and in the best award of his treasure.

In ii. 11, 1, and ii. 11, 12, the locative would likewise be preferable; but there is a decided majority of passages

in which dâváne occurs and where it is to be taken as a
dative*, nor is there any other instance in the Veda of a
nomen actionis being formed by vana. It is better, therefore, in vi. 71, 2, to refer *sreshthe* to sávîmani, and to make
allowance in the other passages for the idiomatic use of such
phrases as dâváne vásûnâm or râyâh dâváne.

The termination váne explains, as has been shown by
Professor Benfey, Greek infinitives such as δοῦναι, i. e.
δοεναι or δοϝεναι = Sanskrit dâ-váne. The termination *mane*
in dâ-mane, for the purpose of giving, explains, as the same
scholar has proved, the ancient infinitives in Greek, such
as δό-μεναι. It may be added that the regular infinitives
in Greek, ending in εναι, as λελοιπ-έναι, are likewise
matched by Vedic forms such as ix. 61, 30. dhûrv-ane, or
vi. 61, 13. vibhv-áne. In the termination ειν, which stands
for εν, like εις for εσι, we have, on the contrary, not a
dative, but a locative of an abstract noun in an, both cases,
as we see from their juxta-position in vi. 71, 2, being equally
applicable to express the relation which we are accustomed
to call infinitive.

Verses 9 and 10, note [1]. Although the names for earth,
sky, and heaven vary in different parts of the Veda, yet the
expression diváh rokanám occurs so frequently that we can
hardly take it in this place in a sense different from its
ordinary meaning. Professor Benfey thinks that rokaná
may here mean ether, and he translates ' come from heaven
above the ether;' and in the next verse, ' come from heaven
above the earth.' At first, every reader would feel inclined
to take the two phrases, diváh vâ rokanât ádhi, and diváh
vâ pârthivât ádhi, as parallel; yet I believe they are not
quite so.

The following passages will show that the two words
rokanám diváh belong together, and that they signify the
light of heaven, or the bright place of heaven.

viii. 98, 3. ágakkhah rokanám diváh.

---

* Rv. i. 61, 10; 122, 5; 134, 2; 139, 6; ii. 1, 10; iv. 29, 5; 32, 9; v. 59,
1; 4; 65, 3; viii. 25, 20; 45, 10; (92, 26); 46, 25; 27; 63, 5; 69, 17; 70,
12; ix. 93, 4; x. 32, 5; 44, 7; 50, 7.

Thou (Indra) wentest to the light of heaven.

i. 155, 3. ádhi rokané diváh.

In the light of heaven.

iii. 6, 8. uraú vâ yé antárikshe—diváh vâ yé rokané.

In the wide sky, or in the light of heaven.

viii. 82, 4. upamé rokané diváh.

In the highest light of heaven.

ix. 86, 27. tritíye prishthé ádhi rokané diváh.

On the third ridge, in the light of heaven. See also i. 105, 5; viii. 69, 3.

The very phrase which we find in our verse, only with *kit* instead of vâ, occurs again, i. 49, 1; viii. 8, 7; and the same sense must probably be assigned to viii. 1, 18, ádha *gmáh* ádha vâ diváh brihatáh rokanât ádhi.

Either from the earth, or from the light of the great heaven, increase, O Indra!

Rokaná also occurs in the plural:

i. 146, 1. vísvâ diváh rokaná.

All the bright regions of heaven.

Sâyana: 'All the bright palaces of the gods.' See iii. 12, 9.

The same word rokaná, and in the same sense, is also joined with sûrya and nâka.

Thus, i. 14, 9. sûryasya rokanât vísvân devân—hótâ ihá vakshati.

May the Hotar bring the Visve Devas hither from the light of the sun, or from the bright realm of the sun.

iii. 22, 3. yáh rokané parástât sûryasya.

The waters which are above, in the bright realm of the sun, and those which are below.

i. 19, 6. yé nâkasya ádhi rokané, diví devásah ásate.

They who in the light of the firmament, in heaven, are enthroned as gods.

Here diví, in heaven, seems to be the same as the light of the firmament, nâkasya rokané.

Thus rokaná occurs also frequently by itself, when it clearly has the meaning of heaven.

It is said of the dawn, i. 49, 4; of the sun, i. 50, 4; and of Indra, iii. 44, 4.

vísvam â bhâti rokanám, they light up the whole sky.

We also read of three rokanas, where, though it is difficult

to say what is really meant, we must translate, the three
skies. The cosmography of the Veda is, as I said before,
somewhat vague and varying. There is, of course, the
natural division of the world into heaven and earth (dyú and
bhúmi), and the threefold division into earth, sky, and heaven,
where sky is meant for the region intermediate between
heaven and earth (prithiví, antáriksha, dyú). There is also
a fourfold division, for instance,

viii. 97, 5. yát vâ ási rokané diváh
        samudrásya ádhi vishtápi,
        yát párthive sádane vritrahan-tama,
        yát antárikshe â gahi.

Whether thou, O greatest killer of Vritra, art in the light
of heaven, or in the basin of the sea, or in the place of the
earth, or in the sky, come hither!

v. 52, 7. yé vavridhánta párthiváh yé uraú antárikshe â,
vrigáne vâ nadínâm sadhá-sthe vâ maháh diváh.

The Maruts who grew, being on the earth, those who are
in the wide sky, or in the compass of the rivers, or in the
abode of the great heaven.

But very soon these three or more regions are each
spoken of as threefold. Thus,

i. 102, 8. tisráh bhúmíh tríni rokaná.

The three earths, the three skies.

ii. 27, 9. trí rokaná divyá dhârayanta.

The Âdityas support the three heavenly skies.

v. 69, 1. trí rokaná varuna trín utá dyún tríni mitra
dhârayathah rágâmsi.

Mitra and Varuna, you support the three lights, and the
three heavens, and the three skies.

Here there seems some confusion, which Sâyana's commentary makes even worse confounded. What can rokaná
mean as distinct from dyú and rágas? The fourth verse of
the same hymn throws no light on the subject, and I should
feel inclined to take divyá-párthivasya as one word, though
even then the cosmic division here adopted is by no means
clear. However, there is a still more complicated division
alluded to in iv. 53, 5:

tríh antáriksham savitá mahi-tvaná trí rágâmsi pari-bhúh
tríni rokaná, tisráh dívah prithivíh tisráh invati.

Here we have the sky thrice, three welkins, three lights, three heavens, three earths.

A careful consideration of all these passages will show, I think, that in our passage we must take diváḥ vâ roḱanât ádhi in its usual sense, and that we cannot separate the two words.

In the next verse, on the contrary, it seems equally clear that diváḥ and pârthivât must be separated. At all events there is no passage in the Rig-veda where pârthiva is joined as an adjective with dyú. Pârthiva as an adjective is frequently joined with ráǥas, never with dyú. See i. 81, 5; 90, 7; viii. 88, 5; ix. 72, 8: in the plural, i. 154, 1; v. 81, 3; vi. 31, 2; 49, 3.

Pârthivâni also occurs by itself, when it means the earth, as opposed to the sky and heaven.

x. 32, 2. ví indra yâsi divyâni roḱanâ ví pârthivâni ráǥasâ.

Indra thou goest in the sky between the heavenly lights and the earthly.

viii. 94, 9. â yé vísvâ pârthivâni papráthan roḱanâ diváḥ.

The Maruts who stretched out all the earthly lights, and the lights of heaven.

vi. 61, 11. â-paprúshî pârthivâni urú ráǥaḥ antáriksham.

Sarasvatî filling the earthly places, the wide welkin, the sky. This is a doubtful passage.

Lastly, pârthivâni by itself seems to signify earth, sky, and heaven, if those are the three regions which Vishṇu measured with his three steps; or east, the zenith, and west, if these were intended as the three steps of that deity. For we read:

i. 155, 4. yáḥ pârthivâni tri-bhíḥ ít vígâma-bhiḥ urú krámishṭa.

He (Vishṇu) who strode wide with his three strides across the regions of the earth.

These two concluding verses might also be taken as containing the actual invocation of the sacrificer, which is mentioned in verse 8. In that case the full stop at the end of verse 8 should be removed.

MANDALA I, SÛKTA 19.

ASHTAKA I, ADHYÂYA 1, VARGA 36–37.

1. Práti tyám kắrum adhvarám go-pîthắya prá
hûyase, marút-bhih agne ắ gahi.

2. Nahí deváh ná mártyah maháh táva krátum
paráh, marút-bhih agne ắ gahi.

3. Yé maháh rágasah vidúh vísve devắsah adrúhah,
marút-bhih agne ắ gahi.

4. Yé ugráh arkám ânrikúh ánâdhrishtâsah ógasâ,
marút-bhih agne ắ gahi.

---

1. WILSON: Earnestly art thou invoked to this perfect rite,
to drink the Soma juice: come, Agni, with the Maruts.

BENFEY: Zu diesem schönen Opfer wirst du gerufen, zum
Trank der Milch!—Mit diesen Marut's, Agni! komm!

LANGLOIS: Le sacrifice est préparé avec soin; nous t'appe-
lons à venir goûter des nos libations: Agni, viens avec les
Marouts.

2. WILSON: No god nor man has power over a rite (dedicated) to thee, who art mighty: come, Agni, with the
Maruts.

BENFEY: Denn nicht ein Gott, kein Sterblicher ragt über
dein, des Grossen, Macht — Mit diesen Marut's, Agni!
komm!

LANGLOIS: Aucun dieu, aucun mortel n'est assez fort pour
lutter contre un être aussi grand que toi: Agni, viens avec
les Marouts.

Hymn to Agni (the God of Fire) and the Maruts (the Storm-gods).

1. Thou art called forth to this fair sacrifice for a draught of milk ;[1] with the Maruts come hither, O Agni !

2. No god indeed, no mortal, is beyond the might[1] of thee, the mighty one ; with the Maruts come hither, O Agni !

3. They who know of the great sky,[1] the Visve Devas[2] without guile ;[3] with those Maruts come hither, O Agni !

4. The wild ones who sing their song,[1] unconquerable by force ; with the Maruts come hither, O Agni !

---

3. Wilson : Who all are divine, and devoid of malignity, and who know (how to cause the descent) of great waters : come, Agni, with the Maruts.

Benfey : Die guten Götter, welche all bestehen in dem weiten Raum—Mit diesen Marut's, Agni ! komm !

Langlois : Tous ces dieux bienfaiteurs (des hommes) connaissent ce vaste monde (où règne la lumière) : Agni, viens avec les Marouts.

4. Wilson : Who are fierce, and send down rain, and are unsurpassed in strength : come, Agni, with the Maruts.

Benfey : Die schrecklich-unbesiegbaren, die mächtiglich Licht angefacht—Mit diesen Marut's, Agni ! komm !

Langlois : Menaçants, doués d'une force invincible, ils peuvent obscurcir la lumière du soleil : Agni, viens avec les Marouts.

5. Yé subhrā́ḥ ghorá-varpasaḥ su-kshatrā́saḥ risā́-dasaḥ, marút-bhiḥ agne ā́ gahi.

6. Yé nā́kasya ádhi roḱané diví devā́saḥ ā́sate, marút-bhiḥ agne ā́ gahi.

7. Yé iṅkháyanti párvatān tiráḥ samudrám arṇa-vám, marút-bhiḥ agne ā́ gahi.

8. Ā́ yé tanvánti rasmí-bhiḥ tiráḥ samudrám ójasā, marút-bhiḥ agne ā́ gahi.

9. Abhí tvā pūrvá-pîtaye sriǵā́mi somyám mádhu, marút-bhiḥ agne ā́ gahi.

---

5. WILSON: Who are brilliant, of terrific forms, who are possessors of great wealth, and are devourers of the malevo-lent: come, Agni, with the Maruts.

BENFEY: Die glänzend-grau'ngestaltigen, hochherrschend-feindvernichtenden—Mit diesen Marut's, Agni! komm!

LANGLOIS: Resplendissants, revêtus d'une forme terrible, ils peuvent donner les richesses, comme ils peuvent aussi détruire leurs ennemis: Agni, viens avec les Marouts.

6. WILSON: Who are divinities abiding in the radiant heaven above the sun: come, Agni, with the Maruts.

BENFEY: Die Götter die im Himmel sind ob dem Lichtkreis des Göttersitz's—Mit diesen Marut's, Agni! komm!

LANGLOIS: Sous la vôute brillante du ciel, ces dieux s'élèvent et vont s'asseoir: Agni, viens avec les Marouts.

7. WILSON: Who scatter the clouds, and agitate the sea (with waves): come, Agni, with the Maruts.

BENFEY: Welche über das wogende Meer hinjagen die Wol-kenschaar—Mit diesen Marut's, Agni! komm!

5. They who are brilliant, of awful shape, powerful, and devourers of foes; with the Maruts come hither, O Agni!

6. They who in heaven are enthroned as gods, in the light of the firmament;[1] with the Maruts come hither, O Agni!

7. They who toss the clouds[1] across the surging sea;[2] with the Maruts come hither, O Agni!

8. They who shoot with their darts across the sea with might; with the Maruts come hither, O Agni!

9. I pour out to thee for the early draught the sweet (juice) of Soma; with the Maruts come hither, O Agni!

LANGLOIS: Ils soulèvent et poussent les montagnes (de nuages) au-dessus de l'abîme des mers: Agni, viens avec les Marouts.

8. WILSON: Who spread (through the firmament), along with the rays (of the sun), and, with their strength, agitate the ocean: come, Agni, with the Maruts.

BENFEY: Die mit Blitzen schleuderen mächtig über das Meer hinaus—Mit diesen Marut's, Agni! komm!

LANGLOIS: Ils étendent avec force les rayons à travers l'Océan (céleste): Agni, viens avec les Marouts.

9. WILSON: I pour out the sweet Soma juice for thy drinking, (as) of old: come, Agni, with the Maruts.

BENFEY: Ich giesse zu dem ersten Trank für dich des Soma Honig aus—Mit diesen Marut's, Agni! komm!

LANGLOIS: A toi cette première libation; je t'offre la douce boisson du soma: Agni, viens avec les Marouts.

This hymn is ascribed to Medhâtithi, of the family of Kan̄va. The metre is Gâyatrî throughout.

Verse 1, note [1]. Gopîthâ is explained by Yâska and Sâyan̄a as drinking of Soma. I have kept to the literal signification of the word, a draught of milk. In the last verse of our hymn the libation offered to Agni and the Maruts is said to consist of Soma, but Soma was commonly mixed with milk. The other meaning assigned to gopîthâ, protection, would give the sense: 'Thou art called for the sake of protection.' But pîtha has clearly the sense of drinking in soma-pîthâ, Rv. i. 51, 7, and must therefore be taken in the same sense in gopîthâ.

Verse 2, note [1]. The Sanskrit krátu expresses power both of body and mind.

Verse 3, note [1]. The sky or welkin (rágas) is the proper abode of the Maruts, and 'they who know of' means simply 'they who dwell' in the great sky. The Vedic poets distinguish commonly between the three worlds, the earth, prithivî, f., or pârthiva, n.; the sky, rágas; and the heaven, dyú: see i. 6, 9, note [1]. The phrase maháh rágasah occurs i. 6, 10; 168, 6, &c. Sâyan̄a takes rágas for water or rain: see on this my article in Kuhn's Zeitschrift, vol. xii. p. 28. The identification of rágas with ἔρεβος (Leo Meyer, in Kuhn's Zeitschrift, vol. vi. p. 19) must remain doubtful until stronger evidence has been brought forward in support of a Greek β representing a Sanskrit g, even in the middle of a word. See my article in Kuhn's Zeitschrift, vol. xv. p. 215; Curtius, Grundzüge, p. 421.

Verse 3, note [2]. The appellation Vísve deváh, all gods together, or, more properly, host-gods, is often applied to the Maruts; cf. i. 23, 8; 10. Benfey connects this line with the preceding verse, considering Vísve deváh, it seems, inappropriate as an epithet of the Maruts.

Verse 3, note [3]. On adrúh, without guile or deceit,

without hatred, see Kuhn's excellent article, Zeitschrift für die Vergleichende Sprachforschung, vol. i. pp. 179, 193. Adrúh is applied to the Maruts again in viii. 46, 4, though in connection with other gods. It is applied to the Visve Devas, Rv. i. 3, 9; ix. 102, 5: the Âdityas, Rv. viii. 19, 34; 67, 13: the Rudras, Rv. ix. 73, 7: to Heaven and Earth, Rv. ii. 41, 21; iii. 56, 1; iv. 56, 2; vii. 66, 18: to Mitra and Varuna, Rv. v. 68, 4: to Agni, Rv. vi. 15, 7; viii. 44, 10. The form adhrúk occurs in the sixth Mandala only.

Verse 4, note [1]. Sâyana explains arká by water. Hence Wilson: 'Who are fierce and send down rain.' But arká has only received this meaning of water in the artificial system of interpretation first started by the authors of the Brâhmanas, who had lost all knowledge of the natural sense of the ancient hymns. The passages in which arká is explained as water in the Brâhmanas are quoted by Sâyana, but they require no refutation. On the singing of the Maruts see note to i. 38, 15. The perfect in the Veda, like the perfect in Homer, has frequently to be rendered in English by the present.

Verse 6, note [1]. Nâka must be translated by firmament, as there is no other word in English besides heaven, and this is wanted to render dyú. Like the Jewish firmament, the Indian nâka, too, is adorned with stars; cf. i. 68, 10. pipésa nâkam stríbhih. Dyú, heaven, is supposed to be above the rágas, sky or welkin. Kuhn's Zeitschrift, vol. xii. p. 28.

Sâyana: 'In the radiant heaven above the sun.' See note [1] to i. 6, 9; p. 34.

Verse 7, note [1]. That párvata (mountain) is used in the sense of cloud, without any further explanation, is clear from many passages:

i. 57, 6. tvám tám indra párvatam mahám urúm vágrena vagrin parva-sáh kakartitha.

Thou, Indra, hast cut this great broad cloud to pieces with thy lightning. Cf. i. 85, 10.

We actually find two similes mixed up together, such

as v. 32, 2. ûdha*h* párvatasya, the udder of the cloud.   In the Edda, too, the rocks, said to have been fashioned out of Ymir's bones, are supposed to be intended for clouds. In Old Norse *klakkr* means both cloud and rock ; nay, the English word *cloud* itself has been identified with the Anglo-Saxon *clûd*, rock.   See Justi, Orient und Occident, vol. ii. p. 62.

Verse 7, note [2]. Whether the surging sea is to be taken for the sea or for the air, depends on the view which we take of the earliest cosmography of the Vedic *R*ishis. Sâya*n*a explains: ' They who make the clouds go, and stir the watery sea.' Wilson remarks that the influence of the winds upon the sea, alluded to in this and the following verse, indicates more familiarity with the ocean than we should have expected from the traditional inland position of the early Hindus, and it has therefore been supposed that, even in passages like our own, samudrá was meant for the sky, the waters above the firmament.   But although there are passages in the Rig-veda where samudrá may be taken to mean the welkin, this word shows in by far the larger number of passages the clear meaning of ocean.   There is one famous passage, vii. 95, 2, which proves that the Vedic poets, who were supposed to have known the upper courses only of the rivers of the Penjâb, had followed the greatest and most sacred of their rivers, the Sarasvatî, as far as the Indian ocean.   It is well known that, as early as the composition of the laws of the Mânavas, and possibly as early as the composition of the Sûtras on which these metrical laws are based, the river Sarasvatî had changed its course, and that the place where that river disappeared under ground was called Vina*s*ana, the loss. This Vina*s*ana forms, according to the laws of the Mânavas, the western frontier of Madhyadesa, the eastern frontier being formed by the confluence of the Gangâ and Yamunâ. Madhyadesa is a section of Âryâvarta, the abode of the Âryas in the widest sense.   Âryâvarta shares with Madhyadesa the same frontiers in the north and the south, viz. the Himâlaya and Vindhya mountains, but it extends beyond Madhyadesa to the west and east as far as the western and eastern seas.   A section of Madhyadesa, again, is the

country described as that of the Brahmarshis, which com-
prises only Kurukshetra, the countries of the Matsyas,
Pañkâlas (Kanyâkubga, according to Kullûka), and Sûrasenas
(Mathurâ, according to Kullûka). The most sacred spot
of all, however, is that section of the Brahmarshi country
which lies between the rivers Drishadvatî and Sarasvatî,
and which in the laws of the Mânavas is called Brahmâvarta.
I have not found any mention of the Vinasana of the Sarasvatî in any of those works which the author of the laws of
the Mânavas may be supposed to have consulted. Madhyadesa is indeed mentioned in one of the Parisishtas (MS. 510,
Wilson) as a kind of model country, but it is there described
as lying east of Dasârna*, west of Kâmpilya†, north of
Pâriyâtra ‡, and south of the Himavat, or again, in a more
general way, as the Duâb of the Gangâ and Yamunâ §.

It is very curious that while in the later Sanskrit literature the disappearance of the Sarasvatî in the desert is a
fact familiar to every writer, no mention of it should occur
during the whole of the Vedic period, and it is still more
curious that in one of the hymns of the Rig-veda we should
have a distinct statement that the Sarasvatî fell into the sea:

vii. 95, 1–2. prá kshódasâ dhâyasâ sasre eshâ sárasvatî
dharúnam âyasî púh, pra-bâbadhânâ rathyâ-iva yâti vísvâh
apáh mahinâ síndhuh anyâh. ékâ aketat sárasvatî nadînâm
súkih yatí girí-bhyah â samudrât, râyáh ketantî bhúvanasya
bhûreh ghritám páyah duduhe náhushâya.

1. With her fertilizing stream this Sarasvatî comes forth—
(she is to us) a stronghold, an iron gate. Moving along as
on a chariot, this river surpasses in greatness all other waters.
2. Alone among all rivers Sarasvatî listened, *she who goes*

---

* See Wilson's Vishnu-purâna, ed. Hall, pp. 154, 155, 159, 160.
† See Wilson's Vishnu-purâna, ed. Hall, p. 161.
‡ l. c. pp. 123, 127.
§ Prâg dasârnât pratyak kâmpilyâd udak pâriyâtrâd, dakshinena himavatah.
Gangâyamunayor antaram eke madhyadesam ity âkakshate. Medhâtithi says
that Madhyadesa, the middle country, was not called so because it was in the
middle of the earth, but because it was neither too high nor too low. Albíruny,
too, remarks that Madhyadesa was between the sea and the northern mountains,
between the hot and the cold countries, equally distant from the eastern and
western frontiers. See Reinaud, Mémoire sur l'Inde, p. 46.

pure from the mountains as far as the sea. She who knows
of the manifold wealth of the world, has poured out to man
her fat milk.

Here we see samudrá used clearly in the sense of sea, the
Indian sea, and we have at the same time a new indication
of the distance which separates the Vedic age from that of
the later Sanskrit literature. Though it may not be possible
to determine by geological evidence the time of the changes
which modified the southern area of the Penjâb and caused
the Sarasvatî to disappear in the desert, still the fact remains
that the loss of the Sarasvatî is later than the Vedic age, and
that at that time the waters of the Sarasvatî reached the
sea. Professor Wilson had observed long ago in reference
to the rivers of that part of India, that there have been, no
doubt, considerable changes here, both in the nomenclature
and in the courses of the rivers, and this remark has been
fully confirmed by later observations. I believe it can be
proved that in the Vedic age the Sarasvatî was a river as
large as the Sutlej, that it was the last of the rivers of the
Penjâb, and therefore the iron gate, or the real frontier
against the rest of India. At present the Sarasvatî is so
small a river that the epithets applied to the Sarasvatî in
the Veda have become quite inapplicable to it. The Vedic
*R*ishis, though acquainted with numerous rivers, including
the Indus and Ganges, call the Sarasvatî the mother of
rivers (vii. 36, 6. sárasvatî saptáthî síndhu-mâtâ), the
strongest of rivers (vi. 61, 13. apásâm apá*h*-tamâ), and in our
passage, vii. 95, 2, we have, as far as I can judge, conclusive
evidence that the old Sarasvatî reached in its course the
Indian sea, either by itself, or united with the Indus.

But this passage, though important as showing the application of samudrá, i. e. *confluvies*, to the Indian sea, and
proving the acquaintance of the Vedic *R*ishis with the
southern coast of India, is by no means the only one in
which samudrá must be translated by sea. Thus we read,
vii. 49, 2:

yâ*h* ấpa*h* divyấ*h* utá vâ srávanti khanítrimâ*h* utá vâ yấ*h*
svayam-*g*â*h*, samudrá-arthâ*h* yấ*h* *s*úkaya*h* pâvakấ*h* tấ*h* ấpa*h*
devî*h* ihá mâm avantu.

The waters which are from heaven, or those which flow

after being dug, or those which spring up by themselves, the bright, pure waters that tend to the sea, may those divine waters protect me here!

i. 71, 7. agním vísvâh abhí príkshah sakante samudrám ná sravátah saptá yahvíh.

All kinds of food go to Agni, as the seven rivers go to the sea.

Cf. i. 190, 7. samudrám ná sravátah ródha-kakráh.

v. 78, 8. yáthâ vátah yáthâ vánam yáthâ samudráh égati.

As the wind moves, as the forest moves, as the sea moves (or the sky).

In hymn x. 58, the same expression occurs which we have in our hymn, and samudrám arnavám there as here admits but of one explanation, the surging sea.

Samudrá in many passages of the Rig-veda has to be taken as an adjective, in the sense of watery or flowing:

vi. 58, 3. yás te pûshan návah antáh samudré hiranyáyîh antárikshe káranti.

Thy golden ships, O Pûshan, which move within the watery sky.

vii. 70, 2. yáh vâm samudrân sarítah píparti.

He who carries you across the watery rivers.

i. 161, 14. at-bhíh yâti várunah samudraíh.

Varuna moves in the flowing waters.

In both these passages samudrá, as an adjective, does not conform to the gender of the noun. See Bollensen, Orient und Occident, vol. ii. p. 467.

ii. 16, 3. ná samudraíh párvataih indra te ráthah (ná pari-bhvé).

Thy chariot, O Indra, is not to be overcome by the watery clouds.

Mandala I, Sûkta 37.
Ashtaka I, Adhyâya 3, Varga 12–14.

1. Krílám vah sárdhah márutam anarvânam rathe-
súbham, kánvâh abhí prá gâyata.

2. Yé príshatîbhih rishtí-bhih sâkám vâsîbhih angí-
bhih, ágâyanta svá-bhânavah.

3. Ihá-iva srinve eshâm kásâh hásteshu yát vádân,
ní yâman kitrám ringate.

4. Prá vah sárdhâya ghríshvaye tveshá-dyumnâya
sushmíne, deváttam bráhma gâyata.

---

1. Wilson: Celebrate, Kañwas, the aggregate strength of
the Maruts, sportive, without horses, but shining in their
car.

Benfey: Kanviden, auf! begrüsst mit Sang, die muntre
Heerschaar der Marut's, die rasch'ste, wagenglänzende.

Langlois: Enfants de Canwa, célébrez la puissance des
Marouts que transporte un char brillant, (puissance) rapide
et inattaquable dont vous ressentez les effets.

2. Wilson: Who, borne by spotted deer, were born self-
radiant, with weapons, war-cries, and decorations.

Benfey: Die mit Hirschen und Speeren gleich mit
Donnern und mit Blitzen auch—selbststrahlende—geboren
sind.

Langlois: Ils viennent de naître, brillants de leur propre
éclat. (Voyez-vous) leurs armes, leurs parures, leur char traîné
par les daims? (entendez-vous) leurs clameurs?

1. Sing forth, O Ka*n*vas, to the sportive host of your Maruts, brilliant on their chariots, and unscathed,[1]—

2. They who were born together, self-luminous, with the spotted deer (the clouds),[1] the spears, the daggers, the glittering ornaments.[2]

3. I hear their[1] whips, almost close by, as they crack them in their hands ; they gain splendour[2] on their way.[3]

4. Sing forth your god-given prayer to the exultant[1] host of your Maruts, the furiously vigorous,[2] the powerful.

---

3. Wilson : I hear the cracking of the whips in their hands, wonderfully inspiring (courage) in the fight.

Benfey : Schier hier erschallt der Peitsche Knall, wenn sie in ihrer Hand erklingt; leuchtend fahr'n sie im Sturm herab.

Langlois : Écoutez, c'est le bruit du fouet qu'ils tiennent dans leurs mains; c'est le bruit qui, dans le combat, anime le courage.

4. Wilson : Address the god-given prayer to those who are your strength, the destroyers of foes, the powerful, possessed of brilliant reputation.

Benfey : Singt eurer Schaar, der wühlenden, der strahlenreichen, kräftigen ein gotterfülletes Gebet !

Langlois : A cette troupe (divine), qui détruit vos ennemis, noble, forte et glorieuse, offrez la part d'hymnes et de sacrifices que lui donnent les Dévas.

5. Prá *saṃsa* góshu ághnyam kri*l*ám yát sárdha*h* mắrutam, *g*ắmbhe rásasya vav*r*idhe.

6. Ká*h* va*h* várshish*th*ah ắ nara*h* divắ*h k*a gmắ*h k*a dhútaya*h*, yát sîm ántam ná dhúnuthá.

7. Ní va*h* yắmâya mắnusha*h* dadhré ugrắya man-yắve, *g*íhîta párvata*h* girí*h*.
8. Yéshâm á*g*meshu p*r*ithivî *g*ugurvân-iva vispáti*h*, bhiyắ yắmeshu ré*g*ate.
9. Sthirám hí *g*ắnam eshâm váya*h* mâtú*h* ní*h*-etave, yát sîm ánu dvitắ sắva*h*.

---

5. Wilson : Praise the sportive and resistless might of the Maruts, who were born amongst kine, and whose strength has been nourished by (the enjoyment of) the milk.

Benfey : Preist hoch die muntre Marutschaar die unbe-siegbar in den Küh'n, im Schlund des Safts wuchs sie heran.

Langlois : Loue donc cette puissance des Marouts, invul-nérable et rapide, qui règne au milieu des vaches (célestes), et ouvre avec force (leurs mamelles pour en faire couler) le lait.

6. Wilson : Which is chief leader among you, agitators of heaven and earth, who shake all around, like the top (of a tree)?

Benfey : Wer, Helden! ist der erste euch—ihr Erd- und Himmel-schütterer!—wenn ihr sie schüttelt Wipfeln gleich?

Langlois : Parmi vous qui remuez si puissamment le ciel et la terre, qui agitez celle-ci comme la cime (d'un arbre), quel est le plus vigoureux?

7. Wilson : The householder, in dread of your fierce and violent approach, has planted a firm (buttress); for the many-ridged mountain is shattered (before you).

5. Celebrate the bull among the cows (the storm among the clouds),[1] for it is the sportive host of the Maruts; he grew as he tasted the rain.[2]

6. Who, O ye men, is the oldest among you here, ye shakers of heaven and earth, when you shake them like the hem of a garment?[1]

7. At your approach the son of man holds himself down; the gnarled cloud[1] fled at your fierce anger.

8. They at whose racings[1] the earth, like a hoary king, trembles for fear on their ways,

9. Their birth is strong indeed: there is strength to come forth from their mother, nay, there is vigour twice enough for it.[1]

BENFEY: Vor eurem Gange beuget sich, vor eurem wilden Zorn der Mann; der Hügel weichet und der Berg;

LANGLOIS: Contre votre marche impétueuse et terrible, l'homme ne peut résister; les collines et les montagnes s'abaissent devant vous.

8. WILSON: At whose impetuous approach earth trembles; like an enfeebled monarch, through dread (of his enemies).

BENFEY: Bei deren Lauf bei deren Sturm die Erde zittert voller Furcht, wie ein altergebeugter Mann.

LANGLOIS: Sous vos pas redoutables, la terre tremble de crainte, telle qu'un roi accablé par l'âge.

9. WILSON: Stable is their birthplace, (the sky); yet the birds (are able) to issue from (the sphere of) their parent: for your strength is everywhere (divided) between two (regions, —or, heaven and earth).

BENFEY: Kaum geboren sind sie so stark, dass ihrer Mutter sie entfliehn: ist ja doch zwiefach ihre Kraft.

LANGLOIS: Le lieu de votre naissance est ferme et stable; vous pouvez, du sein de votre mère, vous élancer, tels que des oiseaux; car, des deux côtés, est un élément solide.

10. Út úm (íti) tyé sûnávaḥ gíraḥ kấshtḥấḥ ấgme-
shu atnata, vâsrấḥ abhi-gñú yấtave.

11. Tyám ḱit gha dîrghám pṛithúm miháḥ nấpâtam
ámṛidhram, prá ḱyavayanti yấma-bhiḥ.
12. Márutaḥ yát ha vaḥ bálam gánân aḱuḱyavîtana,
girĭ̃n aḱuḱyavîtana.

13. Yát ha yẫnti marútaḥ sám ha bruvate ádhvan
ấ, sṛinóti káḥ ḱit eshâm.
14. Prá yâta sĭ̃bham âsú-bhiḥ sánti kánveshu vaḥ
dúvaḥ, tátro (íti) sú mâdayâdhvai.

---

10. Wilson: They are the generators of speech: they
spread out the waters in their courses: they urge the lowing
(cattle) to enter (the water), up to their knees, (to drink.)

Benfey: In ihrem Lauf erheben dann diese Söhne Getös
und Fluth, die bis zum Knie den Kühen geht.

Langlois: Ces (dieux) répandent le son comme on répand
la libation. Leur souffle étend les voies du ciel; (l'eau tombe)
et la vache (en s'y désaltérant), y entre jusqu'aux genoux.

11. Wilson: They drive before them, in their course, the
long, vast, uninjurable, rain-retaining cloud.

Benfey: Dann treiben sie im Sturm heran jenen langen
und breiten Spross der Wolke unerschöpflichen.

Langlois: (Voyez-vous) ce long et large (nuage), fils de
l'onde (qui s'y amoncelle)? (Il semble) invulnérable. (Les
Marouts) savent le chemin par lequel on arrive jusqu'à lui
pour l'ébranler.

12. Wilson: Maruts, as you have vigour, invigorate mankind: give animation to the clouds.

10. And these sons, the singers,[1] enlarged the fences in their coursings;[2] the cows had to walk knee-deep.

11. They cause this long and broad unceasing rain[1] to fall on their ways.

12. O Maruts, with such strength as yours, you have caused men to fall,[1] you have caused the mountains to fall.

13. As the Maruts pass[1] along, they talk together on the way: does any one hear them?

14. Come fast on your quick steeds! there are worshippers[1] for you among the Kaṇvas: may you well rejoice among them.

BENFEY: O Marut's! mit der Kraft, die ihr besitzt, werft ihr Geschöpfe um, die Berge werft ihr um sogar.

LANGLOIS: O Marouts, puisque vous avez la force, faites-la sentir aux hommes, faites-la sentir aux collines.

13. WILSON: Wherever the Maruts pass, they fill the way with clamour: every one hears their (noise).

BENFEY: Wenn die Marut's des Weges ziehn, dann sprechen mit einander sie und mancher mag sie hören.

LANGLOIS: Quand les Marouts sont en marche, le chemin retentit de leur voix: chacun les entend.

14. WILSON: Come quickly, with your swift (vehicles). The offerings of the Kaṇwas are prepared. Be pleased with them.

BENFEY: Auf schnellen kommet schnell herbei, bei Kaṇva's Spross sind Feste euch: da wollt euch schön ergötzen.

LANGLOIS: Accourez, portez ici vos pas rapides. Les enfants de Canwa vous attendent avec leurs offrandes; ici vous serez satisfaits.

15. Ásti hí sma mádâya va*h* smási sma vayám eshâm, vísvam *k*it ǎyu*h* *g*ívâse.

---

15. WILSON : The offering is prepared for your gratification : we are your (worshippers), that we may live all our life.

BENFEY : Gerüstet ist für euren Rausch und wir gehören,

COMMENTARY.

This hymn is ascribed to Ka*n*va, the son of Ghora. The metre is Gâyatrî.

Verse 1, note [1]. Wilson translates anarvâ*n*am by without horses, though the commentator distinctly explains the word by without an enemy. Wilson considers it doubtful whether árvan can ever mean enemy. The fact is, that in the Rig-veda an-arván. never means without horses, but always without hurt or free from enemies ; and the commentator is perfectly right, as far as the sense is concerned, in rendering the word by without an enemy, or unopposed (apraty-*r*ita). An-arván is not formed from árvat, horse, racer, but from árvan ; and this is derived from the same root which yields árus, n. a wound. The accusative of anar-vat, without a horse, would be anarvantam, not anarvâ*n*am.

The root ar, in the sense of hurting, is distantly connected with the root mar : see Lectures on the Science of Language, Second Series, p. 323. It exists in the Greek ὄλλυμι, corresponding to Sanskrit ri*n*omi, i. e. arnomi, I hurt, likewise in οὐλή, wound, which cannot be derived from ὅλη : in οὖλος, οὔλιος, hurtful, and ὀλοός, destructive : see Curtius, Grundzüge der Griechischen Etymologie (zweite Ausgabe), pp. 59, 505. In the Veda ar has the sense of offending or injuring, particularly if preceded by upa.

X. 164, 3. yát â-*s*â*s*â ni*h*-*s*â*s*â abhi-*s*â*s*â upa-árimá *g*â-grata*h* yát svapánta*h*, agní*h* vísvâni ápa du*h*-k*r*itâni á*g*ush*t*âni âré asmát dadhâtu.

15. Truly there is enough for your rejoicing. We always are their servants, that we may live even the whole of life.

traun! euch an für unser ganzes Lebelang.

LANGLOIS: Agréez notre sacrifice, car nous vous sommes dévoués. Daignez nous assurer une longue existence.

If we have offended, or whatever fault we have committed, by bidding, blaming, or forbidding, while waking or while sleeping, may Agni remove all wicked misdeeds far from us.

Hence upârá, injury, vii. 86, 6. ásti *gyấyân* kánîyasa*h* upa-aré, the older man is there to injure, to offend, to mis-lead, the young: (History of Ancient Sanskrit Literature, second edition, p. 541.) Roth translates upârá by *Verfehlung*, missing. Ari, enemy, too, is best derived from this root, and not from râ, to give, with the negative particle, as if meaning originally, as Sâya*n*a supposes, a man who does not give. In árarivân, gen. árarusha*h*, hostile, Rosen recognized many years ago a participle of a really redupli-cated perfect of ar, and he likewise traced aráru, enemy, back to the same root : see his note to i. 18, 3.

From this root ar, to hurt, árvan, hurting, as well as árus, wound, are derived in the same manner as both dhánvan and dhánus, bow, are formed from dhan; yá*g*van and yá*g*us from ya*g*, párvan and párus from par. See Kuhn, Zeitschrift, vol. ii. p. 233.

Anarván, then, is the same as ánarus, Sat. P. Brâhma*n*a iii. 1, 3, 7; and from meaning originally without a wound or without one who can wound, it takes the more general sense of uninjured, invulnerable, perfect, strong, (cf. inte-ger, intact, and entire.) This meaning is applicable to i. 94, 2; 136, 5; ii. 6, 5; v. 49, 4; vii. 20, 3; 97, 5; x. 61, 13; 65, 3. In i. 116, 16, anarván seems to be used as an adverb; in i. 51, 12, as applied to *s*lóka, it may have the more general meaning of irresistible, powerful.

There are two passages in which the nom. sing. árvân, and one in which the acc. sing. árvânam, occur, apparently meaning horse. But in i. 163, 13, and ix. 97, 25, árvân stands in the Pada text only, the Sanhitâ has árvâ ákkha and árvâ iva. In x. 46, 5, the text híri-smasrum ná árvânam dhána-arkam is too doubtful to allow of any safe induction, particularly as the Sâma-veda gives a totally different reading. I do not think therefore that árvat, horse, admits in the nom. and acc. sing. of any forms but árvâ and árvantam. Pânini (vi. 4, 127) allows the forms arvân and arvânam, but in anarvan only, which, as we saw, has nothing in common with árvat, horse. Benfey: ' die rascheste (keinen Renner habend, uneinholbar),' the quickest (having no racer, hence not to be reached).

The masculine anarvânam after the neuter sárdhas is curious; sárdhas means might, but it is here used to express a might or an aggregate of strong men or gods, and the nom. plur. yé, who, in the next verse, shows the same transition of thought, not only from the singular to the plural, but also from the neuter to the masculine, which must be admitted in anarvânam. It would be possible, if necessary, to explain away the irregularity of anarvânam by admitting a rapid transition from the Maruts to Indra, the eldest among the Maruts (cf. i. 23, 8. índra-gyeshthâh márut-ganâh), and it would be easier still to alter sárdhas into sárdham, as an accusative singular of the masculine noun sárdha, which has the same meaning as the neuter sárdhas. There is one passage, v. 56, 9, which would seem to give ample countenance to such a conjecture:

tám vah sárdham rathe-súbham—â huve.

I call hither this your host, brilliant on chariots.

Again, ii. 30, 11, we read:

tám vah sárdham mârutam—girâ úpa bruve.

I call with my voice on this your host of Maruts.

viii. 93, 16. srutám vah vritrahán-tamam prá sárdham karshanînâm, â sushe.

I pant for the glorious, victorious, host of the quick Maruts.

From this sárdha we have also the genitive sárdhasya, vii. 56, 8 (4):

subhráh vah súshmah krúdhmî mánâmsi dhúnih múnih-
iva *sárdhasya* dh*r*ishnóh.

Your strength is brilliant, your minds furious ; the shout
of the daring host is like one possessed.

We have likewise the dative *sárdhâya*, the instrumental
sárdhena, and the acc. plur. *sárdhân*; and in most cases,
except in two or three where *sárdha* seems to be used as
an adjective, meaning strong, these words are applied to the
host of the Maruts.

But the other word *sárdhas* is equally well authenticated, and we find of it, not only the nominative, accusative, and vocative sing. *sárdhas*, but likewise the nom.
plur. *sárdhâmsi*.

The nominative singular occurs in our very hymn :

i. 37, 5. krî*l*ám yát *sárdhah* mã́rutam.

Which is the sportive host of the Maruts.

i. 127, 6. sáh hí *sárdhah* ná mã́rutam tuvi-svánih.

For he (Agni) is strong-voiced like the host of the Maruts.

iv. 6, 10. tuvi-svanásah mã́rutam ná *sárdhah*.

Thy flames (Agni) are strong-voiced like the host of the
Maruts.

v. 46, 5. utá tyát nah mã́rutam *sárdhah* ã́ gamat.

May also that host of the Maruts come to us.

ii. 1, 5. tvám narã́m *sárdhah* asi puru-vásuh.

Thou (Agni), full of riches, art the host of the men.

This host of men seems to me intended again for the
Maruts, although it is true that in thus identifying Agni
with different gods, the poet repeats himself in the next
verse :

ii. 1, 6. tvám *sárdhah* mã́rutam.

Thou art the host of the Maruts.

If this repetition seems offensive, the first narã́m *sárdhas*
might be taken for some other company of gods. Thus
we find :

vii. 44, 5. *sr*inótu nah daívyam *sárdhah* agníh s*ri*nvántu
ví*s*ve mahishấh ámûrâh.

May the divine host, may Agni, hear us, may the Vi*s*ve
hear us, the strong, the wise.

Or iii. 19, 4. sáh ã́ vaha devá-tâtim yavish*th*a *sárdhah*
yát adyá divyám yágâsi.

Bring thou hither, O Agni, the gods, that you may sacrifice to-day to the divine host.

Or i. 139, 1. á nú tát sárdha*h* divyám vri*n*îmahe.

We chose for us now that divine host.

As in these last, so in many other passages, sárdhas is used as a neuter in the accusative. For instance,

i. 106, 1; ii. 11, 14. mârutam sárdha*h*.

ii. 3, 3; vi. 3, 8. sárdha*h* marútâm.

The vocative occurs,

v. 46, 2. ágne índra váru*n*a mítra dévâ*h* sárdha*h* prá yanta mâruta utá vish*n*o (íti).

Agni, Indra, Varu*n*a, Mitra, gods, host of the Maruts, come forth, and Vish*n*u !

We see how throughout all these passages those in which sárdha and sárdhas are applied to the Maruts, or to some other company of gods, preponderate most decidedly. Yet passages occur in the Rig-veda where both sárdha and sárdhas are applied to other hosts or companies. Thus v. 53, 10, sárdha refers to chariots, while in i. 133, 3, sárdhas is applied to evil spirits.

If the passages hitherto examined were all that occur in the Rig-veda, we might still feel startled at the construction of our verse, where sárdhas is not only followed by masculine adjectives in the singular, but, in the next verse, by a pronoun in the plural. But if we take the last irregularity first, we find the same construction, viz. sárdhas followed by yé, in iii. 32, 4:

índrasya sárdha*h* marúta*h* yé âsan.

The host of Indra, that was the Maruts.

As to the change of genders, we find adjectives in the masculine after sárdhas, in

v. 52, 8. sárdha*h* mârutam út sa*m*sa satyá-savasam *r*ibh-vasam.

Celebrate the host of the Maruts, the truly vigorous, the brilliant.

Here, too, the poet afterwards continues in the plural, though as he uses the demonstrative, and not, as in our passage, the relative pronoun, we cannot quote this in support of the irregularity which has here to be explained. Anyhow the construction of our verse, though bold and unusual, is not so unusual as to force us to adopt conjectural remedies, and in v. 58, 2, we find yé after ga*n*á*h*. On the Umbrian Çerfo Martio, as possibly the same as *s* árdha-s mâruta-s, see Grassman, Kuhn's Zeitschrift, vol. xvi. p. 190.

Verse 2, note [1]. The spotted deer (p*r*íshatî) are the recognized animals of the Maruts, and were originally, as it would seem, intended for the rain-clouds. Sâya*n*a is perfectly aware of the original meaning of p*r*íshatî, as clouds. The legendary school, he says, takes them for deer with white spots, the etymological school for the many-coloured lines of clouds : (Rv. Bh. i. 64, 8.) This passage shows that although p*r*íshatî, as Roth observes, may mean a spotted cow or a spotted horse,—the Maruts, in fact, are called sometimes p*r*ishat-asvâ*h*, having piebald horses, vii. 40, 3,—yet the later tradition in India had distinctly declared in favour of spotted deer. The Vedic poets, how-ever, admitted both ideas, and they speak in the same hymn, nay, in the same verse, of the fallow deer and of the horses of the Maruts. Thus v. 58, 1, the Maruts are called âsú-asvâ*h*, possessed of quick horses ; and in v. 58, 6, we read yát prá áyâsish*t*a p*r*íshatîbhi*h* ásvai*h*—ráthebhi*h*, where the gender of p*r*íshatîbhi*h* would hardly allow us to join it with ásvai*h*, but where we must translate : When you come with the deer, the horses, the chariots.

Verse 2, note [2]. The spears and daggers of the Maruts are meant for the thunderbolts, and the glittering ornaments for the lightning. Sâya*n*a takes vâ*s*î in this passage for war-cries on the authority of the Nirukta, where vâ*s*î is given among the names of the voice. From other passages, however, it becomes clear that vâ*s*î is a weapon of the Maruts ; and Sâya*n*a, too, explains it sometimes in that sense : cf. v. 53. 4; 57, 2. Thus i. 88, 3, the vâ*s*îs are spoken of as being on the bodies of the Maruts. In v. 53, 4, the Maruts are said to shine in their ornaments and their vâ*s*îs. Here Sâya*n*a, too, translates vâ*s*î rightly by weapon ; and in his remarks on i. 88, 3, he says that vâ*s*î was a weapon commonly called ârâ, which is a shoe-maker's awl. This reminds one of *framea* which at one time was supposed to be connected with the German *pfrieme*. See, however, Grimm (Deutsche Grammatik, vol. i. p. 128) and Leo Meyer (Kuhn's Zeitschrift, vol. vi. p. 424). In viii. 29, 3, the god Tvasht*ar* is said to carry an iron vấsî in his hand. Grassman (Kuhn's Zeitschrift, vol. xvi. p. 163) translates vấsî by axe. That añ*gí* is to be taken in the sense of ornament, and not in the sense of ointment, is shown by passages like viii. 29, 1, where a golden ornament is mentioned, añ*gí* añkte hira*n*yấyam. Sâkám, together, is used with reference to the birth of the Maruts, i. 64, 4. It should not be connected with vấsîbhi*h*.

Verse 3, note [1]. Eshâm should be pronounced as a creticus; also in verses 9, 13, 15. This is a very common vyûha.

Verse 3, note [2]. I should have taken *k*itrám as an adverb, like Benfey, if ni *riñg* were not usually construed with an accusative. *Riñg* in the 3rd pers. plur. pres. Âtm. is treated like a verb of the Ad-class.

Verse 3, note [3]. The locative yấman is frequently used of the path on which the gods move and approach the sacrifice; hence it sometimes means, as in our passage, in the sky. Yấmam in B. R., s. v. ar*g*, is wrong.

Verse 4, note [1]. Benfey translates gh*r*íshvi by burrowing, and refers it to the thunderbolt that uproots the earth. He points out that gh*r*íshvi means also, for the same reason, the boar, as proved by Kuhn (Die Herabkunft des Feuers, S. 202). I prefer, however, the general sense assigned to the adjective gh*r*íshu and gh*r*íshvi, exuberant, brisk, wild. See Kuhn in Kuhn's Zeitschrift, vol. xi. p. 385. Wilson, after Sâya*n*a, translates destroyers of foes. On the representation of the clouds as boars, see Nir. v. 4.

Verse 4, note [2]. Tveshấ-dyumna is difficult to render. Both tveshấ and dyumnấ are derived from roots that mean to shine, to be bright, to glow. Derivatives from tvish express the idea of fieriness, fierceness, and fury. In iv. 17, 2, tvish is used correlatively with manyú, wrath.

Derivatives from dyu convey the idea of brightness and briskness. Both qualities are frequently applied to the Maruts.

Verse 5, note [1]. This translation is merely conjectural. I suppose that the wind driving the clouds before him, is here compared to a bull among cows, cf. v. 52, 3:

té syandrãsaḥ ná ukshãnaḥ áti skandanti sárvarîḥ.

They, the Maruts, like rushing oxen, mount on the dark cows.

The last sentence states that the wind grows even stronger after it has tasted the rain (i. 85, 2. té ukshitãsaḥ mahimã-nam ãsata).

Verse 5, note [2]. I take gámbhe in the sense of gámbhane. (On the root gabh and its derivatives, see Kuhn, Zeitschrift für vergleichende Sprachwissenschaft, vol. i. p. 123 seq.) It would be better to read mukhe, instead of sukhe, in the commentary. The Maruts were not born of milk for Priśni, as Wilson says in a note, but from the milk of Priśni. Priśni is called their mother, Rudra their father: (v. 52, 16; 60, 5.)

Benfey takes the cows for clouds in which the lightnings dwell; and the abyss of the sap is by him supposed to be again the clouds.

Verse 6, note [1]. Ántam ná, literally, like an end, is explained by Sâyaṇa as the top of a tree. Wilson, Langlois, and Benfey accept that interpretation. Roth proposes, like the hem of a garment, which I prefer; for vastrânta, the end of a garment, is a common expression in later Sanskrit, while anta is never applied to a tree in the sense of the top of a tree. Here agra would be more appropriate.

Verse 7, note [1]. Sâyaṇa translates: ' Man has planted a firm buttress to give stability to his dwelling.' Nidadhré is the perfect Âtmanepada, and expresses the holding down of the head or the cowering attitude of man. I have taken ugrãya manyáve over to gíhîta, because these words could hardly form an apposition to yámáya. As the Vedic poets speak of the very mountains as shaken by the

storms, we might translate párvato girâh by the gnarled or
rocky mount; but there is no authority for translating
gîhîta by it is shattered, and we should have to translate, the
mountain yielded or bent before your anger. Cf. v. 57, 3 :
  ní vah vánâ gihate yâmanah bhiyâ.
The forests get out of your way from fear.
  v. 60, 2. vánâ kit ugrâh gihate ní vah bhiyâ prithivî kit
regate párvatah kit.
Even the forests, ye fearful Maruts, yield from fear of
you : even the earth trembles, even the mountains.

Verse 8, note [1]. Ágma seems to express the act of
racing or running (like âgi, race, battle), while yâma is the
road itself where the racing takes place. A very similar
passage occurs in i. 87, 3. The comparison of the earth
(fem.) to a king (masc.) would be considered a grave offence
in the later Sanskrit literature. In i. 87, 3, vithurâ takes
the place of vispáti.

Verse 9, note [1]. A very difficult verse. The birth of
the Maruts is frequently alluded to, as well as their sur-
passing strength, as soon as born. Hence the first sentence
admits of little doubt. But what follows is very abrupt.
Váyas may be the plural of vi, bird, or it may be váyas, the
neuter, meaning vital strength: see Kuhn's Zeitschrift,
vol. xv. p. 217. The Maruts are frequently compared to
birds (cf. i. 87, 2; 88, 1), but it is usual to indicate the
comparison by ná or iva. I therefore take váyas as a nom.
sing. neut., in the sense of vigour, life. Nir-i is used with
particular reference to the birth of a child (cf. v. 78, 7; 9).

Verse 10, note [1]. If we take sûnávo gírah in the sense of
the sons of voice, i. e. of thunder, the accent of gírah will
have to be changed. Gírah, however, occurs, at least once
more, in the sense of singers or poets, ix. 63, 10, where
gírah can only be a vocative, O ye singers ! In i. 6, 6, the
translation of gírah by singers, i. e. the Maruts, may be
contested, but if we consider that gírah, in the sense of
hymns, is feminine, and is followed by the very word which
is here used, viz. devayántah, as a feminine, viz. devayántîh,

vii. 18, 3, we can hardly doubt that in i. 6, 6, gírah is a masculine and means singers. The same applies to vi. 63, 10. In vi. 52, 9, the construction is, of course, quite different.

Verse 10, note [2]. The expression that the Maruts enlarged or extended the fences of their race-course, can only mean that they swept over the whole sky, and drove the clouds away from all the corners. Kâshthâ may mean the wooden enclosures (*carceres*) or the wooden poles that served as turning and winning-posts (*metæ*). The last sentence expresses the result of this race, viz. the falling of so much rain that the cows had to walk up to their knees in water. This becomes still clearer from the next verse.

Sâyana: 'These, the producers of speech, have spread water in their courses, they cause the cows to walk up to their knees in order to drink the water.'

Verse 11, note [1]. Rain is called the offspring of the cloud, mihó nápât, and is then treated as a masculine.

Verse 12, note [1]. In viii. 72, 8, akukyavît is explained by vyadârayat, he tore open. Akukyavîtana is the Vedic form of the 2nd pers. plur. of the reduplicated aorist.

Verse 13, note [1]. Yânti has to be pronounced as an amphibrachys.

Verse 14, note [1]. Benfey supposes that dúvah stands in the singular instead of the plural. But why should the plural have been used, as the singular (asti) would have created no kind of difficulty? It is better to take dúvah as a nominative plural of a noun dû, worshipper, derived from the same root which yielded dúvah, worship. We certainly find á-duvah in the sense of not-worshipping:

vii. 4, 6. mâ̂ tvâ vayám sahasâ-van avîrâh mâ̂ ápsavah pári sadâma mâ̂ áduvah.

May we not, O hero, sit round thee like men without strength, without beauty (cf. viii. 7, 7), without worship.

Here Sâyana explains áduvah very well by parikarana-hînâh, which seems better than Roth's explanation 'zögernd, ohne Eifer.'

Mandala I, Sûkta 38.
Ashtaka I, Adhyâya 3, Varga 15-17.

1. Kát ha nûnám kadha-priya*h** pitấ putrám ná hástayo*h*, dadhidhvé v*r*ikta-barhisha*h*.

2. Kvā nûnám kát va*h* ártham gánta divấ*h* ná p*r*ithivyấ*h*, kvā va*h* gấva*h* ná † ra*n*yanti.

3. Kvā va*h* sumnấ nâvyâ*m*si márutа*h* kvā suvitấ, kvō (íti) vísvâni saúbhagâ.

4. Yát yûyám pri*s*ni-mâtara*h* mártâsa*h* syấtana, stotấ va*h* am*r*íta*h* syât.

5. Mấ va*h* m*r*igấ*h* ná yávase *g*aritấ bhût ágoshya*h*, pathấ yamásya gât úpa.

6. Mó (íti) sú na*h* párâ-parâ ní*h*-*r*iti*h* du*h*-hánâ vadhît, padîshtấ t*r*íshu*n*ayâ sahấ.

7. Satyám tveshấ*h* áma-vanta*h* dhánvau *k*it ấ rudríyâsa*h*, míham kri*n*vanti avâtấm ‡.

8. Vâ*s*rấ-iva vi-dyút mimâti vatsám ná mâtấ si-*s*akti, yát eshâm v*r*ish*t*í*h* ásar*g*i.

9. Dívâ *k*it táma*h* kri*n*vanti par*g*ányena uda-vâhéna, yát p*r*ithivî́m vi-undánti.

10. Ádha svanất marútâm vísvam ấ sádma pârthi-vam, áre*g*anta prá mấnushâ*h*.

---

1. What then now ? When[1] will you take (us) as a dear father takes his son by both hands, O ye gods, for whom the sacred grass has been trimmed ?[2]

2. Whither now ? On what errand of yours are you going, in heaven, not on earth ?[1] Where are your cows sporting ?[2]

3. Where are your newest favours,[1] O Maruts ? Where the blessings ? Where all delights ?

4. If you, sons of Prisni, were mortals, and your worshipper an immortal,[1]—

5. Then never[1] should your praiser be unwelcome, like a deer in pasture grass,[2] nor should he go on the path of Yama.[3]

6. Let not one sin[1] after another, difficult to be conquered, overcome us ; may it depart[2] together with lust.

7. Truly they are furious and powerful ; even to the desert the Rudriyas bring rain that is never dried up.[1]

8. The lightning lows like a cow, it follows as a mother follows after her young, that the shower (of the Maruts) may be let loose.[1]

9. Even by day the Maruts create darkness with the water-bearing cloud,[1] when they drench the earth.

10. From the shout of the Maruts over the whole space of the earth,[1] men reeled forward.

11. Máruta*h* vî*l*upâ*n*í-bhi*h* * *k*itrâ*h* ródhasvatî*h* ánu, yâtá î*m* ákhidrayâma-bhi*h*.

12. Sthirâ*h* va*h* santu nemáya*h* ráthâ*h* ásvâsa*h* eshâm, sú-sa*m*sk*r*itâ*h* abhîsava*h*.
13. Á*kkh*a vada tánâ girâ *g*arâyai bráhma*n*a*h* pátim, agním mitrám ná darsatám.

14. Mimíhí *s*lókam âsyê par*g*ánya*h*-iva tatana*h*, gâya gâyatrám ukthyâm.
15. Vándasva márutam ga*n*ám tveshám panasyúm arkí*n*am, asmé (íti) v*r*iddhâ*h* asan ihá.

COMMENTARY.

This hymn is ascribed to Ka*n*va, the son of Ghora. The metre is Gâyatrî throughout. Several verses, however, end in a spondee instead of the usual iambus. No attempt should be made to improve such verses by conjecture, for they are clearly meant to end in spondees. Thus in verses 2, 7, 8, and 9, all the three pâdas alike have their final spondee. In verse 7, the ionicus a minore is with an evident intention repeated thrice.

Verse 1, note [1]. Kadha-priya*h* is taken in the Padapâ*th*a as one word, and Sâya*n*a explains it by delighted by or delighting in praise, a nominative plural. A similar compound, kadha-priya, occurs in i. 30, 20, and there too the vocative sing. fem., kadhapriye, is explained by Sâya*n*a as fond of praise. In order to obtain this meaning, kadha has to be identified with kathâ, story, which is simply impossible. There is another compound, adha-priyâ, nom. dual,

---

* vî*l*úpâ*n*i-bhi*h* ?

11. Maruts on your strong-hoofed steeds[1] go on easy roads[3] after those bright ones (the clouds), which are still locked up.[2]

12. May your felloes be strong, the chariots, and their horses, may your reins[1] be well-fashioned.

13. Speak out for ever with thy voice to praise the Lord of prayer,[1] Agni, who is like a friend,[2] the bright one.

14. Fashion a hymn in thy mouth! Expand like a cloud![1] Sing a song of praise.

15. Worship the host of the Maruts, the brisk, the praiseworthy, the singers.[1] May the strong ones stay here among us.[2]

---

which occurs viii. 8, 4, and which Sâyana explains either as delighted here below, or as a corruption of kadha-priyâ.

In Boehtlingk and Roth's Dictionary, kadha-priya and kadha-prî are both explained as compounds of kadha, an interrogative adverb, and priya or prî, to love or delight, and they are explained as meaning kind or loving to whom? In the same manner adha-priya is explained as kind then and there.

It must be confessed, however, that a compound like kadha-prî, kind to whom?, is somewhat strange, and it seems preferable to separate the words, and to write kádha priyá and ádha priyá.

It should be observed that the compounds kadha-prî and kadha-priya occur always in sentences where there is another interrogative pronoun. The two interrogatives kát—kádha, what—where, and kás—kádha, who—where, occurring in the same sentence, an idiom so common in Greek, may have puzzled the author of the Pada text, and the compound once sanctioned by the authority of Sâkalya, Sâyana would explain it as best he could. But if we admit the double use of the interrogative in Sanskrit, as in Greek, then, in our passage, priyá*h* would be an adjective belonging to pitấ, and we might translate: ' What then now? When will you take (us), as a dear father takes his son by both hands, O ye Maruts?' In the same manner we ought to translate i. 30, 20:

ká*h* te usha*h* kádha priye bhu*gé* márta*h* amartye.

Who and where was there a mortal to be loved by thee, O beloved, immortal Dawn?

In viii. 7, 31, where the same words are repeated as in our passage, it is likewise better to write:

kát ha nûnám kádha priyá*h* yát índram á*g*ahâtana, ká*h* va*h* sakhi-tvé ohate.

What then now? Where is there a friend, now that you have forsaken Indra? Who cares for your friendship?

Why in viii. 8, 4, adha priyâ should have been joined into one word is more difficult to say, yet here, too, the compound might easily be separated.

Kádha does not occur again, but would be formed in analogy with ádha. It occurs in Zend as kadha.

The words kát ha nûnám commonly introduce an interrogative sentence, literally, What then now? cf. x. 10, 4.

Verse 1, note [2]. Vrikta-barhis is generally a name of the priest, so called because he has to trim the sacrificial grass. ' The sacred Kuṣa grass (Poa cynosuroides), after having had the roots cut off, is spread on the Vedi or altar, and upon it the libation of Soma-juice, or oblation of clarified butter, is poured out. In other places, a tuft of it in a similar position is supposed to form a fitting seat for the deity or deities invoked to the sacrifice. According to Mr. Stevenson, it is also strewn over the floor of the chamber in which the worship is performed.'

Cf. vi. 11, 5. v*ri*ñ*g*é ha yát námasâ barhí*h* agnaú, áyâmi srúk ghritá-vatî su-v*ri*ktí*h*.

When I reverentially trim the truss for Agni, when the well-trimmed ladle, full of butter, is stretched forth.

In our passage, unless we change the accent, it must be taken as an epithet of the Maruts, they for whom the grass-altar has been prepared. They are again invoked by the same name, viii. 7, 20:

kvā nûnám su-dânava*h* mádatha vrikta-barhisha*h*.

Where do ye rejoice now, you gods for whom the altar is trimmed?

Otherwise, vrikta-barhisha*h* might, with a change of accent, supply an accusative to dadhidhve : ' Will you take the worshippers in your arms?' This, however, is not necessary, as to take by the hand may be used as a neuter verb.

Benfey : ' Wo weilt ihr gern? was habt ihr jetzt—gleichwie ein Vater seinen Sohn—in Händen, da das Opfer harrt?'

Wilson : ' Maruts, who are fond of praise, and for whom the sacred grass is trimmed, when will you take us by both hands as a father does his son?'

Verse 2, note [1]. The idea of the first verse, that the Maruts should not be detained by other pursuits, is carried on in the second. The poet asks, what they have to do in the sky, instead of coming down to the earth. The last sentence seems to mean ' where tarry your herds?' viz. the clouds. Sâya*n*a translates : ' Where do worshippers, like lowing cows, praise you?' Wilson : ' Where do they who worship you cry to you like cattle.' Benfey : ' Wo jauchzt man euch, gleich wie Stiere? (Ihre Verehrer brüllen vor Freude über ihre Gegenwart, wie Stiere.)' The verb ra*n*yati, however, when followed by an accusative, means to love, to accept with pleasure. The gods accept the offerings and the prayers :

v. 18, 1. vísvâni yá*h* ámartya*h* havyấ márteshu rá*n*yati.

The immortal who deigns to accept all offerings among mortals.

v. 74, 3. kásya bráhmâ*n*i ra*n*yatha*h*.

Whose prayers do ye accept?

Followed by a locative ra*n*yati means to delight in. Both the gods are said to delight in prayers (viii. 12, 18; 33, 16), and prayers are said to delight in the gods (viii. 16, 2). I therefore take ra*n*yanti in the sense of tarrying, disporting, and ná, if it is to be retained, in the sense of not; where do they not sport? meaning that they are to be found everywhere, except where the poet desires them to be. We thus get rid of the simile of singing poets and lowing cows, which,

though not too bold for Vedic bards, would here come in
too abruptly. It would be much better, however, if the
negative particle could be omitted altogether. If we retain
it, we must read: kvã váḥ | gâváḥ | na ráṇ | yantí | .
But the fact is that through the whole of the Rig-veda
kvã has always to be pronounced as two syllables, kuva.
There is only one passage, v. 61, 2, where, before a vowel,
we have to read kva : kuva vo 'sváḥ, kvâbhîsavaḥ. In
other passages, even before vowels, we always have to
read kuva, e. g. i. 161, 4. kuvet = kva it; i. 105, 4.
kuvartam = kva ṛitam. In i. 35, 7, we must read either
kuvedânîm sûryaḥ, making sûryaḥ trisyllabic, or kuva idânîm,
leaving a hiatus. In i. 168, 6, kvâvaram is kuvâvaram :
Ŝâkalya, forgetting this, and wishing to improve the metre,
added na, thereby, in reality, destroying both the metre and
the sense. Kva occurs as dissyllabic in the Rig-veda at
least forty-one times.

Verse 3, note [1]. The meanings of sumná in the first five
Maṇḍalas are well explained by Professor Aufrecht in Kuhn's
Zeitschrift, vol. iv. p. 274. As to suvitấ in the plural, see
x. 86, 21, and viii. 93, 29, where Indra is said to bring all
suvita's. It frequently occurs in the singular :
    x. 148, 1. ấ naḥ bhara suvitám yásya kâkán.

· Verse 4, note [1]. One might translate : ' If you, sons of
Pṛisni, were mortals, the immortal would be your worshipper.' But this seems almost too deep and elaborate
a compliment for a primitive age. Langlois translates :
' Quand vous ne seriez pas immortels, (faites toutefois) que
votre panégyriste jouisse d'une longue vie.' Wilson's translation is obscure : ' That you, sons of Pṛisni, may become
mortals, and your panegyrist become immortal.' Sâyaṇa
translates : ' Though you, sons of Pṛisni, were mortal, yet
your worshipper would be immortal.' I think it best to
connect the fourth and fifth verses, and I feel justified in
so doing by other passages where the same or a similar
idea is expressed, viz. that if the god were the poet and the
poet the god, then the poet would be more liberal to the
god than the god is to him. Thus I translated a passage,

vii. 32, 18, in my History of Ancient Sanskrit Literature, p. 545: 'If I were lord of as much as thou, I should support the sacred bard, thou scatterer of wealth, I should not abandon him to misery. I should award wealth day by day to him who magnifies, I should award it to whosoever it be.' Another parallel passage is pointed out by Mr. J. Muir. (On the Interpretation of the Veda, p. 79.) viii. 19, 25: 'If, Agni, thou wert a mortal, and I were an immortal, I should not abandon thee to malediction or to wretchedness; my worshipper should not be miserable or distressed.' Still more to the point is another passage, viii. 44, 23: 'If I were thou, and thou wert I, then thy wishes should be fulfilled.' See also viii. 14, 1, 2.

As to the metre it is clear that we ought to read martâsa*h* syâtana.

Verse 5, note [1]. Mâ, though it seems to stand for ná, retains its prohibitive sense.

Verse 5, note [2]. Yávasa is explained by Sâyana as grass, and Wilson's Dictionary, too, gives to it the meaning of meadow or pasture grass, whereas yava is barley. The Greek ζεά or ζειά is likewise explained as barley or rye, fodder for horses. See i. 91, 13. gávah ná yávaseshu, like cows in meadows.

Verse 5, note [3] The path of Yama can only be the path that leads to Yama, as the ruler of the departed.

x. 14, 8. sám gakkhasva pitrí-bhih sám yaména.
Meet with the fathers, meet with Yama, (x. 14, 10; 15, 8.)
x. 14, 7. yamám pasyâsi várunam ka devám.
Thou wilt see (there) Yama and the divine Varuna.
x. 165, 4. tásmai yamâya námah astu mrityáve.
Adoration to that Yama, to Death!
Wilson: 'Never may your worshipper be indifferent to you, as a deer (is never indifferent) to pasture, so that he may not tread the path of Yama.' Benfey: 'Wer euch besingt, der sei euch nicht gleichgültig, wie das Wild im Gras, nicht wandl' er auf des Yama Pfad.' Ayoshya is translated insatiable by Professor Goldstücker.

Verse 6, note [1]. One of the meanings of nírriti is sin. It is derived from the same root which yielded ritá, in the sense of right. Nírriti was conceived, it would seem, as going away from the path of right, the German *Vergehen*. Nírriti was personified as a power of evil and destruction.

vii. 104, 9. áhaye vâ tấn pra-dádâtu sómaḥ ấ vâ dadhâtu níḥ-riteḥ upá-sthe.

May Soma hand them over to Ahi, or place them in the lap of Nirriti.

i. 117, 5. susupvấṃsam ná níḥ-riteḥ upá-sthe.

Like one who sleeps in the lap of Nirriti.

Here Sâyaṇa explains Nirriti as earth, and he attaches the same meaning to the word in other places which will have to be considered hereafter. Cf. Lectures on the Science of Language, Second Series, pp. 515, 516.

Wilson treats Nirriti as a male deity, and translates the last words, ' let him perish with our evil desires.'

Verse 6, note [2]. Padîshtá is formed as an optative of the Âtmanepada, but with the additional s before the t, which, in the ordinary Sanskrit, is restricted to the so-called benedictive (Grammar, § 385; Bopp, Kritische Grammatik, ed. 1834, § 329, note). Pad means originally to go, but in certain constructions it gradually assumed the meaning of to perish, and native commentators are inclined to explain it by pat, to fall. One can watch the transition •of meaning from going into perishing in such phrases as V. S. xi. 46. mâ pâdy âyushaḥ purâ, literally, ' may he not go before the time,' but really intended for ' may he not die before the time.' In the Rig-veda padîshtá is generally qualified by some words to show that it is to be taken in *malam partem*. Thus in our passage, and in iii. 53, 21; vii. 104, 16; 17. In i. 79, 11, however, padîshtá sáḥ is by itself used in a maledictory sense, *pereat*, may he perish! In another, vi. 20, 5, pấdi by itself conveys the idea of perishing. This may have some weight in determining the origin of the Latin *pestis* (Corssen, Kritische Beiträge, p. 396). for it shows that, even without prepositions, such as *á* or *vi*, pad may have an ill-omened meaning. In the Aitareya-brâhmaṇa vii. 14 (History of

Ancient Sanskrit Literature, p. 471), pad, as applied to a child's teeth, means to go, to fall out. With sam, however, pad has always a good meaning, and this shows that originally its meaning was neutral.

Verse 7, note [1]. The only difficult word is avâtâm. Sâyana explains it, 'without wind.' But it is hardly possible to understand how the Maruts, themselves the gods of the storm, the sons of Rudra, could be said to bring clouds without wind. Langlois, it is true, translates without any misgivings : 'Ces dieux peuvent sur un sol desséché faire tomber la pluie sans l'accompagner de vent.' Wilson : 'They send down rain without wind upon the desert.' Benfey saw the incongruous character of the epithet, and explained it away by saying that the winds bring rain, and after they have brought it, they moderate their violence in order not to drive it away again ; hence rain without wind. Yet even this explanation, though ingenious, and, as I am told, particularly truthful in an Eastern climate, is somewhat too artificial. If we changed the accent, ávâtâm, unchecked, unconquered, would be better than avâtâm, windless. But ávâta, unconquered, does not occur in the Rig-veda, except as applied to persons. It occurs most frequently in the phrase vanván ávâtah, which Sâyana explains well by himsan ahimsitah, hurting, but not hurt : (vi. 16, 20 ; 18, 1; ix. 89, 7.) In ix. 96, 8, we read prit-sú vanván ávâtah, in battles attacking, but not attacked, which renders the meaning of ávâta perfectly clear. In vi. 64, 5, where it is applied to Ushas, it may be translated by unconquerable, intact.

There are several passages, however, where avâta occurs with the accent on the last syllable, and where it is accordingly explained as a Bahuvrîhi, meaning either windless or motionless, from vâta, wind, or from vâta, going, (i. 62, 10.) In some of these passages we can hardly doubt that the accent ought to be changed, and that we ought to read ávâta. Thus in vi. 64, 4, avâte is clearly a vocative applied to Ushas, who is called ávâtâ, unconquerable, in the verse immediately following. In i. 52, 4, the Maruts are called avâtâh, which can only be ávâtâh, unconquerable ; nor can we hesitate in viii. 79, 7, to change avâtâh into ávâtah, as an epithet applied to Soma, and preceded by ádriptakratuh, of unimpaired strength, unconquerable.

But even then we find no evidence that ávâta, uncon-quered, could be applied to rain or to a cloud, and I there-fore propose another explanation, though equally founded on the supposition that the accent of avâtâm in our passage should be on the first syllable.

I take vâta as a Vedic form instead of the later vâna, the past participle of vai, to wither. Similarly we find in the Veda gîta, instead of gîna, the latter form being sanctioned by Pâ*n*ini. Vâ means to get dry, to flag, to get exhausted ; ávâta therefore, as applied to a cloud, would mean not dry, not withered, as applied to rain, not dried up, but remain-ing on the ground. It is important to remark that in one passage, vi. 67, 7, Sâya*n*a, too, explains ávâta, as applied to rivers, by asushka, not dry; and the same meaning would be applicable to avâtâh in i. 62, 10. In this sense of not withered, not dry, ávâtâm in our passage would form a per-fectly appropriate epithet of the rain, while neither windless nor unconquered would yield an appropriate sense. In the famous passage x. 129, 2, ânît avâtám svadháyâ tát ékam, that only One breathed breathless by itself, avâtâm might be taken, in accordance with its accent, as windless or breath-less, and the poet may have wished to give this antithetical point to his verse. But ávâtam, as an adverb, would here be equally appropriate, and we should then have to translate, ' that only One breathed freely by itself.'

Verse 8, note [1]. The peculiar structure of the metre in the seventh and eighth verses should be noted. Though we may scan

$$ - - - - \cup \acute{\cup} - - | - - \cup - - \acute{\cup} - - | \cup - - - \cup \acute{\cup} - - | $$
$$ - - \cup - - \acute{\cup} - - | - - \cup - - \acute{\cup} - - | \cup - - - \cup \acute{\cup} - - $$

by throwing the accent on the short antepenultimate, yet the movement of the metre becomes far more natural by throwing the accent on the long penultimate, thus reading

$$ - \acute{-} - \acute{-} \cup \cup \acute{-} - \ - \acute{-} \cup \acute{-} \cup \cup \acute{-} - \ \cup \acute{-} - \acute{-} \cup \cup \acute{-} - $$
$$ - \acute{-} \cup \acute{-} - \cup \acute{-} - | - \acute{-} \cup \acute{-} - \cup - - \ \cup \acute{-} - \acute{-} \cup \cup \acute{-} - $$

Sâya*n*a : ' Like a cow the lightning roars, (the lightning) attends (on the Maruts) as the mother cow on her calf, because their rain is let loose at the time of lightning and thunder.'

Wilson : 'The lightning roars like a parent cow that bellows for its calf, and hence the rain is set free by the Maruts.'

Benfey : ' Es blitzt—wie eine Kuh brüllt es—die Mutter folgt dem Kalb gleichsam—wenn ihr Regen losgelassen. (Der Donner folgt dem Blitz, wie eine Kuh ihrem Kalbe.)'

Vâsrâ as a masculine means a bull, and it is used as a name of the Maruts in some passages, viii. 7, 3 ; 7. As a feminine it means a cow, particularly a cow with a calf, a milch cow. Hence also a mother, x. 119, 4. The lowing of the lightning must be intended for the distant thunder, and the idea that the lightning goes near or looks for the rain is not foreign to the Vedic poets. See i. 39, 9 : ' Come to us, Maruts, with your entire help, as lightnings (come to, i. e. seek for) the rain !'

Verse 9, note [1]. That pargánya here and in other places means cloud has been well illustrated by Dr. Bühler, Orient und Occident, vol. i. p. 221. It is interesting to watch the personifying process which is very palpable in this word, and by which Parganya becomes at last a friend and companion of Indra.

Verse 10, note [1]. Sádma, as a neuter, means originally a seat, and is frequently used in the sense of altar : iv. 9, 3. sáh sádma pári nîyate hótâ ; vii. 18, 22. hótâ-iva sádma pári cini rébhan. It soon, however, assumed the more general meaning of place, as

x. 1, 1. agníh bhânúnâ rúsatâ vísvâ sádmâni aprâh.

Agni with brilliant light thou filledst all places.

It is lastly used with special reference to heaven and earth, the two sádmanî, i. 185, 6 ; iii. 55, 2. In our passage sádma pârthivam is the same as pârthive sádane in viii. 97, 5. Here the earth is mentioned together with heaven, the sea, and the sky. Sâyana takes sádma as ' dwelling,' so do Wilson and Langlois. Benfey translates ' der Erde Sitz,' and makes it the subject of the sentence : ' From the roaring of the Maruts the seat of the earth trembles, and all men tremble.' Sadman,

with the accent on the last syllable, is also used as a masculine
in the Rig-veda, i. 173, 1; vi. 51, 12. sadmânam divyám.

Verse 11, note ¹. I have translated vîlu-pânibhi*h*, as if it
were vilúpânibhi*h*, for this is the right accent of a Bahuvrîhi
compound. Thus the first member retains its own accent in
prithú-pâni, bhûri-pâni, vrísha-pâni, &c. It is possible that
the accent may have been changed in our passage, because
the compound is used, not as an adjective, but as a kind of
substantive, as the name of a horse. Pâní, hand, means, as
applied to horses, hoof:
    ii. 31, 2. prithivyâ*h* sânau gânghananta pâní-bhi*h*.
When they strike with their hoofs on the summit of the
earth.
    This meaning appears still more clearly in such com-
pounds as dravát-pâni:
    viii. 5, 35. hiranyáyena ráthena dravátpâni-bhi*h* ásvai*h*.
On a golden chariot, on quick-hoofed horses.
    The horses of the Maruts, which in our verse are called
vîlu-pâní, strong-hoofed, are called viii. 7, 27. híranya-pâni,
golden-hoofed:
    ásvai*h* híranyapâni-bhi*h* dévâsa*h* úpa gantana.
On your golden-hoofed horses come hither, O gods.
    Those who retain the accent of the MSS. ought to trans-
late, ' Maruts, with your strong hands go after the clouds.'

Verse 11, note ². Ródhasvatî is explained by Sâyana as
river. It does not occur again in the Rig-veda. Ródhas
is enclosure or fence, the bank of a river; but it does not
follow that ródhasvat, having enclosures or banks, is applicable to rivers only. ii. 15, 8, it is said that he emptied or
opened the artificial enclosures of Bala, these being the
clouds conquered by Indra. Hence I take ródhasvatî in
the sense of a cloud yet unopened, which is followed or
driven on by the Maruts.
    Kitrá, bright or many-coloured, is applied to the clouds,
v. 63, 3. kitrébhi*h* abhrái*h*.

Verse 11, note ³. Roth takes ákhidrayâman for a name of
horse. The word does not occur again in the Rig-veda,

but the idea that the roads of the gods are easy (sugâh
ádhvâ) is of frequent occurrence.

Wilson : 'Maruts, with strong hands, come along the
beautifully-embanked rivers with unobstructed progress.'

Benfey : 'Mit euren starken Händen folgt den hehren
eingeschlossnen nach in unermüd'tem Gang, Maruts.'

Verse 12, note [1]. Abhîsu does not mean finger in the
Rig-veda, though Sâyana frequently explains it so, misled
by Yâska who gives abhîsu among the names of finger.
Wilson : 'May your fingers be well skilled (to hold the reins).'

Verse 13, note [1]. Agni is frequently invoked together
with the Maruts, and is even called marút-sakhâ, the friend
of the Maruts, viii. 92, 14. It seems better, therefore, to
refer bráhmanas pátim to Agni, than, with Sâyana, to the
host of the Maruts (marúdganam). Bráhmanaspáti and
Brihaspáti are both varieties of Agni, the priest and purohita
of gods and men, and as such he is invoked together with
the Maruts in other passages, i. 40, 1. Tánâ is an adverb,
meaning constantly, always, for ever. Cf. ii. 2, 1; viii. 40, 7.

Wilson : 'Declare in our presence (priests), with voice
attuned to praise Brahmanaspati, Agni, and the beautiful
Mitra.'

Benfey : 'Lass schallen immerfort das Lied zu grüssen
Brahmanaspati, Agni, Mitra, den herrlichen.'

Verse 13, note [2]. Mitra is never, as far as I know, invoked together with the Maruts, and it is better to take
mitrám as friend. Besides ná cannot be left here untrans-
lated.

Verse 14, note [1]. The second sentence is obscure. Sâyana
translates : 'Let the choir of priests make a hymn of
praise, let them utter or expand it, like as a cloud sends
forth rain.' Wilson similarly : 'Utter the verse that is in
your mouth, spread it out like a cloud spreading rain.'
Benfey : 'Ein Preislied schaffe in dem Mund, ertöne dem
Parganya gleich.' He takes Parganya for the god of thunder,
and supposes the hymn of praise to be compared to it on

account of its loudness. Tatana*h* can only be the second person singular of the conjunctive of the reduplicated perfect, of which we have also tatánat, tatánâma, tatánan, and tatánanta. Tatana*h* can be addressed either to the host of the Maruts, or to the poet. I take it in the latter sense, for a similar verse occurs viii. 21, 18. It is said there of a patron that he alone is a king, that all others about the river Sarasvatî are only small kings, and the poet adds : 'May he spread like a cloud with the rain,' giving hundreds and thousands, (par*g*ánya*h*-iva tatánat hí vrish*t*yâ.)

Verse 15, note [1]. It is difficult to find an appropriate rendering for arkín. It means praising, celebrating, singing, and it is in the last sense only that it is applicable to the Maruts. Wilson translates, 'entitled to adoration;' Benfey, 'flaming.' Boehtlingk and Roth admit the sense of flaming in one passage, but give to arkín in this place the meaning of praising. If it simply meant, possessed of arká, i. e. songs of praise, it would be a very lame epithet after panasyú. But other passages, like i. 19, 4; 52, 15, show that the conception of the Maruts as singers was most familiar to the Vedic *R*ishis (i. 64, 10; Kuhn, Zeitschrift, vol. i. p. 521, note); and arká is the very name applied to their songs (i. 19, 4). In the Edda, too, ' storm and thunder are represented as a lay, as the wondrous music of the wild hunt. The dwarfs and Elbs sing the so-called Alb-leich which carries off everything, trees and mountains.' See Justi in Orient und Occident, vol. ii. p. 62. There is no doubt therefore that arkín here means musician, and that the arká of the Maruts is the music of the winds.

Verse 15, note [2]. Vriddhá, literally grown, is used in the Veda as an honorific epithet, with the meaning of mighty or great :
iii. 32, 7. yá*g*âma*h* ít námasâ vriddhám índram
brihántam *r*ishvám a*g*áram yúvânam.

We worship with praise the mighty Indra, the great, the exalted, the immortal, the vigorous.

Here neither is vriddhá intended to express old age, nor yúvan young age, but both are meant as laudatory epithets.

Asan is the so-called Let of as, to be. This Let is properly an imperative, which gradually sinks down to a mere subjunctive. Of as, we find the following Let forms : belonging to the present, we have ásasi, ii. 26, 2 ; ásati, vi. 23, 9 ; ásathaḥ, vi. 63, 1 ; and ásatha, v. 61, 4 : belonging to the imperfect, ásaḥ, viii. 100, 2 ; ásat, i. 9, 5 ; ásâma, i. 173, 9 ; ásan, i. 89, 1. Ásam, a form quoted by Roth from Rig-veda x. 27, 4, is really âsam.

We find, for instance, ásaḥ, with an imperative or optative meaning, in

viii. 100, 2. ásaḥ ka tvám dakshiṇatáḥ sákhâ me
ádha vritrấṇi gaṅghanâva bhûri.

And be thou my friend on my right hand, and we shall kill many enemies.

Here we see the transition of meaning from an imperative to the conditional. In English, too, we may say, ' Do this and you shall live,' which means nearly the same as, ' If you do this, you will live.' Thus we may translate this passage : ' And if thou be my friend on my right side, then we shall kill many enemies.'

x. 124, 1. imám naḥ agne úpa yagñám â ihi—
ásaḥ havya-vâṭ utá naḥ puraḥ-gâḥ.

Here we have the imperative ihi and the Let ásaḥ used in the same sense.

Far more frequently, however, ásaḥ is used in relative sentences, such as,

vi. 36, 5. ásaḥ yáthâ naḥ sávasâ kakânáḥ.

That thou mayest be ours, delighting in strength.

vii. 24, 1. ásaḥ yáthâ naḥ avitấ vridhé ka.

That thou mayest be our helper and for our increase.

See also x. 44, 4 ; 85, 26 ; 36.

Wilson : ' May they be exalted by this our worship.'

Benfey : ' Mögen die Hohen hier bei uns sein.'

MA*ND*ALA I, SÛKTA 39.
ASH*T*AKA I, ADHYÂYA 3, VARGA 18–19.

1. Prá yát ithấ parâ-váta*h* so*k*í*h* ná mắnam ásyatha, kásya krátvâ maruta*h* kásya várpasâ kám yâtha kám ha dhûtaya*h*.

2. Sthirấ va*h* santu ấyudhâ parâ-núde vîlú utá prati-skábhe, yushmắkam astu távishî pánîyasî mắ mártyasya mâyína*h*.

3. Pắrâ ha yát sthirám hathá nára*h* vartáyatha gurú, ví yâthana vanína*h* prithivyắ*h* ví ắsâ*h* párvatânâm.

4. Nahí va*h* sátru*h* vividé ádhi dyávi ná bhûmyâm risâdasa*h*, yushmắkam astu távishî tánâ yu*g*ắ rúdrâsa*h* nú *k*it â-dh*r*íshe.

5. Prá vepayanti párvatân vi viñ*k*anti vánaspátîn, pró (íti) ârata maruta*h* durmádâ*h*-iva dévâsa*h* sárvayâ visắ.

6. Úpo (íti) rátheshu príshatí*h* ayugdhvam prásh-ti*h* vahati róhita*h*, ắ va*h* yắmâya prithiví* *k*it a*s*rot ábîbhayanta mắnushâ*h*.

7. Ắ va*h* makshú tánâya kám rúdrâ*h* áva*h* v*r*inî-mahe, gánta nûnám na*h* ávasâ yáthâ purắ itthấ kán-vâya bibhyúshe.

8. Yushmắ-ishita*h* maruta*h* mártya-ishita*h* ắ yắ*h* na*h* ábhva*h* íshate, ví tám yuyota sávasâ ví ó*g*asâ ví yushmắkâbhi*h* ûtí-bhi*h*.

9. Ásâmi hí pra-ya*g*yava*h* kán*v*am dadá pra-*k*etasa*h*, ásâmi-bhi*h* maruta*h* ắ na*h* ûtí-bhi*h* gánta v*r*ishtím ná vi-dyúta*h*.

1. When you thus from afar cast forwards your measure[1] like a blast of fire, through whose wisdom is it, through whose design?[2] To whom do you go, to whom, ye shakers (of the earth)?

2. May your weapons be firm to attack, strong also to withstand. May yours be the more glorious strength, not that of the deceitful mortal.

3. When you overthrow what is firm, O ye men, and whirl about what is heavy, you pass[1] through the trees of the earth, through the clefts of the rocks.[2]

4. No real foe of yours is known in heaven, nor on earth, ye devourers of enemies! May strength be yours, together with your race,[1] O Rudras, to defy even now.[2]

5. They make the rocks to tremble, they tear asunder the kings of the forest.[1] Come on, Maruts, like madmen, ye gods with your whole tribe.

6. You have harnessed the spotted deer to your chariots, a red one draws as leader;[1] even the earth listened at your coming, and men were frightened.

7. O Rudras, we quickly desire your help for our race. Come now to us with help, as of yore; thus now also, for the sake of the frightened Kanva.[1]

8. Whatever fiend, roused by you or roused by men, attacks us, tear him (from us) by your power, by your strength, by your aid.[1]

9. For you, worshipful and wise, have wholly protected[1] Kanva. Come to us, Maruts, with your entire help, as lightnings[2] (go in quest of) the rain.

10. Ásâmi ógah bibhṛitha su-dânavah ásâmi dhû-
tayah sávah, ṛishi-dvíshe marutah pari-manyáve
íshum ná sṛigata dvísham.

COMMENTARY.

This hymn is ascribed to Kaṇva, the son of Ghora. The
metre varies between Brihatî and Satobrihatî, the odd verses
being composed in the former, the even verses in the latter
metre. Each couple of such verses is called a Bârhata
Pragâtha. The Brihatî consists of $8 + 8 + 12 + 8$, the
Satobrihatî of $12 + 8 + 12 + 8$ syllables.

Verse 1, note [1]. Mằna, which I translate by measure, is
explained by Sâyaṇa as meaning strength. Wilson: 'When
you direct your awful vigour downwards from afar, as light
(descends from heaven).' Benfey: 'Wenn ihr aus weiter
Ferne so wie Strahlen schleudert euren Stolz (das worauf
ihr stolz seid: euren Blitz).' Langlois: 'Lorsque vous
lancez votre souffle puissant.' I doubt whether mằna is
ever used in the Rig-veda in the sense of pride, which no
doubt it has, as a masculine, in later Sanskrit: cf. Halâ-
yudha, ed. Aufrecht, iv. 37. Mằna, as a masculine,
means frequently a poet in the Rig-veda, viz. a measurer, a
thinker or maker; as a neuter it means a measure, or what
is measured or made. Thus v. 85, 5, we read:
mằnena-iva tasthi-vẵn antárikshe ví yáh mamé pṛithivím
sûryeṇa.

He (Varuṇa) who standing in the welkin has measured
the earth with the sun, as with a measure.

In this passage, as well as in ours, we must take measure,
not in the abstract sense, but as a measuring line, which is
cast forward to measure the distance of an object, an image,
perfectly applicable to the Maruts, who seem with their
weapons to strike the trees and mountains when they themselves are still far off. Another explanation might be given,

10. Bounteous givers, you possess whole strength, whole power, ye shakers (of the world). Send, O Maruts, against the wrathful enemy of the poets an enemy, like an arrow.[1]

---

if mắna could be taken in the sense of measure, i. e. shape or form, but this is doubtful.

Verse 1, note [2]. Várpas, which generally means body or form, is here explained by praise. Benfey puts *Werk* (i. e. *Gesang, Gebet*) ; Langlois, *maison.* Várpas, which, without much reason, has been compared to Latin *corpus,* must here be taken in a more general sense. Thus vi. 44, 14, asyá madé purú várpâmsi vidvắn, is applied to Indra as knowing many schemes, many thoughts, many things, when he is inspired by the Soma-juice.

Verse 3, note [1]. Benfey takes ví yâthana in a causative sense, you destroy, you cause the trees to go asunder. But even without assigning to yâ a causative meaning, to go through, to pierce, would convey the idea of destruction. In some passages vi-yâ is certainly used in the simple sense of passing through, without involving the idea of destruction:
viii. 73, 13. ráthaḥ viyắti ródasî (íti).
Your chariot which passes through or between heaven and earth.
In other passages the mere passing across implies conquest and destruction :
i. 116, 20. vi-bhindúnâ....ráthena ví párvatân....ayâtam.
On your dissevering chariot you went across the mountains (the clouds).
In other passages, however, a causative meaning seems equally, and even more applicable :
viii. 7, 23. ví vritrám parva-*sáḥ* yayuḥ ví párvatân.
They passed through Vritra piecemeal, they passed through the mountains (the clouds) ; or, they destroyed Vritra, cutting him to pieces, they destroyed the clouds.

G 2

Likewise i. 86, 10. ví yâta vísvam atrínam.

Walk athwart every evil spirit, or destroy every evil spirit !

We must scan vi yâthana vaninaḥ pṛithivyâḥ.

Verse 3, note [2]. It might seem preferable to translate áśâḥ párvatânâm by the spaces of the clouds, for párvata means cloud in many places. Yet here, and still more clearly in verse 5, where párvata occurs again, the object of the poet is to show the strength of the Maruts. In that case the mere shaking or bursting of the clouds would sound very tame by the side of the shaking and breaking of the forest trees. Vedic poets do not shrink from the conception that the Maruts shake even mountains, and Indra is even said to have cut off the mountain tops: iv. 19, 4. áva abhinat kakú-bhaḥ párvatânâm. In the later literature, too, the same idea occurs: Mahâbh. Vana-parva, v. 10974, dyauḥ svit patati kim bhûmir dîryate parvato nu kim, does the sky fall? is the earth torn asunder, or the mountain?   ·

Verse 4, note [1]. Sâyana was evidently without an autho-ritative explanation of tânâ yugá. He tries to explain it by ' through the union of you may strength to resist be quickly extended.' Wilson: ' May your collective strength be quickly exerted.' Benfey takes tánâ as adverb and leaves out yugá: ' Zu allen Zeiten, O Furchtbarn !—sei im Nu zu überwält'gen euch die Macht.' Yugá, an instrumental, if used together with another instrumental, becomes in the Veda a mere preposition: cf. vii. 43, 5; 95, 4. râyâ yugá; x. 83, 3. tápasâ yugá; x. 102, 12. vádhrinâ yugá; vii. 32, 20. púram-dhyâ yugá; vi. 56, 2. sákhyâ yugá; viii. 68, 9. tvâ yugá. As to the meaning of tán, see B. R. s. v., where tán in our passage is explained as continuation. The off-spring or race of the Maruts is mentioned again in the next verse.

Verse 4, note [2]. Nú kit â-dhríshe might possibly be taken as an abrupt interrogative sentence, viz. Can it be defied? Can it be resisted? See v. 87, 2 :

tát vaḥ marutaḥ ná â-dhríshe sávaḥ.

Your strength, O Maruts, is not to be defied.

Verse 5, note [1]. Large trees of the forest are called the kings or lords of the forest.

Verse 6, note [1]. Prâsh*t*i is explained by Sâya*n*a as a sort of yoke in the middle of three horses or other animals, harnessed in a car; róhita as a kind of red deer. Hence Wilson remarks that the sense may be, 'The red deer yoked between them aids to drag the car.' But he adds that the construction of the original is obscure, and apparently rude and ungrammatical. Benfey translates, 'Sie führt ein flammenrothes Joch,' and remarks against Wilson that Sâya*n*a's definition of prâsh*t*i as yoke is right, but that of róhita as deer, wrong. If Sâya*n*a's authority is to be invoked at all, one might appeal from Sâya*n*a in this place to Sâya*n*a viii. 7, 28, where prâsh*t*i is explained by him either by quick or by pramukhe yu*g*yamâna*h*, harnessed in front. The verse is

yát eshâm p*r*íshatî*h* ráthe prásh*t*ih váhati róhita*h*.

When the red leader draws or leads their spotted deer in the chariot.

vi. 47, 24. prásh*t*i*h* is explained as tripada âdhâra*h*; tad-vad vahantîti prash*t*ayo 'svâ*h*. In i. 100, 17, prásh*t*ibhi*h*, as applied to men, means friends or supporters, or, as Sâya*n*a explains, pârsvasthair anyair *r*ishibhi*h*.

Verse 7, note [1]. Ka*n*va, the author of the hymn.

Verse 8, note [1]. A very weak verse, particularly the second line, which Wilson renders by, 'Withhold from him food and strength and your assistance.' Benfey translates ábhva very happily by Ungethüm.

Verse 9, note [1]. The verb dadá is the second pers. plur. of the perfect of dâ, and is used here in the sense of to keep, to protect, as is well shown by B. and R. s. v. dâ 4, base dad. Sâya*n*a did not understand the word, and took it for an irregular imperative; yet he assigned to the verb the proper sense of to keep, instead of to give. Hence Wilson: 'Uphold the sacrificer Kanva.' Benfey, less correctly, 'Den Ka*n*va gabt ihr,' as if Ka*n*va had been the highest gift of the Maruts.

Verse 9, note [2]. The simile, as lightnings go to the
rain, is not very telling. It may have been suggested by
the idea that the lightnings run about to find the rain,
or the *tertium comparationis* may simply be the quickness
of lightning. Wilson : 'As the lightnings bring the rain.'
Benfey: '(So schnell) gleichwie der Blitz zum Regen
kömmt.' Lightning precedes the rain, and may therefore
be represented as looking about for the rain.

Verse 10, note [1]. Wilson : 'Let loose your anger.'
Sâya*na* : 'Let loose a murderer who hates.'

Pari-manyú, which occurs but once in the Rig-veda, cor-
responds as nearly as possible to the Greek περίθυμος.
Manyú, like θυμός, means courage, spirit, anger; and in
the compound parimanyú, as in περίθυμος, the preposition
pári seems to strengthen the simple notion of the word.
That pári is used in that sense in later Sanskrit is well
known; for instance, in parilaghu, *perlevis*, parikshâma,
withered away : see Pott, Etymologische Forschungen,
second edition, vol. i. p. 487. How pári, originally meaning
round about, came to mean excessive, is difficult to explain
with certainty. It may have been, because what surrounds
exceeds, but it may also have been because what is done all
around a thing is done thoroughly. Thus we find in the
Veda, viii. 75, 9, pári-dveshas, lit. one who hates all around,
then a great hater :

    mâ na*h* pári-dveshasa*h* amhatí*h*, ûrmí*h* ná nâvam â vadhît.

May the grasp of the violent hater strike us not, as the
wave strikes a ship.

Again, pari-sprídh means literally one who strives round
about, then an eager enemy, a rival (fem.):

    ix. 53, 1. nudásva yâ*h* pari-sprídha*h*.

Drive away those who are rivals.

Pari-kro*s*á means originally one who shouts at one from
every side, who abuses one roundly, then an angry reviler.
This word, though not mentioned in B. R.'s Dictionary,
occurs in

    i. 29, 7. sárvam pari-krosám *g*ahi.

Kill every reviler !

The same idea which is here expressed by pari-kro*s*á, is

in other places expressed by pari-ráp, lit. one who shouts round about, who defies on every side, a calumniator, an enemy.

ii. 23, 3. ā vi-bā́dhya pari-rápa*h*.
Having struck down the enemies.

ii. 23, 14. ví pari-rápa*h* ardaya.
Destroy the enemies.

In the same way as words meaning to hate, to oppose, to attack, are strengthened by this preposition, which conveys the idea of round about, we also find words expressive of love strengthened by the same preposition. Thus from prîtá*h*, loved, we have pári-prîta*h*, lit. loved all round, then loved very much : i. 190, 6. pári-prîta*h* ná mitrá*h*; cf. x. 27, 12. We also find ix. 72, 1. pari-príya*h*, those who love fully or all around, which may mean great lovers, or surrounding friends.

In all these cases the intensifying power of pári arises from representing the action of the verb as taking place on every side, thoroughly, excessively ; but in other cases, mentioned by Professor Pott, particularly where this preposition is joined to a noun which implies some definite limit, its magnifying power is no doubt due to the fact that what is around, is outside, and therefore beyond. Thus in Greek περίμετρος expresses the same idea as ὑπέρμετρος (loc. cit. p. 488), but I doubt whether pári ever occurs in that sense in Sanskrit compounds.

MANDALA I, SÛKTA 64.
ASHTAKA I, ADHYÂYA 5, VARGA 6-8.

1. Vríshne sárdhâya sú-makhâya vedhâse nódha*h*
su-vriktím prá bhara marút-bhya*h*, apá*h** ná dhî-
ra*h* mánasâ su-hástya*h* gíra*h* sám ange vidátheshu
â-bhúva*h*.

2. Té gagñire divá*h* rishvấsa*h* ukshána*h* rudrásya
máryâ*h* ásurâ*h* arepása*h*, pâvakấsa*h* súkaya*h* sûryâ*h*-
iva sátvana*h* ná drapsína*h* ghorá-varpasa*h*.

3. Yúvâna*h* rudrấh agárâh abhok-hána*h* vavakshúh
ádhri-gâva*h* párvatâ*h*-iva, drilhấ kit vísvâ bhúvanâni
pấrthivâ prá kyavayanti divyấni magmấnâ.

4. Kitraíh angí-bhi*h* vápushe ví angate váksha*h*-su
rukmấn ádhi yetire subhé, ámseshu eshâm ní mi-
mrikshu*h* rishtáya*h* sâkám gagñire svadhấyâ divá*h*
nára*h*.

5. Îsâna-krítah dhúnaya*h* risấdasa*h* vấtân vi-dyúta*h*
tắvishîbhi*h* akrata, duhánti ấdha*h* divyấni dhắtaya*h*
bhắmim pinvanti páyasâ pấri-graya*h*.

6. Pínvanti apá*h* marúta*h* su-dấnava*h* páya*h* ghritá-
vat vidátheshu â-bhúva*h*, ấtyam ná mihó ví nayanti
vấgínam útsam duhanti stanáyantam ákshitam.

7. Mahishẩsa*h* mâyína*h* kitrá-bhânava*h* girẩya*h* ná
─────────────────────────────
* apấh !

1. For the manly host, the majestic, the wise, for the Maruts bring thou, O Nodhas,[1] a pure offering.[2] Like a workman,[3] wise in his mind and handy, I join together words which are useful at sacrifices.

2. They are born, the tall bulls of Dyu[1] (heaven), the boys[2] of Rudra, the divine, the blameless, pure, and bright like suns ; scattering rain-drops, of awful shape, like giants.[3]

3. The youthful Rudras, they who never grow old, the slayers of the demon,[1] have grown irresistible like mountains. They shake with their strength all beings, even the strongest, on earth and in heaven.

4. They deck themselves with glittering ornaments[1] for show ; on their chests they fix gold (chains) for beauty ;[2] the spears on their shoulders pound to pieces ;[3] they were born together by themselves,[4] the men of Dyu.

5. They who confer power,[1] the roarers,[2] the devourers of foes, they made winds and lightnings by their powers. The shakers milk the heavenly udders (clouds), roaming around they fill the earth with milk (rain).

6. The bounteous[1] Maruts fill[2] (with) the fat milk (of the clouds) the waters, which are useful at sacrifices. They seem to lead[3] about the powerful horse, the cloud, to make it rain ; they milk the thundering, unceasing spring.[4]

7. Mighty you are, powerful, of wonderful splendour, firmly rooted[1] like mountains, (yet) lightly

svá-tavasa*h* raghu-syáda*h*, m*r*igâ*h*-iva hastína*h* khâ-
datha vânâ yát âru*n*íshu távishí*h* áyugdhvam.

8. Si*m*hâ*h*-iva nânadati prá-*k*etasa*h* pisâ*h*-iva su-
písa*h* visvá-vedasa*h*, kshápa*h* *g*ínvanta*h* p*r*íshatîbhi*h* *r*ishtí-bhi*h* sám ít sa-bâdha*h* sávasâ áhi-manyava*h*.

9. Ródasî (íti) â vadata ga*n*a-sriya*h* n*r*í-sâ*k*a*h* sûrâ*h*
sávasâ áhi-manyava*h*, â vandhúreshu amáti*h* ná dar-
satâ vi-dyút ná tasthau maruta*h* rátheshu va*h*.

10. Visvá-vedasa*h* rayí-bhi*h* sám-okasa*h* sám-mi-
slâsa*h* távishîbhi*h* vi-rap*s*ína*h*, ástâra*h* íshum dadhire
gábhastyo*h* anantá-sushmâ*h* v*r*ísha-khâdaya*h* nára*h*.

11. Hira*n*yáyebhi*h* pavî-bhi*h* paya*h*-v*r*ídha*h* út
*g*ighnante â-pathyâ*h* ná párvatân, makhâ*h* ayâsa*h*
sva-s*r*íta*h* dhruva-*k*yúta*h* dudhra-k*r*íta*h* marúta*h*
bhrâ*g*at-*r*ish*t*aya*h*.

12. Gh*r*íshum pâvakám vanínam ví-*k*arsha*n*im rudrásya sûnúm havâsâ g*r*i*n*îmasi, ra*g*a*h*-túram tavásam mârutam ga*n*ám *r*i*g*îshí*n*am v*r*ísha*n*am sas*k*ata
sriyé.

13. Prá nú sá*h* mártta*h* sávasâ *g*ánân áti tasthaú
va*h* ûti maruta*h* yám âvata, árvat-bhi*h* vâ*g*am bha-
rate dhánâ n*r*í-bhi*h* â-p*r*í*kkh*yam krátum â ksheti
púshyati.

gliding along ;—you chew up forests, like elephants,[2]
when you have assumed vigour among the red flames.[3]

8. Like lions they roar, the far-sighted Maruts,
they are handsome like gazelles,[1] the all-knowing.
By night[2] with their spotted deer (rain-clouds) and
with their spears (lightnings) they rouse the companions together, they whose ire through strength
is like the ire of serpents.

9. You who march in companies, the friends of
man, heroes, whose ire through strength is like the
ire of serpents, salute heaven and earth![1] On the
seats on your chariots, O Maruts, the lightning stands,
visible like light.[2]

10. All-knowing, surrounded with wealth, endowed
with vigour, singers,[1] men of endless prowess, armed
with strong rings,[2] they, the archers, have placed the
arrow on their arms.

11. The Maruts, who with their golden fellies,
increase the rain, stir up the clouds like wanderers
on the road. They are brisk, indefatigable,[1] they
move by themselves ; they throw down what is firm,
the Maruts with their brilliant spears make (everything) to reel.[2]

12. We invoke with prayer[1] the offspring of Rudra, the brisk, the bright, the worshipful,[2] the active.
Cling[3] for happiness-sake to the strong host of the
Maruts, the chasers of the sky,[4] the vigorous, the
impetuous.[5]

13. The mortal whom ye, Maruts, protected with
your protection, he indeed surpasses people in strength.
He carries off food with his horses, treasures with his
men ; he acquires honourable[1] strength, and he prospers.[2]

14. *K*ark*r*ítyam maruta*h* p*r*it-sú dustáram dyu-mántam *s*úshmam maghávat-su dhattana, dhana-sp*r*ítam ukthyâm vi*s*vá-*k*arsha*n*im tokám pushyema tánayam satám hímâ*h*.

15. Nú sthi*r*ám maruta*h* vírá-vantam *r*iti-sáham rayím asmâsu dhatta, sahasrí*n*am satínam sûsu-vâ*m*-sam prâtá*h* makshú dhiyâ-vasu*h* *g*agamyât.

COMMENTARY.

This hymn is ascribed to Nodhas, of the family of Go-tama. The metre from verse 1–14 is *G*agatî, verse 15 is Trish*t*ubh.

Verse 1, note [1]. The first line is addressed by the poet to himself.

Verse 1, note [2]. Suv*r*iktí is generally explained by a hymn of praise, and it cannot be denied that in this place, as in most others, that meaning would be quite satisfactory. Etymologically, however, suv*r*iktí means the cleaning and trimming of the grass on which, as on a small altar, the oblation is offered: cf. v*r*iktabarhis, i. 38, 1, note [2], page 68. Hence, although the same word might be metaphorically applied to a carefully composed, pure and holy hymn of praise, yet wherever the primary meaning is applicable it seems safer to retain it: cf. iii. 61, 5; vi. 11, 5.

Verse 1, note [3]. Apás, with the accent on the last syllable, is the accusative plural of ap, water, and it is so explained by Sâya*n*a. He translates: 'I show forth these hymns of praise, like water, i. e. everywhere, as Par*g*anya sends down rain at once in every place.' Benfey explains: 'I make these hymns smooth like water, i. e. so that they run smooth

14. Give, O Maruts, to the worshippers strength glorious, invincible in battle, brilliant, wealth-conferring, praiseworthy, known to all men.[1] Let us foster our kith and kin during a hundred winters.

15. Will[1] you then, O Maruts, grant unto us wealth, durable, rich in men, defying all onslaughts?[2]—wealth a hundred and a thousand-fold, always increasing?—May he who is rich in prayers[3] (the host of the Maruts) come early and soon!

---

like water.' He compares ῥυθμός, as derived from ῥέω. Another explanation might be, that the hymns are powerful like water, when it has been banked up. Yet all these similes seem very lame, and I feel convinced that we ought either to change the accent, and read ápah, or the last vowel, and read apấh. In the former case the meaning would be, 'As one wise in mind and clever performs his work, so do I compose these hymns.' In the second case, which seems to me preferable, we should translate: 'Like a workman, wise in mind and handy, I put together these hymns.'

Verse 2, note [1]. It is difficult to say in passages like this, whether Dyu should be taken as heaven or as a personified deity. When the Maruts are called Rudrásya máryâh, the boys of Rudra (vii. 56, 1), the personification is always preserved. Hence if the same beings are called Diváh máryâh, this too, I think, should be translated the boys of Dyu (iii. 54, 13; v. 59, 6), not the sons of heaven. The bulls of Dyu is a more primitive and more vigorous expression for what we should call the fertilising winds of heaven.

Verse 2, note [2]. Márya is a male, particularly a young male, a boy, a young man (i. 115, 2; iii. 33, 10; iv. 20, 5; v. 61, 4, with vîra):

v. 59. 5. máryâh-iva su-vrídhah vavridhuh nárah.
Like boys that grow well they have grown men.

When joined with nára*h* (v. 53, 3), nára*h* máryâ*h* are-pása*h*, it may be taken as an adjective, manly, strong. At last márya assumes the general meaning of man :

i. 91, 13. márya*h*-iva své oky*ê*.
Like a man in his own house.

Verse 2, note [3]. The simile, like giants, is not quite clear. Sátvan means a strong man, but it seems intended here to convey the idea of supernatural strength. Benfey translates, 'like brave warriors ;' Wilson, 'like evil spirits.' Ghorá-varpas is an adjective belonging to the Maruts rather than to the giants, and may mean of awful aspect, i. 19, 5, or of cruel mind ; cf. i. 39, 1, note [2].

Verse 3, note [1]. Abhog-ghána*h*, the slayers of the demon, are the slayers of the clouds, viz. of such clouds as do not yield rain. Abho*g*, not nurturing, is a name of the rainless cloud, like Námu*k*i (na-mu*k*, not delivering rain), the name of another demon killed by Indra ; see Benfey, Glossar, s. v. The cloud which sends rain is called bhu*g*mán :

viii. 50, 2. giri*h* ná bhu*g*mâ maghávat-su pinvate.
Like a feeding cloud he showers his gifts on the wor-shippers.

Verse 4, note [1]. The ornaments of the Maruts are best described v. 54, 11:

á*m*seshu va*h* rish*t*áya*h* pat-sú khâdáya*h* vákshah*h*-su ruk-mâ*h*.

On your shoulders are the spears, on your feet rings, on your chests gold ornaments.

Rukmá as a masc. plur. is frequently used for ornaments which are worn on the breast by the Maruts, but no hint is given as to the exact nature of the ornaments. The Maruts are actually called rukmávakshasa*h*, gold-breasted, (ii. 34, 2 ; v. 55, 1 ; 57, 5.)

Verse 4, note [2]. Vápushe and *s*ubhé, as parallel expres-sions, occur also vi. 63, 6.

Verse 4, note [3]. Ní mim*r*ikshur does not occur again in the Rig-veda, and Roth has suggested to read ní mimikshur instead ; see ni + mar*g*. He does not, however, give our passage under myak, but under mraksh, and this seems indeed preferable. No doubt, there is ample analogy for mimikshuh, and the meaning would be, their spears stick firm to their shoulders. But as the MSS. give mimrikshuh, and as it is possible to find a meaning for this, I do not propose to alter the text. The question is only, what does mimrikshuh mean? Mraksh means to grind, to rub, and Roth proposes to render our passage by 'the spears rub together on their shoulders.' The objections to this translation are the preposition ni, and the active voice of the verb. I take mraksh in the sense of grinding, pounding, destroying, which is likewise appropriate to mraksha-krítvan (viii. 61, 10), and tuvi-mrakshá (vi. 18, 2), and I translate, 'the spears on their shoulders pound to pieces.'

Verse 4, note [4]. The idea that the Maruts owe everything, if not their birth, at least their strength (svá-tavasah, svá-bhânavah, sva-srítah), to themselves is of frequent occurrence in these hymns.

Verse 5, note [1]. They are themselves compared to kings (i. 85, 8), and called îsâná, lords (i. 87, 4).

Verse 5, note [2]. Dhúni is connected with root dhvan, to dun or to din. Sâyana explains it by bending or shaking, and Benfey, too, translates it by *Erschütterer*. Roth gives the right meaning.

Verse 6, note [1]. I translate sudấnavah by bounteous, or good givers, for, if we have to choose between the two meanings of bounteous or endowed with liquid drops or dew, the former is the more appropriate in most passages. We might, of course, admit two words, one meaning, possessed of good water, the other, bounteous; the former derived from dấnu, neuter, water, or rain, the other from dânú, giving. It cannot be denied, for instance, that whenever the Maruts are called sudấnavah, the meaning, possessed of good rain, would be applicable: i. 40, 1; 44, 14; 64, 6; 85, 10; ii. 34, 8; iii. 26, 5; v. 52, 5; 53, 6; 57, 5; viii. 20, 18; x. 78, 5; i. 15, 2; 23, 9; 39, 10. Yet, even in these passages, while sudấnavah in the sense of possessed

of good rain is possible throughout, that of good giver would
sometimes be preferable, for instance, i. 15, 2, as compared
with i. 15, 3.

When the same word is applied to Indra, vii. 31, 2 ;
x. 23, 6 ; to Vishnu, viii. 25, 12 ; to the Asvins, i. 112, 11 ;
to Mitra and Varuna, v. 62, 9 ; to Indra and Varuna, iv. 41,
8, the meaning of giver of good rain might still seem
more natural. But with Agni, vi. 2, 4; the Âdityas, v. 67, 4;
viii. 18, 12 ; 19, 34; 67, 16 ; the Vasus, i. 106, 1; x. 66,
12 ; the Visve, x. 65, 11, such an epithet would not be
appropriate, while sudânavah, in the sense of bounteous
givers, is applicable to all.   The objection that dânu, giver,
does not occur in the Veda, is of no force, for many words
occur at the end of compounds only, and we shall see
passages where sudânu must be translated by good giver.
Nor would the accent of dânú, giver, be an obstacle, considering that the author of the Unâdi-sûtras had no Vedic
authority to guide him in the determination of the accent of
dânú.   Several words in nu have the accent on the first
syllable.` But one might go even a step further, and find
a more appropriate meaning for sudânu by identifying it
with the Zend hudânu, which means, not a good giver,
but a good knower, wise. True, this root dâ, to know, does
not occur in the ordinary Sanskrit, but as it exists both in
Zend and in Greek (δάημι, δάεις), it may have left this one
trace in the Vedic word sudânu.   This, however, is only a
conjecture ; what is certain is this, that apart from the
passages where sudânu is thus applied to various deities, in
the sense of bounteous or wise, it also occurs as applied to
the sacrificer, where it can only mean giver.   This is clear
from the following passages :

i. 47, 8. ísham prinkántâ su-kríte su-dânave.

Bringing food to him who acts well and gives well.

vii. 96, 4. gani-yántah nú ágravah putri-yántah su-dânavah, sárasvantam havâmahe.

We, being unmarried, and wishing for wives and wishing
for sons, offering sacrifices, call now upon Sarasvat.

viii. 103, 7. su-dânavah deva-yávah.

Offering sacrifices, and longing for the gods. Cf. x. 172,
2 ; 3 ; vi. 16, 8.

iv. 4, 7. sá*h* ít agne astu su-bhága*h* su-dánu*h* yá*h* tvâ nítyena havíshâ yá*h* ukthaí*h* píprîshati.

O Agni, let the liberal sacrificer be happy, who wishes to please thee by perpetual offerings and hymns. See also vi. 16, 8; 68, 5; x. 172, 2, 3.

It must be confessed that even the meaning of dânu is by no means quite clear. It is clear enough where it means demon, ii. 11, 18; 12, 11; iv. 30, 7; x. 120, 6, the seven demons. In i. 32, 9; iii. 30, 8, dânu, demon, is applied to the mother of V*r*itra. From this dânu we have the derivative dânavá, meaning again demon. Why the demons, conquered by Indra, were called dânu, is not clear. It may be in the sense of wise, or in the sense of powerful, for this meaning is ascribed to dânú by the author of the U*n*âdi-sûtras. If the latter meaning is authentic, and not only deduced *ex post* from the name of Dânu and Dânava, it might throw light on the Celtic dána, *fortis,* from which Zeuss derives the name of the Danube.

But the sense of the neuter dânu is by no means settled. Sometimes it means Soma :

x. 43, 7. ã́pa*h* ná síndhum abhí yát sam-áksharan sómâsa*h* índram kulyâ*h*-iva hradám, várdhanti víprâ*h* máha*h* asya sádane yávam ná v*r*ish*t*í*h* divyéna dánunâ.

When the Somas run together to Indra, like water to the river, like channels to the lake, then the priests increase his greatness in the sanctuary, as rain the corn, by the heavenly Soma-juice.

⁎ In the next verse *g*îrádânu means the sacrificer whose Soma is always alive, always ready.

In vi. 50, 13, however, dânu pápri*h* is doubtful. As an epithet to Apã́m nápât, it may mean he who wishes for Soma, or he who grants Soma ; but in neither case is there any tangible sense. Again, viii. 25, 5, Mitra and Varu*n*a are called s*r*iprá-dânû, which may mean possessed of flowing rain. And in the next verse, sám yã́ dânûni yemáthu*h* may be rendered by Mitra and Varu*n*a, who brought together rain.

The fact that Mitra-Varu*n*au and the As*v*ins are called dânunaspátî does not throw much more light on the subject, and the one passage where dânu occurs as a feminine,

i. 54, 7, dănu*h* asmai úpará pinvate divá*h*, may be translated by rain pours forth for him, below the sky, but the
translation is by no means certain.

Dănu*k*itra, applied to the dawn, the water of the clouds,
and the three worlds (v. 59, 8; 31, 6; i. 174, 7), means
most likely bright with dew or rain; and dănumat vásu,
the treasure conquered by Indra from the clouds, can be
translated by the treasure of rain. Taking all the evidence
together, we can hardly doubt that dănu existed in the
sense of liquid, rain, or Soma; yet it is equally certain that
dănu existed in the sense of giver, if not of gift, and that
from this, in certain passages, at all events, sudănu must be
derived, as a synonym of sudăvan, sudăman, &c.

Verse 6, note [2]. Cf. vii. 50, 4, (nadyă*h*) páyasá pínva-
mănâ*h*, the rivers swelling with milk. Pinvati is here
construed with two accusatives, the conception being that
they fill or feed the waters, and that the waters take the
food, viz. the rain. The construction is not to be compared with the Greek τρέφειν τροφήν τινα τοιήνδε (Herod.
ii. 2), but rather with διδάσκειν τινά τι.

Cf. vi. 63, 8. dhenúm na*h* ísham pinvatam ásakrâm.

You filled our cow (with) constant food.

Similarly duh, to milk, to extract, is construed with two
accusatives: Pân. i. 4, 51. gâm dogdhi paya*h*, he milks the
cow milk.

Rv. ix. 107, 5. duhânâ*h* ŭdha*h* divyám mádhu priyám.

Milking the heavenly udder (and extracting from it) the
precious sweet, i. e. the rain.

Verse 6, note [3]. The leading about of the clouds is
intended, like the leading about of horses, to tame them,
and make them obedient to the wishes of their riders, the
Maruts. Átya*h* vâgí is a strong horse, possibly a stallion;
but this horse is here meant to signify the cloud. Thus
we read:

v. 83, 6. divá*h* na*h* vrish*t*ím maruta*h* rarídhvam prá
pinvata vríshna*h* ásvasya dhârâ*h*.

Give us, O Maruts, the rain of heaven, pour forth the
streams of the stallion (the cloud).

In the original the simile is quite clear, and no one required to be told that the átya*h* vâg*î* was meant for the cloud. Vâg*í*n by itself means a horse, as i. 66, 2 ; 69, 3. vâg*î* ná prítá*h*, like a favourite horse : i. 116, 6. paidvá*h* vâg*î*, the horse of Pedu. But being derived from vâg*a*, strength, vâg*í*n retained always something of its etymological meaning, and was therefore easily and naturally transferred to the cloud, the giver of strength, the source of food. Even without the ná, i. e. as if, the simile would have been understood in Sanskrit, while in English it is hardly intelligible without a commentary. Benfey discovers some additional idea in support of the poet's comparison : ' Ich bin kein Pferdekenner,' he says, ' aber ich glaube bemerkt zu haben, dass man Pferde, welche rasch gelaufen sind, zum Uriniren zu bewegen sucht. So lassen hier die Maruts die durch ihren Sturm rasch fortgetriebenen Wolken Wasser herab strömen.'

Verse 6, note ¹. U″tsa, well, is meant again for cloud, though we should hardly be justified in classing it as a name of cloud, because the original meaning of útsa, spring, is really retained, as much as that of avatá, well, in i. 85, 10—11. The adjectives stanáyantam and ákshitam seem more applicable to cloud, yet they may be applied also to a spring. Yâska derives utsa from ut-sar, to go forth ; ut-sad, to go out ; ut-syand, to well out ; or from ud, to wet. In v. 32, 2, the wells shut up by the seasons are identified with the udder of the cloud.

Verse 7, note ¹. Svátavas means really having their own independent strength, a strength not derived from the support of others. The yet which I have added in brackets seems to have been in the poet's mind, though it is not expressed. In i. 87, 4, the Maruts are called sva-s*rí*t, going by themselves, i. e. moving freely, independently, wherever they list. See i. 64, 4, note ¹.

Verse 7, note ². M*r*igâ*h* hastína*h*, wild animals with a hand or a trunk, must be meant for elephants, although it has been doubted whether the poets of the Veda were

acquainted with that animal. Hastín is the received name
for elephant in the later Sanskrit, and it is hardly applicable to any other animal. If they are said to eat the
forests, this may be understood in the sense of crushing or
chewing, as well as of eating.

Verse 7, note [3]. The chief difficulty of the last sentence
has been pointed out in B. and R.'s Dictionary, s. v. áruñî.
Áruñî does not occur again in the whole of the Rig-veda.
If we take it with Sâyana as a various reading of aruñî, then
the Aruñîs could only be the ruddy cows of the dawn or of
Indra, with whom the Maruts, in this passage, can have no
concern. Nor would it be intelligible why they should be
called áruñî in this one place only. If, as suggested by
B. and R., the original text had been yadá aruñîshu, it
would be difficult to understand how so simple a reading
could have been corrupted.

Another difficulty is the verb áyugdhvam, which is not
found again in the Rig-veda together with távishî. Távishî,
vigour, is construed with dhâ, to take strength, v. 32, 2.
adhatthâh; v. 55, 2. dadhidhve; x. 102, 8. adhatta; also with
vas, iv. 16, 14; with pat, x. 113, 5, &c. But it is not
likely that to put vigour into the cows could be expressed
in Sanskrit by 'you gain vigour in the cows.' If távishî
must be taken in the sense which it seems always to possess,
viz. vigour, it would be least objectionable to translate,
' when you joined vigour, i. e. when you assumed vigour,
while being among the Aruñîs.' The Aruñîs being the cows
of the dawn, áruñîshu might simply mean in the morning.
Considering, however, that the Maruts are said to eat up
forests, áruñî, in this place, is best taken in the sense of
red flames, viz. of fire or forest-fire (dâvâgni), so that the
sense would be, ' When you, Storms, assume vigour among
the flames, you eat up forests, like elephants.'   Benfey :
' Wenn mit den rothen eure Kraft ihr angeschirrt.   Die
rothen sind die Antilopen, das Vehikel der Maruts, wegen
der Schnelligkeit derselben.'

Verse 8, note [1]. As pisá does not occur again in the Rig-
veda, and as Sâyana, without attempting any etymological

arguments, simply gives it as a name of deer, it seems best
to adopt that sense till something better can be discovered.
Supís, too, does not occur again. In vii. 18, 2, pís is explained by gold, &c.; vii. 57, 3, the Maruts are called
visvapís.

Verse 8, note ². Kshápa*h* can only be the accusative
plural, used in a temporal sense. It is so used in the
expression kshápa*h* usrá*h* ka, by night and by day, lit. nights
and days (vii. 15, 8). In vi. 52, 15, we find kshápa*h* usrá*h*
in the same sense. iv. 53, 7. kshapâbhi*h* áha-bhi*h*, by night
and by day. i. 44, 8, the loc. plur. vyúsh*t*ishu, in the
mornings, is followed by kshápa*h*, the acc. plur., by night,
and here the genitive kshapá*h* would certainly be preferable,
in the sense of at the brightening up of the night. The
acc. plur. occurs again in i. 116, 4, where tisrá*h* is used as
an accusative (ii. 2, 2; viii. 41, 3). Kshapá*h*, with the
accent on the last, must be taken as a *genitivus temporalis*,
like the German *Nachts* (i. 79, 6). In viii. 19, 31, kshapá*h*
vástushu means at the brightening up of the night, i. e. in
the morning. Thus, in iii. 50, 4, Indra is called kshapâm
vastâ *g*anitâ sûryasya, the lighter up of nights, the parent
of the sun. In viii. 26, 3, áti kshapá*h*, the genitive may
be governed by áti. In iv. 16, 19, however, the accusative
kshápa*h* would be more natural, nor do I see how a genitive
could here be accounted for :

dyâva*h* ná dyumnaí*h* abhí sáuta*h* aryá*h* kshapá*h* madema
sarâda*h* ka pûrví*h*.

May we rejoice many years, overcoming our enemies as
the days overcome the nights by splendour.

The same applies to i. 70, 4, where kshapá*h* occurs with
the accent on the last syllable, whereas we expect kshápa*h*
as nom. or acc. plural. Here B. and R. in the Sanskrit
Dictionary, s. v. kshap, rightly, I believe, suppose it to be a
nom. plur. in spite of the accent.

Verse 9, note ¹. Ródasî, a dual, though frequently followed by ubhé (i. 10, 8; 33, 9; 54, 2), means heaven and
earth, excluding the antáriksha or the air between the
two. Hence, if this is to be included, it has to be added :

i. 73, 8. âpapri-vấn ródasî antáriksham. Cf. v. 85, 3. We must scan rŏdã̄sî. See Kuhn, Beiträge, vol. iv. p. 193.

Verse 9, note [2]. The comparison is not quite distinct. Amáti means originally impetus, then power, e. g. v. 69, 1: vavridhânâu amátim kshatríyasya.
Increasing the might of the warrior.
But it is most frequently used of the effulgence of the sun, (iii. 38, 8 ; v. 45, 2 ; 62, 5 ; vii. 38, 1; 2 ; 45, 3.) See also v. 56, 8, where the same companion of the Maruts is called Rodasî. The comparative particle ná is used twice.

Verse 10, note [1]. See i. 38, 14, p. 78.

Verse 10, note [2]. In vrísha-khâdi the meaning of khâdi is by no means clear. Sâyana evidently guesses, and proposes two meanings, weapon or food. In several passages where khâdi occurs, it seems to be an ornament rather than a weapon, yet if derived from khad, to bite, it may originally have signified some kind of weapon. Roth translates it by ring, and it is certain that these khâdis were to be seen not only on the arms and shoulders, but likewise on the feet of the Maruts. There is a famous weapon in India, the kakra or quoit, a ring with sharp edges, which is thrown from a great distance with fatal effect. Bollensen (Orient und Occident, vol. ii. p. 46) suggests for vríshan the meaning of hole in the ear, and then translates the compound as having earrings in the hole of the ear. But vríshan does not mean the hole in the lap of the ear, nor has vrishabhá that meaning either in the Veda or elsewhere. Wilson gives for vrishabha, not for vrishan, the meaning of orifice of the ear, but this is very different from the hole in the lap of the ear. Benfey suggests that the khâdis were made of the teeth of wild animals, and hence their name of biters. Vríshan conveys the meaning of strong, though possibly with the implied idea of rain-producing, fertilising. See p. 121.

Verse 11, note [1]. Formerly explained as 'zum Kampfe wandelnd.' See Kuhn, Zeitschrift, vol. iv. p. 19.

Verse 11, note [2]. Wilson : 'Augmenters of rain, they

drive, with golden wheels, the clouds asunder; as elephants
(in a herd, break down the trees in their way). They are
honoured with sacrifices, visitants of the hall of offering,
spontaneous assailers (of their foes), subverters of what
are stable, immovable themselves, and wearers of shining
weapons.'

Benfey : ' Weghemmnissen gleich schleudern die Fluth-
mehrer mit den goldnen Felgen das Gewölk empor, die nie
müden Kämpfer, frei schreitend-festesstürzenden, die schweres
thu'nden, lanzenstrahlenden Maruts.'

Verse 12, note [1]. Havâsâ, instead of what one should
expect, hávasâ, occurs but once more in another Marut
hymn, vi. 66, 11.

Verse 12, note [2]. Vanín does not occur again as an
epithet of the Maruts. It is explained by Sâya?a as a
possessive adjective derived from vana, water, and Benfey
accordingly translates it by fluthversehn. This, however, is
not confirmed by any authoritative passages. Vanín, unless it
means connected with the forest, a tree, in which sense it occurs frequently, is only applied to the worshippers or priests in
the sense of venerating or adoring (cf. venero, venustus, &c.):

iii. 40, 7. abhí dyumnâni vanína? índram sa?ante ákshitâ.

The inexhaustible treasures of the worshipper go towards
Indra.

viii. 3, 5. índram vanína? havâmahe.

We, the worshippers, call Indra.

Unless it can be proved by independent evidence that
vanín means possessed of water, we must restrict vanín to
its two meanings, of which the only one here applicable,
though weak, is adoring. The Maruts are frequently represented as singers and priests, yet the epithets here applied to
them stand much in need of some definite explanation, as
the poet could hardly have meant to string a number of
vague and ill-connected epithets together. If one might
conjecture, svânínam instead of vanínam would be an im-
provement. It is a scarce word, and occurs but once more
in the Veda, iii. 26, 5, where it is used of the Maruts, in
the sense of noisy, turbulent.

Verse 12, note [3]. Sa*k*ata, which I have here translated literally by to cling, is often used in the sense of following or revering (*colere*) :

ii. 1, 13. tvâm râti-sâ*k*a*h* adhvaréshu sa*k*ire.

The gods who are fond of offerings cling to thee, follow thee, at the sacrifices.

The Soma libation is said to reach the god :

ii. 22, 1. sâ*h* enam sa*s*kat devâ*h* devám. The gods too are said to cling to their worshippers, i. e. to love and protect them : iii. 16, 2 ; vii. 18, 25. The horses are said to follow their drivers: vi. 36, 3 ; vii. 90, 3, &c. It is used very much like the Greek ὀπάζω.

Verse 12, note [4]. Ra*g*astû*h* may mean rousing the dust of the earth, a very appropriate epithet of the Maruts. Sâya*n*a explains it thus, and most translators have adopted his explanation. But as the epithets here are not simply descriptive, but laudatory, it seems preferable, in this place, to retain the usual meaning of rá*g*as, sky. When Soma is called ra*g*astû*h*, ix. 108, 7, Sâya*n*a too explains it by te*g*asâm prerakam, and ix. 48, 4, by udakasya prerakam.

Verse 12, note [5]. *R*i*g*îshín, derived from *r*i*g*îsha. *R*i*g*îsha is what remains of the Soma-plant after it has once been squeezed, and what is used again for the third libation. Now as the Maruts are invoked at the third libation, they were called *r*i*g*îshín, as drinking at their later libation the juice made of the *r*i*g*îsha. This, at least, is the opinion of the Indian commentators. But it is much more likely that the Maruts were invoked at the third libation, because originally they had been called *r*i*g*îshín by the Vedic poets, this *r*i*g*îshín being derived from *r*i*g*îsha, and *r*i*g*îsha from *r*i*g*, to strive, to yearn, like purîsha from pr*î*, manîshâ from man ; (see U*n*âdi-sûtras, p. 273.) This *r*i*g* is the same root which we have in ὀρέγειν, to reach, ὀργή, emotion, and ὄργια, furious transports of worshippers. Thus the Maruts from being called *r*i*g*îshín, impetuous, came to be taken for drinkers of *r*i*g*îsha, the fermenting and overflowing Soma, and were assigned accordingly to the third libation at sacrifices. *R*i*g*îshín, as an epithet, is not confined to the Maruts ; it is given to Indra, with whom it could not have had a purely ceremonial meaning (viii. 76, 5).

Verse 13, note [1]. Âprikkhya, literally to be asked for, to be inquired for, to be greeted and honoured. A word of an apparently modern character, but occurring again in the Rig-veda as applied to a prince, and to the vessel containing the Soma.

Verse 13, note [2]. Púshyati might be joined with krátu and taken in a transitive sense, he increases his strength. But púshyati is also used as an intransitive, and means he prospers :

i. 83, 3. ásam-yatah vraté te ksheti púshyati.

Without let he dwells in thy service and prospers.

Roth reads asamyattah, against the authority of the MSS.

Verse 14, note [1]. The difficulty of this verse arises from the uncertainty whether the epithets dhanaspritam, ukthyâm, and visvákarshanim belong to súshma, strength, or to toká, kith and kin. Roth and Benfey connect them with toká. Now dhanasprít is applicable to toká, yet it never occurs joined with toká again, while it is used with súshma, vi. 19, 8. Ukthyâ, literally to be praised with hymns, is not used again as an epithet of toká, though it is quite appropriate to any gift of the gods. Lastly, visvákarshani is never applied to toká, while it is an epithet used, if not exactly of the strength, súshma, given by the gods, yet of the fame given by them :

x. 93, 10. dhâtam víreshu visvá-karshani srávah.

Give to these men world-wide glory. Cf. iii. 2, 15.

The next difficulty is the exact meaning of visvá-karshani, and such cognate words as visvá-krishti, visvá-manusha. The only intelligible meaning I can suggest for these words is, known to all men ; originally, belonging to, reaching to all men ; as we say, world-wide or European fame, meaning by it fame extending over the whole of Europe, or over the whole world. If Indra, Agni, and the Maruts are called by these names, they mean, as far as I can judge, known, worshipped by all men. Benfey translates allverständig.

Verse 15, note [1]. *R*iti, the first element of *r*iti-sáham, never occurs by itself in the Rig-veda. It comes from the root ar, to hurt, which was mentioned before (p. 54) in connection with ár-van, hurting, árus, wound, and ári, enemy. Sám-*r*iti occurs i. 32, 6. *R*iti therefore means hurting, and *r*iti-sáh means one who can stand an attack. In our passage rayím vîrá-vantam *r*iti-sáham means really wealth consisting in men who are able to withstand all onslaughts.

The word is used in a similar sense, vi. 14, 4:

agní*h* apsám *r*iti-sáham vîrám dadáti sát-patim, yásya trásanti *s*ávasa*h* sam-*k*ákshi *s*átrava*h* bhiyá.

Agni gives a strong son who is able to withstand all onslaughts, from fear of whose strength the enemies tremble when they see him.

In other passages *r*iti-sáh is applied to Indra:

viii. 45, 35. bibháya hí tvá-vata*h* ugrát abhi-prabhaṅgína*h* dasmát ahám *r*iti-sáha*h*.

For I stand in fear of a powerful man like thee, of one who crushes his enemies, who is strong and withstands all onslaughts.

viii. 68, 1. tuvi-kûrmím *r*iti-sáham índra *s*ávish*th*a sát-pate.

Thee, O most powerful Indra, of mighty strength, able to withstand all onslaughts.

viii. 88, 1. tám va*h* dasmám *r*iti-sáham—índram gî*h*-bhí*h* navámahe.

We call Indra the strong, the resisting, with our songs.

Verse 15, note [2]. The last sentence finishes six of the hymns ascribed to Nodhas. It is more appropriate in a hymn addressed to single deities, such as Agni or Indra, than in a hymn to the Maruts. We must supply *s*ardha, in order to get a collective word in the masculine singular.

Nú, as usual, should be scanned n̆ū́.

Verse 15, note [3]. Dhiyá-vasu, as an epithet of the gods, means rich in prayers, i. e. invoked by many worshippers. It does not occur frequently. Besides the hymns of Nodhas, it only occurs independently in i. 3, 10 (Sarasvatî), iii. 3, 2, iii. 28, 1 (Agni), these hymns being all ascribed to the family of Visvâmitra. In the last verse, which forms the burden of the hymns of Nodhas, it may have been intended to mean, he who is rich through the hymn just recited, he who rejoices in the hymn, the god to whom it is addressed.

Nodhas, the poet, belongs, according to the Anukramaṇî, to the family of Gotama, and in the hymns which are ascribed to him, i. 58–64, the Gotamas are mentioned several times :

i. 60, 5. tám tvâ vayám pátim agne rayîṇâm prá saṃsâmah matí-bhih gótamâsah.

We, the Gotamas, praise thee with hymns, Agni, the lord of treasures.

i. 61, 16. evá te hari-yogana su-vriktí índra bráhmâṇi gótamâsah akran.

Truly the Gotamas made holy prayers for thee, O Indra with brilliant horses ! See also i. 63, 9.

In one passage Nodhas himself is called Gotama :

i. 62, 13. sanâ-yaté gótamah indra návyam
átakshat bráhma hari-yóganâya,
su-nîthâya nah savasâna nodhâh—
prâtáh makshú dhiyâ-vasuh gagamyât.

Gotama made a new song for the old (god) with brilliant horses, O Indra ! May Nodhas be a good leader to us, O powerful Indra ! May he who is rich in prayers (Indra) come early and soon !

I feel justified therefore in following the Anukramaṇî and taking Nodhas as a proper name. It occurs so again in

i. 61, 14. sadyáh bhuvat vîryâya nodhâh.

May Nodhas quickly attain to power !

In i. 124, 4, nodhâh-iva may mean like Nodhas, but more likely it may have the more general meaning of poet.

MANDALA I, SÛKTA 85.
ASHTAKA I, ADHYÂYA 6, VARGA 9-10.

1. Prá yé súmbhante ganayah ná sáptayah yâman rudrásya sûnávah su-dámsasah, ródasî (íti) hí marútah kakriré vridhé mádanti vîrấh vidátheshu ghríshvayah.

2. Té ukshitấsah mahimấnam âsata diví rudrấsah ádhi kakriré sádah, árkantah arkám ganáyantah indriyám ádhi sríyah dadhire prísni-mâtarah.

3. Gó-mâtarah yát subháyante angí-bhih tanấshu subhrấh dadhire virúkmatah, vấdhante vísvam abhi-mâtínam ápa vártmâni eshâm ánu ríyate ghritám.

4. Ví yé bhrẵgante sú-makhâsah rishtí-bhih pra-kyaváyantah ákyutâ kit ógasâ, manah-gúvah yát marutah rátheshu ấ vrísha-vrâtâsah príshatîh áyug-dhvam.

5. Prá yát rátheshu príshatîh áyugdhvam vấge ádrim marutah ramháyantah utá arushásya ví syanti dhấrấh kárma-iva udá-bhih ví undanti bhúma.

6. Ấ vah vahantu sáptayah raghu-syádah raghu-pátvânah prá gigâta bâhú-bhih, sídata ấ barhíh urú vah sádah kritám mádáyadhvam marutah mádhvah ándhasah.

7. Té avardhanta svá-tavasah mahi-tvanấ ấ nấkam

1. Those who glance forth like wives and yoke-fellows,[1] they are the powerful sons of Rudra on their way. The Maruts have made heaven and earth to grow,[2] they, the strong and wild, delight in the sacrifices.

2. When grown up,[1] they attained to greatness; the Rudras have established their abode in the sky. While singing their song and increasing their vigour, the sons of Prisni have clothed themselves in beauty.[2]

3. When these sons of the cow (Prisni)[1] adorn themselves with glittering ornaments, the brilliant[2] ones put bright weapons on their bodies.[3] They hurl away every adversary;[4] fatness (rain) runs along their paths;—

4. When you,[1] the powerful, who glitter with your spears, shaking even what is unshakable by strength; when you, O Maruts, the manly hosts,[2] had yoked the spotted deer, swift as thought, to your chariots;—

5. When you had yoked the spotted deer before your chariots, stirring[1] the cloud to the battle, then the streams of the red enemy[2] rush forth: like a skin[3] with water they water the earth.

6. May the swift-gliding, swift-winged horses carry you hither! Come forth with your arms![1] Sit down on the grass-pile; a wide place has been made for you. Rejoice, O Maruts, in the sweet food.[2]

7. They who have their own strength, grew[1] with

tasthú*h* urú *k*akrire sáda*h*, vísh*n*u*h* yát ha ấvat
vrísha*n*am mada-*k*yútam váya*h* ná sîdan ádhi barhíshi priyé.

8. Sấrâ*h*-iva ít yúyudhaya*h* ná *g*ấgmaya*h* srava-
syáva*h* ná prítanâsu yetire, bháyante vísvâ bhúvanâ
marút-bhya*h* rấ*g*âua*h*-iva tveshá-sand*r*isa*h* nára*h*.

9. Tvásh*t*â yát vấ*g*ram sú-k*r*itam hira*n*yáyam
sahásra-bh*r*ishtím su-ápâ*h* ấvartayat, dhatté índra*h*
nári ápâmsi kártave ấhan v*r*itrám ní*h* apấm aub*g*at
ar*n*avám.

10. Ûrdhvám nunudre ấvatám té ó*g*asâ dad*r*i-
hâ*n*ám *k*it bibhidu*h* ví párvatam, dhámanta*h* vâ-
*n*ám marúta*h* su-dấnava*h* máde sómasya rá*n*yâni
*k*ak*r*ire.

11. *G*ihmám nunudre avatám táyâ disấ ásiñ*k*an
útsam gótamâya t*r*ish*n*á-*g*e, ấ ga*kk*hanti îm ávasâ
*k*itrá-bhânava*h* kấmam víprasya tarpayanta dhấma-
bhi*h*.

12. Yấ va*h* sárma sasamânấya sánti tri-dhấtûni
dâsúshe ya*kk*hata ádhi, asmábhyam tấni marúta*h* ví
yanta rayím na*h* dhatta v*r*isha*n*a*h* su-vîram.

COMMENTARY.

This hymn is ascribed to Gotama. The metre is *G*agatî,
except in verses 5 and 12, which are Trish*t*ubh.

Verse 1, note [1]. The phrase *g*ánaya*h* ná sáptaya*h* is
obscure. As *g*áni has always the meaning of wife, and
sápti in the singular, dual, and plural means horse, it might

might; they stepped to the firmament, they made their place wide. When Vishnu[2] descried the enrapturing Soma, the Maruts sat down like birds on their beloved altar.

8. Like heroes indeed thirsting for fight they rush about; like combatants eager for glory they have struggled in battles. All beings are afraid of the Maruts; they are men awful to behold, like kings.

9. When the clever Tvashtar[1] had turned the well-made, golden, thousand-edged thunderbolt, Indra took it to perform his manly deeds;[2] he slew Vritra, he forced out the stream of water.

10. By their power they pushed the well[1] aloft, they clove asunder the cloud, however strong. Sending forth their voice[2] the beneficent Maruts performed, while drunk of Soma, their glorious deeds.

11. They drove the cloud athwart this way, they poured out the well to the thirsty Gotama. The bright-shining Maruts approach him with help, they with their clans fulfilled the desire of the sage.

12. The shelters which you have for him who praises you, grant them threefold to the man who gives! Extend the same to us, O Maruts! Give us, ye heroes,[1] wealth with excellent offspring!

---

be supposed that *gánayah* could be connected with sáptayah, so as to signify mares. But although *gáni* is coupled with patnî, i. 62, 10, in the sense of mother-wife, and though sápti is most commonly joined with some other name for horse, yet *gánayah* sáptayah never occurs, for the simple reason that it would be too elaborate and almost absurd an expression for vadavâh. We find sápti joined with vágín,

i. 162, 1; with ráthya, ii. 31, 7; átyam ná sáptim, iii.
22, 1; sáptî hárî, iii. 35, 2; ásvâ sáptî-iva, vi. 59, 3.

We might then suppose the thought of the poet to have
been this: What appears before us like race-horses, viz. the
storms coursing through the sky, that is really the host of
the Maruts. But then gánayah remains unexplained, and
it is impossible to take gánayah ná sáptayah as two similes,
like unto horses, like unto wives.

I believe, therefore, that we must here take sápti in its
original etymological sense, which would be *ju-mentum*, a
yoked animal, a beast of draught, or rather a follower, a
horse that will follow. Sápti, therefore, could never be
a wild horse, but always a tamed horse, a horse that will
go in harness. Cf. ix. 21, 4. hitáh ná sáptayah ráthe, like
horses put to the chariot; or in the singular, ix. 70, 10.
hitáh ná sáptih, like a harnessed horse. The root is sap,
which in the Veda means to follow, to attend on, to
worship. But if sápti means originally animals that will
go together, it may in our passage have retained the sense
of yoke-fellow (σύζυγος), and be intended as an adjective
to gánayah, wives. There is at least one other passage
where this meaning would seem to be more appropriate,
viz.

viii. 20, 23. yûyám sakhâyah saptayah.

You (Maruts), friends and followers! or you, friends and
comrades!

Here it is hardly possible to assign to sápti the sense of
horse, for the Maruts, though likened to horses, are never
thus barely invoked as saptayah!

If then we translate, 'Those who glance forth like wives
and yoke-fellows,' i. e. like wives of the same husband, the
question still recurs how the simile holds good, and how
the Maruts rushing forth together in all their beauty can be
compared to wives. In answer to this we have to bear in
mind that the idea of many wives belonging to one husband
(sapatnî) is familiar to the Vedic poet, and that their
impetuously rushing into the arms of their husbands, and
appearing before them in all their beauty, are frequent
images in their poetry. Whether in the phrase pátim ná
gánayah or gánayah ná gárbham, the ganis, the wives or

mothers, are represented as running together after their husbands or children. This impetuous approach the poet may have wished to allude to in our passage also, but though it ' might have been understood at once by his hearers, it is almost impossible to convey this implied idea in any other language.

Wilson translates: ' The Maruts, who are going forth, decorate themselves like females: they are gliders (through the air), the sons of Rudra, and the doers of good works, by which they promote the welfare of earth and heaven. Heroes, who grind (the solid rocks), they delight in sacrifices.'

Verse 1, note [2]. The meaning of this phrase, which occurs very frequently, was originally that the storms by driving away the dark clouds, made the earth and the sky to appear larger and wider. It afterwards takes a more general sense of increasing, strengthening, blessing.

Verse 2, note [1]. Ukshitá is here a participle of vaksh or uksh, to grow, to wax; not from uksh, to sprinkle, to anoint, to inaugurate, as explained by Sâyana. Thus it is said of the Maruts, v. 55, 3. sâkám yâtâh—sâkám ukshitâh, born together, and grown up together.

Verse 2, note [2]. The same expression occurs viii. 28, 5. saptó (íti) ádhi sríyah dhire. See also i. 116, 17; ix. 68, 1.

Verse 3, note [1]. Gó-mâtri, like gó-yâta, a name of the Maruts.

Verse 3, note [2]. Subhrá applied to the Maruts, i. 19, 5.

Verse 3, note [3]. Virúkmatah must be an accusative plural. It occurs i. 127, 3, as an epithet of ójas; vi. 49, 5, as an epithet of the chariot of the Asvins. In our place, however, it must be taken as a substantive, signifying something which the Maruts wear, probably armour or weapons. This follows chiefly from x. 138, 4. sátrun asrinât virúkmatâ, Indra tore his enemies with the bright weapon.

In viii. 20, 11, where rukmá occurs as a masculine plural, ví bhrá*g*ante rukmã́sa*h* ádhi bâhúshu, their bright things shine on their arms, it seems likewise to be meant for weapons; according to Sâya*n*a, for chains. In v. 55, 3; x. 78, 3, the Maruts are called vi-rokína*h*, bright like the rays of the sun or the tongues of fire.

Verse 3, note [4]. Observe the short syllable in the tenth syllable of this Pâda.

Verse 4, note [1]. The sudden transition from the third to the second person is not unusual in the Vedic hymns, the fact being that where we in a relative sentence should use the same person as that of the principal verb, the Vedic poets frequently use the third.

Verse 4, note [2]. Vrísha-vrâta is untranslatable for reasons stated p. 121 seq.; it means consisting of companies of vrí-shan's in whatever sense that word be taken. Wilson in his translation mistakes á*k*yutâ for á*k*yutâ*h*, and vrâta for vrata. He translates the former by 'incapable of being overthrown,' the latter by 'entrusted with the duty of sending rain,' both against the authority of Sâya*n*a. Vrísha-vrâta occurs twice in the Rig-veda as an epithet of Soma only, ix. 62, 11; 64, 1.

Verse 5, note [1]. Ra*m*h, to stir up, to urge, to make go:
v. 32, 2. tvám útsân ritú-bhi*h* badbadhânã́n ára*m*ha*h*.
Thou madest the springs to run that had been shut up by the seasons.
viii. 19, 6. tásya ít árvanta*h* ra*m*hayante âsáva*h*.
His horses only run quick.
Ádri, which I here preferred to translate by cloud, means originally stone, and it is used in adriva*h*, wielder of the thunderbolt, a common vocative addressed to Indra, in the sense of a stone-weapon, or the thunderbolt. If we could ascribe to it the same meaning here, we might translate, 'hurling the stone in battle.' This is the meaning adopted by Benfey.

Verse 5, note [2]. The red enemy is the dark red cloud, but arushá has almost become a proper name, and its original meaning of redness is forgotten. Nay, it is possible that arushá, as applied to the same power of darkness which is best known by the names of Vritra, Dasyu, etc., may never have had the sense of redness, but been formed straight from ar, to hurt, from which arvan, arus, etc., (see p. 54.) It would then mean simply the hurter, the enemy, (see p. 17.)

Verse 5, note [3]. Sâyana explains : 'They moisten the whole earth like a hide,' a hide representing a small surface which is watered without great effort. Wilson : 'They moisten the earth, like a hide, with water.' Langlois : 'Alors les gouttes d'eau, perçant comme la peau de ce (nuage) bienfaisant viennent inonder la terre.' Benfey : 'Dann stürzen reichlich aus der rothen (Gewitterwolke) Tropfen, mit Fluth wie eine Haut die Erde netzend. (Dass die Erde so durchnässt wird, wie durchregnetes Leder.)' If the poet had intended to compare the earth, before it is moistened by rain, to a hide, he might have had in his mind the dryness of a tanned skin, or, as Professor Benfey says, of leather. If, on the contrary, the simile refers to the streams of water, then kárma-iva, like a skin, might either be taken in the technical acceptation of the skin through which, at the preparation of the Soma, the streams (dhârâh) of that beverage are squeezed and distilled, or we may take the word in the more general sense of water-skin. In that case the comparison, though not very pointedly expressed, as it would have been by later Sanskrit poets, would still be complete. The streams of the red enemy, i. e. of the cloud, rush forth, and they, whether the streams liberated by the Maruts, or the Maruts themselves, moisten the earth with water, like a skin, i. e. like a skin in which water is kept and from which it is poured out. The cloud itself being called a skin by Vedic poets (i. 129, 3) makes the comparison still more natural.

One other explanation might suggest itself, if the singular of kárma should be considered objectionable on account of the plural of the verb. Vedic poets speak of the skin of the earth. Thus :

x. 68, 4. bhûmyâh udnâ-iva ví tvákam bibheda.

He (Brihaspati) having driven the cows from the cave, cut the skin of the earth, as it were, with water, i. e. saturated it with rain.

The construction, however, if we took *kárma* in the sense of surface, would be very irregular, and we should have to translate : They moisten the earth with water like a skin, i. e. skin-deep.

We ought to scan *kármevodabhih vi undanti bhúma*, for *kármeva udabhih vyundánti bhúma* would give an unusual cæsura.

Verse 6, note [1]. With your arms, i. e. according to Sâyana, with armfuls of gifts. Though this expression does not occur again so baldly, we read i. 166, 10, of the Maruts, that there are many gifts in their strong arms, *bhúrîni bhadrá náryeshu báhúshu*; nor does *báhú*, as used in the plural, as far as I am able to judge, ever convey any meaning but that of arms. The idea that the Maruts are carried along by their arms as by wings, does not rest on Vedic authority, otherwise we might join *raghupátvánah* with *báhúbhih*, come forth swiftly flying on your arms! As it is, and with the accent on the antepenultimate, we must refer *raghupátvánah* to *sáptayah*, horses.

Verse 6, note [2]. The sweet food is Soma.

Verse 7, note [1]. The initial 'a' of *avardhanta* must be elided, or 'té a' be pronounced as two short syllables equal to one long.

Verse 7, note [2]. Vishnu, whose character in the hymns of the Veda is very different from that assumed by him in later periods of Hindu religion, must here be taken as the friend and companion of Indra. Like the Maruts, he assisted Indra in his battle against Vritra and the conquest of the clouds. When Indra was forsaken by all the gods, Vishnu came to his help.

iv. 18, 11. utá mátá mahishám ánu avenat amí (íti) tvâ *ga*hati putra devá*h*,

átha abravît vritrám índra*h* hanishyán sákhe vishno (íti) vi-tarám ví kramasva.

The mother also called after the bull, these gods forsake thee, O son; then, when going to kill Vritra, Indra said, Friend, Vishnu, step forward!

This stepping of Vishnu is emblematic of the rising, the culminating, and setting of the sun; and in viii. 12, 27, Vishnu is said to perform it through the power of Indra. In vi. 20, 2, Indra is said to have killed Vritra, assisted by Vishnu (víshnunâ sakânâh). Vishnu is therefore invoked together with Indra, vi. 69, 8; vii. 99; with the Maruts, v. 87; vii. 36, 9. In vii. 93, 8, Indra, Vishnu, and the Maruts are called upon together. Nay, mâruta, belonging to the Maruts, becomes actually an epithet of Vishnu, v. 46, 2. mâruta utá vishno (íti); and in i. 156, 4, mârutasya vedhásah has been pointed out by Roth as an appellation of Vishnu. The mention of Vishnu in our hymn is therefore by no means exceptional, but the whole purport of this verse is nevertheless very doubtful, chiefly owing to the fact that several of the words occurring in it lend themselves to different interpretations.

The translations of Wilson, Benfey, and others have not rendered the sense which the poet intends to describe at all clear. Wilson says: ' May they for whom Vishnu defends (the sacrifice), that bestows all desires and confers delight, come (quickly) like birds, and sit down upon the pleasant and sacred grass.' Benfey: ' Wenn Vishnu schützt den rauschtriefenden tropfenden (Soma), sitzen wie Vögel sie auf der geliebten Streu.' Langlois: ' Quand Vichnou vient prendre sa part de nos enivrantes libations, eux, comme des oiseaux, arrivent aussi sur le cousa qui leur est cher.'

Whence all these varieties? First, because ấvat may mean, he defended or protected, but likewise he descried, became aware. Secondly, because vríshan is one of the most vague and hence most difficult words in the Veda, and may mean Indra, Soma, or the cloud: (see the note on Vríshan, p. 121.) Thirdly, because the adjective belonging to vríshan, which generally helps us to determine which vríshan is meant, is here itself of doubtful import, and certainly applicable to Indra as well as to Soma and the Asvins, possibly even to the cloud. Mada-kyút. is readily explained by the commentators as bringing down pride, a meaning which the word might well have in modern Sanskrit, but which it clearly has not in the Veda. Even where the thunderbolt of Indra is called madakyút, and where the meaning of 'bringing down pride' would seem most appropriate, we ought to translate 'wildly rushing down.'

viii. 96, 5. ấ yát vágram bâhvóh indra dhátse mada-kyútam áhaye hántavaí úm (íti).

When thou tookest the wildly rushing thunderbolt in thy arms in order to slay Ahi.

When applied to the gods, the meaning of madakyút is by no means certain. It might mean rushing about fiercely, reeling with delight, this delight being produced by the Soma, but it may also mean sending down delight, i. e. rain or Soma. The root kyu is particularly applicable to the sending down of rain; cf. Taitt. Sanh. ii. 4, 9, 2; 10, 3; iii. 3, 4, 1; and Indra and his horses, to whom this epithet is chiefly applied, are frequently asked to send down rain. However, madakyút is also applied to real horses (i. 126, 4) where givers of rain would be an inappropriate epithet. I should therefore translate madakyút, when applied to Indra, to his horses, to the Asvins, or to horses in general by furiously or wildly moving about, as if 'made kyavate,' he moves in a state of delight, or in a state of intoxication such as was not incompatible with the character of the ancient gods. Here again the difficulty of rendering Vedic thought in English, or any other modern language, becomes apparent, for we have no poetical word to express a high state of mental excitement produced by drinking the intoxicating juice of the Soma or other plants, which has not something opprobrious mixed up with it, while in ancient times that state of excitement was celebrated as a blessing of the gods, as not unworthy of the gods them-selves, nay, as a state in which both the warrior and the poet would perform their highest achievements. The German *Rausch* is the nearest approach to the Sanskrit mada.

viii. 1, 21. vísveshâm tarutâram mada-kyútam máde hí sma dádáti nah.

Indra, the conqueror of all, who rushes about in

rapture, for in rapture he bestows gifts upon us. Cf.
i. 51, 2.

The horses of Indra are called mada*k*yút, i. 81, 3; viii. 33,
18; 34, 9. Ordinary horses, i. 126, 4.

It is more surprising to see this epithet applied to the
A*s*vins, who are generally represented as moving about with
exemplary steadiness. However we read:

viii. 22, 16. mána*h*-*g*avasâ v*r*isha*n*â mada-*k*yutâ.

Ye two A*s*vins, quick as thought, powerful, wildly
moving; or, as Sâya*n*a proposes, liberal givers, humblers
of your enemies. See also viii. 35, 19.

Most frequently mada*k*yút is applied to Soma, x. 30, 9;
ix. 32, 1; 53, 4; 79, 2; 108, 11; where particularly the last
passage deserves attention, in which Soma is called mada-
*k*yútam sahásra-dhâram v*r*ishabhám.

Lastly, even the wealth itself which the Maruts are asked
to send down from heaven, most likely rain, is called, viii.
7, 13, rayím mada-*k*yútam puru-kshúm vi*s*vá-dhâyasam.

In all these passages we must translate mada-*k*yút by
bringing delight, showering down delight.

We have thus arrived at the conclusion that v*r*ísha*n*am
mada-*k*yútam, as used in our passage i. 85, 7, might be
meant either for Indra or for Soma. If the A*s*vins can be
called v*r*isha*n*au mada-*k*yútâ, the same expression would
be even more applicable to Indra. On the other hand,
if Soma is called v*r*ishabhá*h* mada-*k*yút, the same Soma
may legitimately be called v*r*íshâ mada-*k*yút. In deciding
whether Indra or Soma be meant, we must now have
recourse to other hymns, in which the relations of the
Maruts with Vish*n*u, Soma, and Indra are alluded to.

If Indra were intended, and if the first words meant
'When Vish*n*u perceived the approach of Indra,' we should
expect, not that the Maruts sat down on the sacrificial
pile, but that they rushed to the battle. The idea that
the Maruts come to the sacrifice, like birds, is common
enough :

viii. 20, 10. v*r*isha*n*a*s*véna maruta*h* v*r*ísha-psunâ ráthena
v*r*ísha-nâbhinâ, â *s*yenâsa*h* ná pakshí*n*a*h* v*r*íthâ nara*h* havyâ
na*h* vîtáye gata.

Come ye Maruts together, to eat our offerings, on your

strong-horsed, strong-shaped, strong-naved chariot, like
winged hawks!

But when the Maruts thus come to a sacrifice it is to
participate in it, and particularly in the Soma that is
offered by the sacrificer. This Soma, it is said in other
hymns, was prepared by Vish*n*u for Indra (ii. 22, 1), and
Vish*n*u is said to have brought the Soma for Indra (x.
113, 2). If we keep these and similar passages in mind,
and consider that in the preceding verse the Maruts have
been invited to sit down on the sacrificial pile and to rejoice
in the sweet food, we shall see that the same train of
thought is carried on in our verse, the only new idea being
that the keeping or descrying of the Soma is ascribed to
Vish*n*u.

Verse 9, note [1]. Tvásh*t*ar, the workman of the gods,
frequently also the fashioner and creator.

Verse 9, note [2]. Nári, the loc. sing. of n*r*i, but, if so,
with a wrong accent, occurs only in this phrase as used
here, and as repeated in viii. 96, 19. nári ápâ*m*si kártâ sá*h*
v*r*itra-há. Its meaning is not clear. It can hardly mean
' on man,' without some more definite application. If n*r*i
could be used as a name of V*r*itra or any other enemy,
it would mean, to do his deeds against the man, on the
enemy. N*r*i, however, is ordinarily an honorific term,
chiefly applied to Indra, iv. 25, 4. náre náryâya n*r*í-tamâya
n*r*i*n*ám, and hence its application to V*r*itra would be
objectionable. Sâya*n*a explains it in the sense of battle. I
believe that nári stands for náryâ, the acc. plur. neut. of nárya,
manly, and the frequent epithet of ápas, and I have translated accordingly. Indra is called nárya-apas, viii. 93, 1.

Verse 10, note [1]. Avatá, a well, here meant for cloud,
like útsa, i. 64, 6.

Verse 10, note [2]. Dhámanta*h* vâ*n*ám is translated by
Sâya*n*a as playing on the lyre, by Benfey as blowing the
flute. Such a rendering, particularly the latter, would
be very appropriate, but there is no authority for vâná
meaning either lyre or flute in the Veda. Vâ*n*á occurs

five times only.   In one passage, viii. 20, 8, góbhi*h* vâ*n*â*h*
a*gy*ate, it means arrow; the arrow is sent forth from the
bow-strings.   The same meaning seems applicable to ix.
50, 1. vâ*n*âsya *k*odaya pavím.   In another passage, ix. 97, 8,
prá vadanti vâ*n*ám, they send forth their voice, is applied
to the Maruts, as in our passage; in iv. 24, 9, the sense
is doubtful, but here too vâ*n*â clearly does not mean a
musical instrument.   See iii. 30, 10.

Vríshan.

Verse 12, note [1].   In vríshan we have one of those words
which it is almost impossible to translate accurately.   It
occurs over and over again in the Vedic hymns, and if we
once know the various ideas which it either expresses or
implies, we have little difficulty in understanding its import
in a vague and general way, though we look in vain for
corresponding terms in any modern language.   In the
Veda, and in ancient languages generally, one and the
same word is frequently made to do service for many.
Words retain their general meaning, though at the same
time they are evidently used with a definite purpose.   This
is not only a peculiar phase of language, but a peculiar
phase of thought, and as to us this phase has become
strange and unreal, it is very difficult to transport ourselves
back into it, still more to translate the pregnant terms of
the Vedic poets into the definite languages which we have
to use.   Let us imagine a state of thought and speech in
which *virtus* still meant manliness, though it might also be
applied to the virtue of a woman; or let us try to speak
and think a language which expressed the bright and the
divine, the brilliant and the beautiful, the straight and the
right, the bull and the hero, the shepherd and the king by
the same terms, and we shall see how difficult it would be to
translate such terms without losing either the key-note that
was still sounding, or the harmonics which were set vibrating
by it in the minds of the poets and their listeners.

Vríshan, being derived from a root vrish, *spargere*,
meant no doubt originally the male, whether applied to
animals or men.   In this sense vríshan occurs frequently

in the Veda, either as determining the sex of the animal
which is mentioned, or as standing by itself and meaning
the male. In either case, however, it implies the idea of
strength and eminence, which we lose whether we translate
it by man or male.

Thus ásva is horse, but vii. 69, 1, we read:

á vâm rátha*h*—vrisha-bhi*h* yâtu ásvai*h*.

May your chariot come near with powerful horses, i. e.
with stallions.

The Háris, the horses of Indra, are frequently called
vrishan*â* :

i. 177, 1. yuktvâ hárî (íti) vrishan*â*.

Having yoked the bay stallions.

Vrishabhá, though itself originally meaning the male
animal, had become fixed as the name of the bull, and in
this process it had lost so much of its etymological import
that the Vedic poet did not hesitate to define vrishabhá itself
by the addition of vríshan.   Thus we find:

viii. 93, 7. sá*h* vríshâ vrishabhá*h* bhuvat.

May he (Indra) be a strong bull.

i. 54, 2. vríshâ vrisha-tvâ vrishabhá*h*.

Indra by his strength a strong bull ; but, literally, Indra
by his manliness a male bull.

Even vrishabhá loses again its definite meaning ; and as
bull in bull-calf means simply male, or in bull-trout, large,
so vrishabhá is added to átya, horse, to convey the meaning of large or powerful :

i. 177, 2. yé te vríshan*ah* vrishabhâsa*h* indra—átyâ*h*.

Thy strong and powerful horses ; literally, thy male bull-
horses.

When vríshan and vrishabhá are used as adjectives,
for instance with súshma, strength, they hardly differ in
meaning :

vi. 19, 8. á na*h* bhara vríshan*am* súshmam indra.

Bring us thy manly strength, O Indra.

And in the next verse :

vi. 19, 9. á te súshma*h* vrishabhá*h* etu.

May thy manly strength come near.

Vám*s*aga, too, which is clearly the name for bull, is
defined by vríshan, i. 7, 8 :

vrísha yûthấ-iva vám̐sagaḥ.

As the strong bull scares the herds.

The same applies to varâha, which, though by itself meaning boar, is determined again by vríshan :

x. 67, 7. vrísha-bhiḥ varâhaiḥ.

With strong boars.

In iii. 2, 11, we read :

vríshâ—nânadat nấ simḥấḥ.

Like a roaring lion.

If used by itself, vríshan, at least in the Rig-veda, can hardly be said to be the name of any special animal, though in later Sanskrit it may mean bull or horse. Thus if we read, x. 43, 8, vríshâ nấ kruddháḥ, we can only translate like an angry male, though, no doubt, like a wild bull, would seem more appropriate.

i. 186, 5. yéna nápâtam apâm ǵunâ̐ma manaḥ-ǵúvaḥ vríshaṇaḥ yấm váhanti.

That we may excite the son of the water (Agni), whom the males, quick as thought, carry along.

Here the males are no doubt the horses or stallions of Agni. But, though this follows from the context, it would be wrong to say that vríshan by itself means horse.

If used by itself, vríshan most frequently means man, and chiefly in his sexual character. Thus :

i. 140, 6. vríshâ-iva pátniḥ abhí eti róruvat.

Agni comes roaring like a husband to his wives.

i. 179, 1. ápi ûm (íti) nú pátniḥ vríshaṇaḥ ǵagamyuḥ.

Will the husbands now come to their wives?

ii. 16, 8. sakrít sú te sumatí-bhiḥ—sám pátnîbhiḥ nấ vríshaṇaḥ nasîmahi.

May we for once cling firmly to thy blessings, as husbands cling to their wives.

v. 47, 6. upa-prakshé vríshaṇaḥ módamânâḥ diváḥ pathâ vadhvâḥ yanti ákkha.

The exulting men come for the embrace on the path of heaven towards their wives.

In one or two passages vríshan would seem to have a still more definite meaning, particularly in the formula sŭraḥ drísîke vríshaṇaḥ ka paúm̐sye, which occurs iv. 41, 6; x. 92, 7. See also i. 179, 1.

In all the passages which we have hitherto examined
vríshan clearly retained its etymological meaning, though
even then it was not always possible to translate it by
male.

The same meaning has been retained in other languages
in which this word can be traced. Thus, in Zend, arshan
is used to express the sex of animals in such expressions
as aspahé arshnô, gen. a male horse; varâzahe arshnô, gen.
a male boar; géus arshnô, gen. a male ox; but likewise in
the sense of man or hero, as arsha husrava, the hero
Husrava. In Greek we find ἄρσην and ἄῤῥην used in the
same way to distinguish the sex of animals, as ἄρσενες ἵπποι,
βοῦν ἄρσενα. In Latin the same word may be recognized
in the proper name Varro, and in váro and báro.

We now come to another class of passages in which
vríshan is clearly intended to express more than merely the
masculine gender. In some of them the etymological
meaning of spargere, to pour forth, seems to come out
again, and it is well known that Indian commentators are
very fond of explaining vríshan by giver of rain, giver of
good gifts, bounteous. The first of these meanings may
indeed be admitted in certain passages, but in others it is
more than doubtful.

i. 181, 8. vríshâ vâm megháh may be translated, your
raining cloud.

i. 129, 3. dasmáh hí sma vríshanam pínvasi tvákam.

Thou art strong, thou fillest the rainy skin, i. e. the
cloud.

See also iv. 22, 6; and possibly v. 83, 6.

It may be that, when applied to Soma too, vríshan
retained something of its etymological meaning, that it
meant gushing forth, poured out, though in many places
it is impossible to render vríshan, as applied to Soma, by
anything but strong. All we can admit is that vríshan,
if translated by strong, means also strengthening and invi-
gorating, an idea not entirely absent even in our expression,
a strong drink.

i. 80, 2. sáh tvâ amadat vríshâ mádah, sómah—sutáh.

This strong draught inspirited thee, the poured out
Soma-juice.

i. 91, 2. tvám vríshâ vrisha-tvébhi*h*.

Thou, Soma, art strong by strength.

i. 175, 1. vríshâ te vrísh*n*e índu*h* vâg*î* sahasra-sâtama*h*.

For thee, the strong one, there is strong drink, powerful, omnipotent.

In the ninth Ma*n*dala, specially dedicated to the praises of Soma, the inspiriting beverage of gods and men, the repetition of vríshan, as applied to the juice and to the god who drinks it, is constant. Indo vríshâ or vríshâ indo are incessant invocations, and become at last perfectly meaningless.

There can be no doubt, in fact, that already in the hymns of the Veda, vríshan had dwindled away to a mere *epitheton ornans*, and that in order to understand it correctly, we must, as much as possible, forget its etymological colouring, and render it by hero or strong. Indra, Agni, the A*s*vins, Vish*n*u, the *R*ibhus (iv. 35, 6), all are vríshan, which means no longer male, but manly, strong.

In the following passages vríshan is thus applied to Indra :

i. 54, 2. yá*h* dh*r*ishnúnâ *s*ávasâ ródasî (íti) ubhé (íti) vríshâ vrisha-tvá vríshabhá*h* ni-*r*iñgáte.

(Praise Indra) who by his daring strength conquers both heaven and earth, a bull, strong in strength.

i. 100, 1. sá*h* yá*h* vríshâ vrísh*n*yebhi*h* sám-okâ*h* mahá*h* divá*h* p*r*ithivyâ*h* *k*a sam-râ*t* satînâ-satvâ hávya*h* bháreshu marútvân na*h* bhavatu índra*h* ûtí.

He who is strong, wedded to strength, who is the king of the great sky and the earth, of mighty might, to be invoked in battles,—may Indra with the Maruts come to our help !

i. 16, 1. â tvâ vahantu hárayú*h* vrísha*n*am sóma-pîtaye, índra tvâ sûra-*k*akshasa*h*.

May the bays bring thee hither, the strong one, to the Soma-draught, may the sunny-eyed horses (bring) thee, O Indra !

iv. 16, 20. evá ít índrâya vrishabhâya vrísh*n*e bráhma akarma bh*r*ígava*h* ná rátham.

Thus we have made a hymn for Indra, the strong bull, as the Bh*r*igus make a chariot.

x. 153, 2. tvám vrishan vríshâ ít asi.

Thou, O hero, art indeed a hero; and not, Thou, O male, art indeed a male; still less, Thou, O bull, art indeed a bull.

i. 101, 1. avasyávah vríshaṇam vágra-dakshiṇam marút-vantam sakhyâya havâmahe.

Longing for help we call as our friend the hero who wields the thunderbolt, who is accompanied by the Maruts.

viii. 6, 14. ní súshṇe indra dharṇasím vágram gaghantha dásyavi, vríshâ hí ugra srìṇvishé.

Thou, O Indra, hast struck the strong thunderbolt against Śushṇa, the fiend; for, terrible one, thou art called hero!

viii. 6, 40. vavridhânáh úpa dyávi vríshâ vagrí aroravît, vritra-hấ soma-pâtamaḥ.

Growing up by day, the hero with the thunderbolt has roared, the Vritra-killer, the great Soma-drinker.

v. 35, 4. vríshâ hí ási râdhase gaghnishé vríshṇi te sávaḥ.

Thou (Indra) art a hero, thou wast born to be bounteous; in thee, the hero, there is might.

It is curious to watch the last stage of the meaning of vríshan in the comparative and superlative várshîyas and várshishṭha. In the Veda, várshishṭha still means excellent, but in later Sanskrit it is considered as the superlative of vriddha, old, so that we see vríshan, from meaning originally manly, vigorous, young, assuming in the end the meaning of old. (M. M., Sanskrit Grammar, § 252.)

Yet even thus, when vríshan means simply strong or hero, its sexual sense is not always forgotten, and it breaks out, for instance, in such passages as,

i. 32, 7. vríshṇaḥ vádhriḥ prati-mấnam búbhûshan puru-trâ vritráḥ aśayat ví-astaḥ.

Vritra, the eunuch, trying to be like unto a man (like unto Indra), was lying, broken to many pieces.

The next passages show vríshan as applied to Agni:

iii. 27, 15. vríshaṇam tvâ vayám vrishan vríshaṇaḥ sám idhîmahi.

O, strong one, let us the strong ones kindle thee, the strong!

v. 1, 12. ávokâma kaváye médhyâya vákaḥ vandấru vrishabhấya vrishṇe.

We have spoken an adoring speech for the worshipful
poet, for the strong bull (Agni).

Vishṇu is called vrîshan, i. 154, 3:
prá víshṇave sûshấm etu mánma giri-kshíte uru-gâyấya
vrîshṇe.

May this hymn go forth to Vishṇu, he who dwells in
the mountain (cloud), who strides wide, the hero!

Rudra is called vrîshan:
ii. 34, 2. rudrấḥ yát vaḥ marutaḥ rukma-vakshasaḥ vrishâ
ágani prísnyâḥ sukré ûdhani.

When Rudra, the strong man, begat you, O Maruts with
brilliant chests, in the bright bosom of Prísni.

That the Maruts, the sons of Rudra, are called vrîshan,
we have seen before, and shall see frequently again,
(i. 165, 1; ii. 33, 13; vii. 56, 20; 21; 58, 6.) The whole
company of the Maruts is called vrishâ gaṇấḥ, the strong
or manly host, i. e. the host of the Maruts, without any
further qualification.

Here lies, indeed, the chief difficulty which is raised
by the common use of vrîshan in the Veda, that when it
occurs by itself, it often remains doubtful who is meant
by it, Indra, or Soma, or the Maruts, or some other deity.
We shall examine a few of these passages, and first some
where vrîshan refers to Indra:

iv. 30, 10. ápa ushấḥ ánasaḥ sarat sám-pishṭât áha
bibhyúshî, ní yát sîm sisnáthat vrîshâ.

Ushas went away from her broken chariot, fearing lest
the hero should do her violence.

Here vrîshan is clearly meant for Indra, who, as we
learn from the preceding verse, was trying to conquer
Ushas, as Apollo did Daphne; and it should be observed
that the word itself, by which Indra is here designated, is
particularly appropriate to the circumstances.

i. 103, 6. bhûri-karmaṇe vrishabhấya vrîshṇe satyá-sush-
mâya sunavâma sómam, yáḥ â-dŕitya paripanthî-iva sûraḥ
áyagvanaḥ vi-bhágan éti védaḥ.

Let us pour out the Soma for the strong bull, the performer of many exploits, whose strength is true, the hero

who, watching like a footpad, comes to us dividing the wealth of the infidel.

Here it is clear again from the context that Indra only can be meant.

But in other passages this is more doubtful:

iii. 61, 7. *ri*tásya budhné ushásâm isha*n*yán v*rí*shâ mahî (íti) ródasî (íti) â vivesa.

The hero in the depth of the heaven, yearning for the dawns, has entered the great sky and the earth.

The hero who yearns for the dawns, is generally Indra; here, however, considering that Agni is mentioned in the preceding verse, it is more likely that this god, as the light of the morning, may have been meant by the poet. That Agni, too, may be called v*rí*shan, without any other epithet to show that he is meant rather than any other god, is clear from such passages as,

vi. 3, 7. v*rí*shâ rukshá*h* óshadhîshu nûnot.

He the wild hero shouted among the plants.

In vii. 60, 9, vrisha*n*au, the dual, is meant for Mitra and Varu*n*a; in the next verse, v*ri*sha*n*a*h*, the plural, must mean the same gods and their companions.

That Soma is called simply v*rí*shan, not only in the ninth Ma*nd*ala, but elsewhere, too, we see from such passages as,

iii. 43, 7. índra píba v*rí*sha-dhûtasya v*rí*sh*n*a*h* (â yám te *s*yená*h* u*s*até *g*abhâra), yásya máde *k*yavâyasi prá k*ri*sh*tí*h yásya máde ápa *g*otrâ vavártha.

Indra drink of the male (the strong Soma), bruised by the males (the heavy stones), inspirited by whom thou makest the people fall down, inspirited by whom thou hast opened the stables.

Here Sâya*n*a, too, sees rightly that ' the male bruised by the males ' is the Soma-plant, which, in order to yield the intoxicating juice, has to be bruised by stones, which stones are again likened to two males. But unless the words, enclosed in brackets, had stood in the text, words which clearly point to Soma, I doubt whether Sâya*n*a would have so readily admitted the definite meaning of v*rí*shan as Soma.

i. 109, 3. mâ *kh*edma ra*s*mî*n* íti nâdhamânâ*h* pit*rí̂n*âm *s*aktî*h* anu-yá*kkh*amânà*h*, indrâgnî-bhyâm kám vrîsha*n*a*h* madanti tâ hí ádrî (íti) dhishâ*n*âyâ*h* upá-sthe.

We pray, let us not break the cords (which, by means of the sacrifices offered by each generation of our forefathers, unite us with the gods); we strive after the powers of our fathers. The Somas rejoice for Indra and Agni ; here are the two stones in the lap of the vessel.

First, as to the construction, the fact that participles are thus used as finite verbs, and particularly when the subject changes in the next sentence, is proved by other passages, such as ii. 11, 4. The sense is that the new generation does not break the sacrificial succession, but offers Soma, like their fathers. The Soma-plants are ready, and, when pressed by two stones, their juice flows into the Soma-vessel. There may be a *double entendre* in dhishânâyâ*h* upá-sthe, which Sanskrit scholars will easily perceive.

When vrîshan is thus used by itself, we must be chiefly guided by the adjectives or other indications before we determine on the most plausible translation. Thus we read :

i. 55, 4. sá*h* ít vánc namasyú-bhi*h* vakasyate *k*áru *y*áneshu pra-bruvâ*n*á*h* indriyám, vrîshâ *kh*ándu*h* bhavati haryatá*h* vrîshâ kshémen*a* dhénâm maghá-vâ yát ínvati.

In the first verse the subject is clearly Indra : ' He alone is praised by worshippers in the forest, he who shows forth among men his fair power.' But who is meant to be the subject of the next verse? Even Sâya*n*a is doubtful. He translates first: ' The bounteous excites the man who wishes to sacrifice; when the sacrificer, the rich, by the protection of Indra, stirs up his voice.' But he allows an optional translation for the last sentences : ' when the powerful male, Indra, by his enduring mind reaches the praise offered by the sacrificer.'

According to these suggestions, Wilson translated : ' He (Indra) is the granter of their wishes (to those who solicit him); he is the encourager of those who desire to worship (him), when the wealthy offerer of oblations, enjoying his protection, recites his praise.'

Benfey : ' The bull becomes friendly, the bull becomes desirable, when the sacrificer kindly advances praise.'

Langlois : ' When the noble Maghavan receives the

homage of our hymns, his heart is flattered, and he
responds to the wishes of his servant by his gifts.'

As far as I know, the adjective *khándu* does not occur
again, and can therefore give us no hint. But haryatá,
which is applied to vríshan in our verse, is the standing
epithet of Soma. It means delicious, and occurs very
frequently in the ninth Mandala. It is likewise applied
to Agni, Pûshan, the Haris, the thunderbolt, but wherever
it occurs our first thought is of Soma. Thus, without
quoting from the Soma-Mandala, we read, x. 96, 1, harya-
tám mádam, the delicious draught, i. e. Soma.

x. 96, 9. pîtvâ mádasya haryatásya ándhasaḥ, means
having drunk of the draught of the delicious Soma.

viii. 72, 18. padám haryatásya ni-dhányàm, means the
place where the delicious Soma resides.

iii. 44, 1. haryatáḥ sómaḥ.

Delicious Soma.

ii. 21, 1. bhara índrâya sómam yagatâya haryatâm.

Bring delicious Soma for the holy Indra.

i. 130, 2. mádâya haryatâya te tuvíḥ-tamâya dhâyase.

That thou mayest drink the delicious and most powerful
draught, i. e. the Soma.

If, then, we know that vríshan by itself is used in the
sense of Soma, haryatá vríshan can hardly be anything
else, and we may therefore translate the second line of
i. 55, 4, 'the strong Soma is pleasing, the strong Soma is
delicious, when the sacrificer safely brings the cow.'

That Indra was thirsting for Soma had been said in the
second verse, and he is again called the Soma-drinker in the
seventh verse. The bringing of the cow alludes to the often
mentioned mixture with milk, which the Soma undergoes
before it is offered.

That the Maruts are called vríshan, without further explanations, will appear from the following passages :

i. 85, 12. rayím naḥ dhatta vrishanaḥ su-víram.

Give us wealth, ye heroes, consisting of good offspring.

viii. 96, 14. íshyâmi vaḥ vrishanaḥ yúdhyata âgaú.

I wish for you, heroes (Maruts), fight in the race !

In all the passages which we have hitherto examined,
vríshan was always applied to living beings, whether

animals, men, or gods. But as, in Greek, ἄρρην means at last simply strong, and is applied, for instance, to the crash of the sea, κτύπος ἄρσην πόντου, so in the Veda vrishan is applied to the roaring of the storms and similar objects.

v. 87, 5. svanáh vrishâ.

Your powerful sound (O Maruts).

x. 47, 1. gagribhmá te dákshinam indra hástam vasu-yávah vasu-pate vásûnâm, vidmá hí tvâ gó-patim súra gónâm asmábhyam kitrám vrishanam rayím dâh.

We have taken thy right hand, O Indra, wishing for trea-sures, treasurer of treasures, for we know thee, O hero, to be the lord of cattle; give us bright and strong wealth.

Should kitrá here refer to treasures, and vrishan to cattle?

x. 89, 9. ní amítreshu vadhám indra túmram vrishan vrishânam arushám sisîhi.

Whet, O hero, the heavy strong red weapon, against the enemies.

The long â in vrishânam is certainly startling, but it occurs once more, ix. 34, 3, where there can be no doubt that it is the accusative of vrishan. Professor Roth takes vrishan here in the sense of bull (s. v. tumra), but he does not translate the whole passage.

iii. 29, 9. krinóta dhûmám vrishanam sakhâyah.

Make a mighty smoke, O friends!

Strength itself is called vrishan, if I am right in trans-lating the phrase vrishanam súshmam by manly strength. It occurs,

iv. 24, 7. tásmin dadhat vrishanam súshmam índrah.

May Indra give to him manly strength.

vi. 19, 8. â nah bhara vrishanam súshmam indra.

Bring to us, O Indra, manly strength.

vii. 24, 4. asmé (íti) dádhat vrishanam súshmam indra.

Giving to us, O Indra, manly strength.

See also vi. 19, 9, súshmah vrishabháh, used in the same sense.

This constant play on the word vrishan, which we have observed in the passages hitherto examined, and which give by no means a full idea of the real frequency of its occurrence in the Veda, has evidently had its influence on the Vedic *Rishis*, who occasionally seem to delight in the most silly and unmeaning repetitions of this word, and its compounds and derivatives. Here no language can supply any adequate translation ; for though we may translate words which express thoughts, it is useless to attempt to render mere idle play with words. I shall give a few instances :

i. 177, 3. â tish*tha* râtham vrísha*n*am vríshâ te sutá*h* sóma*h* pári-siktâ mádhûni, yuktvā́ vrísha-bhyâm vrishabha kshitînấm hári-bhyâm yâhi pra-vâtâ úpa madrík.

Mount the *strong* car, the *strong* Soma is poured out for thee, sweets are sprinkled round; come down towards us, thou bull of men, with the *strong* bays, having yoked them.

But this is nothing yet compared to other passages, when the poet cannot get enough of vríshan and vrishabhá.

ii. 16, 6. vríshâ te vá*gra*h utá te vríshâ rátha*h* vrísha*n*â hárî (íti) vrishabhấ*n*i âyudhâ, vrísh*n*a*h* mádasya vrishabha tvám îsishe índra sómasya vrishabhásya tri*p*ruhi.

Thy thunderbolt is *strong*, and thy car is *strong, strong* are the bays, the weapons are *powerful*, thou, bull, art lord of the *strong* draught, Indra rejoice in the *powerful* Soma!

v. 36, 5. vríshâ tvâ vrísha*n*am vardhatu dyaú*h* vríshâ vrí-sha-bhyâm vahase hári-bhyâm, sá*h* na*h* vríshâ vrísha-ratha*h* su-sipra vrísha-krato (íti) vríshâ vagrin bhâre dhâ*h*.

May the *strong* sky increase thee, the *strong* ; a *strong* one thou art, carried by two *strong* bays ; do thou who art *strong*, with a *strong* car, O thou of *strong* might, *strong* holder of the thunderbolt, keep us in battle !

v. 40, 2–3. vríshâ grấvâ vríshâ máda*h* vríshâ sóma*h* ayám sutá*h*, vríshan indra vrísha-bhi*h* vritrahan-tama, vríshâ tvâ vrísha*n*am huve.

The stone is *strong*, the draught is *strong*, this Soma that has been poured out is *strong*, O thou *strong* Indra, who killest Vritra with the *strong* ones (the Maruts), I, the *strong*, call thee, the *strong*.

viii. 13, 31—33. vríshâ ayám indra te rátha*h* utó (íti) te vrísha*n*â hárî (íti), vríshâ tvám sata-krato (íti) vríshâ háva*h*. vríshâ grấvâ vríshâ máda*h* vríshâ sóma*h* ayám sutá*h*, vríshâ ya*g*ñá*h* yám ínvasi vríshâ háva*h*. vríshâ tvâ vrísha*n*am huve vá*g*rin *k*itrâbhi*h* ûtí-bhi*h*, vavántha hí práti-stutim vríshâ háva*h*.

This thy car is *strong*, O Indra, and thy bays are *strong;* thou art *strong*, O omnipotent, our call is *strong.* The stone is *strong*, the draught is *strong*, the Soma is *strong*, which is here poured out; the sacrifice which thou orderest, is *strong*, our call is *strong.* I, the *strong*, call thee, the *strong*, thou holder of the thunderbolt, with manifold blessings; for thou hast desired our praise; our call is *strong.*

There are other passages of the same kind, but they are too tedious to be here repeated. The commentator, throughout, gives to each vríshan its full meaning either of showering down or bounteous, or male or bull; but a word which can thus be used at random has clearly lost its definite power, and cannot call forth any definite ideas in the mind of the listener. It cannot be denied that here and there the original meaning of vríshan would be appropriate even where the poet is only pouring out a stream of majestic sound, but we are not called upon to impart sense to what are *verba et præterquam nihil.* When we read, i. 122, 3, vâta*h* apâm vrishan-vân, we are justified, no doubt, in translating, 'the wind who pours forth water;' and x. 93, 5, apâm vrishan-vasû (íti) sûryâmâsâ, means 'Sun and Moon, givers of water.' But even in passages where vríshan is followed by the verb vrish, it is curious to observe that vrish is not necessarily used in the sense of raining or pouring forth, but rather in the sense of drinking.

vi. 68, 11. indrâvaru*n*â mádhumat-tamasya vrísh*n*a*h* sómasya vrisha*n*â * â vrishethâm.

---

* The dual vrisha*n*au occurs only when the next word begins with a vowel. Before an initial a, â, i, the au is always changed into âv in the Sanhitâ (i. 108, 7–12; 116, 21; 117, 19; 153, 2; 157, 5; 158, 1; 180, 7; vii. 61, 5). Before u the preceding au becomes â in the Sanhitâ, but the Pada gives au, in order to show that no Sandhi can take place between the two vowels (vii. 60, 9; x. 66, 7). Before consonants the dual always ends in â, both in the Sanhitâ and Pada. But there are a few passages where the final â occurs before initial vowels, and where the two vowels are allowed to form one syllable. In four passages this happens before an initial â (i. 108, 3; vi. 68, 11; i. 177, 1; ii. 16, 5). Once, and once only, it happens before u, in viii. 22, 12.

Indra and Varu*n*a, you strong ones, may you drink of
the sweetest strong Soma.

That â-*v*rish means to drink or to eat, was known to
Sâya*n*a and to the author of the *S*atapatha-brâhma*n*a, who
paraphrases â v*r*ishâyadhvam by a*s*nîta, eat.

The same phrase occurs i. 108, 3.

i. 104, 9. uru-vyá*k*â*h* gath*á*re *ã* v*r*ishasva.

Thou of vast extent, drink (the Soma) in thy stomach.

The same phrase occurs x. 96, 13.

viii. 61, 3. *ã* v*r*ishasva—sutásya indra ándhasa*h*.

Drink, Indra, of the Soma that is poured out.

In conclusion, a few passages may be pointed out in
which v*r*íshan seems to be the proper name of a pious
worshipper:

i. 36, 10. yám tvâ devấsa*h* mánave dadhú*h* ihá yá*g*ish*t*/*h*am
havya-vâhana, yám ká*n*va*h* médhya-atithi*h* dhana-sp*r*ítam
yám v*r*íshâ yám upa-stutấ*h*.

Thee, O Agni, whom the gods placed here for man, the
most worthy of worship, O carrier of oblations, thee whom
Ka*n*va, thee whom Medhyâtithi placed, as the giver of
wealth, thee whom V*r*ishan placed and Upastuta.

Here the commentator takes V*r*ishan as Indra, but this
would break the symmetry of the sentence. That Upastuta*h* is here to be taken as a proper name, as Upastuta,
the son of V*r*ish*t*ihavya, is clear from verse 17:

agní*h* prá âvat mitrấ utá médhya-atithim agní*h* sâtấ upa-
stutám.

Agni protected also the two friends, Medhyâtithi and
Upastuta, in battle.

The fact is that whenever upastutá has the accent on the
last syllable, it is intended as a proper name, while, if used
as a participle, in the sense of praised, it has the accent on
the first.

viii. 5, 25. yáthâ *k*it ká*n*vam ávatam priyá-medham upa-
stutám.

As you have protected Ka*n*va, Priyamedha, Upastuta.
Cf. i. 112, 15.

viii. 103, 8. prá má*m*hish*t*/*h*âya gâyata—úpastutâsa*h* ag-
nâye.

Sing, O Upastutas, to the worthiest, to Agni!

x. 115, 9. íti tvâ agne vrish*t*i-hávyasya putrã*h* upa-
stutãsa*h* ríshaya*h* avo*k*an.

By these names, O Agni, did the sons of Vrish*t*ihavya,
the Upastutas, the *R*ishis, speak to you.

Vrishan occurs once more as a proper name in vi. 16,
14 and 15 :

tám û*m* (íti) tvâ dadhyáṅ *r*íshi*h* putrá*h* îdhe átharva*n*a*h*,
vritra-hánam puram-darám.

tám û*m* (íti) tvâ pâthyá*h* vrîshâ sám îdhe dasyuhán-
tamam, dhanam-*g*ayám rá*n*e-ra*n*e.

Thee, O Agni, did Dadhya*k* kindle, the *R*ishi, the son of
Atharvan, thee the killer of V*r*itra, the destroyer of towns.

Thee, O Agni, did Vrishan Pâthya kindle, thee the best
killer of enemies, the conqueror of wealth in every battle.

Here the context can leave no doubt that Dadhya*k* as
well as Vrishan were both intended as proper names. Yet as
early as the composition of the *S*atapatha-brâhma*n*a, this
was entirely misunderstood. Dadhya*k*, the son of Atharvan,
is explained as speech, Vrishan Pâthya as mind (*S*at. Br.
vi. 3, 3, 4). On this Mahîdhara, in his remarks on Vâ*g*.
Sanh. xi. 34, improves still further. For though he allows
his personality to Dadhya*k*, the son of Atharvan, he says
that Pâthya comes from pathin, path, and means he who
moves on the right path ; or it comes from pâthas, which
means sky, and is here used in the sense of the sky of the
heart. He then takes vrishan as mind, and translates the
mind of the heart. Such is the history of the rise and fall
of the Indian mind !

MANDALA I, SÛKTA 86.
ASHTAKA I, ADHYÂYA 6, VARGA 11–12.

1. Márута*h* yásya hí ksháye pâthá divá*h* vi-maha-
sa*h*, sá*h* su-gopâtama*h* gána*h*.

2. Ya*g*ñai*h* vâ ya*g*ña-vâhasa*h* víprasya vâ matînẫm,
márута*h* sri*n*utá hávam.

3. Utá vâ yásya vâ*g*ína*h* ánu vípram átakshata,
sá*h* gántâ gó-mati vra*g*é.

4. Asyá virásya barhíshi sutá*h* sómah dívish*t*ishu,
ukthám máda*h* *k*a sasyate.

5. Asyá sroshantu ẫ bhúva*h* * vísvâ*h* yá*h* *k*arshan*î*h
abhí, sûram *k*it sasrúshî*h* ísha*h*.

6. Pûrvî'bhi*h* hí dadâsimá sarát-bhi*h* maruta*h*
vayám, áva*h*-bhi*h* *k*arshan̂înẫm.

7. Su-bhága*h* sá*h* pra-ya*g*yava*h* máruta*h* astu
mártya*h*, yásya práyâ*m*si párshatha.

8. *S*asamânásya vâ nara*h* svédasya satya-*s*avasa*h*,
vidá kã̃masya vénata*h*.

9. Yûyám tát satya-savasa*h* âvî*h* karta mahi-tvanã̃,
vídhyata vi-dyútâ ráksha*h*.

10. Gûhata gúhyam táma*h* ví yâta vísvam atrí*n*am,
*g*yóti*h* karta yát usmási.

---

* â-bhúva*h*

1. O Maruts, that man in whose dwelling you drink (the Soma), ye mighty (sons) of heaven, he indeed has the best guardians.[1]

2. You who are propitiated[1] either by sacrifices or from the prayers of the sage, hear the call, O Maruts!

3. Aye, the strong man to whom you have granted a sage, he will live in a stable rich in cattle.[1]

4. On the altar of that strong man Soma is poured out in daily sacrifices; praise and joy are sung.

5. To him let the strong[1] Maruts listen, to him who surpasses all men, as the flowing rain-clouds[2] pass over the sun.

6. For we, O Maruts, have sacrificed in many a harvest, through the mercies[1] of the swift gods (the storm-gods).

7. May that mortal be blessed, O worshipful Maruts, whose offerings you carry off.[1]

8. You take notice either of the sweat of him who praises you, ye men of true strength, or of the desire of the suppliant.[1]

9. O ye of true strength, make this manifest by your greatness! strike the fiend[1] with your thunderbolt!

10. Hide the hideous darkness, destroy[1] every tusky[2] spirit. Create the light which we long for!

COMMENTARY.

This hymn is ascribed to Gotama. The metre is Gâyatrî throughout.

Verse 1, note [1]. Vímahas occurs only once more as an epithet of the Maruts, v. 87, 4. Being an adjective derived from máhas, strength, it means very strong. The strong ones of heaven is an expression analogous to i. 64, 2. diváh rishvásah ukshánah; i. 64, 4. diváh nárah.

Verse 2, note [1]. The construction of this verse is not clear. Yagñá-vâhas has two meanings in the Veda. It is applied to the priest who carries or performs the sacrifice :
iii. 8, 3, and 24, 1. várkah dhâh yagñá-vâhase.
Grant splendour to the sacrificer !
But it is also used of the gods who accept the sacrifice, and in that case it means hardly more than worshipped or propitiated; i. 15, 11 (Asvinau); iv. 47, 4 (Indra and Vâyu); viii. 12, 20 (Indra). In our verse it is used in the latter sense, and it is properly construed with the instrumental yagñaíh. The difficulty is the gen. plur. matînâm, instead of matíbhih. The sense, however, seems to allow of but one construction, and we may suppose that the genitive depends on the yagña in yagñávâhas, ' accepting the worship of the prayers of the priest.' Benfey refers yagñaíh to the preceding verse, and joins hávam to víprasya matînâm : ' Durch Opfer—Opferfördrer ihr !—oder ihr hört —Maruts—den Ruf der Lieder die der Priester schuf.'
The Sanhitâ text lengthens the last syllable of srinutá, as suggested by the metre.

Verse 3, note [1]. The genitive yásya vágínah depends on vípra. Anu-taksh, like anu-grah, anu-gñâ, seems to convey the meaning of doing in behalf or for the benefit of a person. Gántâ might also be translated in a hostile sense, he will go into, he will conquer many a stable full of cows.

Verse 5, note [1]. I have altered â bhúvah into âbhúvah,

for I do not think that bhúva*h*, the second pers. sing.,
even if it were bhúvat, the third pers., could be joined with
the relative pronoun yá*h* in the second pada.   The phrase
vísvâ*h* yá*h* *k*arsha*nî*h abhí occurs more than once, and is
never preceded by the verb bhuva*h* or bhuvat.   Âbhúva*h*,
on the contrary, is applied to the Maruts, i. 64, 6, vidátheshu âbhúva*h*; and as there can be no doubt who are
the deities invoked, âbhúva*h*, the strong ones, is as appropriate an epithet as vímahas in the first verse.

Verse 5, note [2]. Sasrúshî*h* ísha*h*, as connected with súra,
the sun, can only be meant for the flowing waters, the
rain-clouds, the givers of ish or vigour.   They are called
divyâ*h* ísha*h* :
viii. 5, 21. utá na*h* divyâ*h* ísha*h* utá síndhûn varshatha*h*.
You rain down on us the heavenly waters and the rivers.
Wilson translates : ' May the Maruts, victorious over all
men, hear (the praises) of this (their worshipper) ; and may
(abundant) food be obtained by him who praises them.'
Benfey: ' Ihn, der ob alle Menschen ragt, sollen hören
die Labungen, und nahn, die irgend Weisen nahn.'
Langlois : ' Que les Marouts écoutent favorablement la
prière ; qu'ils acceptent aussi les offrandes de ce (mortel) que
sa position élève au-dessus de tous les autres, et même
jusqu'au soleil.'
*S*roshantu does not occur again ; but we find *s*róshan,
i. 68, 5 ; *s*róshamâ*n*a, iii. 8, 10 ; vii. 51, 1 ; vii. 7, 6.

Verse 6, note [1]. The expression ávobhi*h*, with the help,
the blessings, the mercies, is generally used with reference
to divine assistance ; (i. 117, 19; 167, 2; 185, 10; 11;
iv. 22, 7; 41, 6; v. 74, 6; vi. 47, 12; vii. 20, 1; 35, 1, &c.)
It seems best therefore to take *k*arsha*n*í as a name or
epithet of the Maruts, although, after the invocation of the
Maruts by name, this repetition is somewhat unusual.   One
might translate, ' with the help of our men, of our active
and busy companions,' for *k*arsha*n*í is used in that sense
also.   Only ávobhi*h* would not be in its right place then.

Verse 7, note [1]. Par, with ati, means to carry over,

(i. 97, 8; 99, 1; 174, 9; iii. 15, 3; 20, 4; iv. 39, 1; v. 25, 9; 73, 8; vii. 40, 4; 97, 4; viii. 26, 5; 67, 2, &c.); with apa, to remove, (i. 129, 5); with nih, to throw down. Hence, if used by itself, unless it means to overrun, as frequently, it can only have the general sense of carrying, taking, accepting, or accomplishing.

Verse 8, note [1]. Vidá as second pers. plur. perf. is frequent, generally with the final 'a' long in the Sanhitâ, i. 156, 3; v. 41, 13; 55, 2.

Verse 9, note [1]. Observe the long penultimate in rákshah, instead of the usual short syllable. Cf. i. 12, 5, and see Kuhn, Beiträge, vol. iii. p. 456.

Verse 10, note [1]. See note to i. 39, 3, note [1].

Verse 10, note [2]. Atrín, which stands for attrín, is one of the many names assigned to the powers of darkness and mischief. It is derived from atrá, which means tooth or jaw, and therefore meant originally an ogre with large teeth or jaws, a devourer. Besides atrá, we also find in the Veda átra, with the accent on the first syllable, and meaning what serves for eating, or food:

x. 79, 2. átrâni asmai pat-bhíh sám bharanti.

They bring together food for him (Agni) with their feet.

With the accent on the last syllable, atrá in one passage means an eater or an ogre, like atrín:

v. 32, 8. apâdam atrám—mridhrá-vâkam.

Indra killed the footless ogre, the babbler.

It means tooth or jaw:

i. 129, 8. svayám sâ rishayádhyai yâ nah upa-îshé atraíh.

May she herself go to destruction who attacks us with her teeth.

It is probably from atrá in the sense of tooth (cf. ὀδόντες = ἐδόντες) that atrín is derived, meaning ogre or a devouring devil. In the later Sanskrit, too, the Asuras are represented as having large tusks, Mahâbh. v. 3572, damshtrino bhî-mavegâs ka.

Thus we read i. 21, 5, that Indra and Agni destroy the Rakshas, and the poet continues:

áprayâḥ santu atrínaḥ.
May the ogres be without offspring!
ix. 86, 48. gahí víṣvân rakshásaḥ indo (íti) atrínaḥ.
Kill, O Soma, all the tusky Rakshas. Cf. ix. 104, 6;
105, 6.
vi. 51, 14. gahí ní atrínam paṇím.
Kill, O Soma, the tusky Paṇi.
i. 94, 9. vadhaíḥ duḥ-sáṃsân ápa duḥ-dhyâḥ gahi
dûré vâ yé ánti vâ ké kit atrínaḥ.
Strike with thy blows, O Agni, the evil-spoken, evil-
minded (spirits), the ogres, those who are far or who are
near.
See also i. 36, 14; 20; vi. 16, 28; vii. 104, 1; 5; viii.
12, 1; 19, 15; x. 36, 4; 118, 1.

MANDALA I, SÛKTA 87.
ASHTAKA I, ADHYÂYA 6, VARGA 13.

1. Prá-tvakshasa*h* prá-tavasa*h* vi-rapsína*h* ánâna-
tâ*h* ávithurâ*h* *r*igîshína*h*, gúsh*t*a-tamâsa*h* nrí-ta-
mâsa*h* a*ñg*í-bhi*h* ví ânag*r*e ké *k*it usrâ*h*-iva strí-
bhi*h*.

2. Upa-hvaréshu yát á*k*idhvam yayím váya*h*-iva
maruta*h* kéna *k*it pathâ, s*k*ótanti kósâ*h* úpa va*h*
rátheshu â gh*r*itám ukshata mádhu-var*n*am ár-
*k*ate.

3. Prá eshâm ágmeshu vithurâ-iva re*g*ate bhûmi*h*
yâmeshu yát ha yu*ñg*áte *s*ubhé, tó krî*l*áya*h* dhúnaya*h* bhrâ*g*at-*r*ish*t*aya*h* svayám mahi-tvám panayanta
dhûtaya*h*.

4. Sâ*h* hí sva-s*r*ít p*r*íshat-a*s*va*h* yúvâ ga*n*â*h*
ayâ îsânâ*h* távishîbhi*h* â-v*r*ita*h*, ási satyâ*h* *r*i*n*a-
yâvâ ánedya*h* asyâ*h* dhiyâ*h* pra-avitâ átha v*r*íshâ
ga*n*â*h*.

5. Pitú*h* p*r*atnásya *g*ánmanâ vadâmasi sómasya
*g*ihvâ prá *g*igâti *k*ákshasâ, yát îm índram *s*âmi
*r*íkvâ*n*a*h* âsata ât ít nâmâni ya*g*ñíyâni dadhire.

6. *S*riyáse kám bhânú-bhi*h* sám mimikshire té
ra*s*mí-bhi*h* té *r*íkva-bhi*h* su-khâdáya*h*, té vâ*s*í-
manta*h* ishmí*n*a*h* ábhíravâ*h* vidré priyásya mârutá-
sya dhâmna*h*.

1. The active, the strong, the singers, the never flinching, the immovable, the wild, the most beloved and most manly, they have shown themselves with their glittering ornaments, a few only,[1] like the heavens with the stars.

2. When you see your way through the clefts, you are like birds, O Maruts, on whatever road it be.[1] The clouds drop (rain) on your chariots everywhere; pour out the honey-like fat (the rain) for him who praises you.

3. At their ravings the earth shakes, as if broken,[1] when on the (heavenly) paths they harness (their deer) for victory.[2] They the sportive, the roaring, with bright spears, the shakers (of the clouds) have themselves praised their greatness.

4. That youthful company (of the Maruts), with their spotted horses,[1] moves by itself; hence[2] it exercises lordship, and is invested with powers. Thou art true, thou searchest out sin,[3] thou art without blemish. Therefore thou, the strong host, thou wilt cherish this prayer.

5. We speak after the kind of our old father, our tongue goes forth at the sight[1] of the Soma: when the shouting Maruts had joined Indra in the work,[2] then only they received sacrificial honours;—

6. For their glory[1] these well-equipped Maruts obtained splendours, they obtained[2] rays, and men to praise them; nay, these well-armed, nimble, and fearless beings found the beloved home of the Maruts.[3]

COMMENTARY.

This hymn is ascribed to Gotama.   The metre is Gagatî throughout.

Verse 1, note [1].   Ké kit refers to the Maruts, who are represented as gradually rising or just showing themselves, as yet only few in number, like the first stars in the sky. Ké kit, some, is opposed to sarve, all.   The same expression occurs again, v. 52, 12, where the Maruts are compared to a few thieves.   B. and R. translate usrâh iva strí-bhih by ' like cows marked with stars on their foreheads.'   Such cows no doubt exist, but they can hardly be said to become visible by these frontal stars, as the Maruts by their ornaments.   We must take usrâh here in the same sense as dyâvah; ii. 34, 2, it is said that the Maruts were perceived dyâvah ná strí-bhih, like the heavens with the stars.

    i. 166, 11.   dûre-drísah yé divyâh-iva strí-bhih.

    Who are visible far away, like the heavens (or heavenly beings) by the stars.

    And the same is said of Agni, ii. 2, 5. dyaúh ná strí-bhih kitayat ródasî (íti) ánu.   Stríbhih occurs i. 68, 5; iv. 7, 3; vi. 49, 3; 12.   It always means stars, and the meaning of rays (strahl) rests, as yet, on etymological authority only.   The evening sky would, no doubt, be more appropriate than usrâh, which applies chiefly to the dawn.   But in the Indian mind, the two dawns, i. e. the dawn and the gloaming, are so closely united and identified, that their names, too, are frequently interchangeable.

    Verse 2, note [1].   I translate yayí not by a goer, a traveller, i. e. the cloud, (this is the explanation proposed by Sâyana, and adopted by Professor Benfey,) but by path. Etymologically yayí may mean either.   But in parallel passages yayí is clearly replaced by yâma.   Thus:

    viii. 7, 2. yát—yâmam subhrâh ákidhvam.

    When you, bright Maruts, have seen your way.

    See also viii. 7, 4. yát yâmam yânti vâyú-bhih.

    When they (the Maruts) go on their path with the winds.

viii. 7, 14. ádhi-iva yát girî*n*ầm yẩmam *s*ubhrâ*h* â*k*idhvam.
When you, bright Maruts, had seen your way, as it were,
along the mountains.

The same phrase occurs, even without yẩma or yayí, in

v. 55, 7. ná párvatâ*h* ná nadyẩ*h* varanta va*h* yátra
á*k*idhvam maruta*h* gá*kkh*ata ít u tát.

Not mountains, not rivers, keep you back ; where you
have seen (your way), there you go.

Though yayí does not occur frequently in the Rig-veda,
the meaning of path seems throughout more applicable than
that of traveller.

v. 87, 5. tveshâ*h* yayí*h*.
Your path, O Maruts, is brilliant.

v. 73, 7. ugrá*h* vâm kakuhâ*h* yayí*h*.
Fearful is your pass on high.

i. 51, 11. ugrá*h* yayím ní*h* apấ*h* srótasâ as*ri*?at.
The fearful Indra sent the waters forth on their way
streaming.

x. 92, 5. prá—yayínâ yanti síndhava*h*.
The waters go forth on their path.

Verse 3, note [1]. Cf. i. 37, 8, page 51. There is no
authority for Sâya*n*a's explanation of vithurấ-iva, the earth
trembles like a widow. Vithurấ occurs several times in
the Rig-veda, but never in the sense of widow. Thus:

i. 168, 6. yát *k*yaváyatha vithurấ-iva sám-hitam.
When you, Maruts, shake what is compact, like brittle
things.

i. 186, 2 ; vi. 25, 3 ; 46, 6 ; viii. 96, 2 ; x. 77, 4 (vi-
thuryáti). The Maruts themselves are called ávithura in
verse I. As to á*g*ma and yẩma, see i. 37, 8, page 62.

Verse 3, note [2]. *S*úbh is one of those words to which it
is very difficult always to assign a definite special meaning.
Being derived from *s*úbh, to shine, the commentator has
no difficulty in explaining it by splendour, beauty ; sometimes by water. But although *s*úbh means originally
splendour, and is used in that sense in many passages,
yet there are others where so vague a meaning seems very
inappropriate. In our verse Sâya*n*a proposes two trans-

lations, either, 'When the Maruts harness the clouds,' or,
'When the Maruts harness their chariots, for the bright
rain-water.' Now the idea that the Maruts harness their
chariots in order to make the clouds yield their rain, can
hardly be expressed by the simple word *subhé*, i. e. for
brightness' sake. As the Maruts are frequently praised for
their glittering ornaments, their splendour might be intended
in this passage as it certainly is in others. Thus:

i. 85, 3. yát *subh*áyante an*gí*-bhi*h* tanúshu *subh*rá*h*
dadhire virúkmata*h*.

When the Maruts adorn themselves with glittering
ornaments, the brilliant ones put bright weapons on their
bodies.

vii. 56, 6. *subh*á *s*óbhish*th*â*h*, *s*riyá sám-mislâ*h*, ó*g*a*h*-bhi*h*
ugrá*h*.

The most brilliant by their brilliancy, united with
splendour, terrible by strength.

In i. 64, 4, I have translated váksha*h*-su rukmán ádhi
yetire *subh*é by 'they fix gold (chains) on their chests for
beauty.' And the same meaning is applicable to i. 117, 5,
*subh*é rukmám ná dar*s*atám ní-khátam, and other passages:
iv. 51, 6; vi. 63, 6.

But in our verse and others which we shall examine, beauty
and brilliancy would be very weak renderings for *subh*é.
'When they harnessed their chariots or their deer for the sake
of beauty,' means nothing, or, at least, very little. I take,
therefore, *subh*é in this and similar phrases in the sense of
triumph or glory or victory. 'When they harness their chariots
for to conquer,' implies brilliancy, glory, victory, but it conveys at the same time a tangible meaning. Let us now see
whether the same meaning is appropriate in other passages:

i. 23, 11. *y*áyatâm-iva tanyatú*h* marútâm eti dh*r*ish*n*u-yá
yát *s*úbham yáthána nara*h*.

The thundering voice of the Maruts comes fiercely, like
that of conquerors, when you go to conquer, O men!

Sâya*n*a: 'When you go to the brilliant place of sacrifice.'
Wilson: 'When you accept the auspicious (offering).'
Benfey: 'Wenn ihr euren Schmuck nehmt.'

v. 57, 2. yáthana *s*úbham, you go to conquer. Cf. v. 55, 1.

Sâya*n*a: 'For the sake of water, or, in a chariot.'

v. 52, 8. sárdha*h* mắrutam út sa*m*sa — utá sma té subhé nára*h* prá syandrẫ*h* yu*g*ata tmáuâ.

Praise the host of the Maruts, and they, the men, the quickly moving, will harness by themselves (the chariots) for conquest.

Sâya*n*a : 'For the sake of water.' Cf. x. 105, 3.

v. 57, 3. subhé yát ugrẫ*h* p*rí*shatî*h* áyugdhvam.

When you have harnessed the deer for conquest.

Sâya*n*a : 'For the sake of water.'

v. 63, 5. rátham yuñ*g*ate marúta*h* subhé su-khám sữra*h* ná — gó-ish*l*ishu.

The Maruts harness the chariot meet for conquest, like a hero in battles.

Sâya*n*a : 'For the sake of water.'

i. 88, 2. subhé kám yânti — ásvai*h*.

The Maruts go on their horses towards conquest.

Sâya*n*a : 'In order to brighten the worshipper, or, for the sake of water.'

i. 119, 3. sám yát mithẫ*h* paspridhânẫsa*h* ágmata subhé makhẫ*h* ámitẫ*h* *g*âyávah rá*n*e.

When striving with each other they came together, for the sake of glory, the brisk (Maruts), immeasurable (in strength), panting for victory in the fight.

Sâya*n*a : 'For the sake of brilliant wealth.'

vii. 82, 5. marút-bhi*h* ugrá*h* súbham anyá*h* îyate.

The other, the fearful (Indra), goes with the Maruts to glory.

Sâya*n*a : 'He takes brilliant decoration.'

iii. 26, 4. subhé — p*rí*shatî*h* ayukshata.

They had harnessed the deer for victory.

Sâya*n*a : 'They had harnessed in the water the deer together (with the fires).'

i. 167, 6. ẫ asthậpayanta yuvatím yúvâna*h* subhé ní-mislâm.

The Maruts, the youths, placed the maid (lightning on their chariot), their companion for victory, (subhé nímislâm).

Sâya*n*a : 'For the sake of water, or, on the brilliant chariot.' Cf. i. 127, 6 ; 165, 1.

vi. 62, 4. súbham p*rí*ksham ísham ữr*g*am váhantâ.

The Asvins bringing glory, wealth, drink, and food.

L 2

viii. 26, 13. subhé *k*akráte, you bring him to glory.
Subham-yấvan is an epithet of the Maruts, i. 89, 7 ;
v. 61, 13.   Cf. subhra-yâvânâ, viii. 26, 19 (Asvinau).
Subham-yấ, of the wind, iv. 3, 6.
Subham-yú, of the rays of the dawn, x. 78, 7.

Verse 4, note [1]. Sâya*n*a : 'With spotted deer for their
horses.' See i. 37, 2, note [1], page 59.

Verse 4, note [2]. Ayấ is a word of very rare occurrence
in the Rig-veda. It is the instrum. sing. of the feminine
pronominal base â or î, and as a pronoun followed by a
noun it is frequently to be met with; v. 45, 11. ayấ dhiyấ,
&c. But in our verse it is irregular in form as not entering
into Sandhi with îsânâ*h*. This irregularity, however, which
might have led us to suppose an original ayấ*h*, indefatigable,
corresponding with the following ási, is vouched for by the
Pada text, in such matters a better authority than the Sanhitâ text, and certainly in this case fully borne out by the
Prâtisâkhya, i. 163, 10. We must therefore take ayấ as
an adverb, in the sense of thus or hence. In some passages
where ayấ seems thus to be used as an adverb, it would be
better to supply a noun from the preceding verse. Thus in
ii. 6, 2, ayấ refers to samídham in ii. 6, 1. In vi. 17, 15, a
similar noun, samídhâ or girấ, should be supplied. But
there are other passages where, unless we suppose that the
verse was meant to illustrate a ceremonial act, such as the
placing of a samídh, and that ayấ pointed to it, we must
take it as a simple adverb, like the Greek τῷ: Rv. iii.
12, 2 ; ix. 53, 2 ; 106, 14. In x. 116, 9, the Pada reads
áyâ*h*-iva, not áyâ, as given by Roth; in vi. 66, 4, áyâ nú,
the accent is likewise on the first.

Verse 4, note [3]. *R*i*n*a-yấvan is well explained by B. and
R. as going after debt, searching out sin. Sâya*n*a, though
he explains *r*i*n*a-yấvan by removing sin, derives it nevertheless correctly from *r*i*n*a and yâ, and not from yu. The
same formation is found in subham-yấvan, &c. ; and as
t~~here~~ is *r*i*n*a-yấ besides *r*i*n*a-yấvan, so we find subham-yấ
besides subham-yấvan.

Verse 5, note ¹. The Soma-juice inspires the poet with eloquence.

Verse 5, note ². Sámi occurs again in ii. 31, 6; iii. 55, 3; viii. 45, 27; x. 40, 1. In our passage it must be taken as a locative of sám, meaning work, but with special reference to the toil of the battle-field. It is used in the same sense in

viii. 45, 27. ví ânat turvâne sámi.

He (Indra) was able to overcome in battle, lit. he reached to, or he arrived at the overcoming or the victory in battle.

But, like other words which have the general meaning of working or toiling, sám is likewise used in the sense of sacrifice. This meaning seems more applicable in

x. 40, 1. vástoh-vastoh váhamânam dhiyấ sámi.

Your chariot, O Asvins, which through prayer comes every morning to the sacrifice.

ii. 31, 6. apẫm nápât âsu-hémâ dhiyấ sámi.

Apâm napât (Agni) who through prayer comes quickly to the sacrifice.

In these two passages one feels inclined, with a slight alteration of the accent, to read dhiyâ-sámi as one word. Dhiyâ-sâm would mean the sacrificer who is engaged in prayer; cf. dhiyâ-gúr, v. 43, 15. Thus we read:

vi. 2, 4. yáh te su-dânave dhiyấ mártah sasámate.

The mortal who toils for thee, the liberal god, with prayer.

There is no necessity, however, for such a change, and the authority of the MSS. is certainly against it.

In iii. 55, 3, sámi is an acc. plur. neut.:

sámi ákkha dîdye pûrvyẫni.

I glance back at the former sacrifices. See B. R. s.v. dî.

From the same root we have the feminine sámî, meaning work, sacrificial work, but, as far as we can see, not simply sacrifice. Thus the Ribhus and others are said to have acquired immortality by their work or works, sámî or sámîbhih, i. 20, 2; 110, 4; iii. 60, 3; iv. 33, 4. Cf. iv. 22, 8; 17, 18; v. 42, 10; 77, 4; vi. 52, 1; viii. 75, 14; ix. 74, 7; x. 28, 12. In vi. 3, 2, we read:

îgé yagñébhih sasamé sámîbhih.

I have sacrificed with sacrifices, I have worked with pious works.

Here the verb *sam* must be taken in the sense of working, or performing ceremonial worship, while in other places (iii. 29, 16; v. 2, 7) it takes the more special sense of singing songs of praise. The Greek κάμ-νω, to work, to labour, to tire (Sanskrit sâmyati), the Greek κομιδή and κομίζω, to labour for or take care of a person, and possibly even the Greek κῶμος, a song or a festival (not a village song), may all find their explanation in the Sanskrit root *sam*.

The idea that the Maruts did not originally enjoy divine honours will occur again and again : cf. i. 6, 4; 72, 3. A similar expression is used of the *R*ibhus, i. 20, 8, &c. Ya*g*ñíya, properly 'worthy of sacrifice,' has the meaning of divine or sacred. The Greek ἅγιος has been compared with yâ*g*ya, *sacrificio colendus*, not a Vedic word.

Verse 6, note [1]. *S*riyáse kám seems to be the same as the more frequent *s*riyé kám. *S*riyáse only occurs twice more, v. 59, 3. The chief irregularity consists in the absence of Gu*n*a, which is provided for by Pâ*n*ini's kasen (iii. 4, 9). Similar infinitives, if they may so be called, are bhiyáse, v. 29, 4; vridháse, v. 64, 5; dhruváse, vii. 70, 1; tu*g*áse, iv. 23, 7; ri*ñg*áse, viii. 4, 17; vri*ñg*áse, viii. 76, 1; *r*ikáse, vii. 61, 6. In vi. 39, 5, *r*ikáse may be a dat. sing. of the masculine, to the praiser.

Verse 6, note [2]. Mimikshire from myaksh, to be united with. Ra*s*mí, rays, after bhânú, splendour, may seem weak, but it is impossible. to assign to ra*s*mí any other meaning, such as reins, or strings of a musical instrument. In v. 79, 8, ra*s*mí is used in juxta-position with ar*k*í.

Verse 6, note [3]. The bearing of this concluding verse is not quite clear, unless we take it as a continuation of the preceding verse. It was there said that the Maruts (the *r*íkvâ*n*a*h*) obtained their sacrificial honours, after having joined Indra in his work. Having thus obtained a place in the sacrifice, they may be said to have won at the same time splendour and worshippers to sing their praises, and to have established themselves in what became afterwards known as their own abode, their own place among the gods who are invoked at the sacrifice.

The metre requires that we should read dhâmana*h*.

Benfey translates: 'Gedeih'n zu spenden woll'n die schöngeschmücketen mit Lichtern, Strahlen mit Lobsängern regenen; die brüllenden, furchtlosen stürmischen, sie sind bekannt als Glieder des geliebten Marutstamms.'

Wilson: 'Combining with the solar rays, they have willingly poured down (rain) for the welfare (of mankind), and, hymned by the priests, have been pleased partakers of the (sacrificial food). Addressed with praises, moving swiftly, and exempt from fear, they have become possessed of a station agreeable and suitable to the Maruts.'

MANDALA I, SÛKTA 88.

ASHTAKA I, ADHYÂYA 6, VARGA 14.

1. Â vidyúnmat-bhi*h* marut*ah* su-arkaí*h* ráthebhi*h* yâta rish*t*imát-bhi*h** ásva-parnai*h*, â várshish*th*ayâ na*h* ishâ váya*h* ná paptata su-mâyâ*h*.

2. Tó aru*n*óbhi*h* váram â pisángai*h* subhó kám yânti rathatû*h*-bhi*h* ásvai*h*, rukmá*h* ná *k*itrá*h* † svá-dhiti-vân pavyâ ráthasya *g*anghananta bhûma.

3. *S*riyé kám va*h* ádhi tanûshu vâsi*h* medhâ ‡ vânâ ná k*r*i*n*avante ûrdhvâ, yushmábhyam kám marut*ah* su-*g*âtâ*h* tuvi-dyumnâsa*h* dhanayante ádrim.

4. Áhâni g*r*ídhrâ*h* pári â va*h* â agu*h* imâm dhíyam vârkâryâm *k*a devím, bráhma k*r*i*n*vánta*h* gótamâsa*h* arkaí*h* ûrdhvám nunudre utsa-dhím píbadhyai.

5. Etát tyát ná yó*g*anam a*k*eti sasvá*h* ha yát marut*ah* gótama*h* va*h*, pásyan híra*n*ya-*k*akrân áya*h*-dam*sht*rân vi-dhâvata*h* varâhûn.

6. Eshâ syâ va*h* marut*ah* anu-bhartrî práti sto-bhati vâgháta*h* ná vâ*n*î, ástobhayat v*r*íthâ âsâm ánu svadhâm gábhastyo*h*.

---

* rish*t*i-manta*h* ?   † *k*itrá*h* eshâm?   ‡ medhâ*h*

1. Come hither, Maruts, on your chariots charged with lightning, resounding with beautiful songs,[1] stored with spears, and winged with horses! Fly[3] to us like birds, with your best food,[2] you mighty ones!

2. They come gloriously on their red, or, it may be, on their tawny horses which hasten their chariots. He who holds the axe[1] is brilliant like gold;—with the felly[2] of the chariot they have struck the earth.

3. On your bodies there are daggers for beauty; may they stir up our minds[1] as they stir up the forests. For your sake, O well-born Maruts, you who are full of vigour, they (the priests) have shaken[2] the stone (for distilling Soma).

4. Days went round you and came back,[1] O hawks, back to this prayer, and to this sacred rite; the Gotamas making prayer with songs, have pushed up the lid of the well (the cloud) for to drink.

5. No such hymn[1] was ever known as this which Gotama sounded for you, O Maruts, when he saw you on golden wheels, wild boars[2] rushing about with iron tusks.

6. This refreshing draught of Soma rushes towards you, like the voice of a suppliant: it rushes freely from our hands as these libations are wont to do.

COMMENTARY.

This hymn is ascribed to Gotama, the son of Rahûga*n*a. The metre varies. Verses 1 and 6 are put down as Prastâra-pankti, i. e. as 12 + 12 + 8 + 8. By merely counting the syllables, and dissolving semivowels, it is just possible to get twenty-four syllables in the first line of verses 1 and 6. The old metricians must have scanned verse 1 :

ā vidyŭnmāt-bhi*h* mărŭta*h* sŭ-ārkai*h*
rāthĕbhi*h* yāta⁻risht̆imat-bhi*h* āsvā-par*n*ai*h*.

Again verse 6 : eshā syā va*h* mărŭta*h* ănŭ-bhārtrî
prāti stŏbhatĭ vāghata*h* nă vā*n*î.

But the general character of these lines shows that they were intended for hendecasyllabics, each ending in a bacchius, though even then they are not free from irregularities. The first verse would scan :

ā vidyŭnmāt-bhi*h* mărŭta*h* sŭ-ārkai*h*
rāthĕbhi*h* yāta⁻risht̆imāt-(bhi*h*) āsvā-par*n*ai*h*.

And verse 6 : eshā syā va*h* mărŭta*h*⁻ănŭ-bhārtrî
prāti stŏbhatĭ vāghata*h* nă vā*n*î.

Our only difficulty would be the termination bhi*h* of risht̆i-mat-bhi*h*. I cannot adopt Professor Kuhn's suggestion to drop the Visarga of bhi*h* and change i into y (Beiträge, vol. iv. p. 198), for this would be a license without any parallel. It is different with sa*h*, originally sa, or with feminines in i*h*, where parallel forms in î are intelligible. The simplest correction would be to read rāthĕbhih yāta⁻risht̆i-manta*h*⁻asvā-par*n*aih. One might urge in support of this reading that in all other passages where risht̆imat occurs, it refers to the Maruts themselves, and never to their chariots. Yet the difficulty remains, how could so simple a reading have been replaced by a more difficult one?

In the two Gâyatrî pâdas which follow I feel equally reluctant to alter. I therefore scan

ā vărshisht̆hāyā na*h* ĭshā vāya*h* nă pāptătă sŭ-māyā*h*,

taking the dactyl of paptata as representing a spondee, and

admitting the exceptional bacchius instead of the amphimacer at the end of the line.

The last line of verse 6 should be scanned:

ăstŏbhāyăt vr̆ithā̄̆āsām̆ ănŭ svādhām̆ gābhăstyŏh̆.

There are two other verses in this hymn where the metre is difficult. In the last pâda of verse 5 we have seven syllables instead of eleven. Again, I say, it would be most easy to insert one of the many tetrasyllabic epithets of the Maruts. But this would have been equally easy for the collectors of the Veda. Now the authors of the Anukramanîs distinctly state that this fifth verse is virâdrûpâ, i. e. that one of its pâdas consists of eight syllables. How they would have made eight syllables out of vi-dhâvatah varâhûn does not appear, but at all events they knew that last pâda to be imperfect. The rhythm does not suffer by this omission, as long as we scan vi-dhâvatah varâhûn.

Lastly, there is the third pâda of the second verse, rukmah na kitrah svadhiti-vân. It would not be possible to get eleven syllables out of this, unless we admitted vyûha not only in svadhitivân or svadhitî-vân, but also in kitrah. Nothing would be easier than to insert eshâm after kitrah, but the question occurs again, how could eshâm be lost, or why, if by some accident it had been lost, was not so obvious a correction made by Saunaka and Kâtyâyana?

Verse 1, note [1]. Alluding to the music of the Maruts, and not to the splendour of the lightning which is mentioned before. See Wolf, Beiträge zur Deutschen Mythologie, vol. ii. p. 137. ʻDas Ross und den Wagen des Gottes begleitet munterer Hörnerschall, entweder stösst er selbst ins Horn, oder sein Gefolge. Oft vernimmt man auch eine liebliche Musik, der keine auf Erden gleich kommt (Müllenhof, 582). Das wird das Pfeifen und Heulen des Sturmes sein, nur in idealisirter Art.ʼ Ibid. p. 158.

Verse 1, note [2]. Várshishtha, which is generally explained as the superlative of vriddha, old, (Pân. vi. 4, 157,) has in most passages of the Rig-veda the more general meaning of strong or excellent: vi. 47, 9. ísham ắ vakshi ishām várshishthâm; iii. 13, 7 (vásu); iii. 26, 8 (rátna);

iii. 16, 3 (raí); iv. 31, 15; viii. 46, 24 (srávah); iv. 22, 9 (nrimná); v. 67, 1 (kshatrá); vi. 45, 31 (mûrdhán). In some passages, however, it may be taken in the sense of oldest (i. 37, 6; v. 7, 1), though by no means necessarily. Várshishtha is derived in reality from vríshan, in the sense of strong, excellent. See note to i. 85, 12, page 126.

Verse 1, note [3]. Paptata, the second person plural of the Let of the reduplicated base of pat. It is curiously like the Greek πίπτετε, but it has the meaning of flying rather than falling: see Curtius, Grundzüge, p. 190. Two other forms formed on the same principle occur in the Rig-veda, paptah and paptan :

ii. 31, 1. prá yát váyah ná páptan.

That they may fly to us like birds.

vi. 63, 6. prá vâm váyah—ánu paptan.

May your birds fly after you.

x. 95, 15. púrûravah mâ mrithâh mâ prá paptah.

Purûravas, do not die, do not fly away!

Verse 2, note [1]. Though svadhiti-vân does not occur again, it can only mean he who holds the axe, or, it may be the sword or the thunderbolt, the latter particularly, if Indra is here intended. Svadhiti signifies axe :

iii. 2, 10. svá-dhitim ná tégase.

They adorned Agni like an axe to shine or to cut.

The svádhiti is used by the butcher, i. 162, 9; 18; 20; and by the wood-cutter or carpenter, iii. 8, 6; 11; x. 89, 7, &c. In v. 32, 10, a devî svádhitih is mentioned, possibly the lightning, the companion of Indra and the Maruts.

Verse 2, note [2]. The felly of the chariot of the Maruts is frequently mentioned. It was considered not only as an essential part of their chariot, but likewise as useful for crushing the enemy :

v. 52, 9. utá pavyâ ráthânâm ádrim bhindanti ójasâ.

They cut the mountain (cloud) with the felly of their chariot.

i. 166, 10. pavíshu kshurâh ádhi.

On their fellies are sharp edges.

In v. 31, 5, fellies arc mentioned without horses and chariot, which were turned by Indra against the Dasyus, (i. 64, 11.) I doubt, however, whether in India or elsewhere the fellies or the wheels of chariots were ever used as weapons of attack, as detached from the chariot; (see M. M., On Pavîrava, in Beiträge zur vergleichenden Sprachforschung, vol. iii. p. 447.) If we translate the figurative language of the Vedic poets into matter-of-fact terms, the fellies of the chariots of the Maruts may be rendered by thunderbolts; yet by the poets of the Veda, as by the ancient people of Germany, thunder was really supposed to be the noise of the chariot of a god, and it was but a continuation of the same belief that the sharp wheels of that chariot were supposed to cut and crush the clouds; (see M. M., loc. cit. p. 444.)

Verse 3, note [1]. That the vâsîs arc small weapons, knives or daggers, we saw before, p. 59. Sâyana here explains vâsî by a weapon commonly called âra, or an awl. In x. 101, 10, vâsîs are mentioned, made of stone, asman-mâyî.

The difficulty begins with the second half. Medhâ, as here written in the Pada text, could only be a plural of a neuter medhám, but such a neuter does nowhere exist in the Veda. We only find the masculine médha, sacrifice, which is out of the question here, on account of its accent. Hence the passage iii. 58, 2, ûrdhvâh bhavanti pitárâ-iva médhâh, is of no assistance, unless we alter the accent. The feminine medhâ means will, thought, prayer: i. 18, 6; ii. 34, 7; iv. 33, 10; v. 27, 4; 42, 13; vii. 104, 6; viii. 6, 10; 52, 9; ix. 9, 9; 26, 3; 32, 6; 65, 16; 107, 25; x. 91, 8. The construction does not allow us to take medhâ as a Vedic instrumental instead of medhâyâ, nor does such a form occur anywhere else in the Rig-veda. Nothing remains, I believe, than to have recourse to conjecture, and the addition of a single Visarga in the Pada would remove all difficulty. In the next line, if tuvi-dyumnâsah be the subject, it would signify the priests. This, however, is again without any warrant from the Rig-veda, where tuvi-dyumná is always used as an epithet of gods. I therefore take it as referring to the Maruts, as an

adjective in the nominative, following the vocatives maruta*h*
su-*y*âtâ*h*.   The conception that the Maruts stir up the
forests is not of unfrequent occurrence in the Rig-veda:
cf. i. 171, 3; v. 59, 6.   That ûrdhvá is used of the mind,
in the sense of roused, may be seen in i. 119, 2; 134, 1;
144, 1; vii. 64, 4.   The idea in the poet's mind seems to
have been that the thunderbolts of the Maruts rouse up
men to prayer as they stir the tops of the forest trees.

Verse 3, note [2].   On dhan in the sense of to agitate,
see B. and R. s. v.

Verse 4, note [1].   The first question is, which is the
subject, áhâni or grídhrâ*h* ?   If grídhrâ*h* were the subject,
then we should have to translate it by the eager poets,
and take áhâni in the sense of vísvâ ahâni.   The sense
then might be: 'Day by day did the eager poets sing
around you this prayer.'   There would be several objections, however, to this rendering.   First, grídhrâ*h* never
occurs again as signifying poets or priests.   One passage only could be quoted in support, ix. 97, 57, kaváya*h*
ná grídhrâ*h* (not grídhrâ*h*), like greedy poets.   But even
here, if this translation is right, the adjective is explained
by kaví, and does not stand by itself.   Secondly, áhâni
by itself is never used adverbially in the sense of day after
day.   The only similar passage that might be quoted is
iii. 34, 10, and that is very doubtful.   To take áhâni as a
totally different word, viz. as á + hâni, without ceasing,
without wearying, would be too bold in the present state
of Vedic interpretation.   If then we take áhâni as the
subject, grídhrâ*h* would have to be taken as a vocative,
and intended for the Maruts.   Now, it is perfectly true,
that by itself grídhra, hawk, does not occur again as a
name of the Maruts, but *s*yená, hawk, and particularly a
strong hawk (ix. 96, 6), is not only a common simile applied
to the Maruts, but is actually used as one of their names:
    vii. 56, 3. abhí sva-pû̃bhi*h* mithá*h* vapanta vấta-svanasa*h*
*s*yenấ*h* aspridhran.
    They plucked each other with their beaks (?), the hawks,
rushing like the wind, strove together.

Aguh might be the aorist of gai, to sing, or of gâ, to go:

i. 174, 8. sânâ tâ te indra nâvyâh â aguh.
New poets, O Indra, sang these thy old deeds.
iii. 56, 2. gâvah â aguh.
The cows approached.

If then the sense of the first line is, 'Days went and came back to you,' the next question is whether we are to extend the construction to the next words, imâm dhíyam vârkâryâm ka devím, or whether these words are to be joined to krinvántah, like bráhma. The meaning of vârkâryâ is, of course, unknown. Sâyana's interpretation as 'what is to be made by means of water' is merely etymological, and does not help us much. It is true that the object of the hymn, which is addressed to the Maruts, is rain, and that literally vârkâryâ might be explained as 'that the effect of which is rain.' But this is far too artificial a word for Vedic poets. Possibly there was some other word that had become unintelligible and which, by a slight change, was turned into vârkâryâ, in order to give the meaning of rain-producing. It might have been karkârya, glorious, or the song of a poet called Vârkara. The most likely supposition is that vârkâryâ was the name given to some famous hymn, some pæan or song of triumph belonging to the Gotamas, possibly to some verses of the very hymn before us. In this case the epithet devî would be quite appropriate, for it is frequently used for a sacred or sacrificial song: iv. 43, 1. devím su-stutím; iii. 18, 3. imâm dhíyam sata-séyâya devím. See, however, the note to verse 6.

The purport of the whole line would then be that many days have gone for the Maruts as well as for the famous hymn once addressed to them by Gotama, or, in other words, that the Gotamas have long been devoted to the Maruts, an idea frequently recurring in the hymns of the Veda, and, in our case, carried on in the next verse, where it is said that the present hymn is like one that Gotama composed when he saw the Maruts or spoke of them as wild boars with iron tusks. The pushing up the lid of the well for to drink, means that they obtained rain from the cloud, which is here, as before, represented as a covered well.

See another explanation in Haug, Über die ursprüngliche Bedeutung des Wortes Brahma, 1868, p. 5.

Verse 5, note [1]. Yó*g*ana commonly means a chariot: vi. 62, 6. are*n*ú-bhi*h* yó*g*anebhi*h* bhu*g*ántâ. You who possess dustless chariots. viii. 72, 6. á*s*va-vat yó*g*anam brihát. The great chariot with horses.

It then became the name for a distance to be accomplished without unharnessing the horses, just as the Latin *jugum,* a yoke, then a *juger* of land, ‘quod uno jugo boum uno die exarari posset,’ Pliny xviii. 3, 3, 9.

In our passage, however, yó*g*ana means a hymn, lit. a composition, which is clearly its meaning in

viii. 90, 3. bráhma te indra girva*n*a*h* kriyánte ánatid-bhutâ, imấ *g*ushasva hari-a*s*va yó*g*anâ índra yấ te ámanmahi.

Unequalled prayers are made for thee, praiseworthy Indra; accept these hymns which we have devised for thee, O Indra with bright horses!

Verse 5, note [2]. Varâhu has here the same meaning as varâhá, wild boar, (viii. 77, 10; x. 28, 4.) It occurs once more, i. 121, 11, as applied to V*ri*tra, who is also called varâhá, i. 61, 7; x. 99, 6. In x. 67, 7, v*ri*sha-bhi*h* varâhai*h* (with the accent on the penultimate) is intended for the Maruts*. Except in this passage, varâha has the accent on the last syllable: ix. 97, 7, varâhá is applied to Soma.

Verse 6. This last verse is almost unintelligible to me. I give, however, the various attempts that have been made to explain it.

Wilson: ‘This is that praise, Maruts, which, suited (to your merits), glorifies every one of you. The speech of the

---

* See Genthe, Die Windgottheiten, 1861, p. 14; Grimm, Deutsche Mytho-logie, p. 689. Grimm mentions *ebur*ð*rung* (boar-throng) as a name of Orion, the star that betokens storm.

priest has now glorified you, without difficulty, with sacred verses, since (you have placed) food in our hands.'

Benfey: ' Dies Lied — Maruts! — das hinter euch empor-strebt, es klingt zurück gleich eines Beters Stimme Mühlos schuf solche Lieder er, entsprechend eurer Arme Kraft. (Note: Der zum Himmel schallende Lobgesang findet seinen Widerhall (wirklich, " bebt zurück") in dem Sturm-geheul der Maruts, welches mit dem Geheul des Betenden verglichen wird.)'

Langlois : ' O Marouts, la voix qui s'élève aujourd'hui vers vous, vous chante avec non moins de raison que celle qui vous célébra (jadis). Oui, c'est avec justice que nous vous exaltons dans ces (vers), tenant en nos mains les mets sacrés.'

My own translation is to a great extent conjectural. It seems to me from verse 3, that the poet offers both a hymn of praise and a libation of Soma. Possibly vârkâryâ in verse 4 might be taken in the sense of Soma-juice, and be derived from valkala, which in later Sanskrit means the bark of trees. In that case verse 5 would again refer to the hymn of Gotama, and verse 6 to the libation which is to accompany it. Anu-bhartrî does not occur again, but it can only mean what supports or refreshes, and therefore would be applicable to a libation of Soma which supports the gods. The verb stobhati would well express the rushing sound of the Soma, as in i. 168, 8, it expresses the rushing noise of the waters against the fellies of the chariots. The next line adds little beyond stating that this libation of Soma rushes forth freely from the hands, the gabhastîs being specially mentioned in other passages where the crushing of the Soma-plant is described :

ix. 71, 3. ádri-bhi*h* sutá*h* pavate gábhastyo*h*.

The Soma squeezed by the stones runs from the hands.

On svadhấ see p. 19.

MANDALA I, SÛKTA 165.
ASHTAKA II, ADHYÂYA 3, VARGA 24–26.

Indra*h*.

1. Káyâ *s*ubhấ sá-vayasa*h* sá-nîlấ*h* samấnyấ marúta*h* sám mimikshu*h*, káyâ matî́ kúta*h* ấ-itâsa*h* eté
ár*k*anti *s*úshmam vríshana*h* vasu-yấ.

Indra*h*.

2. Kásya bráhmấ*n*i *gug*ushu*h* yúvâna*h* kấ*h* adhvaré
marúta*h* ấ vavarta, *sy*enấn-iva dhrá*g*ata*h* antárikshe
kéna mahấ mánasâ ríramâma.

Maruta*h*.

3. Kútа*h* tvám indra mấhina*h* sán éka*h* yâsi sat-
pate kím te itthấ, sám p*ri*k*kh*ase sam-arấ*n*ấ*h* *s*ubhâ-
naí*h* vo*k*é*h* tát *n*a*h* hari-va*h* yất te asmé (íti).

---

1. WILSON: (Indra speaks): With what auspicious fortune
have the Maruts, who are of one age, one residence, one
dignity, watered (the earth) together: with what intention:
whence have they come: Showerers of rain, they venerate,
through desire of wealth, the energy (that is generated in the
world by rain)?

LANGLOIS: Quel éclat ces Marouts qui parcourent, qui
habitent ensemble (les espaces de l'air) répandent par tout (le
monde)! Que veulent-ils? d'où viennent-ils, généreux et
riches, chercher les offrandes?

2. WILSON: Of whose oblations do the youthful (Maruts)
approve: who attracts them to his (own) sacrifice (from the

The Prologue.

The sacrificer speaks :

1. With what splendour are the Maruts all equally[1] endowed,[2] they who are of the same age, and dwell in the same house? With what thoughts? From whence are they come?[3] Do these heroes sing forth their (own) strength[4] because they wish for wealth?

2. Whose prayers have the youths accepted? Who has turned the Maruts to his own sacrifice? By what strong devotion[1] may we delight them, they who float through the air like hawks?

The Dialogue.

The Maruts speak :

3. From whence,[1] O Indra, dost thou come alone, thou who art mighty? O lord of men,[2] what has thus happened to thee? Thou greetest (us)[3] when thou comest together with (us), the bright (Maruts).[4] Tell us then, thou with thy bay horses, what thou hast against us!

---

rites of others): with what powerful praise may we propitiate (them), wandering like kites in the mid-air?

Langlois: Quel est celui qui, par ses hommages, plaît à ces jeunes (divinités)? qui, par son sacrifice, attire les Marouts? Par quelle prière parviendrons-nous à retenir ces (dieux qui) comme des éperviers, parcourent les airs?

3. Wilson: (The Maruts): Indra, lord of the good, whither dost thou, who art entitled to honour, proceed alone: what means this (absence of attendance): when followed (by us), thou requirest (what is right). Lord of fleet horses, say to us, with pleasant words, that which thou (hast to say) to us.

Langlois : (Les Marouts parlent): Indra, maître des

M 2

Indra*h.*

4. Bráhmá*n*i me matáya*h* sám sutása*h* súshma*h* iyarti prá-bh*r*ita*h* me ádri*h*, á̱ sásate práti haryanti ukthá̱ imá̱ hárî (íti) vahata*h* tá̱ na*h* á*kkh*a.

Maruta*h.*

5. Áta*h* vayám antamébhi*h* yugá̱ná̱*h* svá-kshatre-bhi*h* tanvá̱*h* súmbhamá̱ná̱*h* má̱ha*h*-bhi*h* óta̱n úpa yu*g*-mahe nú índra svadhá̱m á̱nu hí na*h* babhútha.

Indra*h.*

6. Kvã̱ syá̱ va*h* maruta*h* svadhá̱ â̱sît yát má̱m ékam sam-á̱dhatta ahi-hátye, ahá̱m hí ugrá̱*h* tavi-shá̱*h* túvishmâ̱n vísvasya sá̱tro*h* á̱namam vadha-sna*íh.*

---

hommes pieux, d'où viens-tu, grand et unique? Que veux-tu? Toi qui est notre compagnon, tu peux nous répondre avec bonté. O dieu, traîné par des coursiers azurés, dis-nous ce que tu nous veux.

4. WILSON.: (Indra): Sacred rites are mine : (holy) praises give me pleasure : libations are for me : my vigorous thunder-bolt, hurled (against my foes), goes (to its mark): me, do (pious worshippers) propitiate : hymns are addressed to me; these horses bear us to the presence (of those worshippers, and worship).

LANGLOIS : (Indra parle): Les cérémonies, les prières, les hymnes, les libations, les offrandes, tout est à moi. Je porte la foudre. Des invocations, des chants se sont fait entendre. Mes chevaux m'amènent. Voilà ce que je veux ici.

5. WILSON : (The Maruts): Therefore we also, decorating our persons, are ready, with our docile and nigh-standing

Indra speaks:

4. The sacred songs are mine, (mine are) the prayers;[1] sweet[2] are the libations! My strength rises,[3] my thunderbolt is hurled forth. They call for me, the prayers yearn for me. Here are my horses, they carry me towards them.

The Maruts speak:

5. Therefore, in company with our strong friends,[1] having adorned our bodies, we now harness our fallow deer[2] with all our might;[3]—for, Indra, according to thy custom, thou hast been with us.

Indra speaks:

6. Where, O Maruts, was that custom of yours, that you should join me who am alone in the killing of Ahi? I indeed am terrible, strong, powerful,—I escaped from the blows of every enemy.[1]

---

steeds, (to attend thee) with all our splendour, to those rites; verily, Indra, thou appropriatest our (sacrificial) food.

LANGLOIS: (Les Marouts parlent): Et nous, sur les puissants coursiers que voici, plaçant nos corps légers et brillants, nous joignons nos splendeurs aux tiennes. Et tu veux, Indra, t'approprier notre offrande?

6. WILSON: (Indra): Where, Maruts, has that (sacrificial) food been assigned to you, which, for the destruction of Ahi, was appropriated to me alone; for I indeed am fierce and strong and mighty, and have bowed down all mine enemies with death-dealing shafts.

LANGLOIS: (Indra parle): Et comment cette offrande serait-elle pour vous, ô Marouts, quand vous reconnaissez ma supériorité en réclamant mon secours pour la mort d'Ahi? Je suis grand, fort et redoutable, et de mes traits, funestes à tous mes ennemis, j'ai tué Ahi.

Maruta*h*.

7. Bhûri *k*akartha yú*g*yebhi*h* asmé (íti) samâné-
bhi*h* v*r*ishabha paúm*syebhi*h*, bhûrî*n*i hí k*r*i*n*ávâma
savish*th*a índra krátvâ maruta*h* yát vásâma.

Indra*h*.

8. Vádhîm v*r*itrám maruta*h* indriyé*n*a svéna
bhâmena tavishá*h* babhûvã́n, ahám etã́*h* mánave vi-
svá-*k*andrâ*h* su-gã́*h* apá*h* *k*akara vá*g*ra-bâhu*h*.

Maruta*h*.

9. Ánuttam ã́ te magha-van nákí*h* nú ná tvã́-vân
asti devátâ vídâna*h*, ná *g*ã́yamâna*h* násate ná *g*âtá*h*
yã́ni karishyã́ * k*r*i*n*uhí pra-v*r*iddha.

Indra*h*.

10. Ékasya *k*it me vi-bhú astu ó*g*a*h* yã́ nú

---

7. WILSON: (Maruts): Showerer (of benefits) thou hast
done much; but it has been with our united equal energies;
for we, too, most powerful Indra, have done many things, and
by our deeds (we are, as) we desire to be, Maruts.

LANGLOIS: (Les Marouts parlent): Tu as beaucoup fait,
(dieu) généreux en venant nous seconder de ta force héroïque.
Mais, ô puissant Indra, nous pouvons aussi beaucoup, quand,
nous autres Marouts, nous voulons prouver notre vaillance.

8. WILSON: (Indra): By my own prowess (Maruts) I,
mighty in my wrath, slew Vritra; armed with my thunderbolt, I created all these pellucid, gently-flowing waters for
(the good of) man.

---

* kari*sh*yã́*h* '

The Maruts speak:

7. Thou hast achieved much with us as companions.[1] With the same valour, O hero! let us achieve then many things, O thou most powerful, O Indra! whatever we, O Maruts, wish with our heart.[2]

Indra speaks:

8. I slew V*r*itra, O Maruts, with (Indra's) might, having grown strong through my own vigour; I, who hold the thunderbolt in my arms, I have made these all-brilliant waters to flow freely for man.[1]

The Maruts speak:

9. Nothing, O powerful lord, is strong before thee: no one is known among the gods[1] like unto thee. No one who is now born[2] will come near, no one who has been born. Do what has to be done,[3] thou who art grown so strong.

Indra speaks:

10. Almighty power be mine alone, whatever I

_____

LANGLOIS: (Indra parle): Marouts, j'ai tué Vritra, et je n'ai eu besoin que de ma colère et de ma force d'Indra. C'est moi, qui, la foudre à la main, ai ouvert un chemin à ces ondes qui font le bonheur de Manou.

9. WILSON: (Maruts): Verily, Maghavat, nothing (done) by thee is unavailing, there is no divinity as wise as thou; no one being born, or that has been born, ever surpasses the glorious deeds which thou, mighty (Indra), hast achieved.

LANGLOIS: (Les Marouts parlent): O Maghavan, nous n'attaquons pas ta gloire. Personne, ô dieu, quand on connaît tes exploits, ne peut se croire ton égal. Aucun être, présent ou passé ne saurait te valoir. Tu es grand, fais ce que tu dois faire.

10. WILSON: (Indra): May the prowess of me alone be

dadhrishvắn krinávai maníshắ, ahám hí ugrá*h* maruta*h* vídâna*h* yắni *k*yávam índra*h* ít íse eshâm.

Indra*h*.

11. Ámandat mâ maruta*h* stóma*h* átra yát me
nara*h* srútyam bráhma *k*akrắ, índrâya vri*shne* sú-
makhâya máhyam sákhyo sákhâya*h* tanvè tanûbhi*h*.

Indra*h*.

12. Evá ít eté práti mâ ró*k*amânâ*h* ánedya*h* *
sráva*h* ắ ísha*h* dádhânâ*h*, sam-*k*ákshya maruta*h*
*k*andrá-var*nâh* á*kkh*ânta me *kh*adáyâtha *k*a nûnám.

Agastya*h*.

13. Kắ*h* nú átra maruta*h* mamahe va*h* prắ yâtana

irresistible, may I quickly accomplish whatever I contemplate
in my mind, for verily, Maruts, I am fierce and sagacious,
and to whatever (objects) I direct (my thoughts), of them I
am the lord, and rule (over them).

LANGLOIS: (Indra parle): Ma force est assez grande, pour
que, seul, je puisse exécuter ce que je veux tenter. Je suis
redoutable, ô Marouts, je sais ce que j'ai à faire, moi, Indra,
maître de vous tous.

11. WILSON: Maruts, on this occasion praise delights me;
that praise which is to be heard (by all), which men have
offered me. To Indra, the showerer (of benefits), the object
of pious sacrifice; to me, (endowed) with many forms, (do
you) my friends (offer sacrifices) for (the nourishment of my)
person.

---

* ánedyam ?

may do, daring in my heart;[1] for I indeed, O Maruts, am known as terrible: of all that I threw down, I, Indra, am the lord.

Indra speaks:

11. O Maruts, now your praise has pleased me, the glorious hymn which you have made for me, ye men!—for me, for Indra, for the powerful hero, as friends for a friend, for your own sake and by your own efforts.[1]

Indra speaks:

12. Truly, there they are, shining towards me, assuming blameless glory, assuming vigour. O Maruts, wherever I have looked for you, you have appeared to me in bright splendour: appear to me also now!

The Epilogue.

The sacrificer speaks:

13. Who has magnified you here, O Maruts? Come

LANGLOIS: O Marouts, l'éloge que vous avez fait de moi m'a flatté et surtout votre attention à me laisser votre part du sacrifice. Indra est généreux, et fêté par de nombreux hommages. Soyez mes amis, et développez vos corps (légers).

12. WILSON: Maruts, verily, glorifying me, and enjoying boundless fame and food (through my favour), do you, of golden colour, and invested with glory, cover me in requital, verily, (with renown.)

LANGLOIS: Ainsi brillant à mes côtés, prenez dans les offrandes et dans les hymnes la part conforme à votre rang, O Marouts, vos couleurs sont merveilleuses. Resplendissons ensemble, et couvrez-moi (de vos corps) comme vous l'avez fait jusqu'à présent.

13. WILSON: (Agastya): What mortal, Maruts, worships you in this world: hasten, friends, to the presence of your

sákhin *ákkha* sakhâya*h*, mánmâni *kitrá*h api-vátá-
yanta*h* eshấm bhûta návedấ*h* me *r*itấnâm.

Agastya*h*.
14. Ấ yất duvasyất duváse ná kârú*h* asmấn *k*akré
mânyásya medhẫ, ó (íti) sú varta maruta*h* vípram
ákkha imẫ bráhmấ*n*i *g*aritẫ va*h* ar*k*at.

Agastya*h*.
15. Eshấ*h* va*h* stómah maruta*h* iyám gî*h* mândâr-
yásya mânyásya kâró*h*, ẫ ishẫ yâsîsh*t*a tanvẽ vayẫm
vidyẫma ishấm v*r*i*g*ánam *g*îrá-dânum.

---

friends; wonderful (divinities), be to them the means of acquiring riches; and be not uncognisant of my merits.
LANGLOIS: (Le poëte parle): Quel est celui qui vous chante
en ce moment, ô Marouts? Soyez-nous agréables, et venez
vers des amis. D'un souffle propice favorisez nos vœux. Pos-
sesseurs de biens variés, daignez visiter notre sacrifice.
14. WILSON: Since the experienced intellect of a venerable
(sage), competent to bestow praise upon (you), who deserve
praise, has been exerted for us: do you, Maruts, come to the
presence of the devout (worshipper) who, glorifying (you),
worships you with these holy rites.
LANGLOIS: Si la science d'un sage nous a, comme un

COMMENTARY.

According to the Anukrama*n*ikâ this hymn is a dialogue
between Agastya, the Maruts, and Indra. A careful consideration of the hymn would probably have led us to a similar
conclusion, but I doubt whether it would have led us to
adopt the same distribution of the verses among the poet,
the Maruts, and Indra, as that adopted by the author of the

hither, O friends, towards your friends. Ye brilliant Maruts, cherish[1] these prayers, and be mindful of these my rites.

14. The wisdom of Mânya has brought us to this, that he should help as the poet helps the performer of a sacrifice: bring (them) hither quickly! Maruts, on to the sage! these prayers the singer has recited for you.[1]

15. This your praise, O Maruts, this your song comes from Mândârya, the son of Mâna,[1] the poet. Come hither with rain! May we find for ourselves offspring,[2] food, and a camp[3] with running water.

---

artiste habile, façonnés au culte pompeux que nous vous rendons, ô Marouts, traitez avec bonté l'homme qui, par ses prières et ses chants, vous a honorés.

15. WILSON: This praise, Maruts, is for you: this hymn is for you, (the work) of a venerable author, capable of conferring delight (by his laudations). May the praise reach you, for (the good of your) persons, so that we may (thence) obtain food, strength, and long life.

LANGLOIS: O Marouts, cet éloge et cet hymne d'un respectable poëte s'addressent à vous. Il a voulu vous plaire. Venez avec l'abondance, en étendant vos réseaux. Que nous connaissions la prospérité, la force et l'heureuse vieillesse!

Anukramanikâ. He assigns the first two verses to Indra, the third, fifth, seventh, and ninth to the Maruts, the fourth, sixth, eighth, tenth, eleventh, and twelfth to Indra, and the three concluding verses to Agastya. I think that the two verses in the beginning, as well as the three concluding verses, belong certainly to Agastya or to whoever else the real performer of the sacrifice may have been. The two verses in the beginning cannot be ascribed to Indra, who, to judge from his language, would never say: 'By what strong devotion may we delight the Maruts?' It might seem, in fact, as if the three following verses, too, should be ascribed to the sacrificer, so that the dialogue between Indra and the Maruts would begin only with the sixth verse. The third verse might well be addressed to Indra by the sacrificer, and in the fourth verse we might see a description of all that he had done for Indra. What is against this view, however, is the phrase prábhrita*h* me ádri*h*. If used by the sacrificer, it might seem to mean, 'my stone, i. e. the stone used for squeezing the Soma, has been brought forth.' But though Professor Roth assigns this meaning to prábhrita in our passage, I doubt whether, in connection with ádri, or with vá*g*ra, prábh*r*ita can mean anything but hurled. Thus we read:

i. 61, 12. asmaí ít û*m* (íti) prá bhara — vritráya vá*g*ram.

Hurl thou, Indra, the thunderbolt against this Vritra.

v. 32, 7. yát îm vá*g*rasya prá-bhritau dadábha.

When Indra conquered him in the hurling of the thunderbolt.

I therefore suppose the dialogue to begin with verse 3, and I find that Langlois, though it may be from different reasons, arrived at the same conclusion.

There can be little doubt that the other verses, to verse 12, are rightly apportioned between Indra and the Maruts. Verse 12 might perhaps be attributed again to the worshipper of the Maruts, but as there is no absolute necessity for assigning it to him, it is better to follow the tradition and to take it as the last verse of Indra's speech. It would seem, in fact, as if these ten verses, from 3 to 12, formed an independent poem, which was intended to show the divine power of the Maruts. That their divine power was sometimes denied, and that Indra's occasional contempt of them was well known to the Vedic poets, will become evident from other hymns. This dialogue seems therefore to have been distinctly intended to show that, in spite of occasional misunderstandings between the Maruts and the all-powerful Indra, Indra himself had fully recognized their power and accepted their friendship. If we suppose that this dialogue was repeated at sacrifices in honour of the

Maruts, or that possibly it was acted by two parties, one representing Indra, the other the Maruts and their followers, then the two verses in the beginning and the three at the end ought to be placed in the mouth of the actual sacrificer, whoever he was. He begins by asking, who has attracted the Maruts to his sacrifice, and by what act of praise and worship they can be delighted. Then follows the dialogue in honour of the Maruts, and after it the sacrificer asks again, 'Who has magnified the Maruts, i.e. have not we magnified them?' and he implores them to grant him their friendship in recognition of his acts of worship. If then we suppose that the dialogue was the work of Mândârya Mânya, the fourteenth verse, too, would lose something of its obscurity. Coming from the mouth of the actual sacrificer, it would mean, 'the wisdom, or the poetical genius, of Mânya has brought us to this, has induced us to do this, i.e. to perform this dialogue of Mânya, so that he, Mânya, should assist, as a poet assists the priest at a sacrifice.' If Mânya himself was present, the words ó sú varta, 'bring hither quickly,' would have to be taken as addressed to him by the sacrificer; the next, 'Maruts, on to the sage!' would be addressed to the Maruts, the sage (vípra) being meant for Mânya; and in the last words, too, 'these prayers the singer has recited for you,' the singer (garitâ) might again be Mânya, the powerful poet whose services the sacrificer had engaged, and whose famous dialogue between Indra and the Maruts was considered a safe means of winning their favour. It would be in keeping with all this, if in the last verse the sacrificer once more informed the Maruts that this hymn of praise was the work of the famous poet Mândârya, the son of Mâna, and if he then concluded with the usual prayer for safety, food, and progeny.

Verse 1, note ¹. As samânî occurs in the Veda as the feminine of samâna (cf. iv. 51, 9; x. 191, 3; 4), samânyâ might, no doubt, be taken as an instrumental, belonging to subhâ. We should then have to translate: 'With what equal splendour are the Maruts endowed?' Sâyana adopts the same explanation, while Wilson, who seems to have read samânyâ*h*, translates 'of one dignity.' Professor Roth, s. v. myaksh, would seem to take samânyâ as some kind of substantive, and he refers to another passage, i. 167, 4, sâdhâra*n*yâ-iva marúta*h* mimikshu*h*, without, however, detailing his interpretation of these passages.

It cannot be said that Sâya*n*a's explanation is objectionable, yet there is something awkward in qualifying by an adjective, however indefinite, what forms the subject of an interrogative sentence, and it would be possible to avoid this, by taking samânyâ as an adverb. It is clearly used as an adverb in iii. 54, 7 ; viii. 83, 8.

Verse 1, note [2]. Mimikshu*h* is the perfect of myaksh, in the sense of to be firmly joined with something. It has therefore a more definite meaning than the Latin *miscere* and the Greek μίσγειν, which come from the same source, i. e. from a root *mik* or *mig*, in Sanskrit also mis in mis-ra ; (see Curtius, Grundzüge, p. 300.) There may be indeed one or two passages in the Veda where myaksh seems to have the simple meaning of mixing, but it will be seen that they constitute a small minority compared with those where myaksh has the meaning of holding to, sticking to ; I mean

x. 104, 2. mimikshú*h* yám ádraya*h* indra túbhyam.

The Soma which the stones have mixed for thee.

This form cannot be derived from mimiksh, but is the 3rd pers. plur. perf. Parasm. of myaksh. It may, however, be translated, 'This Soma which the stones have grasped or squeezed for thee,' as may be seen from passages quoted hereafter, in which myaksh is construed with an accusative.

ii. 3, 11. gh*r*itám mimikshe.

The butter has been mixed.

This form cannot be derived from mimiksh, but is the 3rd pers. sing. perf. Âtm. of myaksh. If the meaning of mixing should be considered inadmissible, we might in this verse translate, 'The butter has become fixed, solid, or coagulated.'

Leaving out of consideration for the present the forms which are derived from mimiksh, we find the following passages in which myaksh occurs. Its original meaning must have been to be mixed with, to be joined to, and in many passages that original sense is still to be recognized, only with the additional idea of being firmly joined, of sticking to, or, in an active sense, laying hold of, grasping firmly.

1. Without any case:

i. 169, 3. ámyak sấ te indra *r*ish*t*í*h* asmé (íti).

This thy spear, O Indra, sits firm for us.

This would mean that Indra held his weapon well, as a soldier ought to hold his spear. Ámyak is the 3rd pers. sing. of a second aor. Parasm., ámyaksham, ámyak(sht); (Sây. prâpnoti.) Cf. viii. 61, 18.

2. With locative:

x. 44, 2. mimyáksha vá*g*ra*h* nri-pate gabhástau.

In thy fist, O king, the thunderbolt rests firmly.

i. 167, 3. mimyáksha yéshu sú-dhitâ—*r*ish*t*í*h*.

With whom the spear (lightning) rests well placed (*gut eingelegt*), i. e. the Maruts who hold the spear firmly, so that it seems to stick fast to them. (Sây. sa*m*ga*t*âbhût.)

vi. 50, 5. mimyáksha yéshu rodasî̌ nú devî̌.

To whom the goddess Rodasî clings. (Sây. sa*m*ga*kkh*ate.)

vi. 11, 5. ámyakshi sádma sádane p*r*ithivyấ*h*.

The seat was firmly set on the seat of the earth. (Sây. gamyate, parig*r*ihyate). It is the 3rd pers. sing. aor. pass.

vi. 29, 2. ấ yásmin háste náryâ*h* mimikshú*h* ấ ráthe hira*n*yáye rathe-sthấ*h*, ấ ra*s*máya*h* gábhastyo*h* sthûráyo*h* ấ ádhvan á*s*vâsa*h* v*r*ísha*n*a*h* yu*g*ânấ*h*.

To whose hand men cling, in whose golden chariot the drivers stand firm, in whose strong fists the reins are well held, on whose path the harnessed stallions hold together. (Sây. âsi*k*yante, âpûryante ; or âsiñ*k*anti, pûrayanti.)

x. 96, 3. índre ní rûpấ háritâ mimikshire.

Bright colours stuck or clung or settled on Indra. (Sây. nishiktâni babhûvu*h* ; mihe*h* sanantât karma*n*i rûpam.)

3. With instrumental:

i. 165, 1. káyâ *s*ubhấ marúta*h* sám mimikshu*h*.

To what splendour do the Maruts cling; or, what splendour clings to them?

v. 58, 5. sváyâ matyấ marúta*h* sám mimikshu*h*. (See also i. 165, 1.)

The Maruts cling to their own thought or will. (Sây. vrish*t*yâ samyak siñ*k*anti.)

i. 167, 4. yavyâ (i. e. yavîyâ) sâdhâra*n*yâ-iva marúta*h* mimikshu*h*.

A difficult passage which receives little light from i. 173, 12; viii. 98, 8; or vi. 27, 6.

i. 87, 6. bhânú-bhi*h* sám mimikshire.

The Maruts were joined with splendour. (Sây. me*dh*um i*kk*anti.)

4. With accusative:

viii. 61, 18. ní yâ vá*g*ram mimikshátu*h*.

Thy two arms which have firmly grasped the thunder-bolt. (Sây. parig*r*ih*n*îta*h*.)

Here I should also prefer to place vii. 20, 4, if we might explain mímikshan as a participle present of myaksh in the Hu-class:

ní vá*g*ram índra*h* mímikshan.

Grasping firmly the thunderbolt. (Sây. *s*atrushu prâ-payan.)

vi. 29, 3. sriyé te pâdâ dúva*h* â mimikshu*h*.

Thy servants embrace thy feet for their happiness. (Sây. âsiñ*k*anti, samarpayanti.)

Like other verbs which mean to join, myaksh, if accompanied by prepositions expressive of separation, means to separate. (Cf. vi-yukta, *se-junctus*.)

ii. 28, 6. ápo (íti) sú myaksha varu*n*a bhiyásam mát.

Remove well from me, O Varu*n*a, terror. (Sây. apa-gamaya.)

Quite distinct from this is the desiderative or inchoative verb mimiksh, from mih, in the sense of to sprinkle, or to shower, chiefly used with reference to the gods who are asked to sprinkle the sacrifice with rain. Thus we read:

i. 142, 3. mádhvâ ya*g*ñám mimikshati.

(Narâ*s*a*m*sa) sprinkles the sacrifice with rain.

ix. 107, 6. mádhvâ ya*g*ñám mimiksha na*h*.

Sprinkle (O Soma) our sacrifice with rain.

i. 34, 3. trí*h* adyá ya*g*ñám mádhunâ mimikshatam.

O Asvins, sprinkle the sacrifice with rain thrice to-day!

i. 47, 4. mádhvâ ya*g*ñám mimikshatam.

O Asvins, sprinkle the sacrifice with rain!

5. Without mádhu :

i. 22, 13. mahí dyaúh prithiví ka nah imám yagñám mimikshatâm.

May the great heaven and earth sprinkle this our sacrifice.

6. With mádhu in the accusative :

vi. 70, 5. mádhu nah dyávâprithiví (íti) mimikshatâm.

May heaven and earth shower down rain for us.

Very frequently the Asvins are asked to sprinkle the sacrifice with their whip. This whip seems originally, like the whip of the Maruts, to have been intended for the cracking noise of the storm, preceding the rain. Then as whips had probably some similarity to the instruments used for sprinkling butter on the sacrificial viands, the Asvins are asked to sprinkle the sacrifice with their whip, i. e. to give rain :

i. 157, 4. mádhu-matyâ nah kásayâ mimikshatam.
O Asvins, sprinkle us with your rain-giving whip.

i. 22, 3. táyâ yagñám mimikshatam.
O Asvins, sprinkle the sacrifice with it (your whip).

7. Lastly, we find such phrases as,

i. 48, 16. sám nah râyá—mimikshvá.

Sprinkle us with wealth, i. e. shower wealth down upon us. Here mih is really treated as a Hu-verb in the Âtmanepada.

As an adjective, mimikshú is applied to Indra (iii. 50, 3), and mimikshá to Soma (vi. 34, 4).

Verse 1, note [3]. I do not see how étâsah can here be taken in any sense but that suggested by the Pada, â-itâsah, come near. Professor Roth thinks it not impossible that it may be meant for étâh, the fallow deer, the usual team of the Maruts. These Etas are mentioned in verse 5, but there the Pada gives quite correctly étân, not â-itân, and Sâyana explains it accordingly by gantûn.

Verse 1, note [4]. The idea that the Maruts proclaim their own strength occurred before, i. 87, 3. It is a perfectly natural conception, for the louder the voice of the wind, the greater its strength.

Verse 2, note [1]. Mánas here, as elsewhere, is used in the
sense of thought preceding speech, devotion not yet expressed in prayer. See Taitt. Sanh. v. 1, 3, 3. yat purusho
manasâbhiga*kkh*ati tad vâ*k*â vadati, what a man grasps in
his mind that he expresses by speech. Professor Roth
suggests an emendation which is ingenious, but not necessary, viz. mahā námasâ, with great adoration, an expression
which occurs, if not in vi. 52, 17, at least in vii. 12, 1. We
find, however, the phrase mahā mánasâ in

vi. 40, 4. ā yâhi *sá*svat u*s*atā yayâtha índra mahā mánasâ
soma-péyam,

úpa bráhmâ*n*i *sr*i*n*ava*h* imā na*h* átha te ya*gñá*h tanv*e*
váya*h* dhât.

Come hither, thou hast always come, Indra, to our
libation through our yearning great devotion. Mayest
thou hear these our prayers, and may then the sacrifice
place vigour in thy body.

It is curious to observe that throughout the Rig-
veda the instrumental singular mahā is always used
as an adjective belonging to some term or other for
praise and prayer. Besides the passages mentioned, we
find :

ii. 24, 1. ayā vidhema návayâ mahā girā.

Let us sacrifice with this new great song.

vi. 52, 17. su-ukténa mahā námasâ ā vivâse.

I worship with a hymn with great adoration, or I worship
with a great hymn in adoration.

viii. 46, 14. gâya girā mahā ví-*k*etasam.

Celebrate the wise Indra with a great song.

Verse 3, note [1]. We ought to scan kŭta*h* tvăm índră
māhĭna*h* săn, because yâsi, being anudâtta, could not begin
a new pâda. It would be more natural to translate kúta*h*
by why? for the Maruts evidently wish to express their
surprise at Indra's going to do battle alone and without
their assistance. I do not think, however, that in the
Rig-veda, even in the latest hymns, kúta*h* has ever a causal
meaning, and I have therefore translated it in the same
sense in which it occurs before in the poet's address to
the Maruts.

Verse 3, note [2]. Sat-pati, lord of men, means lord of real men, of heroes, and should not be translated by good lord. Sat by itself is frequently used in the sense of heroes, of men physically rather than morally good :

ii. 1, 3. tvám agne índra*h* v*r*ishabhá*h* satā́m asi.

Thou, Agni, art Indra, the hero among heroes.

i. 173, 7. samát-su tvâ *s*úra satā́m urā́*n*ám.

Thee, O hero, in battles the protector of (good and true) men.

Verse 3, note [3]. The meaning of sám p*r*ik*kh*ase is very much the same as that of sám vadasva in i. 170, 5.

Verse 3, note [4]. Subhâná evidently is meant as a name for the Maruts, who thus speak of themselves in the third person. This is by no means unusual in the Rig-veda; see, for instance,

i. 170, 2. tébhi*h* kalpasva sâdhu-yā́ mā́ na*h* sam-ára*n*e vadhî*h*.

Be thou good with these (with us, the Maruts), do not kill us in battle!

Verse 4. Indra certainly addresses his old friends, the Maruts, very unceremoniously, but this, though at first startling, was evidently the intention of the poet. He wished to represent a squabble between Indra and the Maruts, such as they were familiar with in their own village life, and this was to be followed by a reconciliation. The boorish rudeness, selfishness, and boastfulness here ascribed to Indra may seem offensive to those who cannot divest themselves of the modern meaning of deities, but looked upon from the right point of view, it is really full of interest.

Verse 4, note [1]. Bráhmâ*n*i and matáya*h* are here mentioned separately in the same way as a distinction is made between bráhman, stóma, and ukthá, iv. 22, 1 ; vi. 23, 1 ; between bráhmâ*n*i and gíra*h*, iii. 51, 6 ; between bráhma, gíra*h*, and stóma*h*, vi. 38, 3; between bráhma, gíra*h*, ukthā́, and mánma, vi. 38, 4, &c.

Verse 4, note [2]. *Sám*, which I have here translated by sweet, is a difficult word to render. It is used as a substantive, as an adjective, and as an adverb; and in several instances it must remain doubtful whether it was meant for one or the other. The adverbial character is almost always, if not always, applicable, though in English there is no adverb of such general import as *sám*, and we must therefore render it differently, although we are able to perceive that in the mind of the poet it might still have been conceived as an adverb, in the sense of 'well.' I shall arrange the principal passages in which *sám* occurs according to the verbs with which it is construed.

1. With bhû :

viii. 79, 7. bháva na*h* soma *sám* h*r*idé.

Be thou, Soma, well (pleasant) to our heart. Cf. viii. 82, 3.

viii. 48, 4. *sám* na*h* bhava h*r*idé â pítâ*h* indo (íti).

Be thou well (sweet) to our heart, when drunk, O Soma! Cf. x. 9, 4.

i. 90, 9. *sám* na*h* bhavatu ar*y*amâ.

May Aryaman be well (kind) to us!

vi. 74, 1. *sám* na*h* bhûtam dvi-pâde *sám* *k*átu*h*-pade.

May Soma and Rudra be well (kind) to *our* men and cattle.

Here *sám* might be rendered as an adverb, or as an adjective, or even as a substantive, in the sense of health or blessing.

Cf. vii. 54, 1; ix. 69, 7. The expression dvipád and *k*átu*h*-pad is curiously like what occurs in the prayers of the Eugubian tables, Fisovic Sansie, ditu ocre Fisi, tote Jovine, ocrer Fisic, totar Jovinar *dupursus, peturpursus* fato fito, (Umbrische Sprachdenkmäler, von Aufrecht, p. 198.)

ii. 38, 11. *sám* yát stot*r*í-bhya*h* âpáye bhávâti.

What may be well (a pleasure) for the praisers, for the friend.

x. 37, 10. *sám* na*h* bhava *k*ákshasâ.

Be kind to us with thy light!

2. With as .

viii. 17, 6. sóma*h* *sám* astu te h*r*idé.

May the Soma be well (agreeable) to thy heart!

i. 5, 7. *sám* te santu prá-*k*etase.

May the Somas be well (pleasing) to thee, the wise!

v. 11, 5. túbhyam manîshā iyám astu *sám* hridé.
May this prayer be well (acceptable) to thy heart !
i. 114, 1. yáthā *sám* ásat dvi-páde *kátuh*-pade.
That it may be well for our men and cattle.   Cf. x.
165, 1 ; 3.
vii. 86, 8. *sám* na*h* kshéme *sám* û*m* (íti) yóge na*h* astu.
May it be well with us in keeping and acquiring !
v. 7, 9. ā́ yá*h* te—agne *sám* ásti dhāyase.
He who is lief to thee to support, i. e. he whom thou
likest to support.
v. 74, 9. *sám* û*m* (íti) sú vâm—asmâkam astu *karkritíh*.
Let there be happiness to you—glory to us !

3. With as or bhû understood :
vi. 45, 22. *sám* yát gáve ná sâkíne.
A song which is pleasant to the mighty Indra, as food
to an ox.
viii. 13, 11. *sám* ít hí te.
For it is well for thee.
x. 86, 15. manthá*h* te indra *sám* hridé.
The mixture is pleasant to thy heart, O Indra !
x. 97, 18. áram kāmâya, *sám* hridé.
Enough for love, pleasant to the heart.
vi. 34, 3. *sám* tát asmai.
That is pleasant to him.
vi. 21, 4. ká*h* te ya*g*ñá*h* mánase *sám* várâya.
What sacrifice seems to thy mind pleasant to select?

4. With kar :
i. 43, 6. *sám* na*h* karati árvate.
May he do well to our horse, i.e. may he benefit our horses.
iv. 1, 3. tokáya tu*g*é—*sám* kridhi.
Do good to our children and progeny, or bless us for
the procreation of children.
viii. 18, 8. *sám* na*h* karata*h* asvínâ.
May the two A*s*vins do us good !

5. With vah :
i. 157, 3. *sám* na*h* ā́ vakshat dvi-páde *kátuh*-pade.
May he bring blessing to us for man and cattle.
viii. 5, 20. téna na*h*—pásve tokáya *sám* gáve, váhatam
pī́vari*h* ísha*h*.

Bring to us rich food, a blessing to cattle, to children, and to the ox.

6. With other verbs, such as pû, vâ, and others, where
it is clearly used as an adverb:

ix. 11, 3. sá*h* na*h* pavasva *s*ám gáve *s*ám *g*ánâya *s*ám árvate, *s*ám râ*g*an óshadhîbhya*h*.

Do thou, king Soma, stream upon us, a blessing for the ox, a blessing for man, a blessing for the horse, a blessing for the plants. Cf. ix. 11, 7; 60, 4; 61, 15; 109, 5.

vii. 35, 4. *s*ám na*h* ishirá*h* abhí vâtu vâta*h*.

May the brisk wind blow kindly upon us, or blow a blessing upon us.

vii. 35, 6. *s*ám na*h* tvásh*t*â gnâbhi*h* ihá *s*ri*n*otu.

May Tvash*t*ar with the goddesses hear us here well, i. e. auspiciously!

vii. 35, 8. *s*ám na*h* sûrya*h*—út etu.

May the sun rise auspiciously for us!

viii. 18, 9. *s*ám na*h* tapatu sûrya*h*.

May the sun warm us well!

iii. 13, 6. *s*ám na*h* *s*o*k*a—ágne.

Shine well for us, O Agni!

*S*ám also occurs in a phrase that has puzzled the interpreters of the Veda very much, viz. *s*ám yó*h*. These are two words, and must both be taken as substantives, though originally they may have been adverbs. Their meaning seems to have been much the same, and in English they may safely be rendered by health and wealth, in the old acceptation of these words:

i. 93, 7. dhattam yá*g*amânâya *s*ám yó*h*.

Give, Agni and Soma, to the sacrificer health and wealth.

i. 106, 5. *s*ám yó*h* yát te mánu*h*-hitam tát îmahe.

*B*rihaspati, we ask for health and wealth which thou gavest to Manu.

i. 114, 2. yát *s*ám *k*a yó*h* *k*a mánu*h* â-ye*g*é pitâ tát asyâma táva rudra prá-nîtishu.

Rudra, the health and wealth which Manu, the father, obtained, may we reach it under thy guidance.

ii. 33, 13. yâni mánu*h* ávri*n*îta pitâ na*h* tâ *s*ám *k*a yó*h* *k*a rudrásya vasmi.

The medicines which our father Manu chose, those I
desire, the health and wealth of Rudra.

i. 189, 2. bháva tokãya tánayâya sám yóh.
Be to our offspring health and wealth !

iv. 12, 5. yákkha tokãya tánayâya sám yóh.
Give to our offspring health and wealth !

v. 69, 3. íle tokãya tánayâya sám yóh.
I ask for our offspring health and wealth.

vi. 50, 7. dhãta tokãya tánayâya sám yóh.
Give to our offspring health and wealth !

x. 182, 1. átha karat yágamânâya sám yóh.
May he then produce for the sacrificer health and
wealth.

vii. 69, 5. téna nah sám yóh—ní asvinâ vahatam.
On that chariot bring to us, Asvins, health and wealth.

iii. 17, 3. átha bhava yágamânâya sám yóh.
Then, Agni, be health and wealth to the sacrificer.

iii. 18, 4. brihát váyah sasamânéshu dhehi, revát agne
visvãmitreshu sám yóh.

Give, Agni, much food to those who praise thee, give to
the Visvâmitras richly health and wealth.

x. 15, 4. átha nah sám yóh arapáh dadhãta.
And give us health and wealth without a flaw! Cf. x. 59, 8.

x. 37, 11. tát asmé sám yóh arapáh dadhâtana.
And give to us health and wealth without a flaw !

v. 47, 7. tát astu mitra-varunâ tát agne sám yóh asmábhyam idám astu sastám.

Let this, O Mitra-Varuna, let this, O Agni, be health
and wealth to us ; may this be auspicious !

v. 53, 14. vrishtví sám yóh ãpah usrí bheshagám syãma
marutah sahá.

Let us be together, O Maruts, after health, wealth, water,
and medicine have been showered down in the morning.

viii. 39, 4. sám ka yóh ka máyah dadhe.
He gave health, wealth, and happiness.

viii. 71, 15. agním sám yóh ka dãtave.
We ask Agni to give us health and wealth.

x. 9, 4. sám yóh abhí sravantu nah.
May the waters bring to us health and wealth, or may
they run towards us auspiciously.

Verse 4, note [3]. If we retain the reading of the MSS.
súshma*h* iyarti, we must take it as an independent phrase,
and translate it by 'my strength rises.' For súshma, though
in this and other places it is frequently explained as an
adjective, meaning powerful, is, as far as I can see, always
a substantive, and means power, strength. There may be
a few passages in which, as there occur several words for
strength, it might be possible to translate súshma by strong.
But even there it is better to keep to the general meaning
of súshma, and translate it as a substantive.

Iyarti means to rise and to raise. It is particularly
applied to prayers raised by the poet in honour of the gods,
and the similes used in connection with this, show clearly
what the action implied by iyarti really is. For instance,

i. 116, 1. stómân iyarmi abhríyâ-iva vâta*h*.

I stir up hymns as the wind stirs the clouds.

x. 116, 9. su-va*k*asyâm iyarmi síndhau-iva prá îrayam
nâvam.

I stir up sweet praise, as if rowing a ship on the river.

In the sense of rising it occurs,

x. 140, 2. pâvaká-var*k*â*h* *s*ukrá-var*k*â*h* ánûna-var*k*â*h* út
iyarshi bhânúnâ.

Thou risest up with splendour, Agni, thou of bright,
resplendent, undiminished majesty.

We might therefore safely translate in our verse 'my
strength rises,' although it is true that such a phrase does
not occur again, and that in other passages where iyarti and
súshma occur together, the former governs the latter in the
accusative. Cf. iv. 17, 12; x. 75, 3.

Verse 5, note [1]. If, as we can hardly avoid, we ascribe
this verse to the Maruts, we must recognize in it the usual
offer of help to Indra on the part of the Maruts. The
question then only is, who are the strong friends in whose
company they appear? It would be well if one could
render antamébhi*h* by horses, as Sâya*n*a does, but there is
no authority for it. Svá-kshatra is an adjective, meaning
endowed with independent strength, synonymous with
svá-tavas, i. 166, 2. It is applied to the mind of Indra,
i. 54, 3; v. 35, 4; to the Maruts, v. 48, 1, but never to

horses. As it stands, we can only suppose that a distinction is made between the Maruts and their followers, and that after calling together their followers, and adorning themselves for battle, they proceed to harness their chariots. Cf. i. 107, 2.

Verse 5, note [2]. Étân, in all MSS. which I consulted, has here the accent on the first syllable, and Professor Aufrecht ought not to have altered the word into etấn. If the accent had not been preserved by the tradition of the schools, the later interpreters would certainly have taken etân for the demonstrative pronoun. As it is, in spite of accent and termination, Sâya*n*a in i. 166, 10, seems to take étâ*h* for eté. In other passages, however, Sâya*n*a, too, has perceived the difference, and in i. 169, 6, he explains the word very fully as p*r*ishadvar*n*â gantâro vâ a*s*vâ vâ. In this passage the Etas are clearly the deer of the Maruts, the P*r*ishatîs:

i. 169, 6. ádha yát eshâm p*r*ithu-budhnãsa*h* étâ*h*.

In the next verse, however, éta seems applied to the Maruts themselves:

i. 169, 7. práti ghorấ*n*âm étânâm ayấsâm marútâm *s*rí*n*ve â-yatấm upabdí*h*.

The shout of the terrible, speckled, indefatigable Maruts is heard, as they approach; unless we translate:

The noise of the terrible deer of the indefatigable Maruts is heard, as they approach.

In i. 166, 10, á*m*seshu étâ*h*, I adopt Professor Roth's conjecture, that étâ*h* means the skins of the fallow deer, so that we should have to translate: On their shoulders are the deer-skins.

In the other passages where éta occurs, it is used as a simile only, and therefore throws no light on the relation of the Etas to the Maruts. In both passages, however (v. 54, 5; x. 77, 2), the simile refers to the Maruts, though to their speed only, and not to their colour.

Verse 5, note [3]. Máha*h*-bhi*h*, which I have translated 'with all our might,' seems to be used almost as an adverb, mightily or quickly (makshu), although the original meaning, with our powers, through our might, is likewise applicable. The original meaning is quite perceptible in passages like

v. 62, 3. ádhârayatam p*r*ithiv*î*m utá dy*ā*m mítra-râ*g*ânâ varu*n*â máha*h*-bhi*h*.

Kings Mitra and Varu*n*a, you have supported heaven and earth by your powers.

vii. 3, 7. tébhi*h* na*h* agne ámitai*h* máha*h*-bhi*h* *s*atám pûr-bhí*h* *ă*yasîbhi*h* ní pâhi.

With those immeasurable powers, O Agni, protect us, with a hundred iron strongholds.

i. 90, 2. té—máha*h*-bhi*h*, vrat*ā* rakshante vi*s*v*ā*hâ.

They always protect the laws by their powers.

vii. 71, 1. tvám na*h* agne máha*h*-bhi*h* pâhí.

Protect us, Agni, with thy power.

In other passages, however, we see máha*h*-bhi*h* used of the light or of the flames of Agni and of the dawn :

iv. 14, 1. devá*h* ró*k*amâna*h* máha*h*-bhi*h*.

Agni, the god, brilliant with his powers.

vi. 64, 2. devi ró*k*amânâ máha*h*-bhi*h*.

O goddess, brilliant with thy powers.

The powers of the Maruts are referred to by the same name in the following passages :

v. 58, 5. prá-pra *g*âyante—máha*h*-bhi*h*.

The Maruts are born with their powers.

vii. 58, 2. prá yé máha*h*-bhi*h* ó*g*asà utá sánti.

The Maruts who excel in power and strength.   Cf. iii. 4, 6.

Verse 6, note [1]. Indra in this dialogue is evidently repre-sented as claiming everything for himself alone. He affects contempt for the help proffered by the Maruts, and seems to deny that he was at any time beholden to their assistance. By asking, Where was that custom of yours that you should join me in battle? he implies that it never was their custom before, and that he can dispense with their succour now. He wants to be alone in his battle with Ahi, and does not wish that they should join him : (cf. i. 33, 4.) Professor Roth takes sam-ádhatta in the sense of implicating, but it can hardly be said that the Maruts ever implicated Indra in his fight against Ahi. Certainly this is not in keeping with the general tenor of this dialogue, where, on the contrary, Indra shuns the company of the Maruts. But while on this point I differ from Professor Roth, I think he has rightly interpreted the meaning of ánamam. Out of the four passages in which badha-snai*h* occurs, it is three times joined with nam, and every time has the sense of to bend away from, to escape from. See also Sonne, in Kuhn's Zeitschrift, vol. xii. p. 348.

Verse 7, note [1]. See vii. 39, 6. sakshîmáhi yú*gy*ebhi*h* nú devaí*h*.

Verse 7, note [2]. The last words leave no doubt as to their meaning, for the phrase is one of frequent occurrence. The only difficulty is the vocative maruta*h*, where we should expect the nominative. It is quite possible, however, that the Maruts should here address themselves, though, no doubt, it would be easy to alter the accent. As to the phrase itself, see

viii. 61, 4. táthâ ít asat índra krátvâ yáthâ vá*sah*.

May it be so, O Indra, as thou desirest by thy mind.

viii. 66, 4. va*grï*—ít karat índra*h* krátvâ yáthâ vá*s*at.

May Indra with the thunderbolt act as he desires in his mind. Cf. viii. 20, 17 ; 28, 4, &c.

Verse 8, note [1]. Here again Indra claims everything for himself, denying that the Maruts in any way assisted him while performing his great deeds. These deeds are the killing of V*r*itra, who withholds the waters, i. e. the rain from the earth, and the consequent liberation of the waters so that they flow down freely for the benefit of Manu, that is, of man.

When Indra says that he slew V*r*itra indriyé*n*a, he evidently chooses that word with a purpose, and we must therefore translate it, not only by might, but by Indra's peculiar might. Indriyá, as derived from índra, means originally Indra-hood, then power in general, just as vere-thraghna in Zend means victory in general, though origin-ally it meant the slaying of V*r*itra.

Verse 9, note [1]. Devâtâ in the ordinary sense of a deity never occurs in the Rig-veda. The word, in fact, as a

feminine substantive occurs but twice, and in the tenth
Mandala only. But even there it does not mean deity.
In x. 24, 6, devâh devátayâ means, O gods, by your godhead, i. e. by your divine power. In x. 98, 1, bríhaspate
práti me devátâm ihi, I take devâtâ in the same sense as
devátâti, and translate, O Brihaspati, come to my sacrifice.

In all other places where devâtâ occurs in the Rig-veda
it is a local adverb, and means among the gods. I shall
only quote those passages in which Professor Roth assigns
to devâtâ a different meaning:

i. 55, 3. prá vîryĕna devátâ áti kekite.
He is pre-eminent among the gods by his strength.

i. 22, 5. sáh kéttâ devátâ padám.
He knows the place among the gods.

i. 100, 15. ná yásya devâh devátâ ná mártâh âpah kaná
sávasah ántam âpúh.

He, the end of whose power neither the gods among the
gods, nor mortals, nor even the waters have reached.

Here the translation of devâtâ in the sense of 'by their
godhead,' would be equally applicable, yet nothing would
be gained as, in either case, devâtâ is a weak repetition.

vi. 4,,7. índram ná tvâ sávasâ devátâ vâyúm prinanti
râdhasâ nrí-tamâh.

The best among men celebrate thee, O Agni, as like
unto Indra in strength among the gods, as like unto Vâyu
in liberality.

Verse 9, note ². The juxta-position of gâyamânah and
gâtáh would seem to show that, if the latter had a past,
the former had a future meaning. To us, 'No one who
will be born and no one who has been born,' would certainly sound more natural. The Hindu, however, is
familiar with the idea as here expressed, and in order to
comprehend all beings, he speaks of those who are born
and those who are being born. Thus in a Padasishta of
the Pâvamânîs (ix. 67) we read:

> yan me garbhe vasatah pâpam ugram,
> yag gâyamânasya ka kimkid anyat,
> gâtasya ka yak kâpi vardhato me,
> tat pâvamânîbhir aham punâmi.

Verse 9, note [3]. Karishyấ is written in all the MSS. without a Visarga, and unless we add the Visarga on our own authority, we should have to take it as an accusative plur. neut. of a passive participle of the future, karishyấm standing for kâryấm, *faciendum*. It would be much easier, however, to explain this form if we added the Visarga, and read karishyấ*h*, which would then be a second person singular of a Vedic conjunctive of the future. This form occurs at least once more in the Veda:

iv. 30, 23. utá núnắm yát indriyắm karishyấ*h* indra paú*m*syam, adyá nákí*h* tát ẫ minat.

O Indra, let no man destroy to-day whatever manly feat thou art now going to achieve.

Verse 10, note [1]. As 1 have translated these words, they sound rather abrupt. The meaning, however, would be clear enough, viz. almighty power belongs to me, therefore I can dare and do. If this abrupt expression should offend, it may be avoided, by taking the participle dadh*r*ishvẫn as a finite verb, and translating, Whatever I have been daring, I shall do according to my will.

Verse 11, note [1]. In this verse Indra, after having declined with no uncertain sound the friendship of the Maruts, repents himself of his unkindness towards his old friends. The words of praise which they addressed to him in verse 9, in spite of the rebuff they had received from Indra, have touched his heart, and we may suppose that after this, their reconciliation was complete. The words of Indra are clear enough, the only difficulty occurs in the last words, which are so idiomatic that it is impossible to render them in English. In tanvẽ tanẫbhí*h*, literally for the body by the bodies, tanú is used like the pronoun self. Both must therefore refer to the same subject. We cannot translate 'for myself made by your-selves,' but must take the two words together, so that they should mean, 'the hymn which you have made for your own sake, freely, and by your own exertions, honestly.'

Verse 13, note [1]. I translate api-vâtáyanta*h* by cherish-ing, a meaning equally applicable to i. 128, 2, and x. 25, 1.

I suppose the original meaning was really to blow upon a
person, to cool or refresh a person by a draught of air,
which, in countries like India, was and is the office of the
attendants of a prince. It would then take the meaning of
honouring, worshipping or cherishing, though I confess the
hymns of the Veda seem almost too early for such a courtly
metaphor.

Verse 14, note [1]. This is a verse which, without some
conjectural alterations, it seems impossible to translate.
Sâyana, of course, has a translation ready for it, so has
M. Langlois, but both of them offend against the simplest
rules of grammar and logic. The first question is, who is
meant by asmân (which is here used as an amphimacer),
the sacrificers or the Maruts? The verb â kakré would well
apply to the medhâ mânyâsya, the hymn of Mânya, which is
intended to bring the Maruts to the sacrifice, this bringing
to the sacrifice being the very meaning of â kar. But then
we have the vocative marutah in the next line, and even if
we changed the vocative into the accusative, we should not
gain much, as the Maruts could hardly call upon anybody
to turn them towards the sage.

If, on the contrary, we admit that asmân refers to those
who offer the sacrifice, then we must make a distinction,
which, it is true, is not an unusual one, between those who
here speak of themselves in the first person, and who provide the sacrifice, and the poet Mândârya Mânya, who was
employed by them to compose or to recite this hymn.

But even if we adopt this alternative, many difficulties
still remain. First of all, we have to change the accent of
kakré into kakre, which may seem a slight change, but is
not the less objectionable when we consider that in our
emendations of the Vedic hymns we must think rather of
accidents that might happen in oral traditions than of the
lapsus calami of later scribes. Secondly, we must suppose
that the hymn of Mândârya Mânya ends with verse 13, and
that the last verses were supplied by the sacrificers themselves. Possibly the dialogue only, from verse 3 to verse 12,
was the work of Mânya, and the rest added at some solemn
occasion.

Other difficulties, however, remain. Duvasyât is taken by Sâyana as an ablative of duvasyâ, worthy of dúvas, i. e. of worship, of sacrifice. Unfortunately this duvasyâ does not occur again, though it would be formed quite regularly, like namasyâ, worthy of worship, from námas, worship.

If we take duvasyât as the 3rd pers. sing. of the present in the Vedic conjunctive, we must also confess that this conjunctive does not occur again. But the verb duvasyati occurs frequently. It seems to have two meanings. It is derived from dúvas, which in the Vedic language means worship or sacrifice, just as karma, work, has assumed the special sense of sacrifice. Derived from dúvas in this sense, duvasyati means to worship. But dúvas meant originally any *opus operatum*. The root from which dúvas is derived, is lost in Sanskrit, but it exists in other languages. It must have been *du* or *dû* in the sense of acting, or sedulously working. It exists in Zend as *du*, to do, in Gothic as *táujan, yataujan*, Old High German *zawjan*, Modern German *zauen* (Grimm, Gram. i². p. 1041). The Gothic *tavi*, opus, Old High German *zouwi*, Middle High German *gezöuwe* (Grimm, Gram. iii. p. 499), come from the same source; and it is possible, too, that the Old Norse *töfrar*, incantamenta, the Old High German *zoupar*, Middle High German *zouber*, both neuter, and the modern *Zauber*, may find their explanation in the Sanskrit dúvas. Derived from dúvas, in the sense of work, we have duvasyati in the sense of helping, providing, the German *schaffen* and *verschaffen*.

In the sense of worshipping, duvasyati occurs,

iii. 2, 8. duvasyáta—gâtá-vedasam.

Worship *G*âtavedas.

v. 28, 6. â *g*uhota duvasyáta agním.

Invoke, worship Agni. Cf. iii. 13, 3; 1, 13.

iii. 3, 1. agníh hí devân—duvasyáti.

Agni performs the worship of the gods. Cf. vii. 82, 5.

i. 167, 6. sutá-somah duvasyán.

He who has poured out Soma and worships.

In many passages duvasyati is joined with an instrumental:

v. 42, 11. námaḥ-bhiḥ devám—duvasya.
Worship the god with praises.
i. 78, 2. tám u tvâ gótamaḥ girâ—duvasyati.
Gotama worships thee with a song.
v. 49, 2. su-uktaíḥ devám—duvasya.
Worship the god with hymns.
vi. 16, 46. vîtî́ yáḥ devám—duvasyét.
He who worships the god with food.
x. 14, 1. yamám—havíshâ duvasya.
Worship Yama with an oblation.
vi. 15, 6. agním-agnim vaḥ samídhâ duvasyata.
Worship Agni with your log of wood. Cf. viii. 44, 1.
iii. 1, 2. samít-bhiḥ agním námasâ duvasyan.
They worshipped Agni with logs of wood, with praise.

In the more general and, I suppose, more original sense of caring for, attending, we find duvasyati:

iii. 51, 3. anehásaḥ stúbhaḥ índraḥ duvasyati.
Indra provides for the matchless worshippers.
i. 112, 15. kalím yâbhiḥ—duvasyáthaḥ.
By the succours with which you help Kali. Cf. i. 112, 21.
i. 62, 10. duvasyánti svásâraḥ áhrayâṇam.
The sisters attend the proud (Agni).
i. 119, 10. yuvám pedáve—svetám—duvasyathaḥ.
You provide for Pedu the white horse.

If, then, we take duvasyati in the sense of working for, assisting, it may be with the special sense of assisting at a sacred act, like διακονεῖν; and if we take duvás, as it has the accent on the last syllable, as the performer of sacrifice, we may venture to translate, 'that he should help, as the singer helps the performer of the sacrifice *.' The singer or the poet may be called the assistant at a sacrifice, for his presence was not necessary at all sacrifices, the songs constituting an ornament rather than an essential in most sacred acts. But though I think it right to offer this conjectural interpretation, I am far from supposing that it gives us the real sense of this difficult verse. Duvasyât may be, as Sâyaṇa suggests, an ablative of duvasyá; and

---

* Kar in the sense of officiating at a sacrifice is equally construed with a dative, x. 97. 22. yásmai krinóti brâhmaṇáḥ, he for whom a Brâhmaṇa performs a sacrifice.

duvasyá, like namasyã, if we change the accent, may mean
he who is to be worshipped, or worshipping. In this way
a different interpretation might suggest itself, in which the
words duvasyất duváse could be taken to mean 'from one
worshipper to another.' Some happy thought may some
day or other clear up this difficulty, when those who have
toiled, but toiled in a wrong direction, will receive scant
thanks for the trouble they have taken.

In the second line, the words ó sú varta remind one of
similar phrases in the Veda, but we want an accusative,
governed by varta; whereas marutaḥ, to judge from its
accent, can only be a vocative. Thus we read:

i. 138, 4. ó (íti) sú tvấ vavṛitîmahi stómebhiḥ.
May we turn thee quickly hither by our praises!
viii. 7, 33. ó (íti) sú vṛíshṇaḥ—vavṛityấm.
May I turn the heroes quickly hither!
Compare also passages like iii. 33, 8:
ó (íti) sú svasâraḥ kâráve sṛiṇota.
Listen quickly, O sisters, to the poet.
i. 139, 7. ó (íti) sú naḥ agne sṛiṇuhi.
Hear us quickly, O Agni.
Cf. i. 182, 1; ii. 34, 15; vii. 59, 5; viii. 2, 19; x. 179, 2.

Unless we change the accent, we must translate, ' Bring
hither quickly!' and we must take these words as addressed
to the kârú, the poet, whose hymn is supposed to attract the
gods to the sacrifice. By a quick transition, the next words,
marutaḥ vípram ákkḥa, would then have to be taken as
addressed to the gods, ' Maruts, on to the sage!' and the
last words would become intelligible by laying stress on
the vaḥ, ' for you, and not for Indra or any other god, has
the singer recited these hymns.'

Verse 15, note [1]. I translate Mânya, the son of Mâna,
because the poet, so called in i. 189, 8, is in all probability
the same as our Mândârya Mânya.

Verse 15, note [2]. The second line is difficult, owing to
the uncertain meaning of vayấm. First of all, it might
seem as if the two hemistichs must be kept distinct, because
the second is so often used independently of the first.

There are passages, however, where this very hemistich carries on the sentence of a preceding hemistich, as, for instance, i. 177, 5; 182, 8. We may therefore join tanvĕ vayãm with the following words, and it certainly seems more difficult to elicit any sense if we join them with the preceding words.

Á ishã * yâsîsh*t*a might be rendered, 'Come hither with water or drink or rain,' yâsîsh*t*a being the aorist without the augment and with the intermediate vowel lengthened. The indicative occurs in

v. 58, 6. yát prá áyâsish*t*a príshatîbhi*h* á*s*vai*h*.

When you Maruts come forth with your fallow deer and your horses.

But what is the meaning of vayãm? Vayã́ means a germ, a sprout, an offshoot, a branch, as may be seen from the following passages :

ii. 5, 4. vidvã́n asya vratã́ dhruvã́ vayã́*h*-iva ánu rohate.

He who knows his eternal laws, springs up like young sprouts.

vi. 7, 6. tásya ít û*m* (íti) ví*s*vâ bhúvanâ ádhi mûrdháni vayã́*h*-iva ruruhu*h*.

From above the head of Vai*s*vanara all worlds have grown, like young sprouts.

viii. 13, 6. stotã́—vayã́*h*-iva ánu rohate.

The worshipper grows up like young sprouts.

viii. 13, 17. índram kshonḯ*h* avardhayan vayã́*h*-iva.

The people made Indra to grow like young sprouts.

viii. 19, 33. yásya te agne anyé agnáya*h* upa-kshíta*h* vayã́*h*-iva.

Agni, of whom the other fires are like parasitical shoots.

i. 59, 1. vayã́*h* ít agne agnáya*h* te anyé.

O Agni, the other fires are indeed offshoots of thee.

ii. 35, 8. vayã́*h* ít anyã́ bhúvanâni asya.

The other worlds are indeed his (the rising sun's) offshoots.

vi. 13, 1. tvát ví*s*vâ—saúbhagâni ágne ví yanti vanína*h* nã́ vayã́*h*.

From thee, O Agni, spring all happinesses, as the sprouts of a tree.

---

vi. 24, 3. vrikshásya nú (ná?) te—vayâḥ ví ûtáyaḥ ruruhuḥ.
Succours sprang from thee, like the branches of a tree.

v. 1, 1. yahvâḥ-iva prá vayâm ut-gîhânâḥ prá bhânávaḥ
sisrate nâkam ákkḥa.

Like birds (?) flying up to a branch, the flames of Agni
went up to heaven.

vi. 57, 5. tắm pûshnáḥ su-matím vayám vrikshásya prá
vayâm-iva índrasya ka ấ rabhâmahe.

Let us reach this favour of Pûshan and of Indra, as one
reaches forth to the branch of a tree.

There remain some doubtful passages in which vayấ
occurs, vii. 40, 5, and x. 92, 3; 134, 6. In the first passage, as in our own, vayâḥ is trisyllabic.

If vayấ can be used in the sense of offshoot or sprout,
we may conclude that the same word, used in the
singular, might mean offspring, particularly when joined
with tanvê. ' Give a branch to our body,' would be understood even in languages less metaphorical than that of the
Vedas; and as the prayer for ' olive branches ' is a constant
theme of the Vedic poets, the very absence of that prayer
here, might justify us in assigning this sense to vayâm.
In vi. 2, 5, the expression vayâvantam kshâyam, a house
with branches, means the same as nrivántam, a house with
children and men. See M. M., On Βίος and váyas, in
Kuhn's Zeitschrift, vol. xv. p. 215.

If the third pâda is to be kept as an independent sentence,
we must take yâsîshṭa as the third pers. sing. of the benedictive, and refer it to stómaḥ or gíḥ. Grammatically this may
seem preferable, and I have given this alternative translation
in the next hymn, where the same verse occurs again.

Verse 15, note [3]. Vrigána means an enclosure, a νομός,
whether it be derived from vrig, to ward off, like are from
arcere, or from vrig, in the sense of clearing, as in vrikta-
barhis, barhíḥ prá vriñge, i. 116, 1. In either case the meaning remains much the same, viz. a field, cleared for pasture
or agriculture,—a clearing, as it is called in America, or a
camp,—enclosed with hurdles or walls, so as to be capable
of defence against wild animals or against enemies. Other
meanings of vrigána will be discussed in other places.

MANDALA I, SÛKTA 166.

ASHTAKA II, ADHYÂYA 4, VARGA 1-3.

1. Tát nú voꞯâma rabhasâya gánmane pûrvam mahi-tvám vrishabhásya ketáve, aidhấ-iva yấman marutaꞯ tuvi-svanaꞯ yudhấ-iva sakrâꞯ tavishấni kartana.

2. Nítyam nᔠsûnúm mᔠdhu bíbhrataꞯ úpa kríꞯanti krîꞯâꞯ vidátheshu ghríshvayah, nákshanti rudrâꞯ ᔠvasâ namasvínam nᔠmardhanti svá-tavasaꞯ haviꞯ-krítam.

3. Yᔠsmai ûmâsaꞯ amrítâꞯ ᔠrâsata râyᔠꞯ pósham ꞯa havíshâ dadâsúshe, ukshánti asmai marútaꞯ hitấꞯ-iva purú rágâꞯsi páyasâ mayaꞯ-bhúvaꞯ.

4. Ấ yé rágâꞯsi távishîbhiꞯ ᔠvyata prᔠvaꞯ évâsaꞯ svá-yatâsaꞯ adhragan, bháyante vísvâ bhú-vanâni harmyấ ꞯitrâꞯ vaꞯ yấmaꞯ prᔠ-yatâsu rishꞯíshu.

5. Yᔠt tveshá-yâmâꞯ nadáyanta párvatân divᔠꞯ vâ prishꞯám náryâ * ᔠꞯuꞯyavuꞯ, vísvaꞯ vaꞯ ᔠgman bhayate vánaspátiꞯ rathiyántî-iva prᔠ gihîte ósha-dhiꞯ.

6. Yûyám naꞯ ugrâꞯ marutaꞯ su-ꞯetúnâ ᔠrishꞯa-grâmâꞯ su-matín pipartana, yátra vaꞯ didyút rádati kríviꞯ-datî riꞯấti pasváꞯ súdhitâ-iva bar-hấꞯâ.

HYMN TO THE MARUTS (THE STORM-GODS).

1. Let us now proclaim for the robust[1] host, for
the herald[2] of the powerful (Indra), their ancient
greatness! O ye strong-voiced Maruts, you heroes,
show your powers on your way as with a torch, as
with a sword![3]

2. Like parents bringing sweet to[1] their own[2]
son, the wild (Maruts) play playfully at the sacrifices. The Rudras reach the worshipper with their
protection, powerful by themselves, they do not hurt
the sacrificer.

3. For the giver of oblations, for him to whom
the immortal guardians, too, have given plenty of
riches, the Maruts, who gladden men with the milk
(of rain), pour out, like friends, many clouds.

4. You who have stirred[1] up the clouds with
might, your horses rushed[2] forth, self-guided. All
beings who dwell in houses[3] are afraid of you, your
coming is brilliant with your spears thrust forth.

5. When they whose path is fiery have caused the
rocks to tremble,[1] or when the manly Maruts have
shaken the back of the sky, then every lord of the
forest fears at your racing, the shrubs get out of
your way,[2] quick like chariots.[3]

6. You, O terrible Maruts, whose ranks are never
broken, favourably[1] fulfil our prayer![2] Wherever
your gory-toothed[3] lightning bites,[4] it crunches[5] all
living beings, like a well-aimed bolt.[6]

7. Prá skambhá-deshnâ*h* anavabhrá-râdhasa*h* alâ-
t*ri*nâsa*h* vidátheshu sú-stutâ*h*, ár*k*anti arkám madi-
rásya pîtáye vidú*h* vîrásya prathamâni paúmsyâ.

8. *S*atábhu*gi*-bhi*h* tám abhí-hrute*h* aghất pû*h*-
bhí*h* rakshata maruta*h* yám ấvata, *g*ánam yám
ugrâ*h* tavasa*h* vi-rapsina*h* pâthána *s*ámsât tána-
yasya push*t*íshu.

9. Vísvâni bhadrấ maruta*h* rátheshu va*h* mitha-
spr*í*dhyâ-iva tavishâ*ni* ấ-hitâ, ámseshu ấ va*h* prá-
patheshu khâdáya*h* áksha*h* va*h* *k*akrấ samáyâ ví
vavrite.

10. Bhûrî*ni* bhadrấ náryeshu bâhúshu váksha*h*-su
rukmấ*h* rabhasâsa*h* añ*g*áyah, ámseshu étâ*h* pavíshu
kshurấ*h* ádhi váya*h* nấ pakshấn ví ánu *s*ríya*h*
dhire.

11. Mahấnta*h* mahnấ vi-bhvâ*h* ví-bhútaya*h*
dûre-dr*í*sah yé divyấ*h*-iva str*í*-bhi*h*, mandrấ*h* su-
*g*ihvâ*h* sváritâra*h* âsá-bhi*h* sám-mislâ*h* índre marúta*h* pari-stúbha*h*.

12. Tát va*h* su-*g*âtâ*h* maruta*h* mahi-tvanám
dîrghám va*h* dâtrám ádite*h*-iva vratám, índra*h*
*k*aná tyá*g*asâ ví hru*n*âti tát *g*ánâya yásmai su-
kr*í*te árâdhvam.

13. Tát va*h* *g*âmi-tvám maruta*h* páre yugé
purú yát *s*ámsam amr*i*tâsa*h* ấvata, ayấ dhiyấ

7. The Maruts whose gifts are firm, whose bounties are never ceasing, who do not revile,[1] and who are highly praised at the sacrifices, they sing forth their song[2] for to drink the sweet juice : they know the first manly deeds of the hero (Indra).

8. The man whom you guarded, O Maruts, shield him with hundredfold strongholds from injury[1] and mischief,—the man whom you, O fearful, powerful singers, protect from reproach in the prosperity of his children.

9. On your chariots, O Maruts, there are all good things, strong weapons[1] are piled up clashing against each other. When you are on your journeys, you carry the rings[2] on your shoulders, and your axle turns the two wheels at once.[3]

10. In your manly arms there are many good things, on your chests golden chains,[1] flaring[2] ornaments, on your shoulders speckled deer-skins,[3] on your fellies sharp edges ;[4] as birds spread their wings, you spread out your splendour behind you.

11. They, mighty by might, all pervading, powerful,[1] visible from afar like the heavens[2] with the stars, sweet-toned, soft-tongued singers with their mouths,[3] the Maruts, united with Indra, shout all around.

12. This is your greatness,[1] O well-born Maruts!— your bounty[2] extends as far as the sway[3] of Aditi.[4] Not even[5] Indra in his scorn[6] can injure that bounty, on whatever man you have bestowed it for his good deeds.

13. This is your kinship (with us), O Maruts, that you, immortals, in former years have often regarded

mánave *s*rush*t*ím ávya sâkám nára*h* da*m*sánai*h* ã
*k*ikitrire.

14. Yéna dîrghám maruta*h* susâvâma yush-
mākena pârînasâ turâsa*h*, ã yát tatánan v*r*igáne
*g*ánâsa*h* ebh*î*/ ya*g*ñébhi*h* tát abhí ísh*t*im a*s*yâm.

15. Eshâ*h* va*h* stóma*h* maruta*h* iyám gî*h* mândâr-
yásya mânyásya kâró*h*, ã i*s*hã yâsish*t*a tanvē vayām
vidyãma ishám v*r*i*g*ánam *g*irâ-dânum.

COMMENTARY.

This hymn is ascribed to Agastya, the reputed son of
Mitrâvaru*n*au, and brother of Vasish*th*a. The metre in
verses 1–13 is *G*agatî, in 14, 15 Trish*t*ubh.

Verse 1, note [1]. Rabhasá, an adjective of rábhas, and
this again from the root rabh, to rush upon a thing, â-rabh,
to begin a thing. From this root rabh we have the Latin
robur, in the general sense of strength, while in *rabies* the
original meaning of impetuous motion has been more clearly
preserved. In the Vedic Sanskrit, derivatives from the
root rabh convey the meaning both of quickness and of
strength. Quickness in ancient language frequently implies
strength, and strength implies quickness, as we see, for
instance, from the German *snël*, which, from meaning
originally strong, comes to mean in modern German quick,
and quick only. Thus we read:

    i. 145, 3. *s*í*s*u*h* ã adatta sám rábha*h*.

The child (Agni) acquired vigour.

Indra is called rabha*h*-dâ*h*, giver of strength; and
rabhasá, vigorous, is applied not only to the Maruts, who

our call.[1] Having through this prayer granted a hearing to man, these heroes become well known by their valiant deeds.

14. That we may long flourish, O Maruts, with your wealth, O ye racers, that our men may spread in the camp, therefore let me achieve the rite with these offerings.

15. May this praise, O Maruts, may this song of Mândârya, the son of Mâna, the poet, approach you (asking) for offspring to our body together with food! May we find food, and a camp with running water!

=====

in v. 58, 5, are called rábhishthâh, the most vigorous, but also to Agni, ii. 10, 4, and to Indra, iii. 31, 12.

In the sense of rabid, furious, it occurs in

x. 95, 14. ádha enam vríkâh rabhasâsah adyúh.

May rabid wolves eat him!

In the next verse rabhasá, the epithet of the wolves, is replaced by âsiva, which means unlucky, uncanny.

In our hymn rabhasá occurs once more, and is applied there, in verse 10, to the angí or glittering ornaments of the Maruts. Here Sâyana translates it by lovely, and it was most likely intended to convey the idea of lively or brilliant splendour. See also ix. 96, 1.

Verse 1, note [2]. Ketú, derived from an old root ki, in Sanskrit ki, to perceive, means originally that by which a thing is perceived or known, whether a sign, or a flag, or a herald. It then takes the more general sense of light and splendour. In our passage, herald seems to me the most appropriate rendering, though B. and R. prefer the sense of banner. The Maruts come before Indra, they announce the arrival of Indra, they are the first of his army.

Verse 1, note ³. The real difficulty of our verse lies in
the two comparisons aidhã-iva and yudhã-iva. Neither of
them occurs again in the Rig-veda. B. and R. explain
aidhã as an instrumental of aídh, flaming, or flame, and
derive it from the root idh, to kindle, with the preposition â.
Professor Bollensen in his excellent article Zur Herstellung
des Veda (Orient und Occident, vol. iii. p. 473) says:
'The analysis of the text given in the Pada, viz. aidhã-
iva and yudhã-iva, is contrary to all sense. The common
predicate is tavishãni kartana, exercise your power, you
roarers, i. e. blow as if you meant to kindle the fire on the
altar, show your power as if you went to battle. We ought
therefore to read aidhé | va and yudhé | va. Both are
infinitives, aidh is nothing but the root idh + â, to kindle,
to light.' Now this is certainly a very ingenious explanation, but it rests on a supposition which I cannot consider
as proved, viz. that in the Veda, as in Pali, the comparative
particle iva may be abbreviated to va. It must be admitted,
I believe, that the two short syllables of iva are occasionally
counted in the Veda as one, but yudhé-iva, though it
might become yudhá iva, would never in the Veda become
yudhéva.

As yudhã occurs frequently in the Veda, we may begin
by admitting that the parallel form aidhã must be explained
in analogy to yudhã. Now yúdh is a verbal noun and
means fighting. We have the accusative yúdham, i. 53, 7;
the genitive yudháh, viii. 27, 17; the dative yudhé, i. 61, 13;
the locative yudhí, i. 8, 3; the instrumental yudhã, i. 53, 7,
&c.; loc. plur. yut-sú, i. 91, 21. As long as yúdh retains
the general predicative meaning of fighting, some of these
cases may be called infinitives. But yúdh soon assumes
not only the meaning of battle, battle-ground, but also of
instrument of fighting, weapon. In another passage,
x. 103, 2, yúdhah may be taken as a vocative plural,
meaning fighters. Passages in which yúdh means clearly
weapon, are, for instance,

v. 52, 6. â rukmaíh â yudhã nárah rishvãh rishtíh
asrikshata.

With your gold chains, with your weapon, you have
stretched forth the uplifted spears.

x. 55, 8. pîtví sómasya diváḥ á vŕidhânáḥ śúraḥ níḥ
yudhá adhamat dásyûn.
The hero, growing, after drinking the Soma, blew away
from the sky the enemies with his weapon. See also
x. 103, 4.

I therefore take yúdh in our passage also in the sense of
weapon or sword, and, in accordance with this, I assign
to aídh the meaning of torch. Whether aídh comes from
idh with the preposition â, which after all, would only give
edh, or whether we have in the Sanskrit aídh the same
peculiar strengthening which this very root shows in Greek
and Latin*, would be difficult to decide. The torch of the
Maruts is the lightning, the weapon the thunderbolt, and
by both they manifest their strength.

Wilson: 'We proclaim eagerly, Maruts, your ancient
greatness, for (the sake of inducing) your prompt appearance, as the indication of (the approach of) the showerer
(of benefits). Loud-roaring and mighty Maruts, you exert
your vigorous energies for the advance (to the sacrifice),
as if it was to battle.'

Langlois: 'Le généreux (Agni) a donné le signal;
chantons l'hymne du matin en l'honneur d'une race impétueuse. O puissants et rapides Marouts, que la marche
accroisse votre éclat; que l'élan du combat augmente vos
forces!'

Verse 2, note [1]. That úpa can be construed with the
accusative is clear from many passages:
iii. 35, 2. úpa imám yagñám á vahâtaḥ índram.
Bring Indra to this sacrifice!
i. 25, 4. váyaḥ ná vasatíḥ úpa.
As birds (fly) to their nests.

Verse 2, note [2]. Nítya, from ni + tya, means originally
what is inside, internus, then what is one's own; and is
opposed to níshtya, from nis + tya, what is outside, strange,
or hostile. Nítya has been well compared with nigá, literally

---

* Schleicher, Compendium, § 36, αἴθω, αἰθήρ, αἴθουσα; and § 49, aídos,
aídilis, œstas.

eingeboren, then, like nítya, one's own. What is inside, or in a thing or place, is its own, is peculiar to it, does not move or change, and hence the secondary meanings of nítya, one's own, unchanging, eternal. Thus we find nítya used in the sense of internal or domestic:

i. 73, 4. tám tvâ nára*h* dáme ấ nítyam iddhám ágne sá*k*anta kshitíshu dhruvấsu.

Our men worshipped thee, O Agni, lighted within the house in safe places.

This I believe to be a more appropriate rendering than if we take nítya in the sense of always, continuously lighted, or, as some propose, in the sense of eternal, everlasting.

vii. 1, 2. dakshâyya*h* yâ*h* dáme ấsa nítya*h*.

Agni who is to be pleased within the house, i.e. as belonging to the house, and, in that sense, who is to be pleased always. Cf. i. 140, 7; 141, 2; x. 12, 2, and iii. 25, 5, where nítya*h*, however, may have been intended as an adjective belonging to the vocative sûno.

Most frequently nítya occurs with sûnú, i. 66, 1; 185, 2; tánaya, iii. 15, 2; x. 39, 14; toká, ii. 2, 11; âpí, vii. 88, 6; páti, i. 71, 1, and has always the meaning of one's own, very much like the later Sanskrit ni*g*a, which never occurs in the Rig-veda, though it makes its appearance in the Âtharvа*n*a.

Nísh*t*ya, *extraneus*, occurs three times in the Rig-veda:

vi. 75, 19. yâ*h* na*h* svá*h* ára*n*a*h* yâ*h* *k*a nísh*t*ya*h* *g*ighâ*m*sati.

Whoever wishes to hurt us, our own friend or a stranger from without.

x. 133, 5. yâ*h* na*h* indra abhi-dásati sá-nâbhi*h* yâ*h* *k*a nísh*t*ya*h*.

He who infests us, O Indra, whether a relative or a stranger.

viii. 1, 13. mấ bhûma nísh*t*yâ*h*-iva índra tvád ára*n*â*h*-iva.

Let us not be like outsiders, O Indra, not like strangers to thee.

Wilson: 'Ever accepting the sweet (libation), as (they would) a son, they sport playfully at sacrifices, demolishing (all intruders).'

Langlois: 'Acceptant la douce libation sans cesse renouvelée, comme (un père adopte) un nouveau-né, ils se livrent à leurs jeux au milieu des sacrifices, terribles (pour leurs ennemis).'

Verse 4, note [1]. A'vyata, a Vedic second aorist of vî (ag), to stir up, to excite. From it pravayaṇa, a goad, pra-vetar, a driver. The Greek οἶ-σ-τρος, gad-fly, has been referred to the same root. See Fick, Wörterbuch, p. 170.

Verse 4, note [2]. Adhragan, from dhrag, a root which, by metathesis of aspiration, would assume the form of dragh or dragh. In Greek, the final medial aspirate being hardened, reacts on the initial media, and changes it to t, as bâhu becomes πῆχυς, budh πυθ, bandh πενθ. This would give us τρεχ, the Greek root for running, Goth. thrag-jan.

Verse 4, note [3]. Harmyá is used here as an adjective to bhúvana, and can only mean living in houses. It does not, however, occur again in the same sense, though it occurs several times as a substantive, meaning house. Its original meaning is fire-pit, then hearth, then house, a transition of meaning analogous to that of ædes. Most of the ancient nations begin their kitchen with a fire-pit. ' They dig a hole in the ground, take a piece of the animal's raw hide, and press it down with their hands close to the sides of the hole, which thus becomes a sort of pot or basin. This they fill with water, and they make a number of stones red-hot in a fire close by. The meat is put into the water, and the stones dropped in till the meat is boiled. Catlin describes the process as awkward and tedious, and says that since the Assinaboins had learnt from the Mandans to make pottery, and had been supplied with vessels by the traders, they had entirely done away the custom, "excepting at public festivals; where they seem, like all others of the human family, to take pleasure in cherishing and perpetuating their ancient customs*." ' This pit was

* Tylor, Early History of Mankind, p. 262.

called harmyá, which is the Zend zairimya*, or gharmá, which is the Latin *formus*. Thus we read:

vii. 56, 16. té harmye-sthã́*h* *s*isava*h* ná *s*ubhrã́*h*.

The Maruts bright like boys standing by the hearth.

From meaning fire-pit, or hearth, harmyá afterwards takes the more general sense of house:

vii. 55, 6. téshãm sám hanma*h* akshã́*n*i yáthá idám harmyám táthá.

We shut their eyes as we shut this house, (possibly, this oven.)

vii. 76, 2. prat*i*k*i* ã́ agãt ádhi harmyébhya*h*.

The dawn comes near, over the house-tops.

x. 46, 3. *y*átã́*h* ã́ harmyéshu.

Agni, born in the houses.

x. 73, 10. manyó*h* iyáya harmyéshu tasthau.

He came from Manyu, he remained in the houses.

In some of these passages harmyá might be taken in the sense of householder; but as harmyá in vii. 55, 6, has clearly the meaning of a building, it seems better not to assign to it unnecessarily any new significations.

But there is one other meaning which harmyá has clearly assumed in the Veda, and that is pit, or the region of darkness, the abode of evil spirits, lastly the abode of the departed. The transition of meaning is intelligible enough, the fiery oven becoming naturally the symbol of any other place of torment:

v. 32, 5. yúyutsantam támasi harmyé dhã́*h*.

When thou, Indra, hadst placed *S*ush*n*a, who was anxious to fight, in the darkness of the pit.

In the next verse we find

asûryé támasi, in the ghastly darkness.

viii. 5, 23. yuvám kã́*n*vãya nâsatyã́ ápi-riptãya harmyé *s*á*s*vat ûtî́*h* da*s*asyatha*h*.

You, Nâsatyas, always grant your aid to Ka*n*va when thrown into the pit.

* Justi, Handbuch, p. 119, zairimyañura, adj. in der Tiefe essend, Name eines Daêva oder, da er dem Hund gegenüber genannt wird, eines ahrimanischen Thieres, Spiegel (Av. übers. vol. i. p. 190) vermuthet des Hamsters.

This fiery pit into which Atri is thrown, and where he, too, was saved by the Asvins, is likewise called gharmá, i. 112, 7; 119, 6; viii. 73, 3; x. 80, 3.

Lastly we find:

x. 114, 10. yadá yamáh bhávati harmyé hitáh.

When Yama is seated in his house, or in the nether world.

The Pitars, too, the spirits of the departed, the Manes, are called gharma-sád, dwelling in the abode of Yama, x. 15, 9, and 10.

Wilson: 'Those, your coursers, which traverse the regions in their speed, proceed, self-guided : all worlds, all dwellings are alarmed, for marvellous is your coming : (such fear as is felt) when spears are thrust forth (in battle).'

Kuhn, Zeitschrift, vol. ii. p. 234 : 'Die ihr die Luft erfüllt mit eurer Kraft, hervorstürmt ihr selbst-gelenkten Laufes.'

Verse 5, note [1]. Nad certainly means to sound, and the causative might be translated by 'to make cry or shriek.' If we took párvata in the sense of cloud, we might translate, 'When you make the clouds roar ;' if we took párvata for mountain, we might, with Professor Wilson, render the passage by 'When your brilliant coursers make the mountains echo.' But nad, like other roots which afterwards take the meaning of sounding, means originally to vibrate, to shake ; and if we compare analogous passages where nad occurs, we shall see that in our verse, too, the Vedic poet undoubtedly meant nad to be taken in that sense :

viii. 20, 5. ákyutâ kit vah ágman á nânadati párvatâsah vánaspátih, bhůmih yâmeshu regate.

At your racing even things that are immovable shake, the rocks, the lord of the forest ; the earth trembles on your ways. (See i. 37, 7, note [1], page 62.)

Verse 5, note [2]. See i. 37, 7, note [1], page 62.

Verse 5, note [3]. Rathiyántî-iva does not occur again.

Sâyaṇa explains it, like a woman who wishes for a chariot, or who rides in a chariot. I join it with óshadhi, and take it in the sense of upamânâd âkâre (Pâṇ. iii. 1, 10), i. e. to behave like or to be like a chariot, whether the comparison is meant to express simply the quickness of chariots or the whirling of their wheels. The Pada has rathiyánti, whereas the more regular form is that of the Sanhitâ, rathîyánti. Cf. Prâtisâkhya, 587.

Verse 6, note [1]. Su-ketúnâ, the instrumental of su-ketú, kindness, good-mindedness, favour. This word occurs in the instrumental only, and always refers to the kindness of the gods; not, like sumatí, to the kindness of the worshipper also:

i. 79, 9. â naḥ agne su-ketúnâ rayím visvâyu-poshasam, mârdikám dhchi gívâse.

Give us, O Agni, through thy favour wealth which supports our whole life, give us grace to live.

i. 127, 11. sáḥ naḥ nédishṭham dádrisânaḥ â bhara ágne devébhiḥ sá-kanâḥ su-ketúnâ mahâḥ râyâḥ su-ketúnâ.

Thou, O Agni, seen close to us, bring to us, in company with the gods, by thy favour, great riches, by thy favour!

i. 159, 5. asmábhyam dyâvâprithivî (íti) su-ketúnâ rayím dhattam vásu-mantam sata-gvínam.

Give to us, O Dyâvâprithivî, by your favour, wealth, consisting of treasures and many flocks.

v. 51, 11. svastí dyâvâprithivî (íti) su-ketúnâ.

Give us, O Dyâvâprithivî, happiness through your favour!

v. 64, 2. tâ bâhávâ su-ketúnâ prá yantam asmai árkate.

Stretch out your arms with kindness to this worshipper!

In one passage of the ninth Maṇḍala (ix. 65, 30) we meet with su-ketúnam, as an accusative, referring to Soma, the gracious, and this would pre-suppose a substantive ketúna, which, however, does not exist.

Verse 6, note [2]. Sumatí has, no doubt, in most passages in the Rig-veda, the meaning of favour, the favour of the gods. 'Let us obtain your favour, let us be in your favour,' are familiar expressions of the Vedic poets. But there are also numerous passages where that meaning is

inapplicable, and where, as in our passage, we must translate sumatí by prayer or desire.

In the following passages sumatí is clearly used in its
original sense of favour, blessing, or even gift:

i. 73, 6 (7). su-matím bhíkshamâ*n*â*h*.

Begging for thy favour.

i. 171, 1. su-ukténa bhikshe su-matím turâ*n*âm.

With a hymn I beg for the favour of the quick Maruts.

i. 114, 3. asyâina te su-matím.

May we obtain thy favour! Cf. i. 114, 9.

i. 114, 4. su-matím ít vayám asya â vri*n*îmahe.

We choose his favour. Cf. iii. 33, 11.

i. 117, 23. sâdâ kavî (íti) su-matím â *k*ake vâm.

I always desire your favour, O ye wise Asvins.

i. 156, 3. mahâ*h* te vish*n*o (íti) su-matím bha*g*âmahe.

May we, O Vish*n*u, enjoy the favour of thee, the mighty!

Bhiksh, to beg, used above, is an old desiderative form
of bha*g*, and means to wish to enjoy.

iii. 4, 1. su-matím râsi vâsva*h*.

Thou grantest the favour of wealth.

vii. 39, 1. ûrdhvá*h* agní*h* su-matím vâsva*h* asret.

The lighted fire went up for the favour of wealth.
Cf. vii. 60, 11 ; ix. 97, 26.

iii. 57, 6. váso (íti) râsva su-matím visvá-*g*anyâm.

Grant us, O Vasu, thy favour, which is glorious among
men !

vii. 100, 2. tvám vish*n*o (íti) su-matím visvá-*g*anyâm —
dâ*h*.

Mayest thou, Vish*n*u, give thy favour, which is glorious
among men !

x. 11, 7. yá*h* te agne su-matím márta*h* ákshat.

The mortal who obtained thy favour, O Agni.

ii. 34, 15. arvâ*k*î sâ maruta*h* yâ va*h* ûtí*h* ó (íti) sú vâsrâ-
iva su-matí*h* *g*igâtu.

Your help, O Maruts, which is to usward, your favour
may it come near, like a cow !

viii. 22, 4. asmân á*kk*ha su-matí*h* vâm subha*h* patî (íti)
â dhenú*h*-iva dhâvatu.

May your favour, O Asvins, hasten towards us, like a
cow !

But this meaning is by no means the invariable meaning of sumatí, and it will easily be seen that, in the following passages, the word must be translated by prayer.   Thus when Sarasvatî is called (i. 3, 11) *kétantî su-matînấm, this can only mean she who knows of the prayers, as before she is called *kodayitrí sûn*r*itânâm, she who excites songs of praise :

i. 151, 7. á*kkh*a gíra*h* su-matím gantam asma-yú (íti).

Come towards the songs, towards the prayer, you who are longing for us. Cf. x. 20, 10.

ii. 43, 3. tûsh*n*ím ãsîna*h* su-matím *k*ikiddhi na*h*.

Sitting quiet, listen, O *S*akuni (bird), to our prayer !

v. 1, 10. ã bhándish*th*asya su-matím *k*ikiddhi.

Take notice of the prayer of thy best praiser ! Cf. v. 33, 1.

vii. 18, 4. ã na*h* índra*h* su-matím gantu á*kkh*a.

May Indra come to our prayer !

vii. 31, 10. prá-*k*etase prá su-matím kri*n*udhvam.

Make a prayer for the wise god !

ix. 96, 2. su-matím yâti á*kkh*a.

He (Soma) goes near to the prayer.

x. 148, 3. *r*íshî*n*âm vípra*h* su-matím *k*akâná*h*.

Thou, the wise, desiring the prayer of the *R*ishis.

viii. 22, 6. tã vâm adyá sumatí-bhi*h* *s*ubha*h* patî (íti) á*s*vinâ prá stuvîmahi.

Let us praise to-day the glorious A*s*vins with our prayers.

ix. 74, 1. tám îmahe su-matí.

We implore him with prayer.

In our passage the verb pipartana, fill or fulfil, indicates in what sense sumatí ought to be taken.   Su-matím pipar-tana is no more than kãmam pipartana, fulfil our desire ! See vii. 62, 3. ã na*h* kãmam pûpurantu ; i. 158, 2. kãma-pré*n*a-iva mánasâ.   On sumná, see Aufrecht, in Kuhn's Zeitschrift, vol. iv. p. 274.

Verse 6, note [3]. Krívi*h*-datî has been a crux to ancient and modern interpreters.   It is mentioned as a difficult word in the Nigha*nt*u, and all that Yâska has to say is that it means possessed of cutting teeth ; (Nir. vi. 30. krivirdatî vikartanadantî.)   Professor Roth, in his note to this passage, says that krivi can never have the meaning of well, which is ascribed to it in the Nighantu iii. 23, but seems rather to mean an animal, perhaps the wild boar, κάπρος, with metathesis of v and r. He translates our passage : 'Where your lightning with boar-teeth tears.' In his Dictionary, however, he only says, ' krivis, perhaps the name of an animal, and dant, tooth.' Sâyana contents himself with explaining krívirdatî by vikshepanasîladantî, having teeth that scatter about.

My own translation is founded on the supposition that krívis, the first portion of krívirdatî, has nothing to do with krivi, but is a dialectic variety of kravís, raw flesh, the Greek κρέας, Latin caro, cruor. It means what is raw, bloody, or gory. From it the adjective krûra, horrible, cruentus; (Curtius, Grundzüge, p. 142 ; Kuhn, Zeitschrift, vol. ii. p. 235.) A name of the goddess Durgâ in later Sanskrit is krûradantî, and with a similar conception the lightning, I believe, is here called krívirdatî, with gory teeth.

Verse 6, note [1]. It should be observed that in rádati the simile of the teeth of the lightning is carried on. For rádati may be supposed to have had in the Veda, too, the original meaning of râdere and rôdere, to scratch, to gnaw. Rada and radana in the later Sanskrit mean tooth. It is curious, however, that there is no other passage in the Rig-veda where rad clearly means to bite. It means to cut, in

i. 61, 12. góh ná párva ví rada tiraskâ.

Cut his joint through, as the joint of an ox.

But in most passages where rad occurs in the Veda, it has the meaning of giving, and is in fact a different root, but hardly the same which we have in the Zend râd, to give, and which Justi rightly identifies with the root râdh.

This meaning is evident in the following passages :

vii. 79, 4. távat ushah râdhah asmábhyam râsva yâvat stotrí-bhyah áradah grinânâ.

Grant us, Ushas, so much wealth as thou hast given to the singers.

i. 116, 7. kakshîvate aradatam púram-dhim.

You gave wisdom to Kakshîvat.

i. 169, 8. ráda marút-bhih surúdhah gó-agrâh.

Give to the Maruts gifts, rich in cattle.

vii. 62, 3. ví na*h* sahásram *s*urúdha*h* radantu.
May they (the gods) give to us a thousand gifts.
i. 117, 11. vá*g*am víprâya—rádantâ.
Giving sustenance to the sage!
vi. 61, 6. ráda pûshâ-iva na*h* saním.
Give us, Sarasvatî, wealth, like Pûshan!
ix. 93, 4. rada índo (íti) rayím.
Give us, O Indra, wealth!
vii. 32, 18. rada-vaso (íti).
Indra, thou who givest wealth!

In many passages, however, this verb rad is connected
with words meaning way or path, and it then becomes a
question whether it simply means to grant a way, or to cut
a way open for some one. In Zend, too, the same idiom
occurs, and Professor Justi explains it by ' prepare a way.'
I subjoin the principal passages :

vi. 30, 3. yát âbhya*h* árada*h* gâtúm indra.
That thou hast cut a way for them (the rivers).
iv. 19, 2. prá vartaní*h* arada*h* vi*s*vá-dhenâ*h*.
Thou (Indra) hast cut open the paths for all the cows.
vii. 47, 4. yâbhya*h* índra*h* áradat gâtúm.
The rivers for which Indra cut a way.
x. 75, 2. prá te aradat váru*n*a*h* yâtave pathâ*h*.
Varu*n*a cut the paths for thee to go.
vii. 87, 1. rádat pathâ*h* váru*n*a*h* sûryâya.
Varu*n*a cut paths for Sûrya.
v. 80, 3. pathâ*h* rádantî suvitâya devî́.
She, the dawn, cutting open the paths for wealth.
vii. 60, 4. yásmai âdityâ*h* ádhvana*h* rádanti.
For whom the Âdityas cut roads.
ii. 30, 2. pathâ*h* rádantî*h*—dhúnaya*h* yanti ártham.
Cutting their paths, the rivers go to their goal.

This last verse seems to show that the cutting open of
a road is really the idea expressed by rad in all these
passages. And thus we find the rivers themselves saying
that Indra cut them out or delivered them :

iii. 33, 6. índra*h* asmấn aradat vá*g*ra-bâhu*h*. Cf. x. 89, 7.

Verse 6, note [6]. Ri*n*âti, like the preceding expressions
krívirdati and rádati, is not chosen at random, for though

it has the general meaning of crushing or destroying, it is
used by the Vedic poets with special reference to the
chewing or crunching by means of the teeth.   For
instance,

i. 148, 4. purûni dasmáh ní rináti gámbhaih.
Agni crunches many things with his jaws.
i. 127, 4. sthirấ kit ánnâ ní rináti ógasâ.
Even tough morsels he (Agni) crunches fiercely.
In a more general sense we find it used,
v. 41, 10. sokíh-kesah ní rináti vânâ.
Agni with flaming hair swallows or destroys the forests.
iv. 19, 3. áhim vágrena ví rinâh.
Thou destroyedst Ahi with the thunderbolt.
x. 120, 1. sadyáh gagñânáh ní rináti sátrûn.
As soon as born he destroys his enemies.

Verse 6, note[6]. Súdhitâ-iva barhánâ. I think the explanation of this phrase given by Sâyana may be retained.
He explains súdhitâ by suhitâ, i. e. sushthu preritâ, well
thrown, well levelled, and barhánâ by hatis, tatsâdhanâ hetir
vâ, a blow or its instrument, a weapon.   Professor Roth
takes barhánâ as an instrumental, used abverbially, in the
sense of powerfully, but he does not explain in what sense
súdhitâ-iva ought then to be taken.   We cannot well refer
it to didyút, lightning, on account of the iva, which requires
something that can form a simile of the lightning. Nor is
su-dhitâ ever used as a substantive so as to take the place
of svâdhitîva.   Sú-dhita has apparently many meanings, but
they all centre in one common conception.   Sú-dhita means
well placed, of a thing which is at rest, well arranged, well
ordered, secure ; or it means well sent, well thrown, of a
thing which has been in motion. Applied to human beings,
it means well disposed or kind.

iii. 23, 1. níh-mathitah sú-dhitah ấ sadhá-sthe.
Agni produced by rubbing, and well placed in his
abode.

vii. 42, 4. sú-prîtah agníh sú-dhitah dáme ấ.
Agni, who is cherished and well placed in the house.

iii. 29, 2. arányoh ní-hitah gâtâ-vedâh gárbhah-iva sú-
dhitah garbhínîshu.

Agni placed in the two fire-sticks, well placed like an embryo in the mothers. Cf. x. 27, 16.

viii. 60, 4. abhí práyâ*m*si sú-dhitâ ấ vaso (íti) gahi.

Come, O Vasu, to these well-placed offerings. Cf. i. 135, 4; vi. 15, 15; x. 53, 2.

x. 70, 8. sú-dhitâ havî*m*shi.

The well-placed offerings.

iv. 2, 10 (adhvarám). vii. 7, 3 (barhí*h*).

As applied to ấyus, life, súdhita may be translated by well established, safe :

ii. 27, 10. asyấma ấyû*m*shi sú-dhitâni pûrvâ.

May we obtain the happy long lives of our forefathers.

iv. 50, 8. sá*h* ít ksheti sú-dhita*h* ókasi své.

That man dwells secure in his own house.

Applied to a missile weapon, súdhita may mean well placed, as it were, well shouldered, well held, before it is thrown ; or well levelled, well aimed, when it is thrown :

i. 167, 3. mimyáksha yéshu sú-dhitâ—*r*ish*t*íh.

To whom the well held spear sticks fast.

vi. 33, 3. tvám tấn indra ubháyân amítrân dấsâ vritrâ*n*i ấryâ *k*a *s*úra, vádhî*h* vánâ-iva sú-dhitebhi*h* átkai*h*.

Thou, Indra, O hero, strikest both enemies, the barbarous and the Aryan fiends, like forests with well-aimed weapons.

Applied to a poem, súdhita means well arranged or perfect :

i. 140, 11. idám agne sú-dhitam dú*h*-dhitât ádhi priyât û*m* (íti) *k*it mánmana*h* préya*h* astu te.

May this perfect prayer be more agreable to thee than an imperfect one, though thou likest it.

vii. 32, 13. mántram ákharvam sú-dhitam.

A poem, not mean, well contrived.

As applied to men, súdhita means very much the same as hitá, well disposed, kind :

iv. 6, 7. ádha mitrá*h* ná sú-dhita*h* pâvaká*h* agní*h* dîdâya mấnushîshu vikshú.

Then, like a kind friend, Agni shone among the children of man.

v. 3, 2. mitrám sú-dhitam.

vi. 15, 2. mitrám ná yám sú-dhitam.

viii. 23, 8. mitrám ná *g*áne sú-dhitam *r*itá-vani.

x. 115, 7. mitrãsa*h* ná yé sú-dhitã*h*.

At last sú-dhita, without reference to human beings, takes the general sense of kind, good :

iii. 11, 8. pári vísvãni sú-dhitã agné*h* asyãma mánma-bhi*h*. May we obtain through our prayers all the goods of Agni.

Here, however, práyãmsi may have to be supplied, and in that case this passage, too, should be classed with those mentioned above, viii. 60, 4, &c.

If then we consider that súdhita, as applied to weapons, means well held or well aimed, we can hardly doubt that barhá*n*ã is here, as Sáya*n*a says, some kind of weapon. I should derive it from barhayati, to crush, which we have, for instance,

i. 133, 5. pisánga-bh*r*ish*t*im ambhri*n*ám pisã*k*im indra sám m*r*i*n*a, sárvam rákshah ní barhaya.

Pound together the fearful Pi*s*ã*k*i with his fiery weapons, strike down every Rakshas.

ii. 23, 8. b*r*íhaspate deva-nídah ní barhaya.

B*r*ihaspati strike down the scoffers of the gods. Cf. vi. 61, 3.

Barhá*n*ã would therefore mean a weapon intended to crush an enemy, a block of stone, it may be, or some other missile, and in that sense barhá*n*ã occurs at least once more :

viii. 63, 7. yát páñka-*g*anyayã visã índre ghóshã*h* ás*r*ikshata, ást*r*i*n*ãt barhá*n*ã vipá*h*.

When shouts have been sent up to Indra by the people of the five clans, then the weapon scattered the enemies; or, then he scattered the enemies with his weapon.

In other passages Professor Roth is no doubt right when he assigns to barhá*n*ã an adverbial meaning, but I do not think that this meaning would be appropriate in our verse.

Verse 7, note [1]. Alát*r*inãsa*h*, a word which occurs but once more, and which had evidently become unintelligible even at the time of Yáska. He (Nir. vi. 2) explains it by alamãtardano meghah, the cloud which opens easily. This, at least, is the translation given by Professor Roth, though not without hesitation. Alamãtardana*h*, as a compound, is explained by the commentator as âtardanaparyâpta*h*, alam âtardayitum udakam, i. e. capable of letting off the water. But Devarâ*g*aya*g*van explains it differently. He says: alam paryâptam âtardanam hi*m*sâ yasya, bahûdakatvât *s*abalo megho vi*s*eshyate, i. e. whose injuring is great; the dark cloud is so called because it contains much water. Sâya*n*a, too, attempts several explanations. In iii. 30, 10, he seems to derive it from t*r*ih, to kill, not, like Yâska, from t*r*id, and he explains its meaning as the cloud which is exceedingly hurt by reason of its holding so much water. In our passage he explains it either as anât*r*i*n*a, free from injury, or good hurters of enemies, or good givers of rewards.

From all this I am afraid we gain nothing. Let us now see what modern commentators have proposed in order to discover an appropriate meaning in this word. Professor Roth suggests that the word may be derived from râ, to give, and the suffix t*r*i*n*a, and the negative particle, thus meaning, one who does not give or yield anything. But, if so, how is this adjective applicable to the Maruts, who in this very verse are praised for their generosity? Langlois in our passage translates, 'heureux de nos louanges;' in iii. 30, 10, 'qui laissait flétrir les plantes.' Wilson in our passage translates, 'devoid of malevolence;' but in iii. 30, 10, 'heavy.'

I do not pretend to solve all these difficulties, but I may say this in defence of my own explanation that it fulfils the condition of being applicable both to the Maruts and to the demon Bala. The suffix t*r*i*n*a is certainly irregular, and I should much prefer to write alât*r*i*n*a, for in that case we might derive lâtrin from lâtra, and to this lâtra, i. e. râtra, I should ascribe the sense of barking. The root rai or râ means to bark, and has been connected by Professor Aufrecht with Latin *rire, inrire*, and possibly *inritare* *, thus showing a transition of meaning from barking, to provoking or attacking. The same root râ explains also the Latin *lâtrare*, to bark, *allatrare*, to assail; and, whatever ancient etymologists may say to the contrary, the Latin *latro*, an assailer. The old derivation ' latrones eos

---

* Kuhn, Zeitschrift, vol. ix. p. 233.

antiqui dicebant, qui conducti militabant, ἀπὸ τῆς λατρείας,' seems to me one of those etymologies in which the scholars of Rome, who had learnt a little Greek, delighted as much as scholars who know a little Sanskrit delight in finding some plausible derivation for any Greek or Latin word in Sanskrit. I know that Curtius (Grundzüge, p. 326) and Corssen (Kritische Nachträge, p. 239) take a different view; but a foreign word, derived from λάτρον, pay, hire, would never have proved so fertile as *latro* has been in Latin.

If then we could write alâtriṇâsaḥ, we should have an appropriate epithet of the Maruts, in the sense of not assailing or not reviling, in fact, free from malevolence, as Wilson translated the word, or rather Sâyaṇa's explanation of it, âtardanarahita. What gives me some confidence in this explanation is this, that it is equally applicable to the other passage where alâtriṇa occurs, iii. 30, 10 :

alâtriṇáḥ valáḥ indra vragáḥ góḥ purắ hántoḥ bháyamânaḥ ví âra.

Without barking did Vala, the keeper of the cow, full of fear, open, before thou struckest him.

If it should be objected that vragá means always stable, and is not used again in the sense of keeper, one might reply that vragáḥ, in the nom. sing., occurs in this one single passage only, and that bháyamânaḥ, fearing, clearly implies a personification. Otherwise, one might translate : 'Vala was quiet, O Indra, and the stable of the cow came open, full of fear, before thou struckest.' The meaning of alâtriṇá would remain the same, the not-barking being here used as a sign that Indra's enemy was cowed, and no longer inclined to revile or defy the power of Indra. Hom. hymn. in Merc. 145, οὐδὲ κύνες λελάκοντο.

Verse 7, note [2]. See i. 38, 15, note [1], page 78.

Verse 8, note [1]. Abhí-hruti seems to have the meaning of assault, injury, insult. It occurs but once, but abhí-hrut, a feminine substantive with the same meaning, occurs several times. The verb hru, which is not mentioned in the Dhâtupâṭha, but has been identified with hvar, occurs in our hymn, verse 12 :

i. 128, 5. sá*h* na*h* trâsate du*h*-itã́t abhi-hrúta*h* sá*m*sât
aghã́t abhi-hrúta*h*.

He protects us from evil, from assaults, from evil speaking, from assaults.

x. 63, 11. trấyadhvam na*h* du*h*-évâyâ*h* abhi-hrúta*h*.

Protect us from mischievous injury !

i. 189, 6. abhi-hrútâm ási hí deva vishpá*t*.

For thou, god, art the deliverer from all assaults. Vishpá*t*,
deliverer, from vi and spas, to bind.

Ví-hruta, which occurs twice, means evidently what has
been injured or spoiled :

viii. 1, 12. íshkartâ ví-hrutam púnar (íti).

He who sets right what has been injured. Cf. viii. 20, 26.

A͏́vi-hruta again clearly means uninjured, intact, entire:

v. 66, 2. tã́ hí kshatrám ávi-hrutam — ã́sâte.

For they both have obtained uninjured power.

x. 170, 1. ã́yu*h* dádhat ya*g*ñá-patau ávi-hrutam.

Giving uninjured life to the lord of the sacrifice.

Verse 9, note [1]. Tavishá certainly means strength, and
that it is used in the plural in the sense of acts of strength,
we can see from the first verse of our hymn and other
passages. But when we read that tavishá*n*i are placed on
the chariots of the Maruts, just as before bhadrẫ, good
things, food, &c., are mentioned, it is clear that so abstract
a meaning as strength or powers would not be applicable
here. We might take it in the modern sense of forces,
i. e. your armies, your companions are on your chariots,
striving with each other; but as the word is a neuter,
weapons, as the means of strength, seemed a preferable
rendering.

Verse 9, note [2]. The rendering of this passage must
depend on the question whether the khâdís, whatever they
are, can be carried on the shoulders or not. We saw before
(p. 102) that khâdís were used both as ornaments and as
weapons, and that, when used as weapons, they were most
likely rings or quoits with sharp edges. There is at least
one other passage where these khâdís are said to be worn
on the shoulders :

vii. 56, 13. ámseshu ā́ marutaḥ khādáyaḥ vaḥ vákshaḥ-su rukmā́ḥ upa-sisriyā́nā́ḥ.

On your shoulders are the quoits, on your chests the golden chains are fastened.

In other places the khádís are said to be in the hands, hásteshu, but this would only show that they are there when actually used for fighting. Thus we read :

i. 168, 3. ā́ eshām ámseshu rambhínî-iva rarabhe, háste-shu khā́díḥ ka kṛitíḥ ka sám dadhe.

To their shoulders (the spear) clings like a creeper, in their hands the quoit is held and the dagger.

In v. 58, 2, the Maruts are called khā́di-hasta, holding the quoits in their hands. There is one passage which was mentioned before (p. 94), where the khā́dís are said to be on the feet of the Maruts, and on the strength of this passage Professor Roth proposes to alter prá-patheshu to prá-padeshu, and to translate, 'The khā́dís are on your forefeet.' I do not think this emendation necessary. Though we do not know the exact shape and character of the khā́dí, we know that it was a weapon, most likely a ring, occasionally used for ornament, and carried along either on the feet or on the shoulders, but in actual battle held in the hand. The weapon which Vishṇu holds in one of his right hands, the so-called kakra, may be the modern representation of the ancient khā́dí. What, however, is quite certain is this, that khā́dí in the Veda never means food, as Sâyaṇa optionally interprets it. This interpretation is accepted by Wilson, who translates, 'At your resting-places on the road refreshments (are ready).' Nay, he goes on in a note to use this passage as a proof of the advanced civilisation of India at the time of the Vedic Rishis. 'The expression,' he says, 'is worthy of note, as indicating the existence of accommodations for the use of travellers : the Prapatha is the choltri of the south of India, the sarái of the Mohammedans, a place by the road-side where the travellers may find shelter and provisions.'

Verse 9, note [3]. This last passage shows that the poet is really representing to himself the Maruts as on their journey, and he therefore adds, 'your axle turns the two

(iv. 30, 2) wheels together,' which probably means no more than, ' your chariot is going smoothly or quickly.' Though the expression seems to us hardly correct, yet one can well imagine how the axle was supposed to turn the wheels as the horses were drawing the axle, and the axle acted on the wheels. Anyhow, no other translation seems possible. Samâyâ in the Veda means together, at once, and is the Greek ὁμῆ, generally ὁμοῦ or ὁμῶς, the Latin *simul*. Cf. i. 56, 6; 73, 6; 113, 10; 163, 3; vii. 66, 15; ix. 75, 4; 85, 5; 97, 56.

Vrit means to turn, and is frequently used with reference to the wheels :

viii. 46, 23. dása syâvâ*h*—nemím ní vav*ri*tu*h*.

The ten black horses turn the felly or the wheel.

iv. 30, 2. satrấ te ánu krish*t*áya*h* vísvâ*h* kakrấ-iva vav*ri*tu*h*.

All men turn always round thee, like wheels.

That the Âtmanepada of v*ri*t may be used in an active sense we see from

i. 191, 15. táta*h* vishám prá vavrite.

I turn the poison out from here.

All the words used in this sentence are very old words, and we can with few exceptions turn them into Greek or Latin. In Latin we should have *axis vos(ter) circos simul divertit*. In Greek ἄξων ὑ(μῶν) κύκλω ὁμῆ . . . .

Verse 10, note [1]. See i. 64, 4, note [1], page 94. I ought to have mentioned there that in the Âsvalâyana *S*rauta-sûtras ix. 4, rukma occurs as the fee to be given to the Hotar, and is explained by âbhara*n*aviseslo v*ri*ttâkâra*h*, a round ornament.

Verse 10, note [2]. See i. 166, 1, note [1], page 200.

Verse 10, note [3]. On éta in the sense of fallow deer, or, it may be, antelope, see i. 165, 5, note [2], page 185.

Éta originally means variegated, and thus becomes a name of any speckled deer, it being difficult to say what exact species is meant. Sâya*n*a in our passage explains éta*h* by suklavar*n*â mâlâ*h*, many-coloured wreaths or chains, which may be right. Yet the suggestion of Professor Roth that étâ*h*, deer, stands here for the skins of fallow deer, is certainly more poetical, and quite in accordance with the Vedic idiom, which uses, for instance, go, cow, not only in the sense of milk,—that is done even in more homely English,—but also for leather, and thong. It is likewise in accordance with what we know of the earliest dress of the Vedic Indians, that deer-skins should here be mentioned. We learn from Âsvalâyana's Grihya-sûtras, of which we now possess an excellent edition by Professor Stenzler, and a reprint of the text and commentary by Râma Nârâyana Vidyâratna, in the Bibliotheca Indica, that a boy when he was brought to his tutor, i. e. from the eighth to possibly the twenty-fourth year, had to be well combed, and attired in a new dress. A Brâhma*n*a should wear the skin of an antelope (ai*n*eya), the Kshatriya the skin of a deer (raurava), the Vaisya the skin of a goat (â*g*a). If they wore dresses, that of the Brâhma*n*a should be dark red (kâshâya), that of the Kshatriya bright red (mâñ*g*ish*th*a), that of the Vaisya yellow (hâridra). The girdle of the Brâhma*n*a should be of Muñ*g*a grass, that of the Kshatriya a bow-string, that of the Vaisya made of sheep's wool. The same regulations occur in other Sûtras, as, for instance, the Dharma-sûtras of the Âpastambîyas and Gautamas, though there are certain characteristic differences in each, which may be due either to local or to chronological causes. Thus according to the Âpa-stambîya-sûtras, which have just been published by Professor Bühler, the Brâhma*n*a may wear the skin of the• hari*n*a deer, or that of the antelope (ai*n*eyam), but the latter must be from the black antelope (krish*n*am), and, a proviso is added, that if a man wears the black antelope skin, he must never spread it out to sit or sleep on it. As materials for the dress, Âpastamba allows sa*n*a, hemp*, or kshumâ,

---

* Sa*n*a is an old Aryan word, though its meanings differ. Hesychius and Eustathius mention κάννα as being synonymous with ψίαθος, reed. Pollux gives two forms, κάννα and κάνα, (Pollux x. 166. πτανάκα δέ ἐστι ψίαθος ἡ ἐν τοῖς ἀκατίοις ἦν καὶ κάναν καλοῦσιν. vii. 176. κάνναι δὲ τὸ ἐκ κανάβων πλέγμα.) This is important, because the same difference of spelling occurs also in

flax, and he adds that woollen dresses are allowed to all
castes, as well as the kambala (masc.), which seems to be
any cloth made of vegetable substances (darbhâdinirmitam
kîram kambalam). He then adds a curious remark, which
would seem to show that the Brâhma*n*as preferred skins,
and the Kshatriyas clothes, for he says that those who wish
well to the Brâhma*n*as should wear a*g*ina, skins, and those
who wish well to the Kshatriyas should wear vastra, clothes,
and those who wish well to both should wear both, but, in
that case, the skin should always form the outer garment.
The Dharma-sûtras of the Gautamas, which were published
in India, prescribe likewise for the Brâhma*n*a the black
antelope skin, and allow clothes of hemp or linen (*sâna-
kshaumakîra*) as well as kutapas (woollen cloth) for all.
What is new among the Gautamas, is, that they add the
kârpâsa, the cotton dress, which is important as showing

κάνναβις and *κάναβος* or *κάνναβος*, a model, a lay figure, which Lobeck derives
from *κάνναι*. In Old Norse we have *hanp-r*, in A. S. *henep*, hemp, Old High
Germ. *hanaf*.

The occurrence of the word *sana* is of importance as showing at how early a
time the Aryans of India were acquainted with the uses and the name of
hemp. Our word hemp, the A. S. *henep*, the Old Norse *hanp-r*, are all borrowed from Latin *cannabis*, which, like other borrowed words, has undergone
the regular changes required by Grimm's law in Low German, and also in
High German, *hanaf*. The Slavonic nations seem to have borrowed their
word for hemp (Lith. *kanapē*) from the Goths, the Celtic nations (Ir. *canaib*)
from the Romans; (cf. Kuhn, Beiträge, vol. ii. p. 382.) The Latin *cannabis*
is borrowed from Greek, and the Greeks, to judge from the account of
Herodotus, most likely adopted the word from the Aryan Thracians and
Scythians; (Her. iv. 74; Pictet, Les Aryens, vol. i. p. 314.) *Κάνναβις* being
a foreign word, it would be useless to attempt an explanation of the final
element *bis*, which is added to *sana*, the Sanskrit word for hemp. It may be
visa, fibre, or it may be anything else. Certain it is that the main element in
the name of hemp was the same among tho settlers in Northern India, and
among the Thracians and Scythians through whom the Greeks first became
acquainted with hemp.

The history of the word *κάνναβις* must be kept distinct from that of the
Greek *κάννα* or *κάνα*, reed. Both spellings occur, for Pollux, x. 166, writes
πτανάκα δέ έστι ψίαθος ἡ ἐν τοῖς ἀκατίοις ἦν καὶ κάναν καλοῦσιν, but vii. 176,
κάνναι δὲ τὸ ἐκ κανάβων πλέγμα. This word *κάννα* may be the same as the
Sanskrit *sana*, only with this difference, that it was retained as common
property by Greeks and Indians before they separated, and was applied
differently in later times by the one and the other.

an early knowledge of this manufacture. The kârpâsa dress occurs once more as a present to be given to the Potar priest (Âsv. Srauta-sûtras ix. 4), and evidently considered as a valuable present, taking precedence of the kshaumî or linen dress. It is provided that the cotton dress should not be dyed, for this, I suppose, is the meaning of avikrita. Immediately after, however, it is said, that some authorities say the dress should be dyed red (kâshâyam apy eke), the very expression which occurred in Âpastamba, and that, in that case, the red for the Brâhmana's dress should be taken from the bark of trees (vârksha). Manu, who here, as elsewhere, simply paraphrases the ancient Sûtras, says, ii. 41 :

kârshnarauravavâstâni karmâni brahmakârinah
vasîrann ânupûrvyena sânakshaumâvikâni ka.

' Let Brahmakârins wear (as outer garments) the skins of the black antelope, the deer, the goat, (as under garments) dresses of hemp, flax, and sheep's wool, in the order of the three castes.'

The Sanskrit name for a dressed skin is agina, a word which does not occur in the Rig-veda, but which, if Bopp is right in deriving it from agâ, goat, as αἰγίς from αἴξ, would have meant originally, not skin in general, but a goat-skin. The skins of the éta, here ascribed to the Maruts, would be identical with the aineya, which Âsvalâyana ascribes to the Brâhmana, not, as we should expect, to the Kshatriya, if, as has been supposed, aineya is derived from ena, which is a secondary form, particularly in the feminine enî, of eta. There is, however, another word, eda, a kind of sheep, which, but for Festus, might be hœdus, and by its side ena, a kind of antelope. These two forms pre-suppose an earlier erna, and point therefore in a different direction.

Verse 10, note [4]. I translate kshurá by sharp edges, but it might have been translated literally by razors, for, strange as it may sound, razors were known, not only during the Vedic period, but even previous to the Aryan separation. The Sanskrit kshurá is the Greek ξυρός or ξυρόν. In the Veda we have clear allusions to shaving :

x. 142, 4. yadắ te vấta*h* anu-vắti so*kíh*, vấptâ-iva *s*mấsru vapasi prá bh*ŭ*ma.

When the wind blows after thy blast, then thou shavest the earth as a barber shaves the beard.   Cf. i. 65, 4.

If, as B. and R. suggest, vaptar, barber, is connected with the more modern name for barber in Sanskrit, viz. nâpita, we should have to admit a root svap, in the sense of tearing or pulling, *vellere*, from which we might derive the Vedic svap*ŭ* (vii. 56, 3), beak.   Corresponding to this we find in Old High German *snabul*, beak, (*schnepfe*, snipe,) and in Old Norse *nef*.   The Anglo-Saxon *neb* means mouth and nose, while in modern English *neb* or *nib* is used for the bill or beak of a bird *.   Another derivation of nâpita, proposed by Professor Weber (Kuhn's Beiträge, vol. i. p. 505), who takes nâpita as a dialectic form of snâpitar, *balneator*, or lavator, might be admitted if it could be proved that in India also the barber was at the same time a *balneator*.

Verse 11, note [1]. Ví-bhûtaya*h* is properly a substantive, meaning power, but, like other substantives †, and particularly substantives with prepositions, it can be used as an adjective, and is, in fact, more frequently used as an adjective than as a substantive.   It is a substantive,

i. 8, 9. evá hí te ví-bhûtaya*h* ûtáya*h* indra mấ-vate sadyá*h* *k*it sánti dấsúshe.

For indeed thy powers, O Indra, are at once shelters for a sacrificer, like me.

But it is an adjective,

i. 30, 5. ví-bhûti*h* astu sûn*rí*tâ.

May the prayer be powerful.

vi. 17, 4. mahắm ánûnam tavásam ví-bhûtim matsarấsa*h* *g*ar*h*rishanta pra-sáham.

———   · · · ·

* Grimm, Deutsche Grammatik, vol. iii. pp. 400, 409.   There is not yet sufficient evidence to show that Sanskrit sv, German sn, and Sanskrit n are interchangeable, but there is at least one case that may be analogous.   Sanskrit svañg, to embrace, to twist round a person, German *slango*, *Schlange*, snake, and Sanskrit nâga, snake.   Grimm, Deutsche Grammatik, vol. iii. p. 364.

† See Benfey, Kuhn's Zeitschrift, vol. ii. p. 216.

The sweet draughts of Soma delighted the great, the
perfect, the strong, the powerful, the unyielding Indra.
Cf. viii. 49, 6; 50, 6.

Vibhvâ*h*, with the Svarita on the last syllable, has to be
pronounced vibhúâ*h*.   In iii. 6, 9, we find vi-bhâva*h*.

Verse **11**, note [2]. See i. 87, 1, note [1], page 144.

Verse **11**, note [3]. See i. 6, 5, note [1], page 29.

Verse **12**, note [1]. Mahi-tvanám, greatness, is formed by
the suffix tvaná, which Professor Aufrecht has identified
with the Greek σύνη (συνον); see Kuhn's Zeitschrift, vol. i.
p. 482. The origin of this suffix has been explained by
Professor Benfey, ibid. vol. vii. p. 120, who traces it back to
the suffix tvan, for instance, i-tvan, goer, in prâta*h*-ítvâ =
prâta*h*-yấvâ.

Verse **12**, notes [2] and [3]. Vratá is one of those words which,
though we may perceive their one central idea, and their
original purport, we have to translate by various terms in
order to make them intelligible in every passage where they
occur.   Vratá, I believe, meant originally what is enclosed,
protected, set apart, the Greek νομός :
    v. 46, 7. yấ*h* pârthivâsa*h* yấ*h* apâm ápi vraté tấ*h* na*h*
devî*h* su-havâ*h* sárma ya*kkh*ata.

O ye gracious goddesses, who are on the earth or in the
realm of the waters, grant us your protection !
    Here vratá is used like vri*g*ána, see i. 165, 15, note [3],
page 195.
    x. 114, 2. tấsâm ní *k*ikyu*h* kavấya*h* ni-dấnam pâreshu yấ*h*
gúhyeshu vratéshu.

The poets discovered their (the Nir*r*itis') origin, who are
in the far hidden chambers.
    i. 163, 3. ási tritá*h* gúhyena vraténa.
    Thou art Trita within the hidden place, or with the
secret work.
    Secondly, vratá means what is fenced off, what is deter-
mined, what is settled, and hence, like dhárman, law,
ordinance.   In this sense vratá occurs very frequently :
    i. 25, 1. yát *k*it hí te vísa*h* yathâ prá deva varu*n*a vratáni,
minîmási dyávi-dyavi.

Whatever law of thine we break, O Varu*n*a, day by day, men as we are.

ii. 8, 3. yásya vratám ná mî*y*ate.

Whose law is not broken.

iii. 32, 8. índrasya kárma sú-*k*ritâ purû*n*i vratâni devâ*h* ná minanti vísve.

The deeds of Indra are well done and many, all the gods do not break his laws, or do not injure his ordinances.

ii. 24, 12. vísvam satyám maghavânâ yuvó*h* ít â*p*a*h* *k*aná prá minanti vratám vâm.

All that is yours, O powerful gods, is true; even the waters do not break your law.

ii. 38, 7. náki*h* asya tâni vratâ devásya savitú*h* minanti.

No one breaks these laws of this god Savitar. Cf. ii. 38, 9.

i. 92, 12. áminatî daívyâni vratâni.

Not injuring the divine ordinances. Cf. i. 124, 2.

x. 12, 5. kát asya áti vratám *k*akrima.

Which of his laws have we overstepped?

viii. 25, 16. tásya vratâni ánu va*h* *k*arâmasi.

His ordinances we follow.

x. 33, 9. ná devânâm áti vratám satá-âtmâ *k*aná *g*îvati.

No one lives beyond the statute of the gods, even if he had a hundred lives.

vii. 5, 4. táva tri-dhâtu p*r*ithiví utá dyaú*h* vaisvânara vratám agne sa*k*anta.

The earth and the sky followed thy threefold law, O Agni Vaisvânara.

vii. 87, 7. yá*h* m*r*ilá*y*âti *k*akrúshe *k*it âga*h* vayám syâma váru*n*e ánâgâ*h*, ánu vratâni áditc*h* *r*idhânta*h*.

Let us be sinless before Varu*n*a, who is gracious even to him who has committed sin, let us perform the laws of Aditi!

ii. 28, 8. náma*h* purấ te varu*n*a utá nûnám utá aparám tuvi-*g*âta bravâma, tvé hí kam párvate ná *r*itâni ápra-*k*yutâni du*h*-dabha vratâni.

Formerly, and now, and also in future let us give praise to thee, O Varu*n*a; for in thee, O unconquerable, all laws are grounded, immovable as on a rock.

A very frequent expression is ánu vratám, according to

the command of a god, ii. 38, 3; 6; viii. 40, 8; or simply áⁿu vratám, according to law and order:

i. 136, 5. tám aryamâ abhí rakshati riǵu-yántam áⁿu vratám.

Aryaman protects him who acts uprightly according to law. Cf. iii. 61, 1; iv. 13, 2; v. 69, 1.

The laws or ordinances or institutions of the gods are sometimes taken for the sacrifices which are supposed to be enjoined by the gods, and the performance of which is, in a certain sense, the performance of the divine will.

i. 93, 8. yáⁿ agníshómâ havíshâ saparyât devadrîkâ mánasâ yáⁿ ghriténa, tásya vratám rakshatam pâtám áⁿhasaⁿ.

He who worships Agni and Soma with oblations, with a godly mind, or with an offering, protect his sacrifice, shield him from evil!

i. 31, 2. tvám agne prathamáⁿ áṅgiraⁿ-tamaⁿ kavíⁿ devânâm pári bhûshasi vratám.

Agni, the first and wisest of poets, thou performest the sacrifice of the gods.

iii. 3, 9. tásya vratâni bhúri-poshíⁿaⁿ vayám úpa bhûshema dáme â suvⁿiktí-bhiⁿ.

Let us, who possess much wealth, perform with prayers the sacrifices of Agni within our house.

In another acceptation the vratas of the gods are what they perform and establish themselves, their own deeds:

iii. 6, 5. vratâ te agne mahatáⁿ mahâni táva krátvâ ródasî (íti) â tatantha.

The deeds of thee, the great Agni, are great, by thy power thou hast stretched out heaven and earth.

viii. 42, 1. ástabhnât dyâm ásuraⁿ visvá-vedâⁿ ámimîta varimâⁿam pⁿithivyâⁿ, â asîdat vísvâ bhúvanâni sam-râⁿ vísvâ ít tâni váruⁿasya vratâni.

The wise spirit established the sky, and made the width of the earth, as king he approached all beings,—all these are the works of Varuⁿa.

vi. 14, 3. tûrvantaⁿ dásyum âyávaⁿ vrataíⁿ síkshantaⁿ avratám.

Men fight the fiend, trying to overcome by their deeds him who performs no sacrifices; or, the lawless enemy.

Lastly, vratá comes to mean sway or power, and the expression vraté táva signifies, at thy command, under thy auspices :

i. 24, 15. átha vayám âditya vraté táva ánâgasa*h* áditaye syâma.

Then, O Âditya, under thy auspices may we be guiltless before Aditi.

vi. 54, 9. pûshan táva vraté vayám ná rishyema kádâ *k*anấ.

O Pûshan, may we never fail under thy protection.

x. 36, 13. yé savitú*h* satyá-savasya ví*s*ve mitrásya vraté váru*n*asya devẫ*h*.

All the gods who are in the power of Savitar, Mitra, and Varu*n*a.

v. 83, 5. yásya vraté p*r*ithiví námnamîti yásya vraté saphấ-vat *g*árbhurîti, yásya vraté óshadhî*h* vi*s*vá-rûpâ*h* sá*h* na*h* par*g*anya máhi *s*árma ya*kkh*a.

At whose command the earth bows down, at whose command the earth is as lively as a hoof (?), at whose command the plants assume all shapes, mayest thou, O Par*g*anya, yield us great protection !

In our passage I take vratá in this last sense.

Dâtrá, if derived from dâ, would mean gift, and that meaning is certainly the most applicable in some passages where it occurs :

ix. 97, 55. ási bhága*h* ási dâtrásya dâtẫ.

Thou art Bhaga, thou art the giver of the gift.

In other passages, too, particularly in those where the verb dâ or some similar verb occurs in the same verse, it can hardly be doubted that the poet took dâtrá, like dátra or dáttra, in the sense of gift, bounty, largess :

i. 116, 6. yám a*s*vinâ dadáthu*h* *s*vetám á*s*vam—tát vâm dâtrám máhi kîrtényam bhût.

The white horse, O A*s*vins, which you gave, that your gift was great and to be praised.

i. 185, 3. anehấ*h* dâtrám áditе*h* anarvám huvé.

I call for the unrivalled, the uninjured bounty of Aditi.

vii. 56, 21. mẫ va*h* dâtrẩt maruta*h* ní*h* arâma.

May we not fall away from your bounty, O Maruts !

iii. 54, 16. yuvám hí sthá*h* rayi-daú na*h* rayî*n*ãm dâtrám rakshethe.

For you, Nâsatyas, are our givers of riches, you protect the gift.

vi. 20, 7. *rigí*svane dâtrám dâsúshe dâ*h*.

To *Rigi*svan, the giver, thou givest the gift.

viii. 43, 33. tát te sahasva îmahe dâtrám yát ná upadásyati, tvát agne vấryam vásu.

We ask thee, strong hero, for the gift which does not perish; we ask from thee the precious wealth.

x. 69, 4. dâtrám rakshasva yát idám te asmé (íti).

Protect this gift of thine which thou hast given to us.

viii. 44, 18. *í*sishe vấryasya hí dâtrásya agne svã*h*-pati*h*.

For thou, O Agni, lord of heaven, art the master of the precious gift. Cf. iv. 38, 1.

Professor Roth considers that dâtrá is derived rather from dâ, to divide, and that it means share, lot, possession. But there is not a single passage where the meaning of gift or bounty does not answer all purposes. In vii. 56, 21, mấ va*h* dâtrất maruta*h* ní*h* arâma, is surely best translated by, 'let us not fall away from your bounty,' and in our own passage the same meaning should be assigned to dâtrá. The idea of dâtrá, bounty, is by no means incompatible with vratá, realm, dominion, sway, if we consider that the sphere within which the bounty of a king or a god is exercised and accepted, is in one sense his realm. What the poet therefore says in our passage is simply this, that the bounty of the Maruts extends as far as the realm of Aditi, i. e. is endless, or extends everywhere, Aditi being in its original conception the deity of the unbounded world beyond, the earliest attempt at expressing the Infinite.

As to dấtra occurring once with the accent on the first syllable in the sense of sickle, see M. M., 'Über eine Stelle in Yâska's Commentar zum Naigha*n*tuka,' Zeitschrift der Deutschen Morgenländischen Gesellschaft, 1853, vol. vii. p. 375.

viii. 78, 10. táva ít indra ahám â-*s*ásâ háste dấtram *k*aná ấ dade.

Trusting in thee alone, O Indra, I take the sickle in my hand.

This dấtra, sickle, is derived from do, to cut.

Aditi, the Infinite.

Verse 12, note [4]. Aditi, an ancient god or goddess, is in reality the earliest name invented to express the Infinite; not the Infinite as the result of a long process of abstract reasoning, but the visible Infinite, visible by the naked eye, the endless expanse beyond the earth, beyond the clouds, beyond the sky. That was called A-diti, the un-bound, the un-bounded; one might almost say, but for fear of misunderstandings, the Absolute, for it is derived from *diti*, bond, and the negative particle, and meant therefore originally what is free from bonds of any kind, whether of space or time, free from physical weakness, free from moral guilt. Such a conception became of necessity a being, a person, a god. To us such a name and such a conception seem decidedly modern, and to find in the Veda Aditi, the Infinite, as the mother of the principal gods, is certainly, at first sight, startling. But the fact is that the thoughts of primitive humanity were not only different from our thoughts, but different also from what we think their thoughts ought to have been. The poets of the Veda indulged freely in theogonic speculations without being frightened by any contradictions. They knew of Indra as the greatest of gods, they knew of Agni as the god of gods, they knew of Varuṇa as the ruler of all, but they were by no means startled at the idea that their Indra had a mother, or that their Agni was born like a babe from the friction of two fire-sticks, or that Varuṇa and his brother Mitra were nursed in the lap of Aditi. Some poet would take hold of the idea of an unbounded power, of Aditi, originally without any reference to other gods. Very soon these ideas met, and, without any misgivings, either the gods were made subordinate to, and represented as the sons of Aditi, or where Indra was to be praised as supreme, Aditi was represented as doing him homage.

viii. 12, 14. utá sva-rā́ǵe áditiḥ stómam índrāya ǵíǵanat.

And Aditi produced a hymn for Indra, the king. Here Professor Roth takes Aditi as an epithet of Agni, not as the name of the goddess Aditi, while Dr. Muir rightly takes it in the latter sense, and retains stómam instead of sómam, as printed by Professor Aufrecht. Cf. vii. 38, 4.

The idea of the Infinite, as I have tried to show elsewhere, was revealed, was most powerfully impressed on the
awakening mind, by the East*. 'It is impossible to enter
fully into all the thoughts and feelings that passed through
the minds of the early poets when they formed names for
that far, far East from whence even the early dawn, the
sun, the day, their own life, seemed to spring. A new life
flashed up every morning before their eyes, and the fresh
breezes of the dawn reached them like greetings from the
distant lands beyond the mountains, beyond the clouds,
beyond the dawn, beyond "the immortal sea which brought
us hither." The dawn seemed to them to open golden
gates for the sun to pass in triumph, and while those gates
were open, their eyes and their mind strove in their childish
way to pierce beyond the limits of this finite world. That
silent aspect awakened in the human mind the conception
of the Infinite, the Immortal, the Divine.' Aditi is a name
for that distant East, but Aditi is more than the dawn.
Aditi is beyond the dawn, and in one place (i. 113, 19)
the dawn is called 'the face of Aditi,' áditer ánîkam. Thus
we read:

v. 62, 8. híranya-rûpam ushása*h* ví-ush*t*au áya*h*-sthû*n*am
út-itâ sûryasya, â rohatha*h* varu*n*a mitra gártam áta*h*
*k*akshâthe (íti) áditim dítim *k*a.

Mitra and Varu*n*a, you mount your chariot, which is
golden, when the dawn bursts forth, and has iron poles
at the setting of the sun: from thence you see Aditi and
Diti, what is yonder and what is here.

If we keep this original conception of Aditi clearly before
us, the various forms which Aditi assumes, even in the
hymns of the Veda, will not seem incoherent. Aditi is not
a prominent deity in the Veda, she is celebrated rather in
her sons, the Âdityas, than in her own person. While
there are so many hymns addressed to Ushas, the dawn,
or Indra, or Agni, or Savitar, there is but one hymn, x. 72,
which from our point of view, though not from that of
Indian theologians, might be called a hymn to Aditi.
Nevertheless Aditi is a familiar name; a name of the past,

---

* Lectures on the Science of Language, Second Series, p. 499.

whether in time or in thought only, and a name that lives on in the name of the Âdityas, the sons of Aditi, including the principal deities of the Veda.

Aditi and the Âdityas.

Thus we read:

i. 107, 2. úpa nah devâh ávasâ â gamantu ángirasâm sáma-bhih stûyámânâh, índrah indriyaíh marútah marút-bhih âdityaíh nah áditih sárma yamsat.

May the gods come to us with their help, praised by the songs of the Angiras,—Indra with his forces, the Maruts with the storms, may Aditi with the Âdityas give us protection!

x. 66, 3. índrah vásu-bhih pári pâtu nah gáyam âdityaíh nah áditih sárma yakkhatu, rudráh rudrébhih deváh mrilayâti nah tvásh/â nah gnâbhih suvitâya ginvatu.

May Indra with the Vasus watch our house, may Aditi with the Âdityas give us protection, may the divine Rudra with the Rudras have mercy upon us, may Tvash/ar with the mothers bring us to happiness!

iii. 54, 20. âdityaíh nah áditih srinotu yákkhantu nah marútah sárma bhadrám.

May Aditi with the Âdityas hear us, may the Maruts give us good protection!

In another passage Varuna takes the place of Aditi as the leader of the Âdityas:

vii. 35, 6. sám nah índrah vásu-bhih deváh astu sám âdityébhih várunah su-sámsah, sám nah rudráh rudrébhih gálâshah sám nah tvásh/â gnâbhih ihá srinotu.

May Indra bless us, the god with the Vasus! May Varuna, the glorious, bless us with the Âdityas! May the relieving Rudra with the Rudras bless us! May Tvash/ar with the mothers kindly hear us here!

Even in passages where the poet seems to profess an exclusive worship of Aditi, as in

v. 69, 3. prâtáh devím áditim gohavîmi madhyándine út-itâ sûryasya,

I invoke the divine Aditi early in the morning, at noon, and at the setting of the sun,

Mitra and Varuṇa, her principal sons, are mentioned immediately after, and implored, like her, to bestow blessings on their worshipper.

Her exclusive worship appears once, in viii. 19, 14.

A very frequent expression is that of âdityâ*h* âditi*h* without any copula, to signify the Âdityas and Aditi:

iv. 25, 3. ká*h* devânâm áva*h* adyá vriṇíte ká*h* âdityắn áditim *gy*óti*h* ítte.

Who does choose now the protection of the gods? Who asks the Âdityas, Aditi, for their light?

vi. 51, 5. vísve âdityâ*h* adite sa-*g*óshâ*h* asmábhyam *s*árma bahulám ví yanta.

All ye Âdityas, Aditi together, grant to us your manifold protection!

x. 39, 11. ná tám râ*g*ânau adite kúta*h* *k*aná ná áṃha*h* aṣnoti du*h*-itám nákih bhayám.

O ye two kings (the Aṣvins), Aditi, no evil reaches him from anywhere, no misfortune, no fear (whom you protect). Cf. vii. 66, 6.

x. 63, 5. tắn â vivâsa námasâ suv*r*iktí-bhi*h* mahá*h* âdityắn áditim svastáye.

I cherish them with worship and with hymns, the great Âdityas, Aditi, for happiness' sake.

x. 63, 17. evá platé*h* sûnú*h* avîv*r*idhat va*h* vísve âdityâ*h* adite manîshî'.

The wise son of Plati magnified you, all ye Âdityas, Aditi!

x. 65, 9. par*g*ányâvâtâ v*r*ishabhấ purîshíṇâ indravâyú (íti) váruṇa*h* mitrá*h* aryamấ, devấn âdityắn áditim havâmahe yé pârthivâsa*h* divyấsa*h* ap-sú yé.

There are Par*g*anya and Vâta, the powerful, the givers of rain, Indra and Vâyu, Varuṇa, Mitra, Aryaman, we call the divine Âdityas, Aditi, those who dwell on the earth, in heaven, in the waters.

We are not justified in saying that there ever was a period in the history of the religious thought of India, a period preceding the worship of the Âdityas, when Aditi, the Infinite, was worshipped, though to the sage who first coined this name, it expressed, no doubt, for a time the principal, if not the only object of his faith and worship.

Aditi and Daksha.

Soon, however, the same mental process which led on later speculators from the earth to the elephant, and from the elephant to the tortoise, led the Vedic poets beyond Aditi, the Infinite. There was something beyond that Infinite which for a time they had grasped by the name of Aditi, and this, whether intentionally or by a mere accident of language, they called dáksha, literally power or the powerful. All this, no doubt, sounds strikingly modern, yet, though the passages in which this dáksha is mentioned are few in number, I should not venture to say that they are necessarily modern, even if by modern we mean only later than 1000 B. C. Nothing can bring the perplexity of the ancient mind, if once drawn into this vortex of speculation, more clearly before us than if we read :

x. 72, 4–5. áditeh dákshah ağâyata dákshât ûm (íti) áditih pári,—áditih hí ağanishta dáksha yâ duhitâ táva, tâm devâh ánu ağâyanta bhadrâh amríta-bandhavah.

Daksha was born of Aditi, and Aditi from Daksha. For Aditi was born, O Daksha, she who is thy daughter ; after her the gods were born, the blessed, who share in immortality.

Or, in more mythological language :

x. 64, 5. dákshasya vâ adite ğánmani vraté râğânâ mitrâ-váruṇâ â vivâsasi.

Or thou, O Aditi, nursest in the birthplace of Daksha the two kings, Mitra and Varuṇa.

Nay, even this does not suffice. There is something again beyond Aditi and Daksha, and one poet says :

x. 5, 7. ásat ka sát ka paramé ví-oman dákshasya ğánman áditeh upá-sthe.

Not-being and Being are in the highest heaven, in the birthplace of Daksha, in the lap of Aditi.

At last something like a theogony, though full of contradictions, was imagined, and in the same hymn from which we have already quoted, the poet says :

x. 72, 1–4. devânâm nú vayám ğânâ prá vokâma vipanyáyâ, ukthéshu sasyámâneshu yáh (yát ?) pásyât út-tare yugé. 1.

bráhma*n*a*h* páti*h* etã́ sám karmã́ra*h*-iva adhamat, devã́nãm
pûrvyé yugé ásata*h* sát a*g*âyata. 2.

devã́nãm yugé prathamé ásata*h* sát a*g*âyata, tát ã́sâ*h* ánu
a*g*âyanta tát uttânâ-*p*ada*h* pári. 3.

bhû́*h* *g*a*g*ñe uttâná-*p*ada*h* bhuvá*h* ã́sâ*h* a*g*âyanta, áditc*h*
dáksha*h* a*g*âyata, dákshât û*m* (íti) áditi*h* pári. 4.

1. Let us now with praise proclaim the births of the
gods, that a man may see them in a future age, whenever
these hymns are sung.

2. Brahma*n*aspati* blew them together like a smith
(with his bellows); in a former age of the gods, Being
was born from Not-being.

3. In the first age of the gods, Being was born from
Not-being, after it were born the Regions, from them
Uttânapada;

4. From Uttânapad the Earth was born, the Regions
were born from the Earth. Daksha was born of Aditi, and
Aditi from Daksha.

The ideas of Being and Not-being (τὸ ὄν and τὸ μὴ ὄν)
are familiar to the Hindus from a very early time in their
intellectual growth, and they can only have been the result
of abstract speculation. Therefore dáksha, too, in the
sense of power or *potentia*, may have been a metaphysical
conception. But it may also have been suggested by a
mere accident of language, a never-failing source of ancient
thoughts. The name dáksha-pitara*h*, an epithet of the
gods, has generally been translated by 'those who have
Daksha for their father.' But it may have been used
originally in a very different sense. Professor Roth has,
I think, convincingly proved that this epithet dáksha-pitar,
as given to certain gods, does not mean, the gods who
have Daksha for their father, but that it had originally
the simpler meaning of fathers of strength, or, as he

---

* Bráhma*n*aspáti, literally the lord of prayer, or the lord of the sacrifice,
sometimes a representative of Agni (i. 38, 13, note), but by no means identical
with him (see vii. 41, 1); sometimes performing the deeds of Indra, but again
by no means identical with him (see ii. 23, 18. Índrena yug*ã́*—ni*h* apã́m
au*h*ga*h* arnavám; cf. viii. 96, 15). In ii. 26, 3, he is called father of the gods
(devã́nâm pitáram); in ii. 23, 2, the creator of all beings (vísveshâm *g*anitã́).

translates it, 'preserving, possessing, granting faculties*.'
This is particularly clear in one passage:

iii. 27, 9. bhûtânâm gárbham â dadhe, dákshasya pitáram.

I place Agni, the source of all beings, the father of
strength . . . . .

After this we can hardly hesitate how to translate the
next verse:

vi. 50, 2. su-*gy*ótisha*h*—dáksha-pit*r*in—devân.

The resplendent gods, the fathers of strength.

It may seem more doubtful when we come to gods like
Mitra and Varu*n*a, whom we are so much accustomed to
regard as Âdityas, or sons of Aditi, and who therefore,
according to the theogony mentioned before, would have
the best claim to the name of sons of Daksha; yet here,
too, the original and simple meaning is preferable; nay, it
is most likely that from passages like this, the later explanation, which makes Mitra and Varu*n*a the sons of
Daksha, may have sprung.

vii. 66, 2. yâ—su-dákshâ dáksha-pitarâ.

Mitra and Varu*n*a, who are of good strength, the fathers
of strength.

Lastly, even men may claim this name; for, unless we
change the accent, we must translate:

viii. 63, 10. avasyáva*h* yushmâbhi*h* dáksha-pitara*h*.

We suppliants, being, through your aid, fathers of
strength.

But whatever view we take, whether we take dáksha in
the sense of power, as a personification of a philosophical
conception, or as the result of a mythological misunder-
standing occasioned by the name of dáksha-pitar, the fact
remains that in certain hymns of the Rig-veda (viii. 25, 5)
Dáksha, like Âditi, has become a divine person, and has
retained his place as one of the Âdityas to the very latest
time of Pura*n*ic tradition.

---

* The accent in this case cannot help us in determining whether dáksha-
pitar means having Daksha for their father (Λοκροπάτωρ), or father of
strength. In the first case dáksha would rightly retain its accent (dáksha-
pitar) as a Bahuvrîhi; in the second, the analogy of such Tatpurusha compounds as grihá-pati (Pân. vi. 2, 18) would be sufficient to justify the pûrva-
padaprakritisvaratvam.

But to return to Aditi. Let us look upon her as the Infinite personified, and most passages, even those where she is presented as a subordinate deity, will become intelligible.

Aditi, in her cosmic character, is the beyond, the unbounded realm beyond earth, sky, and heaven, and originally she was distinct from the sky, the earth, and the ocean. Aditi is mentioned by the side of heaven and earth, which shows that, though in more general language she may be identified with heaven and earth in their unlimited character, her original conception was different. This we see in passages where different deities or powers are invoked together, particularly if they are invoked together in the same verse, and where Aditi holds a separate place by the side of heaven and earth :

i. 94, 16 (final). tát na*h* mitrá*h* váru*n*a*h* mamahantâm áditi*h* síndhu*h* p*r*ithiví utá dyaú*h*.

May Mitra and Varu*n*a grant us this, may Aditi, Sindhu (sea), the Earth, and the Sky !

In other passages, too, where Aditi has assumed a more personal character, she still holds her own by the side of heaven and earth ; cf. ix. 97, 58 (final) :

i. 191, 6. dyaú*h* va*h* pitấ p*r*ithiví mâtấ sómah bhrấtâ áditi*h* svásâ.

The Sky is your father, the Earth your mother, Soma your brother, Aditi your sister.

viii. 101, 15. mâtấ rudrấ*n*âm duhitấ vásûnâm svásâ âdityấnâm am*r*ítasya nâbhi*h*, prá nú vo*k*am *k*ikitúshe *g*ánâya mấ gấm ánâgâm áditim vadhish*t*a.

The mother of the Rudras, the daughter of the Vasus, the sister of the Âdityas, the source of immortality, I tell it forth to the man of understanding, may he not offend the cow, the guiltless Aditi ! Cf. i. 153, 3 ; ix. 96, 15 ; Vâ*g*asan. Sanhitâ xiii. 49.

vi. 51, 5. dyaú*h* pítar (íti) p*r*íthivi mâta*h* ádhruk ágne bhrâta*h* vasava*h* m*r*i*l*áta na*h*, vísve âdityấ*h* adite sa-*g*óshâ*h* asmábhyam *s*árma bahulấm vi yanta.

Sky, father, Earth, kind mother, Fire, brother, bright

gods, have mercy upon us! All Âdityas (and) Aditi together, grant us your manifold protection!

x. 63, 10. su-trâmâ*n*am p*r*ithiv*ī*m dyâm anehásam su-sármâ*n*am áditim su-pránîtim, daívîm nâvam su-aritrâm ánâgasam ásravantîm â ruhema svastáye.

We invoke the well-protecting Earth, the unrivalled Sky, the well-shielding Aditi, the good guide. Let us enter for safety into the divine boat, with good oars, faultless and leakless!

x. 66, 4. áditi*h* dyâvâp*r*ithiv*ī* (íti).

Aditi, and Heaven and Earth.

Where two or more verses come together, the fact that Aditi is mentioned by the side of Heaven and Earth may seem less convincing, because in these Nivids or long strings of invocations different names or representatives of one and the same power are not unfrequently put together. For instance,

x. 36, 1–3. ushásânâktâ b*r*ihatî (íti) su-pésasâ dyâvâkshâmâ váru*n*a*h* mitrá*h* aryamâ, índram huve marúta*h* párvatân apá*h* âdityân dyâvâp*r*ithiv*ī* (íti) apá*h* svâr (íti svâ*h*). 1.

dyaú*h* *k*a na*h* p*r*ithiv*ī* *k*a prá-*k*etasâ *r*itávarî (íty ritávarî) rakshatâm *áṁ*hasa*h* rishá*h*, mâ du*h*-vidátrâ ní*h*-*r*iti*h* na*h* îsata tát devânâm áva*h* adyá v*r*i*n*îmahe. 2.

vísvasmât na*h* áditi*h* pâtu *áṁ*hasa*h* mâtâ mitrásya váru*n*asya reváta*h* svâ*h*-vat *g*yóti*h* avrikám nasîmahi. 3.

1. There are the grand and beautiful Morning and Night, Heaven and Earth, Varu*n*a, Mitra, Aryaman, I call Indra, the Maruts, the Waters, the Âdityas, Heaven and Earth, the Waters, the Heaven.

2. May Heaven and Earth, the provident, the righteous, preserve us from sin and mischief! May the malevolent Nir*r*iti not rule over us! This blessing of the gods we ask for to-day.

3. May Aditi protect us from all sin, the mother of Mitra and of the rich Varu*n*a! May we obtain heavenly light without enemies! This blessing of the gods we ask for to-day.

Here we cannot but admit that Dyâvâkshâmâ, heaven and earth, is meant for the same divine couple as

Dyâvâpr*ithivî*, heaven and earth, although under slightly differing names they are invoked separately. The waters are invoked twice in the same verse and under the same name; nor is there any indication that, as in other passages, the waters of the sky are meant as distinct from the waters of the sea. Nevertheless even here, Aditi, who in the third verse is called distinctly the mother of Mitra and Varu*n*a, cannot well have been meant for the same deity as Heaven and Earth, mentioned in the second verse; and the author of these two verses, while asking the same blessing from both, must have been aware of the original independent character of Aditi.

Aditi as Mother.

In this character of a deity of the far East, of an Orient in the true sense of the word, Aditi was naturally thought of as the mother of certain gods, particularly of those that were connected with the daily rising and setting of the sun. If it was asked whence comes the dawn, or the sun, or whence come day and night, or Mitra and Varu*n*a, or any of the bright, solar, eastern deities, the natural answer was that they come from the Orient, that they are the sons of Aditi. Thus we read in

ix. 74, 3. urvî gávyûti*h* áditе*h r*itám yaté.

Wide is the space for him who goes on the right path of Aditi.

In viii. 25, 3, we are told that Aditi bore Mitra and Varu*n*a, and these in verse 5 are called the sons of Daksha (power), and the grandsons of *S*avas, which again means might: nápâtâ *s*ávasa*h* mahá*h* sûn*û* (íti) dákshasya su-krátû (íti). In x. 36, 3, Aditi is called the mother of Mitra and Varu*n*a; likewise in x. 132, 6; see also vi. 67, 4. In viii. 47, 9, Aditi is called the mother of Mitra, Aryaman, Varu*n*a, who in vii. 60, 5, are called her sons. In x. 11, 1, Varu*n*a is called yahvá*h* áditе*h*, the son of Aditi (cf. viii. 19, 12); in vii. 41, 2, Bhaga is mentioned as her son. In x. 72, 8, we hear of eight sons of Aditi, but it is added that she approached the gods with seven sons only, and that the eighth (mârtân*d*á, addled egg) was thrown away: ash*t*aú putrā́sa*h* ā́dite*h* yé *g*ā́tā*h* tanvā̀*h* pári, devā́n úpa prá ait saptá-bhi*h* párâ mârtâ*nd*ám âsyat.

In x. 63, 2, the gods in general are represented as born from Aditi, the waters, and the earth : yé sthá *g*ā́tā*h* ā́dite*h* at-bhyā́*h* pári yé prithivyā̀*h* té me ihá *s*ruta hávam.

You who are born of Aditi, from the water, you who are born of the earth, hear ye all my call !

The number seven, with regard to the Âdityas, occurs also in

ix. 114, 3. saptá dí*s*a*h* nânâ-sûryā̀*h* saptá hótâra*h* *r*itví*g*ah, devā́*h* âdityā̀*h* yé saptá tébhi*h* soma abhí raksha na*h*.

There are seven regions with their different suns, there are seven Hotars as priests, those who are the seven gods, the Âdityas, with them, O Soma, protect us !

The Seven Âdityas.

This number of seven Âdityas requires an explanation which, however, it is difficult to give. To say that seven is a solemn or sacred number is to say very little, for however solemn or sacred that number may be elsewhere, it is not more sacred than any other number in the Veda. The often-mentioned seven rivers have a real geographical foundation, like the seven hills of Rome. The seven flames or treasures of Agni (v. 1, 5) and of Soma and Rudra (vi. 74, 1), the seven paridhis or logs at certain sacrifices (x. 90, 15), the seven Harits or horses of the sun, the seven Hotar priests (iii. 7, 7 ; 10, 4), the seven cities of the enemy destroyed by Indra (i. 63, 7), and even the seven *R*ishis (x. 82, 2 ; 109, 4), all these do not prove that the number of seven was more sacred than the number of one or three or five or ten used in the Veda in a very similar way. With regard to the seven Âdityas, however, we are still able to see that their number of seven or eight had something to do with solar movements. If their number had always been eight, we should feel inclined to trace the number of the Âdityas back to the eight regions, or the eight cardinal points of the heaven. Thus we read :

i. 35, 8. ash*t*aú ví akhyat kakúbha*h* prithivyā̀*h*.

The god Savitar lighted up the eight points of the earth (not the eight hills).

But we have seen already that though the number of Âdityas was originally supposed to have been eight, it was reduced to seven, and this could hardly be said in any sense of the eight points of the compass. Cf. Taitt. Âr. i. 7, 6.

As we cannot think in ancient India of the seven planets, I can only suggest the seven days or tithis of the four parvans of the lunar month as a possible prototype of the Âdityas. This might even explain the destruction of the eighth Âditya, considering that the eighth day of each parvan, owing to its uncertainty, might be represented as exposed to decay and destruction. This would explain such passages as,

iv. 7, 5. yágishtham saptá dhâma-bhih.

Agni, most worthy of sacrifice in the seven stations.

ix. 102, 2. yagñásya saptá dhâma-bhih.

In the seven stations of the sacrifice.

The seven threads of the sacrifice may have the same origin :

ii. 5, 2. â yásmin saptá rasmáyah tatâh yagñásya netári, manushvát daívyam ashtamám.

In whom, as the leader of the sacrifice, the seven threads are stretched out,—the eighth divine being is manlike (?).

The sacrifice itself is called, x. 124, 1, saptá-tantu, having seven threads.

x. 122, 3. saptá dhâmâni pari-yán ámartyah.

Agni, the immortal, who goes round the seven stations.

x. 8, 4. ushâh-ushah hí vaso (íti) ágram éshi tvám yamá-yoh abhavah vi-bhâvâ, ritâya saptá dadhishe padâni ganâyan mitrám tanvê svâyai.

For thou, Vasu (Agni), comest first every morning, thou art the divider of the twins (day and night). Thou takest for the rite the seven names, creating Mitra (the sun) for thy own body.

x. 5, 6. saptá maryâdâh kaváyah tatakshuh tâsâm ékâm ít abhí amhurâh gât.

The sages established the seven divisions, but mischief befel one of them.

i. 22, 16. áta*h* devá*h* avantu na*h* yáta*h* víshnu*h* vi-*k*akramé prithivyá*h* saptá dhá͞ma-bhi*h*.

May the gods protect us from whence Vish*n*u strode forth, by the seven stations of the earth!

Even the names of the seven or eight Âdityas are not definitely known, at least not from the hymns of the Rig-veda. In ii. 27, 1, we have a list of six names: Mitrá, Aryamán, Bhága, Váru*n*a, Dáksha, *A͞*msa*h*. These with *A͞*diti would give us seven. In vi. 50, 1, we have *A͞*diti, Váru*n*a, Mitrá, Agní, Aryamán, Savitár, and Bhága. In i. 89, 3, Bhága, Mitrá, *A͞*diti, Dáksha, Aryamán, Váru*n*a, Sóma, Asvínâ, and Sárasvatî are invoked together with an old invocation, pú͞rvayâ ni-vídâ. In the Taittirîya-âra*n*yaka, i. 13, 3, we find the following list: 1. Mitra, 2. Varu*n*a, 3. Dhâtar, 4. Aryaman, 5. A*m*sa, 6. Bhaga, 7. Indra, 8. Vivasvan, but there, too, the eighth son is said to be Mârtâ*n*da, or, according to the commentator, Âditya.

The character of Aditi as the mother of certain gods is also indicated by some of her epithets, such as rá*g*a-putrâ, having kings for her sons; su-putrá͞, having good sons; ugra-putrâ, having terrible sons:

ii. 27, 7. pípartu na*h* áditi*h* rá*g*a-putrâ áti dvéshâ*m*si aryamá͞ su-gébhi*h*, brihát mitrásya váru*n*asya *s*árma úpa syâma puru-ví͞râ*h* árish*t*â*h*.

May Aditi with her royal sons, may Aryaman carry us on easy roads across the hatreds; may we with many sons and without hurt obtain the great protection of Mitra and Varu*n*a!

iii. 4, 11. barhí*h* na*h* âstâm áditi*h* su-putrá͞.

May Aditi with her excellent sons sit on our sacred pile!

viii. 67, 11. pá͞rshi dîné gabhîré á͞ ugra-putre *g*íghâ*m*sata*h*, má͞ki*h* tokásya na*h* rishat.

Protect us, O goddess with terrible sons, from the enemy in shallow or deep water, and no one will hurt our offspring!

Aditi identified with other Deities.

Aditi, however, for the very reason that she was originally intended for the Infinite, for something beyond the visible world, was liable to be identified with a number of finite deities which might all be represented as resting on Aditi, as participating in Aditi, as being Aditi. Thus we read:

i. 89, 10 (final). áditi*h* dyaú*h* áditi*h* antárik*s*ham áditi*h* mâtấ sá*h* pitấ sá*h* putrá*h*, vísve devấ*h* áditi*h* páñka *g*ánâ*h* áditi*h* *g*âtám áditi*h* *g*áni-tvam.

Aditi is the heaven, Aditi the sky, Aditi the mother, the father, the son. All the gods are Aditi, the five clans, the past is Aditi, Aditi is the future.

But although Aditi may thus be said to be everything, heaven, sky, and all the gods, no passage occurs, in the Rig-veda at least, where the special meaning of heaven or earth is expressed by Aditi. In x. 63, 3, where Aditi seems to mean sky, we shall see that it ought to be taken as a masculine, either in the sense of Âditya, or as an epithet, unbounded, immortal. In i. 72, 9, we ought pro-bably to read prithvî́ and pronounce prithuvî́, and translate 'the wide Aditi, the mother with her sons;' and not, as Benfey does, ' the Earth, the eternal mother.'

It is more difficult to determine whether in one passage Aditi has not been used in the sense of life after life, or as the name of the place whither people went after death, or of the deity presiding over that place. In a well-known hymn, supposed to have been uttered by *S*una*h*sepa when on the point of being sacrificed by his own father, the following verse occurs:

i. 24, 1. ká*h* na*h* mahyaí áditaye púna*h* dât, pitáram *k*a d*r*iséyam mâtáram *k*a.

Who will give us back to the great Aditi, that I may see father and mother?

As the supposed utterer of this hymn is still among the living, Aditi can hardly be taken in the sense of earth, nor would the wish to see father and mother be intelligible in the mouth of one who is going to be sacrificed by his own father. If we discard the story of *S*una*h*sepa, and take the hymn as uttered by any poet who craves for the protection of the gods in the presence of danger and death, then we may choose between the two meanings of earth or liberty, and translate, either, Who will give us back to the great earth? or, Who will restore us to the great Aditi, the goddess of freedom?

Aditi and Diti.

There is one other passage which might receive light if we could take Aditi in the sense of Hades, but I give this translation as a mere guess :

iv. 2, 11. râyé *ka* na*h* su-apatyấya deva dítim *ka* rấsva ấditim urushya.

That we may enjoy our wealth and healthy offspring, give us this life on earth, keep off the life to come ! Cf. i. 152, 6.

It should be borne in mind that Diti occurs in the Rig-veda thrice only, and in one passage it should, I believe, be changed into Aditi. This passage occurs in vii. 15, 12. tvấm agne vîrá-vat yá*sah* devá*h* *ka* savitấ bhágah, díti*h* *ka* dấti vấryam. Here the name of Diti is so unusual, and that of Aditi, on the contrary, so natural, that I have little doubt that the poet had put the name of Aditi; and that later reciters, not aware of the occasional license of putting two short syllables instead of one, changed it into Aditi. If we remove this passage, then Diti, in the Rig-veda at least, occurs twice only, and each time together or in contrast with Aditi; cf. v. 62, 8, page 231. I have no doubt, therefore, that Professor Roth is right when he says that Diti is a being without any definite conception, a mere reflex of Aditi. We can clearly watch her first emergence into existence through what is hardly more than a play of words, whereas in the epic and paura*n*ic literature this Diti has grown into a definite person, one of the daughters of Daksha, the wife of Ka*s*yapa, the mother of the enemies of the gods, the Daityas. Such is the growth of legend, mythology, and religion !

Aditi in her Moral Character.

Besides the cosmical character of Aditi, which we have hitherto examined, this goddess has also assumed a very prominent moral character. Aditi, like Varu*n*a, delivers from sin. Why this should be so, we can still understand if we watch the transition which led from a purely cosmical to a moral conception of Aditi. Sin in the Veda is frequently conceived as a bond or a chain from which the repentant sinner wishes to be freed :

vii. 86, 5. áva drugdhâni pítryâ srí*g*a na*h* áva yẫ vayám *k*ak*r*imâ tanûbhi*h*, áva râ*g*an pa*s*u-trípam ná tâyúm srí*g*â vatsám ná dẫmna*h* vásish*th*am.

Absolve us from the sins of our fathers, and from those which we have committed with our own bodies. Release Vasish*th*a, O king, like a thief who has feasted on stolen cattle ; release him like a calf from the rope *.

viii. 67, 14. té na*h* âsnấ*h* vrîkâ*n*âm ẫdityâsa*h* mumó*k*ata stenám baddhám-iva adite.

O Âdityas, deliver us from the mouth of the wolves, like a bound thief, O Aditi ! Cf. viii. 67, 18.

*Suna*h*sepa, who, as we saw before, wishes to be restored to the great Aditi, is represented as bound by ropes, and in v. 2, 7, we read :

*s*úna*h*-sépam *k*it ní-ditam sahásrât yûpât amu*ñk*a*h* á*s*a-mish*t*a hí sâ*h*, evá asmát agne ví mumugdhi pẫ*s*ân hótar (íti) *k*ikitva*h* ihá tú ni-sâdya.

O Agni, thou hast released the bound *Suna*h*sepa from the pale, for he had prayed ; thus take from us, too, these ropes, O sagacious Hotar, after thou hast settled here.

Expressions like these, words like dẫman, bond, ní-dita, bound, naturally suggested á-diti, the un-bound or un-bounded, as one of those deities who could best remove the bonds of sin or misery. If we once realise this con-catenation of thought and language, many passages of the Veda that seemed obscure, will become intelligible.

vii. 51, 1. âdityẫnâm ávasâ nûtanena sakshîmáhi sárma*n*â sám-tamena, anâgâ*h*-tvé aditi-tvé turẫsa*h* imám ya*g*ñám dadhatu sróshamâ*n*â*h*.

May we obtain the new favour of the Âdityas, their best protection ; may the quick Maruts listen and place this sacrifice in guiltlessness and Aditi-hood.

I have translated the last words literally, in order to make their meaning quite clear. Ã́gas has the same meaning as the Greek ἄγος, guilt, abomination ; an-âgâs-tvá, therefore, as applied to a sacrifice or to the man who makes it, means guiltlessness, purity. Aditi-tvá, Aditi-hood, has a similar meaning, it means freedom from bonds, from anything that hinders the proper performance of a religious act; it may come to mean perfection or holiness.

Aditi having once been conceived as granting this adititvá, soon assumed a very definite moral character, and hence the following invocations:

i. 24, 15. út ut-tamám varuna pásam asmát áva adhamám ví madhyamám srathaya, átha vayám áditya vraté táva ánâgasah áditaye syâma.

O Varuna, lift the highest rope, draw off the lowest, remove the middle; then, O Âditya, let us be in thy service free of guilt before Aditi.

v. 82, 6. ánâgasah áditaye devásya savitúh savé, vísvâ vâmâni dhîmahi.

May we, guiltless before Aditi, and in the keeping of the god Savitar, obtain all goods! Professor Roth here translates Aditi by freedom or security.

i. 162, 22. anâgâh-tvám nah áditih krinotu.

May Aditi give us sinlessness! Cf. vii. 51, 1.

iv. 12, 4. yát kit hí te purusha-trâ yavishtha ákitti-bhih kakrimá kát kit ágah, kridhí sú asmân áditeh ánâgân ví énâmsi sisrathah víshvak agne.

Whatever, O youthful god, we have committed against thee, men as we are, whatever sin through thoughtlessness, make us guiltless of Aditi, loosen the sins on all sides, O Agni!

vii. 93, 7. sáh agne enâ námasâ sám-iddhah ákkha mitrám várunam índram vokeh, yát sîm ágah kakrimá tát sú mrila tát aryamâ áditih sisrathantu.

O Agni, thou who hast been kindled with this adoration, greet Mitra, Varuna, and Indra. Whatever sin we have committed, do thou pardon it! May Aryaman, Aditi loose it!

Here the plural sisrathantu should be observed, instead of the dual.

viii. 18, 6—7. áditih nah dívâ pasúm áditih náktam ádvayâh, áditih pâtu ámhasah sadâ-vridhâ.

utá syâ nah dívâ matíh áditih ûtyâ â gamat, sâ sám-tâti máyah karat ápa srídhah.

May Aditi by day protect our cattle, may she, who never deceives, protect by night; may she, with steady increase, protect us from evil!

And may she, the thoughtful Aditi, come with help to

us by day; may she kindly bring happiness to us, and carry away all enemies! Cf. x. 36, 3, page 239.

x. 87, 18. ā vriskyantâm âditaye duḥ-ĕvâḥ.

May the evil-doers be cut off from Aditi! or literally, may they be rooted out before Aditi!

ii. 27, 14. âdite mítra váruṇa utá mriḷa yát vaḥ vayám kakrimá kát kit âgaḥ, urú asyâm âbhayam gyótiḥ indra mâ naḥ dîrghấḥ abhí naṣan tâmisrâḥ.

Aditi, Mitra, and also Varuṇa forgive, if we have committed any sin against you. May I obtain the wide and fearless light, O Indra! May not the long darkness reach us!

vii. 87, 7. yáḥ mriḷáyâti kakrúshe kit âgaḥ vayám syâma váruṇe ánâgâḥ, ánu vratấni âditeḥ ridhántaḥ yuyám pâta svastí-bhiḥ sádâ naḥ.

May we be sinless before Varuṇa, who is gracious even to him who has committed sin, and may we follow the laws of Aditi! Protect us always with your blessings!

Lastly, Aditi, like all other gods, is represented as a giver of worldly goods, and implored to bestow them on her worshippers, or to protect them by her power:

i. 43, 2. yáthâ naḥ áditiḥ kárat pásve nrí-bhyaḥ yáthâ gáve, yáthâ tokấya rudríyam.

That Aditi may bring Rudra's favour to our cattle, our men, our cow, our offspring.

i. 153, 3. pîpâya dhenúḥ áditiḥ ritấya gánâya mitrâvaruṇâ haviḥ-dé.

Aditi, the cow, gives food to the righteous man, O Mitra and Varuṇa, who makes offerings to the gods. Cf. viii. 101, 15.

i. 185, 3. anchấḥ dâtrám áditeḥ anarvám huvé.

I call for the unrivalled, uninjured gift of Aditi. Here Professor Roth again assigns to Aditi the meaning of freedom or security.

vii. 40, 2. dídeshṭu devî́ áditiḥ réknaḥ.

May the divine Aditi assign wealth!

x. 100, 1. ā sarvá-tâtim áditim vriṇîmahe.

We implore Aditi for health and wealth.

i. 94, 15. yásmai tvám su-draviṇaḥ dádâsaḥ anâgâḥ-tvám adite sarvá-tâtâ, yám bhadréṇa sávasâ kodâyâsi pragấ-vatâ rấdhasâ té syâma.

To whom thou, possessor of good treasures, grantest guiltlessness, O Aditi, in health and wealth[*], whom thou quickenest with precious strength and with riches in progeny, may we be they!   Cf. ii. 40, 6; iv. 25, 5; x. 11, 2.

The principal epithets of Aditi have been mentioned in the passages quoted above, and they throw no further light on the nature of the goddess. She was called devî, goddess, again and again; another frequent epithet is anarván, un- injured, unscathed. Being invoked to grant light (vii. 82, 10), she is herself called luminous, gyótishmatî, i. 136, 3; and svârvatî, heavenly. Being the goddess of the infinite expanse, she, even with greater right than the dawn, is called úrúkî, viii. 67, 12; uruvyákas, v. 46, 6; uruvragâ, viii. 67, 12; and possibly prithvî in i. 72, 9. As supporting everything, she is called dhârayátkshiti, supporting the earth, i. 136, 3; and visvágyanyâ, vii. 10, 4. To her sons she owes the names of rágaputrâ, ii. 27, 7; suputrấ, iii. 4, 11; and ugraputrâ, viii. 67, 11: to her wealth that of sudraviñas, i. 94, 15, though others refer this epithet to Agni. There remains one name pastyấ, iv. 55, 3; viii. 27, 5, meaning housewife, which again indicates her character as mother of the gods.

I have thus given all the evidence that can be collected from the Rig-veda as throwing light on the character of the goddess Aditi, and I have carefully excluded everything that rests only on the authority of the Yagur- or Atharva-vedas, or of the Brâhmañas and Âranyakas, because in all they give beyond the repetitions from the Rig-veda, they seem to me to represent a later phase of thought that ought not to be mixed up with the more primitive conceptions of the Rig- veda. Much valuable material for an analytical study of Aditi may be found in B. and R.'s Dictionary, and in several of Dr. Muir's excellent contributions to a knowledge of Vedic theogony and mythology.

---

[*] On sarvâtâti, salus, see Benfey's excellent remarks in Orient und Occident, vol. ii. p. 519. Professor Roth takes aditi here as an epithet of Agni.

But although the foregoing remarks give as complete a description of Aditi as can be gathered from the hymns of the Rig-veda, a few words have to be added on certain passages where the word áditi occurs, and where it clearly cannot mean the goddess Aditi, as a feminine, but must be taken either as the name of a corresponding masculine deity, or as an adjective in the sense of unrestrained, independent, free.

v. 59, 8. mímâtu dyaúh áditih vîtáye nah.

May the boundless Dyú (sky) help us to our repast!

Here áditi must either be taken in the sense of Âditya, or better in its original sense of unbounded, as an adjective belonging to Dyú, the masculine deity of the sky.

Dyú or the sky is called áditi or unbounded in another passage, x. 63, 3:

yébhyah mâtấ mádhu-mat pínvate páyah pîyúsham dyaúh áditih ádri-barhâh.

The gods to whom their mother yields the sweet milk, and the unbounded sky, as firm as a rock, their food.

iv. 3, 8. kathấ sárdhâya marútâm ritâya kathấ súré brihaté prikkhyámânah, práti bravah áditaye turấya.

How wilt thou tell it to the host of the Maruts, how to the bright heaven, when thou art asked? How to the quick Aditi?

Here Aditi cannot be the goddess, partly on account of the masculine gender of turấya, partly because she is never called quick. Aditi must here be the name of one of the Âdityas, or it may refer back to súré brihaté. It can hardly be joined, as Professor Roth proposes, with sárdhâya marútâm, owing to the intervening súré brihaté.

In several passages áditi, as an epithet, refers to Agni:

iv. 1, 20 (final). vísveshâm áditih yagñíyânàm vísveshâm átithih mânushânâm.

He, Agni, the Aditi, or the freest, among all the gods; he the guest among all men.

The same play on the words áditi and átithi occurs again:

vii. 9, 3. ámûra*h* kaví*h* áditi*h* vivásvân su-sa*m*sát mitrá*h* átithi*h* sivá*h* na*h*, *k*itrá-bhânu*h* ushásâm bhâti ágre.

The wise poet, Aditi, Vivasvat, Mitra with his good company, our welcome guest, he (Agni) with brilliant light came at the head of the dawns.

Here, though I admit that several renderings are possible, Aditi is meant as a name of Agni, to whom the whole hymn is addressed; and who, as usual, is identified with other gods, or, at all events, invoked by their names. We may translate áditi*h* vivásvân by 'the brilliant Aditi,' or 'the unchecked, the brilliant,' or by 'the boundless Vivasvat,' but on no account can we take áditi here as the female goddess. The same applies to viii. 19, 14, where Aditi, unless we suppose the goddess brought in in the most abrupt way, must be taken as a name of Agni; while in x. 92, 14, áditim anarvá*n*am, to judge from other epithets given in the same verse, has most likely to be taken again as an appellative of Agni. In some passages it would, no doubt, be possible to take Aditi as the name of a female deity, if it were certain that no other meaning could be assigned to this word. But if we once know that Aditi was the name of a male deity also, the structure of these passages becomes far more perfect if we take Aditi in that sense:

iv. 39, 3. ánâgasam tám áditi*h* kri*n*otu sá*h* mitré*n*a váru*n*ena sa-*g*óshâ*h*.

May Aditi make him free from sin, he who is allied with Mitra and Varu*n*a.

We have had several passages in which Aditi, the female deity, is represented as sa*g*óshâ*h* or allied with other Âdityas, but if sá*h* is the right reading here, Aditi in this verse can only be the male deity. The pronoun sá cannot refer to tám.

With regard to other passages, such as ix. 81, 5; vi. 51, 3, and even some of those translated above in which Aditi has been taken as a female goddess, the question must be left open till further evidence can be obtained. There is only one more passage which has been often discussed, and where áditi was supposed to have the meaning of earth:

vii. 18, 8. du*h*-âdhyâ*h* áditim srevâyanta*h* a*k*etása*h* ví
*g*agribhre párusb*n*îm.

Professor Roth in one of his earliest essays translated
this line, 'The evil-disposed wished to dry the earth, the
fools split the Parush*n*î,' and he supposed its meaning to
have been that the enemies of Sudâs swam across the
Parush*n*î in order to attack Sudâs. We might accept this
translation, if it could be explained how by throwing themselves into the river, the enemies made the earth dry,
though even then there would remain this difficulty that,
with the exception of one other doubtful passage, discussed
before, áditi never means earth. I should therefore propose
to translate : 'The evil-disposed, the fools, laid dry and
divided the resistless river Parush*n*î.' This would be a
description of a strategem very common in ancient warfare,
viz. diverting the course of a river and laying its original
bed dry by digging a new channel, and thus dividing the
old river. This is also the sense accepted by Sâya*n*a, who
does not say that vigraha means dividing the waves of a
river, as Professor Roth renders kûlabheda, but that it
means dividing or cutting through its banks. In the
Dictionary Professor Roth assigns to áditi in this passage
the meaning of endless, inexhaustible.

Verse 12, note [5]. Nothing is more difficult in the interpretation of the Veda than to gain an accurate knowledge
of the power of particles and conjunctions. The particle
*k*anâ, we are told, is used both affirmatively and negatively,
a statement which shows better than anything else the
uncertainty to which every translation is as yet exposed.
It is perfectly true that in the text of the Rig-veda, as we
now read it, *k*anâ means both indeed and no. But this
very fact shows that we ought to distinguish where the first
collectors of the Vedic hymns have not distinguished, and
that while in the former case we read *k*anâ, we ought in the
latter to read *k*a nâ.

I begin with those passages in which *k*anâ is used
emphatically and as one word.

   I *a*. In negative sentences :
   i. 18, 7. yásmât *r*ité ná sídhyati ya*gñáh* vipa*h*-*k*íta*h* *k*anâ.

Without whom the sacrifice does not succeed, not even that of the sage.

v. 34, 5. ná ásunvatâ sakate púshyatâ kaná.

He does not cling to a man who offers no libations, even though he be thriving.

i. 24, 6. nahí te kshatrám ná sáhah ná manyúm váyah kaná amî́ (íti) patáyantah âpúh.

For thy power, thy strength, thy anger even these birds which fly up, do not reach. Cf. i. 100, 15.

i. 155, 5. tritī́yam asya nákih â̂ dadharshati váyah kaná patáyantah patatrí́nah.

This third step no one approaches, not even the winged birds which fly up.

i. 55, 1. diváh kit asya varimấ ví papratha, índram ná mahnấ prithivî́ kaná práti.

The width of the heavens is stretched out, even the earth in her greatness is no match for Indra.

I b. In positive sentences :

vii. 32, 13. pûrvî́h kaná prá-sitayah taranti tấm yáh índre kármanâ bhúvat.

Even many snares pass him who is with Indra in his work.

viii. 2, 14. ukthám kaná sasyámânam ágoh aríh â̂ kiketa, ná gâyatrám gîyámânam.

A poor man may learn indeed a prayer that is recited, but not a hymn that is sung.

viii. 78, 10. táva ít indra ahám â-sásâ háste dấtram kaná â̂ dade.

Trusting in thee alone, O Indra, I take even this sickle in my hand.

i. 55, 5. ádha kaná srát dadhati tvíshi-mate índrâya vágram ni-ghánighnate vadhám.

Then indeed they believe in Indra, the majestic, when he hurls the bolt to strike.

i. 152, 2. etát kaná tvah ví kiketat eshâm.

Does one of them understand even this?

iv. 18, 9. mámat kaná used in the same sense as mámat kit.

i. 139, 2. dhîbhíh kaná mánasâ svébhih akshá-bhih.

v. 41, 13. váyah kaná su-bhvãh â̂ áva yanti.

vii. 18, 9. âsúḥ kaná ít abhi-pitvám yagâma.

viii. 91, 3. ấ kaná tvâ kikitsâmaḥ ádhi kaná tvâ ná imasi.

We wish to know thee, indeed, but we cannot understand thee.

x. 49, 5. ahám randhayam mrígayam srutárvaṇe yát mâ áyihîta vayúnâ kaná ânu-shák.

vi. 26, 7. ahám kaná tát sûrí-bhiḥ ânasyâm.

May I also obtain this with my wise friends.

I c. Frequently kaná occurs after interrogative pronouns, to which it imparts an indefinite meaning, and principally in negative sentences:

i. 74, 7. ná yóḥ upabdíḥ ásvyaḥ srinvé ráthasya kát kaná, yát agne yâsi dûtyâm.

No sound of horses is heard, and no sound of the chariot, when thou, O Agni, goest on thy message.

i. 81, 5. ná tvấ-vân indra kúḥ kaná ná yâtáḥ ná yanishyaté.

No one is like thee, O Indra, no one has been born, no one will be!

i. 84, 20. mấ te râdhâṃsi mấ te ûtáyaḥ vaso (íti) asmấn kádâ kaná dabhan.

May thy gifts, may thy help, O Vasu, never fail us!

Many more passages might be given to illustrate the use of kaná or kás kaná and its derivatives in negative sentences. Cf. i. 105, 3; 136, 1; 139, 5; ii. 16, 3; 23, 5; 28, 6; iii. 36, 4; iv. 31, 9; v. 42, 6; 82, 2; vi. 3, 2; 20, 4; 47, 1; 3; 48, 17; 54, 9; 59, 4; 69, 8; 75, 16; vii. 32, 1; 19; 59, 3; 82, 7; 104, 3; viii. 19, 6; 23, 15; 24, 15; 28, 4; 47, 7; 64, 2; 66, 13; 68, 19; ix. 61, 27; 69, 6; 114, 4; x. 33, 9; 39, 11; 48, 5; 49, 10; 59, 8; 62, 9; 85, 3; 86, 11; 95, 1; 112, 9; 119, 6; 7; 128, 4; 129, 2; 152, 1; 168, 3; 185, 2.

I d. In a few passages, however, we find the indefinite pronoun kás kaná used in sentences which are not negative:

i. 113, 8. ushấḥ mritám kám kaná bodháyantî.

Ushas, who wakes even the dead, (or one who is as if dead.)

i. 191, 7. úd*r*ish*t*â*h* kím *k*aná ihá va*h* sárve sâkám ní *g*asyata.

Invisible ones, whatever you are, vanish all together!

II. We now come to passages in which *k*aná stands for *k*a ná, and therefore renders the sentence negative without any further negative particle :

ii. 16, 2. yásmât índrât b*r*ihatâ*h* kím *k*aná îm *r*ité.

Beside whom, (beside) the great Indra, there is not anything.

ii. 24, 12. vísvam satyám magha-vânâ yuvó*h* ít â*p*a*h* *k*aná prá minanti vratám vâm.

Everything, you mighty ones, belongs indeed to you; even the waters do not transgress your law.

iii. 30, 1. títikshante abhí-*s*astim *g*ánânâm índra tvát â kâ*h* *k*aná hí pra-ketâ*h*.

They bear the scoffing of men ; for Indra, away from thee there is no wisdom.

iv. 30, 3. vísve *k*aná ít anẫ tvâ devẫsa*h* indra yuyu-dhu*h*.

Even all the gods together do not fight thee, O Indra.

v. 34, 7. du*h*-gé *k*aná dhriyate vísva*h* ẫ purú *g*ána*h* yâ*h* asya távishîm â*k*ukrudhat.

Even in a stronghold many a man is not often preserved who has excited his anger.

vii. 83, 2. yásmin â*g*ẫ bhâvati kím *k*aná priyám.

In which struggle there is nothing good whatsoever.

vii. 86, 6. svápna*h* *k*aná ít á*n*ritasya pra-yotẫ.

Even sleep does not remove all evil.

In this passage I formerly took *k*aná as affirmative, not as negative, and therefore assigned to prayotẫ the same meaning which Sâya*n*a assigns to it, one who brings or mixes, whereas it ought to be, as rightly seen by Roth, one who removes.

viii. 1, 5. mahé *k*aná tvâm adri-va*h* párâ *s*ulkẫya deyâm, ná sahásrâya ná ayútâya va*g*ri-va*h* ná satẫya sata-magha.

I should not give thee up, wielder of the thunderbolt, even for a great price, not for a thousand, not for ten thousand (?), not for a hundred, O Indra, thou who art possessed of a hundred powers!

viii. 51, 7. kadā *kaná* starī*h* asi.
Thou art never sterile.
viii. 52, 7. kadā *kaná* prá *yukkhasi*.
Thou art never weary.
viii. 55, 5. *kákshushā* *kaná* sam-nâse.
Even with my eye I cannot reach them.
x. 56, 4. mahimnâ*h* eshâm pitára*h* *kaná* îsire.

Verse 12, note [6]. Considering the particular circumstances mentioned in this and the preceding hymn, of
Indra's forsaking his companions, the Maruts, or even
scorning their help, one feels strongly tempted to take
tyá*g*as in its etymological sense of leaving or forsaking,
and to translate, by his forsaking you, or if he should
forsake you. The poet may have meant the word to convey
that idea, which no doubt would be most appropriate here;
but then it must be confessed, at the same time, that in
other passages where tyá*g*as occurs, that meaning could
hardly be ascribed to it. Strange as it may seem, no one
who is acquainted with the general train of thought in the
Vedic hymns can fail to see that tyá*g*as in most passages
means attack, onslaught; it may be even the instrument of
an attack, a weapon. How it should come to take this
meaning is indeed difficult to explain, and I do not wonder
that Professor Roth in his Dictionary simply renders the
word by forlornness, need, danger, or by estrangement,
unkindness, malignity. But let us look at the passages,
and we shall see that these abstract conceptions are quite
out of place:

viii. 47, 7. ná tám tigmám *kaná* tyá*g*a*h* ná drâsad abhí
tám gurú.

No sharp blow, no heavy one, shall come near him whom
you protect.

Here the two adjectives tigmá, sharp, and gurú, heavy,
point to something tangible, and I feel much inclined to
take tyá*g*as in this passage as a weapon, as something that
is let off with violence, rather than in the more abstract
sense of onslaught.

i. 169, 1. mahá*h* *k*it asi tyá*g*asa*h* varûtā.
Thou art the shielder from a great attack.

iv. 43, 4. ká*h* vâm mahá*h* *k*it tyá*g*asa*h* abhî́ke urushyátam mâdhvî dasrâ na*h* ûtî́.

Who is against your great attack? Protect us with your help, ye givers of sweet drink, ye strong ones.

Here Professor Roth seems to join mahá*h* *k*it tyá*g*asa*h* abhî́ke urushyátam, but in that case it would be impossible to construe the first words, ká*h* vâm.

i. 119, 8. ága*kkh*atam k*rí*pamâ*n*am parâ-váti pitú*h* svásya tyá*g*asâ ní-bâdhitam.

You went from afar to the suppliant, who had been struck down by the violence of his own father.

According to Professor Roth tyá*g*as would here mean forlornness, need, or danger. But níbâdhita is a strong verb, as we may see in

viii. 64, 2. padấ pa*n*î́n arâdhása*h* ní bâdhasva mahấn asi.

Strike the useless Pa*n*is down with thy foot, for thou art great.

x. 18, 11. út *s*vañ*k*asva p*r*ithivi mấ ní bâdhathâ*h*.

Open, O earth, do not press on him (i. e. the dead, who is to be buried; cf. M. M., Über Todtenbestattung, Zeitschrift der D. M. G., vol. ix. p. xv).

vii. 83, 6. yátra rấ*g*a-bhi*h* dasá-bhi*h* ní-bâdhitam prá su-dấsam ấvatam t*rí*tsu-bhi*h* sahá.

When you protected Sudâs with the T*r*itsus, when he was pressed or set upon by the ten kings.

Another passage in which tyá*g*as occurs is,

vi. 62, 10. sánutyena tyá*g*asâ mártyasya vanushyatấm ápi *s*írshấ vav*r*iktam.

By your covert attack turn back the heads of those even who harass the mortal.

Though this passage may seem less decisive, yet it is difficult to see how tyá*g*asâ could here, according to Professor Roth, be rendered by forlornness or danger. Something is required by which enemies can be turned back. Nor can it be doubtful that *s*írshấ is governed by vav*r*iktam, meaning turn back their heads, for the same expression occurs again in i. 33, 5. párâ *k*it *s*írshấ vav*r*iguh té indra áya*g*vânah yá*g*va-bhi*h* spárdhamânâ*h*.

Professor Benfey translates this verse by, ' Kopfüber flohn sie alle vor dir;' but it may be rendered more literally, 'These lawless people fighting with the pious turned back their heads.'

x. 144, 6. evá tát índra*h* índunâ devéshu *k*it dhârayâte máhi tyága*h*.

Indeed through this draught Indra can hold out against that great attack even among the gods.

.x. 79, 6. kím devéshu tyága*h* éna*h* *k*akartha.

What insult, what sin hast thou committed among the gods?

In these two passages the meaning of tyágas as attack or assault is at least as appropriate as that proposed by Professor Roth, estrangement, malignity.

There remains one passage, vi. 3, 1. yám tvám mitré*n*a váru*n*a*h* sa-*g*óshâ*h* déva pâsi tyágasâ mártam á*m*ha*h*.

I confess that the construction of this verse is not clear to me, and I doubt whether it is possible to use tyágasâ as a verbal noun governing an accusative. If this were possible, one might translate, 'The mortal whom thou, O God (Agni), Varu*n*a, together with Mitra, protectest by pushing back evil.' Anyhow, we gain nothing here, if we take tyágas in the sense of estrangement or malignity.

If it be asked how tyágas can possibly have the meaning which has been assigned to it in all the passages in which it occurs, viz. that of forcibly attacking or pushing away, we can only account for it by supposing that tya*g*, before it came to mean to leave, meant to push off, to drive away with violence, (verstossen instead of verlassen.) This meaning may still be perceived occasionally in the use of tya*g*; e. g. devâs tya*g*antu mâm, may the gods forsake me! i. e. may the gods drive me away! Even in the latest Sanskrit tya*g* is used with regard to an arrow that is let off. 'To expel' is expressed by nis-tya*g*. Those who believe in the production of new roots by the addition of prepositional prefixes might possibly see in tya*g* an original ati-a*g*, to drive off; but, however that may be, there is evidence enough to show that tya*g* expressed originally a more violent act of separation than it does in ordinary Sanskrit.

Verse 13, note [1]. Sá*m*sa, masc., means a spell whether for good or for evil, a blessing as well as a curse. It means a curse, or, at all events, a calumny :

i. 18, 3. mā na*h* sá*m*sa*h* árarusha*h* dhûrtí*h* prá*n*ak mártyasya.

Let not the curse of the enemy, the onslaught of a mortal hurt us.

i. 94, 8. asmākam sá*m*sa*h* abhí astu du*h*-dhyā*h*.

May our curse fall on the wicked!

ii. 26, 1. *r*igú*h* ít sá*m*sa*h* vanavat vanushyatá*h*.

May the straight curse strike the enemies! Cf. vii. 56, 19.

iii. 18, 2. tápa sá*m*sam árarusha*h*.

Burn the curse of the enemy!

vii. 25, 2. âré tám sá*m*sam k*r*i*n*uhi ninitsó*h*.

Take far away the curse of the reviler! Cf. vii. 34, 12.

It means blessing:

ii. 31, 6. utá va*h* sá*m*sam u*sígâm-iva *smasi.

We desire your blessing as a blessing for suppliants.

x. 31, 1. ā́ na*h* devā́nâm úpa vetu sá*m*sa*h*.

May the blessing of the gods come to us!

x. 7, 1. urushyá na*h* urú-bhi*h* deva sá*m*sai*h*.

Protect us, god, with thy broad blessings!

ii. 23, 10. mā́ na*h* du*h*-sá*m*sa*h* abhi-dipsú*h* îsata prá su-sá*m*sâ*h* matí-bhi*h* târishîmahi.

Let not an evil-speaking enemy conquer us; may we, enjoying good report, increase by our prayers!

Lastly, sá*m*sa means praise, the spell addressed by men to the gods, or prayer:

i. 33, 7. prá sunvatá*h* stuvatá*h* sá*m*sam âva*h*.

Thou hast regarded the prayer of him who offers libation and praise.

x. 42, 6. yásmin vayám dadhimá sá*m*sam índre.

Indra in whom we place our hope. Cf. â*sa*m*s, Westergaard, Radices Linguæ Sanscritæ, s. v. *sa*m*s.

TABLE OF CONTENTS.

	PAGE
HYMN I. 6	2
Commentary	6
Arushá	6
Arushá as an adjective	6
Arushá as an appellative	9
1. Of the horse of the sun, or of the horses of Agni	9
2. Of Vritra	10
Arushá as the proper name of a solar deity	11
The feminine Árushî as an adjective	13
The feminine Árushî as a substantive	14
Remarks on the classification of the different meanings of arushá and árushî in the Dictionary of Boehtlingk and Roth	15
The vocative maryâh	18
Ushádbhih and similar forms	19
Át as two syllables	19
Svadhá, its origin and different meanings	19
Garbhatvám of the Maruts	25
Váhni and its different meanings	25

	PAGE
1. Fire	26
2. Agni	26
3. Luminous	26
4. Vehicle, carrier, horse	27
5. Priest	28
Meaning of váhnih âsấ	29
Is váhni a name of the Maruts ?	30
Derivation of âs and âsya	30
Vílú and Ἴλιος	31
Dríkshase and similar forms	32
Arkati	32
Makhá	33
Makhásya dâváne	33
The terminations mane, váne, ane	34
Rokanám	34
Rokanám diváh	34
Súryasya, nákasya	35
Heaven, earth, and sky	36
Rokanâni trí	36
Pấrthivâni	37
HYMN I. 19	38
Commentary	42
Gopîthá	42
Rágas, ἔρεβος	42
Adrúh	42
Arká	43

S 2

260   TABLE OF CONTENTS.

	PAGE
Nâka	43
Párvata, cloud	43
Samudrá, the sea or the sky	44
Sárasvatî as reaching the sea	45
Samudrá as an adjective	47
HYMN I. 37	48
Commentary	54
Anarván	54
Ar, árvan, árus, upârá, ari	54
Sárdhas and sárdha	56
Masculine gender of the adjective after sárdhas	58
Príshatî	59
Vâsî (p. 157)	59
Riñg	60
Yâman	60
Ghríshvi	60
Tveshá-dyumna	60
Gámbha	61
Anta	61
Gíhite	62
Agina and yáma	62
Váyah	62
Gíruh	62
Káshthá	63
Dúvah	63
HYMN I. 38	64
Commentary	66
Kadhapriyah	66
Vriktabarhis	68
Ránhyati	69
Kvá and kuva	70
Sumná, suvitá	70
Yávasa	71
Yamásya pathâ	71
Nírriti	72

	PAGE
Padîshtá, pad	72
Avâtá and ávâta	73
Vâsrá	75
Pargánya	75
Sádman and sadmán	75
Vilupâní and vilúpâni	76
Ródhasvatî	76
Akhidrayâman	76
Abhísu	77
Bráhmanaspáti	77
Tánâ	77
Tatanah	78
Arkín, Alb-leich	78
Vriddhá	78
As, its Let forms	79
HYMN I. 39	80
Commentary	82
Mâna	82
Várpas	83
Yâ with vi	83
Párvatânâm âsâh	84
Tânâ yugâ	84
Prâshti	85
Dadá	85
Parimanyú	86
Pári, like Lat. per, an adjectival prefix	86
HYMN I. 64	88
Commentary	92
Suvríktí	92
Apás and ápas	92
Dyu or Rudra, father of the Maruts	93
Márya	93
Sátvan	94
Abhogghánah	94
Rukmá (p. 220)	94
Vápushe and subhé	94

	PAGE
Mraksh, mimrikshuh .	94
Dhúni	95
Sudánu	95
Dâ, dânú	96
Dânu	97
Pinvati	98
Átya vâgín	98
Útsa	99
Hastín, elephant . . .	99
Árunî	100
Távishî	100
Pisá	100
Kshápah and kshapáh . .	101
Ródasî	101
Amáti	102
Khâdí (p. 218)	102
Vanín	103
Sask	104
Ragastúh	104
Rigîshín	104
Áprikkhya	105
Púshyati	105
Dhanaspŕt, ukthyâ, vîsvá-karshani	105
Ríti	106
Dhiyâvasu	106
Nodhas Gotama . . .	107
HYMN I. 85	108
Commentary	110
Gánayah sáptayah . . .	110
Ukshitá	113
Virúkmat	113
Vríshavrâta	114
Ramh	114
Ádri	114
Arushá	115
Kárma-iva	115
Víshnu	116
Madakyút	118

	PAGE
Nári, nrí . . .	120
Vâná	120
Vríshan, its etymology .	121
Its various meanings, Male	122
Man	123
Fertilising, strengthening .	124
Epitheton ornans . . .	125
Várshishtha (p. 155) . .	126
Vríshan, applied to certain deities	126
Vríshan, an appellative of certain deities . . .	127
Vríshan haryatá . . .	130
Vríshan, applied to inanimate things . . .	131
Vríshan, an empty word .	132
Â-vrish	133
Vríshan, a proper name .	134
Upastutá and Úpastuta .	134
Vríshan and Dadhyak, their latest phase . .	135
HYMN I. 86	136
Commentary	138
Vímahas	138
Yagñávâhas	138
Á bhúvah or âbhúvah . .	138
Íshah sasrúshih . .	139
Srosh	139
Ávobhih	139
Par, with áti, ápa, níh .	139
Atrín	140
HYMN I. 87	142
Commentary	144
Usráh, stríbhih . . .	144
Yayí	144
Vithurá	145
Súbh	145
Ayá	148

	PAGE		PAGE
*Ri*nayā́van	148	*S*úshma	184
*S*ámi, *s*ám, *s*ámî	149	Iyarti	184
*S*riyáse kám, datives in áse	150	É̃ta	185
Myaksh, mimikshire (p.174)	150	Máha*h*-bhi*h*	185
		Vas	187
HYMN I. 88	152	Indriyá	187
Commentary	154	Devátâ	187
Metre of the hymn	154	Karishyá̃(*h*)	189
Svarká	155	Tanvē̆ tanū́bhi*h*	189
Várshish*tha*	155	Api-vátayati	189
Paptata	156	Duvasyát, dúvas, duvasyáti	191
Svádhitivân	156	Vayá̃	194
Pavi	156	Yâsîsh*ta*	195
Vā́*s*î	157	V*ri*gána	195
Medhá̃	157		
Tuvidyumná	157	HYMN I. 166	196
Ûrdhvá	158	*Commentary*	200
G*ri*dhra	158	Rabhasá	200
A'hâni	158	Ketú	201
Agu*h*	159	Aidhá̃-iva, yudhá̃-iva	202
Vârkâryá̃	159	Ní-tya, nish-*t*ya, ápa-tya	203
Deví̃	159	Ví́, ávyata	205
Yógana	160	Dhra*g*	205
Varã́hu	160	Harmyá, zairimya, *formus*	206
Anubhartrí̃	161	Nad	207
Stobhati	161	Rathiyati	207
		Su*k*etú	208
HYMN I. 165	162	Sumatí	208
Commentary	170	Krívi*h*-datî	210
*A*dri*h* prábh*ri*ta*h*	172	Rad	211
Samânyá̃	173	Rinâti	212
Myaksh	174	Súdhita	213
Mimiksh	176	Barbá́nâ	215
X-itâsa*h*	177	Alâtri*n*á	215
Mánas	178	Abhíhruti	217
Kúta*h*	178	Tavishá	218
Sat-pati	179	Khâdí	218
Bráhmâ*n*i and matáya*h*	179	Samâyâ, ὀμῇ	220
*S*ám	180	É̃ta	220
*S*ám yó*h*	182	Ancient dresses	221

	PAGE		PAGE
Kshurá	223	Áditi as mother	239
Váp-tar, nâpita, svap, snap	224	The seven Ádityas	240
Nâga, svañg, snake	224	Áditi identified with other	
Víbhûti	224	deities	242
Vibhváh	225	Áditi and Díti	244
Mahi-tvanám	225	Áditi in her moral	
Vratá	225	character	244
Dâtrá	228	Áditi as an adjective	249
Dâtra	229	The particles kaná and	
Áditi, the Infinite	230	ka ná	251
Áditi and the Ádityás	232	Tyágas	255
Áditi and Dáksha	234	Nibâdh	256
Áditi in her cosmic		Vrig (sîrshâ)	256
character	237	Sámsa	257

OXFORD:

BY T. COMBE, M.A., E. B. GARDNER, E. P. HALL, AND H. LATHAM, M.A.,

PRINTERS TO THE UNIVERSITY.